To Viviana and Francisco May the' guide your ...

Violet Descends
A Seven Lights Novel

Angel Fuentes

Edited by Le-Andrea Sylvester

Based on the characters created by
Angel Fuentes and Ivonne Falcón

To my insecurities and laziness

Ha! I beat you!

CONTENTS

ACKNOWLEDGMENTS

Thank you for reading my book.

It may sound a little bit cliché, but when characters become clear in my head, they sort of speak to me and guide me through their tale. In the case of Violet, this was no exception. After many years of hearing her voice in my head, I was beginning to believe that I was becoming a girly emo angel. If you ever do find yourself in my predicament, that is to hear girly voices in your head as you read this tale, I recommend that you create a fake profile in any of the many social media venues and use it as an outlet for your inner girly angel thoughts. Mine are @emoangelviolet on Twitter and Facebook.com/VioletDescends.

I remember I met Ivonne Falcón in 2004 at a mall in Guaynabo, Puerto Rico. I don't think either of us thought how long and meaningful our ongoing creative collaboration and friendship would become. Many failed starts and so many long phone calls later, we came up with the basic idea for Violet Descends, a quirky apocalyptic rump that playfully and very loosely reinterpreted parts of the Judeo-Christian mythology. Violet Descends was meant to be a comic book series. Sadly, we only managed to publish the first issue; with art and scripts of the next few issues still hiding in a closet somewhere as of this writing. When it came to making comics, life just got in the way for Ivonne and me. But here it is, Ivonne, the story from beginning to end. Done!

Thankfully, my good friend and creative partner AC Osorio was always there to kick some sense into me and remind me that I am not just a comic book writer; I am a writer, period. His guidance and support pushed me to evolve as a writer. It was AC that championed for me to deliver this story as a novel. So blame him if you don't enjoy this book. It's his fault! ☺

I also wish to thank the following people whose contributions helped make my first novel possible: My girlfriend Leticia Díaz, who said she would not read the novel until I publish it and give her the signed first edition printed copy (I love you, baby doll!); Bill Álvarez (my brother from another mother), who ignited my imagination as we sat next to each other in first grade and drew awesome little cartoons on the back of our notebooks; my family: Yussef A. Fuentes (my awesome son); Alex Fuentes (my brother from the same mother); Pedro Menéndez, and Ángela Rivera (mis abuelos); all my cousins and uncles and aunts and such; Michelle Denise Soto, editor of the original comic book and hardcore Violet fan; David Arroyo, who invited me to dinner and helped me come up with a grand twist for my story. My focus group: Zamaly Díaz, Jorge Berríos, Milo Adorno, and Heidy Castillo, for their vast feedback and encouragement. My friends: Carlos M. Mangual, Ramón Valle, Elisabet Díaz-Cintrón, Claudia Blanco, Vivian González, Brian Blake, Vanessa Febres, Érika Lugo, Mitch Hyman, Juan Lapaix, Amanda Pacheco, José R. Román, J.C. Velázquez, Jorge Resto, Ángel Camacho, Rikky Carrión, Ozzy Fernández, Guillermo Martínez, and Rangely García. Special thanks to everyone at Berlitz US, Spring Bank NY and Banco Popular de Puerto Rico.

Oh, and my mom. I have to thank my mom, Carmen Ada Menéndez. Nothing I ever accomplished could have been possible without her continued support and love. Hi, mom!

PROLOGUE

There were days back at school… there were days when it felt worse than usual. It was one of those days. I held on to my books hard 'cause I couldn't stop my hands from shaking. Never looked anybody in the eyes… Blocked their taunting. It was just me, walking through the busy hallways. I could hear them laughing. Making fun of my looks. Calling me names. That's what I hated most.

Ruth. My name is Ruth.

I was the girl the boys didn't mind pushing around as if I were another boy. I was the one they all ganged up to throw snowballs at, always aiming at my face. I had no friends- I never had any friends. I had people who pretended to be my friend to get something from me, or help the other kids embarrass me in front of everyone. I was the one they cornered at school and reached under my skirt…touching me, while I got my school stuff broken. They said I should be thankful, that no guy would ever want to be with me. And I believed them.

. . . .

He was standing in front of the library with a book in his hands. He seemed happy. He pulled me by the hand and we sat at one of the tables. He opened the book and showed me some pictures on it.

It was a book about angels.

"This is the one I was looking for. It finally got here." he said, "I'm going to do a paper on this. You'll see."

I stared at him glowing as he showed me through the different casts of angels and their stories.

"These here, these seven are the most important ones." He went on, "The Archangels; Gabriel, Michael, Raphael, these three are there in all versions. And then the other four; Abaddon, Metatron, Jophiel and Zadkiel. Sometimes the names change on these last four, depending on the source, but I think- I think I'm going to do my paper on these seven. This book is referenced a lot by the other ones I have. I think I'm good. The Archangels, also known as the warriors of light, have often been represented by different colors-"

Then his hand touched mine…

"I need to tell you something." He said. "Not here, though. Could we meet after school? Can I…Could I walk you home today?"

I stood waiting at the bus stop in front of the school. Some girls passed by and called me names… made fun of me. It started raining. He never came and I walked myself home.

I'm in my bed and he's gone. I never got to see him again. God, it's been so long… Why do I still think about him?

I don't want to get up… I don't want to go to work… Not today, not ever...

I just want it all to end…

1 SILENT PARADE

Thousands of people roamed the always busy streets of Sao Paulo City, in Brazil. The overcrowded metropolis was a melting pot of diverse economic classes. Some of its high class areas; like the glamorous 5 de Marco Avenue, full of boutiques, café's, discos, and restaurants; clashed with low end favelas that lacked proper sanitation, clean water and electricity. Hazardous power cables hung almost at ground level at the slums. As always, traffic was a nightmare because the street lights almost never worked.

Ibirapuera Park, one of the country's largest parks, was particularly crowded that morning. The city had been planning its first annual Children's Day celebration for weeks and workers were relieved that the non-stop rain showers finally receded to allow a sunny day outside. Hundreds of school buses and cars lined at the designated drop off areas for the thousands of families that had come to participate in the day's activities. The park had never seen so many clowns, balloons, rides, sketch artists, food vendors and attractions for families before. The air was full of the clamor of birds singing, popular music buzzing out of loudspeakers and the laughter of children at play. It was even said that the President of Brazil would soon make an appearance to give a few motivational words to the public.

Seven year old Yara wasn't interested in clowns, balloons or food, much less the President. She saw a small blue hummingbird fluttering its wings over the grass covered hill and followed it. The hummingbird

3

hovered over a single red rose at the top of the hill. It was the most beautiful flower Yara had ever seen. She wanted to pick it and show it to her mother, but she also wanted to keep the pretty bird to herself. The girl carefully crawled up the hill making sure her steps wouldn't scare the small bird away. Once at the top, she slowly reached out to catch the hummingbird, and curiously enough, it flew right to Yara's fingertips, as if it knew she wouldn't harm it.

The little girl sat in front of the rose and played happily with the hummingbird for a few moments. Yara was so ecstatic she didn't notice the small crack that opened on the ground in front of the shiny red rose. The crack grew longer and wider until Yara felt her shoe slip off and fall away. As the crack in the ground grew larger, the girl quickly stood up and tried to run, but the earth opened up under her feet and swallowed her whole.

The crack widened and stretched across Ibirapuera Park, through the city, until it became a schism rifting the metropolis in half. It was the first earthquake Sao Paulo had ever experienced, its horror measuring 9.5 on the Richter scale, toppling buildings, destroying vehicles and homes. For almost thirty minutes the rumbles were felt throughout Brazil and other neighboring countries. A cloud of dust engulfed the entire city of Sao Paulo causing thousands of citizens to succumb to confusion and panic. The air became a grey mist of thick pungent dirt. The authorities rushed to assist the public, but they were overwhelmed by the devastation. All streets were impenetrable. No one knew where to run for safety as the earth seemed to crumble from all directions. That day, an estimated seventeen thousand people died and twice that amount were injured.

The small blue hummingbird had flown away. Yara stood at the bottom of a dark rocky void. She kept looking up wondering how she'd manage to climb all the way up and out of the hole. She thought of yelling for her mother, but the topside seemed too distant for anyone to hear her, so it seemed natural for her to keep silent. She wanted to climb up just as soon as she figured out how to do it. After all, Yara didn't feel she was hurt from the fall... she didn't feel anything at all.

A small white hand touched Yara's shoulder from behind. She turned around and saw a pale little girl with black hair and deep black eyes smiling innocently while waving at her. The girl looked younger than her and wore an old grey dress with a dead flower tied by a black ribbon to her chest and worn out schoolgirl shoes. Yara saw that the little girl also wore what seemed like a silly looking bright hat. Sometimes it was floppy and other times it would spin around like a pinwheel behind the little girl's head. She couldn't tell for sure what kind of hat it was because of the bright light emanating from it.

Yara was happy. At least now she had someone to play with. She felt she could trust this girl and was at peace with her. Just when Yara opened her mouth to express her delight to see her, the little girl silenced her with a finger over her lips as she signaled Yara to follow her into the darkness. Yara complied because she thought it was a game and she was very eager to play.

. . . .

The rose at the origin of the crack was still intact. Evergreen gently picked the flower up and took a whiff of it before carefully placing it next to her ear.

"Thy will be done" she whispered to the sky. If mortals could see her, they would describe her as a stunningly beautiful, voluptuous, ebony skinned, naked goddess. Looking into her emerald eyes was hypnotic. But even more breathtaking was her ever-changing hair from which all sorts of colorful flowers and small animals grew. A caterpillar would grow from her head and crawl into a cocoon from which a butterfly would emerge. The leaves sprouting from her head would change colors like the seasons. The only thing that would remain unchanged on her head was a single, white, feather worn as her emblem.

Evergreen marveled at the destruction around her. Where others saw desolation and despair, she could see opportunity.

"We should grow some trees over there," she considered, "maybe a mountain. A mountain would be nice…" For her, the only constant in nature was change. Where there were once oceans, deserts now stood and where there were empty plains, forests would rise. As the angel of nature, it was her duty to make sure to guard Earth's evolutionary process. Her control over the elements would allow her to create hurricanes, snowstorms or any other kind of catalyst she could use on the planet to bring forth flora and fauna, as long as it was the will of God. This time, it was an earthquake. She treated her ministry as a labor of love and a true work of art. What excited her most about her duty was that she could never quite predict the outcome of nature's change. Every moment of her life she'd be the witness of God's Creation. Ever changing... Evergreen. This was her true blessing and only love.

Evergreen's excitement was cut short immediately when she heard a familiar iPhone ringtone followed by a delicate male voice.

"... I'm thinking five interconnected skyscrapers and one hundred and twenty floors each. That's about seven or eight years of work right there. Can you build them in five? Oh, could you be a darling and throw in a lighted fountain too? Thank youuuuuu, love your face! Gotta go."

Clearly annoyed, the green angel turned around and looked up, already expecting to see her brother Blue. He hovered over Evergreen as the sunlight reflected brightly off of the silver plates covering his futuristic cobalt bodysuit, a white feather engraved on the right side of his chest plate marked his angelic insignia. Unlike the other angels, he followed the latest trends and wore his slick blonde hair spiked on top, which Evergreen found irritating. His cobalt eyes shined with the reflection of the hologram light screens that floated around him with images of building plans, power grid layouts and video games. He was the angel of the future, a spaceman years ahead of humanity, yet his existence relied on them.

Blue was the protector and enabler of humankind's technological advancement; his ministry was progress. From the discovery of fire, the wheel and hunting tools to the Internet, smart phones and hybrid cars, all were part of an organized sequence for which there is always a plan and a non-divertible timetable.

"What do you think you're doing?" asked Evergreen.

"It's called progress. Look it up, sis" he answered without moving his stare from the light hologram screens, "I'm sorry, but do you really think you can get away with a mountain in the middle of the largest city in Brazil? That's so tacky, puh-lease!"

Evergreen despised Blue's cockiness, but she knew just how to shut him up. Up in the sky, an eagle flew over the park. She called to it, diverting its trajectory. The bird flew rapidly towards Blue, preparing to attack him. He covered his head with his arms while looking at Evergreen.

"STOP THAT," he yelled at her.

The blue angel let out a low girly squeak as the eagle flew right over him. The bird let out a loud screech and it pooped on Blue's shoulder before flying away. Blue wiped the droppings off his shoulder.

"Very mature…" he mumbled, rolling his eyes.

"I am in charge of renewing this place, not you. White herself gave me this task." Evergreen argued.

"Of course she did!" Blue responded, "But she also thought you might need a little assistance, so she asked *moi* to lend a hand. And I have got to say, honey; she was wrong. You need a *lot* of help!"

An intense blinding white light saturated the skies. Blue and Evergreen heard a beautiful harmony coming from all directions. If mortals could hear it, they would be enthralled by its hypnotic melody like sailors enchanted by the song of sirens. Though this was not a melody at all, it was the voice of an angel speaking.

"I will only ask once for both of you to stop your bickering" proclaimed the voice. The two angels squinted as they tried to locate the voice through the blinding light.

"White is here" whispered Evergreen.

The angel White descended gracefully from beyond. She was the right hand of God and the sight of her - arms wide open embracing all of Creation; her face exuding compassion and peace- was nothing short of messianic. A single luminous white feather adorned her long, flowing platinum hair with a bright, white halo over her head. She wore a long dress made out of solid white light with lace trim covered in pearls, as were the sandals dressing her feet. White was a messenger angel and all others looked up to her with respect because she was entrusted to guard God's most precious creation. Her ministry was life itself, to protect all living beings from the moment of their inception, to the moment they last drew breath.

Two more figures appeared hovering from behind White. The first was Scarlet, the mighty warrior and protector of free will. She wore an impeccable, chromium red medieval knight armor and a grey cape, along with a red, metallic helmet that proudly displayed her angelic feather.

However, Scarlet seemed anxious as she pulled her sword in and out of its scabbard again and again.

"We're wasting time," she complained, "We have a lot of work to do."

"Oh, yeah, we do!" responded Goldie, the other hovering figure. Sporting a black top hat, a golden pantsuit and black high-heels, she was the likes of a circus ringmaster or vaudeville entertainer and she wore her angelic feather as a bow tie. Oddly enough, she wore a white glove on her left hand while her right hand remained naked. She joined fingers from both hands to make a square frame and looked through it like a movie director.

"Oooh! This is gonna be great, kids! I'll fix these buildings right as rain, see?" she said excitedly, "I'll paint the skies red and the clouds'll form the shape of hands! And those'll be the hands of God! Why, it'll be a genuine spectacle! Dogs'll fly, and cats'll dance-," Goldie rambled on. Even though she was in charge of miracles, a very important ministry within God's Divine Plan, the other angels didn't pay much attention to her at all and found her to be rather strange. Blue often called it A.D.D. But to Goldie, her ministry meant putting on a great show, making the impossible possible and leaving her audience craving for more.

"Creation needs a little pizzazz!" She often thought.

White held Goldie's hand with tenderness.

"No need for miracles this time, Goldie. We must play this with subtlety."

"Again?! Dammit! Why I oughta…" Goldie said as she threw her top hat to the ground.

"No cursing." White commanded.

"Now, see here, ya mook. Why ya benching me again, sis?! It's been like a million trillion years since my last good miracle! Ya haven't let me put on a good show since the resurrection of Christ! I wanna do more than just cure some old fart's cancer, see?! Or save a bunch of nobodies from a plane crash!"

"Yours is an important task, child. You'll get your chance to shine in the End of Times."

Goldie sighed in frustration. White gently placed her hand on her shoulder and spoke softly into her ear.

"Have a little patience. This'll all be over soon." White turned to Evergreen and Blue, noticing that Scarlet was no longer with them.

"I think you and your brother should work together on the reconstruction," she said, "I trust Scarlet has gone to take care of the riots and Black is already collecting lost souls. ...Where is Violet?" Blue and Evergreen looked at each other puzzled. None of them had seen Violet since the last major disaster. Evergreen guessed that maybe she was already assisting Scarlet. Blue disagreed:

"I bet that girl is out there cutting her wrists somewhere."

. . . .

The streets of Sao Paulo were burning. With no electricity and night about to fall, amidst the destroyed buildings and vehicles men and women were breaking store display windows and taking whatever they could. They fought for TV screens and laptops, many times killing each other for them. Scarlet marched up hill in the middle of the main street while watching humans revolt. The angel already knew the true machinations behind the mortals' behavior. She could see all the things that humans couldn't, such as the demon goblins in full possession of their bodies. The goblins were small and bestial looking creatures with multiple poisoned fangs coming out of their mouths and skin rough like sandpaper with small boney horns poking from their heads. Their eyes were like a red abyss, a sign that they themselves were possessed by a greater, more powerful demon.

One of the demons rested on a human's shoulders, secreting gooey spider webs from its claws that it used to control the human, like a puppet. Scarlet looked to her right and saw three men attacking a young woman. Taking her sword from its scabbard she walked over to the men and swung it precisely at the demons that possessed the men with their oozing webs. It is said that Scarlet's sword is one of its kind as it can kill any being in existence. The goblins were cut in half as green slime splattered on Scarlet's armor. The men became confused as they came out of a trance and ran away from the girl.

"It was as good of a place to start as any." Scarlet thought, trying to resist her boredom. Other demons nearby panicked and retreated.

"SCARLET!" They screamed in fear as they scattered.

"Boys," she called with a smirk, "try to make it fun please!"

She followed after them slashing her way through the demons, cutting limbs and heads while freeing humans from their possession. Some of them tried surrounding her, attacking from different directions but she disposed of them easily. One of the demons tried to crawl away from the red angel's warpath. She found it quite amusing and put her boot on its chest, making sure not to kill it. The crushed demon could barely breathe as it uttered what it knew would be its last words.

"You think that by killing ussss the humans will stop being evil?"

"I am not here to judge if humans have been good or bad." She replied. "I am here to protect their free will, the freedom to act for themselves. Something your possessions seem to preclude."

"You- you can't stop us all!" the demon smiled defiantly.

Scarlet pressed her foot deeper against the demon's chest making a crunching sound, but she miscalculated how much force she used and her boot got stuck inside the creature's ribcage. She shook her leg a few times to try to free her foot, but the demon's ribcage wouldn't budge.

The demon let out a cry, still alive. Scarlet raised her head, taking her sight away from the demon and back to the streets where thousands of people that were possessed were running wild, killing each other and wreaking havoc upon the city, leaving the angel bewildered.

"So many demons... something's not right..." She said. The armored angel realized she was encircled by hordes of demons. An army like this would only be possible in the final battle at the end of times. As she raised her sword she quickly resolved that neither one nor one thousand demons would matter as she would slaughter them all the same.

Thousands of demons left their human hosts to unite against Scarlet. This was the opportunity they needed to be rid of her once and for all and they finally had the numbers. Scarlet managed to fight off the first wave of demons easily, but as more and more appeared and swarmed upon her, the warrior angel felt overwhelmed.

"There are too many of them," she realized. "Violet! I need you!"

A demon climbed up Scarlet's back and yanked the helmet off her head. More and more demons piled up on Scarlet, pushing her to the ground as they attacked her relentlessly.

"VIOLET!!!" Scarlet cried.

....

Violet was hiding in New York City. She walked towards a subway station ignoring her sister's cries. The purple angel stopped in front of an outdoor café and saw a couple leave a table with dirty dishes and tip money. There was a cream cheese bagel on a plate that was only bitten once. Violet stared at it with curiosity for a few seconds and then grabbed it while she continued her stride towards the stair entrance of the subway station.

....

Yara tightly held the hand of the little girl with the glowing hat as they walked through a dark tunnel in the ground. It seemed strange to her that she hadn't noticed the tunnel before, but she was glad it was there and that her new friend was leading her through it. The tunnel was so dark that Yara couldn't see anything except the little girl in front of her and that was only because of the glowing hat that spun around her head. Sometimes the girl would look back at Yara and smile, even winking at her once. They were playing a game, Yara thought. The rules were simple: she had to follow the little girl through the pitch-black tunnel and stay quiet to avoid waking up the ugly nameless monsters that ate people there.

As they moved through the dark tunnel, Yara noticed they were being followed. At one point Yara thought she saw a tall man in overalls holding a rake behind her till she blinked and then he wasn't there. Seconds later she saw an old lady smiling at her, but then she also disappeared. The little girl considered that maybe there were other people in the tunnel and that for some reason they were hiding. Maybe it was part of the game. Countless people kept appearing and disappearing: a clown, a bus driver, a jogger, a park ranger, a nun, a boy, and so on. The disappearing people were clearly following the little girl with the glowing silly hat. Yara thought this was a fun game. They all marched quietly through the tunnel though none of them knew exactly where they were going. Even animals joined the silent parade.

The little girl with the glowing hat stopped for a moment. They had reached a rocky wall at the end of the tunnel. She stood next to Yara and stared at a rock in front of her. The rock crumbled and as daylight slipped through the cracks, the wall of rock gave way and took the form of a door through which the pale skinned quiet girl led everyone from the parade. They were all outside at Ibirapuera Park again, but the park, and everything else around it, was destroyed. Yara saw that the little girl with the glowing hat walked towards a blue spaceman and a pretty naked lady with butterflies and leaves on her head. There was also a wacky looking blonde lady with a top hat sitting on a bench. The naked lady complained angrily to the blue spaceman. Yara could barely understand what she was saying...

....

"Sister," Evergreen exclaimed, "can you talk some sense into White when you see her? She wants Blue and I to collaborate on Sao Paulo's restoration."

Evergreen was half joking. She knew Black had never intervened in her sibling's affairs. Furthermore, the Black Angel was mute, or at least had never chosen to speak since she knew that there was no need for words when it came to the recently deceased. Whatever had been left unsaid by the bereft of life became the burden of the living to say it. The only necessity of the recently departed was to reach their final resting place be it Heaven or Hell, and the Black Angel was their guide. She knew her way through the darkness and how to avoid the evil residing there that fed on people's souls. If she had to defend these souls against this evil, she knew how to do that too, for her ministry was death itself.

"Are we still having this argument?" Blue interrupted. "I went green! I came up with recycling! What more do you want?"

"The fountain idea is not bad," Evergreen admitted, "but wouldn't a waterfall look nicer?"

"Here we go again! Ok, look, princess, you want your waterfall? Well, I want a monorail. That's the best deal you're going to get!"

"A monouh-raaaaail? Ugh! This isn't Epcot Center! Why do I put up with this? I should grow a cactus up your ass!"

"Don't you dare!"

Evergreen and Blue continued their discussion. Since Black felt they were ignoring her, she left her siblings to their own devices and walked away.

"Alright, alright! No Monorail." Blue continued. "Even I have to admit that's too eighties. We could try a skywalk, like the one they have over at the Grand Canyon. I'm thinking we could build one over the crater, like a memorial. What do you think? …Evergreen?"

Evergreen was no longer paying attention to her brother. She heard people arguing from far away and paused when she saw a young Brazilian man standing between a tree and a group of disaster relief workers and police. The head of the workers stood angrily in front of the young man's face.

"Not you again!" said the worker, "We just had a major earthquake two days ago! Don't you have any respect? There are living, breathing people out there that need help and you'd rather chain yourself to this tree? You hippie types really are something else. Cut off that damned hair of yours and get a job!"

"My job is here, fighting for the planet!" the young man responded, "With all the destruction brought by the earthquake we cannot afford to lose one more tree, don't you understand? Can't you find another place to store all the rubble?"

"That's enough talk, Paolo, we are cutting down this tree whether you're tied to it or not."

"Paolo…" Evergreen repeated, intrigued by the young man.

"Hey, flora head, are you listening to me?" Blue called, pulling his sister's arm away from the scene. "Come oooon, sis! We're on the clock here. That little tree was doomed anyway."

After a while, the authorities removed Paolo from the tree and the workers began to take it down. Evergreen followed Blue, keeping her eyes on Paolo until he was seated in the back of the police car.

. . . .

The Black Angel made her way towards Goldie whom had been sitting bored on a park bench, her top hat resting beside her. Once again, Goldie had been left out of the restoration process. She saved one or two people from dying in the earthquake, but those were small miracles that she performed with her eyes closed and there was nothing left to do for her but to whine and wait. The Black Angel knew this and she wasn't going to waste her time listening to her golden sister complain. She was more interested on a small violet-capped hummingbird that fluttered and hopped near Goldie's bench. The bird was badly injured and in the throes of death. Black happily enjoyed seeing it flap its wings unsuccessfully and she got on her fours and crawled behind the animal to watch it closely. Suddenly, the bird flapped its wings faster, its wounds completely healed. Black was devastated as she saw the hummingbird take flight, a healthy living creature again. It was a miracle. It was-

The angel of death quickly turned her attention to Goldie, staring at her angrily as Goldie smiled. Black stood up in front of Goldie as she pouted her lips and furrowed her brow.

"Suit yaself, doll face. Clearly you're as stale as a day old post." Goldie remarked. "That was a classy prank. I don't think Bozo could'a come up with one bettah."

The Black Angel kept staring at her silent. Goldie sighed and rolled her eyes.

"Have it your way, ya mug!" Goldie conceded.

The hummingbird fell from the sky and splattered right in front of Black making her smile again as she leaned over the dead bird. Black watched the spirit of the creature spread its wings and climb onto her pale hand.

Yara watched all of this from a distance. She looked at the bird's carcass next to the bench and then at the girl with the glowing spinning hat playing with the animal's soul. The Brazilian girl looked at herself and the other people standing with her. It was then that Yara realized she was dead.

2 JONAH'S WHALE

This is me:

In God's name, I am the guardian of the ministry of emotions. It is my duty to guide humanity's destiny through their sensations. My given name is Uriel, sixth of seven Archangels of peace proclaimed in the Pax Dei.

But to them…I am Violet. I wrote that. And I wrote this:

Underneath the lilac drags that cover my pale white flesh, I exist. My purple hair flows over my eyes, matching their light color. My nails, mauve. Heliotrope strapless shirt with black Capris, purple striped socks and amethyst flats. And a single white feather tied to the belt on my hips. This is how I want them to know me.

I write and sometimes I draw. I mostly record my exploits as an angel, or work on my poetry (I suck really bad!), and sketch and stuff. I always carry a small purple book on me to make sure to use my idle time and improve my craft. I'd like to be an artist one day, to create my own universe on paper and be, sort of, like God, all heresies aside or whatever. But my holy ministry always took priority and most of my time so I only get like small windows of creativity here and there.

Listen:

They speak of happiness, they speak of sorrow. They speak of all those fears and insecurities and of little joyful moments that shape their existence. They speak of hopes and dreams that cast a long shadow in their every action. They speak of nostalgia and of regrets. There are no louder noises, no higher notes, no longer-lasting echoes, than the throes of their emotions. They are humanity. They speak. …And I listen to each and every one of them.

The day I wrote those lines I sat at the plaza. It was a sunny day at Union Square Park in New York City. It smelled of humidity and sewer vapors and old stuff by the hoary small buildings that were turned to clothing stores or cafés. The cheap but trendy dressed college students hung out around the steps of the plaza in the center of the crossing of Broadway and Fifth avenues with Fourteen and Sixteen streets. Some of them danced like maniacs being electrocuted while others tried idiotic tricks with skate boards or soccer balls or whatever. I got hit with a ball a couple of times, but I didn't blame the players since they couldn't see me. Humans cannot see angels unless we choose to reveal ourselves to them. I moved from where I was sitting to another area where people walked their dogs or sat down on benches under the trees to watch the old buildings around them and I listened to their peaceful thoughts. I could, like, listen to what people felt. Their emotions flowed through me and responded to me…

I wished I could've stayed there forever, writing at that park, but I was getting as far away as I could from Brazil. Something bad was going to happen there and I didn't want to see - I mean, I didn't want to listen to the suffering. My angel siblings needed me to help restore order by helping survivors cope and feel hopeful and compassionate towards each other and stuff. I can do that. That's my thing. But I chose to abandon them all.

I walked down to the subway station and ate a bagel with cream cheese. No, angels don't need to eat or sleep or go to the bathroom, but we sometimes do it out of boredom, I guess, or to try to connect with humanity? I don't know. I've been eating fruits in Heaven since I was of Cherubim form. Anyway, the station was crowded. I bumped into so many souls while waiting for the train.

A man with no arms sat on the dirty floor of the station. He sang and played a guitar with his feet. He smelled like piss and wore dirty clothes. There was a little cup with a few bucks and some change next to him. But he was happy. At the time I thought that couldn't be right. I could've thought of a billion other souls with much more blessings going for them who wouldn't even crack half a smile on their faces. It didn't make sense to me. He made me feel ashamed of myself. I altered his thoughts a bit. I made him feel hopeless and suicidal, because I thought those were the feelings a man with no arms and nothing to himself but a cup of spare change should feel. He stopped singing and cried. He tried to throw himself to the train tracks, but two husky ladies stopped him and held him down to the floor until a police man came to take him away. The armless man wouldn't stop crying. It was a sad thing to watch. I didn't know why I did that. Why I took his hope away.

Just before I got on the train, my sister Scarlet called me from far away. She was in Sao Paulo.

"Violet! Violet, I need you!" her voice beckoned.

The train was full of people, but I found a seat and pretended not to hear my sister's louder summons: "VIOLET!!!" I finished my bagel with cream cheese. It tore me inside to betray Scarlet like that, but I decided not to suffer again in the service of my ministry. I wanted to quit being the angel of emotions. I came to New York to find the only one who could release me from my burden and stuff, but I could've dug a hole in the ground and bury my head for all it mattered, because the strain of humanity's passions followed me to the underground train.

The moment tragedy struck Sao Paulo, millions of voices cried to me at once. I listened to the feedback of collective panic from those affected by the disaster. I stumbled into confusion, despair, and anger. So many feelings passed through me... I struggled not to drown in an ocean of mixed emotions. What words to describe the relentless pain of infinite broken hearts striking my own all at once?

I fell from my seat and on my knees and I wrapped myself in my arms as hard as I could.

I screamed and contorted and tensed up, sweating off my soul. Sometimes I shook my arms violently. I moved side to side, trying to find a comfortable position to ride it all off. There was no other way to ease the pain but to wait for it to die down. I was tempted to just transfer these piercing emotions to the people around me. I could've done it, too. I could've had the train commuters share my pain, but the massive sorrow would've just killed them. I spent a couple of hours on the floor of that train rolled into myself, people passing me by.

I prayed to God and I begged Him to make the agony go away, but out of all the thousands of voices I made out, God's was the only one I couldn't hear. So I blamed Him for granting me this ministry. I wanted to kill myself. I really did. I felt so alone.

A few hours passed by and I managed to get up from the floor. The pain had mostly gone and I felt more resolved about quitting my ministry and going where I had to go. That's when I noticed a string of intense fright coming from someone on the train. A chubby girl with eyeglasses and a huge funny looking nose was staring at me. She wore a green blouse over a pink and black striped long sleeved shirt with black Capri's like mine. And she had her orange colored hair cut uneven, long on the right side of her head and shaved on the left. She looked at me directly, and I could tell she witnessed my agony because of the horror in her eyes. I tried to face her directly, but she would quickly turn her face away from me when I caught her.

"You're looking at me!" I said to her, "I know you're looking at me!"

The girl turned her head away from me again pretending not to see me. That made me angry. At the next train stop, I tinkered with the feelings of the train passengers to make them feel the need to get off and leave me alone with her. When everyone left and the empty train doors closed, the weird looking chubby girl and I faced each other.

"Stop pretending you can't see me!" I yelled.

"Oh my God! Oh my God! Oh my God!" she repeated, like she had seen a wraith.

I walked up to her and looked her in the eyes. She turned her eyes away avoiding mine.

"I'm talking to you. Look, I'm not going to hurt you or whatever."

"Okay…"

"You shouldn't be able to see me."

"I - I see things no one should see. Like a medium."

"Ah, you're a prophet. That's a good thing. There aren't that many of you anymore. I'm an angel… or was. I quit. Sort of. I haven't told anyone yet, but yes. I'm Violet."

"I'm… um… Spiral Dark…" she mumbled.

"Really? I thought your name was Ruth."

"How-How do you know my name?"

"Didn't you just tell me? It's a pretty name. Why do you call yourself Spiral Dark?"

"It's... I used to have a blog..."

"Anyway, I get it. I hate my name, too. I hate my entire life... and stuff... Listen, does this train stop at 2nd Avenue?"

"Um, no, you're going uptown. You need to get off at the next stop and um... are you alright? I kind of saw you screaming on the floor and-"

Suddenly the space around Ruth and I became terrifying. The lights went out and the train stopped moving. I heard a loud "VIOLET!!!" It was my sister Scarlet! She came all the way to New York to haunt me. There she was, standing at the door, wearing her breathtaking red armor and majestic grey cape of hers that reached under the back of her knees. Her long red hair was a bit messed up and she was dirty with disgusting demonic green goo all over her face and body. Her left boot dragged the body of an ugly little demon goblin that got stuck to it. The critter was still alive!

And of course, on her right hand she held that awesome sword she always carried around. It is required for her mission. My ministry was guiding emotions; Scarlet's was protecting free will. She fought demons that possessed people and enslaved their consciousness. And Scarlet excelled at combating the bastards. They were all seriously scared of her in Hell. The way she looked at you and the way she walked were very intimidating. Some called her the angry fist of God. This was the entire purpose of her life. She had no other passions (at least that I knew of).

I ran to the next empty train car and on to the next one.

"Don't run away, you little coward!" she screamed.

Scarlet was not so much of an angel as she was a force of nature. She ran after me raising her sword and making it glow with crackling electric blue light. When I reached for the next door, she threw the sword and it flew over my head. The blade stuck on the door, jamming it close. I freaked out and fell to the ground screaming. She pulled out the sword from the door and pointed it at me.

"I'm tired of your childish games." She said.

My sister grabbed me by the arm and lifted me.

"Let gooooo!" I yelled. She wouldn't.

"Again and again you neglect your duty. Do you know how many people died in Brazil? They should want to help each other, not loot and riot! I fought an entire demon horde by myself while taking care of your sorry mess! I'm always bailing you out!"

"You're always blaming me for everything! You don't care about me! I'm just your scapegoat!"

"That's it! We're leaving!"

Scarlet yanked my arm hard and walked away. The pull was so strong that I fell to the floor as she dragged me. I came to be face to face with the little demon stuck on her foot. It looked at me scared and moved its lips like saying "Help me!"

"You've never felt what these people feel! The loneliness and dread inside them! It's too painful! I hate it!" I screamed at Scarlet. She did not flinch.

"That is your God given ministry. Attend to it!" She responded.

I got desperate. I was too close to my goal and I wasn't coming back. I lifted my head towards the arm that she was grabbing me with and I pressed my teeth really hard on her fingers. Scarlet quickly let go of me and I fell to the floor. She was furious.

"I SHOULD KILL YOU RIGHT NOW!" she screamed while pointing her sword to my neck.

She held back, struggling to control her rage.

And then… And then she punished me.

Scarlet raised her sword and the crackling electric blue light coming out of it transformed into some sort of glowing liquid energy. Everything around me changed and I was no longer on the train, but inside this gigantic watery IMAX screen. I saw an image of the past. Somehow I knew it was the past, hundreds of years before Christ.

It was a small boat in the middle of the ocean and a man wearing a short tunic. He was rowing, scared. He was trying to get away from the moving dark stormy clouds high up in the sky that were catching up to him.

As lightning hit the boat, the man fell to the water sinking deeper even though he tried desperately to swim up. I could hear Scarlet's voice. It was serious and grave, like a thunderous trembling echo:

"So long as you deny your sacred duty, the ministry granted to you by the Great Divine," she said, "you will be imprisoned…"

I saw an enormous black monster whale, ten times bigger than the biggest blue whale, coming up from under the man's boat. The creature had small limbs with claws and centipede-like legs coming from its sides. That's when I knew the man was the prophet Jonah. The story goes, the Lord wanted Jonah to announce His prophecy in the town of Nineveh. Jonah got cold feet and ran away from God. As chastisement, Jonah was imprisoned inside the belly of the beast until he repented. The monster whale came from underneath the small wooden boat and opened its huge mouth. Jonah saw the monster getting nearer and he paddled faster, trying to escape it, but the whale swallowed him whole…

And that was it. I was back on the floor of the train facing Scarlet. I found it ironic that the angel who fought for humanity's free will would show me this specific allegory, but I wasn't going to ask her about it. She was armed and already too pissed at me. My sister pointed her sword towards the train door behind us.

"Like Jonah was bonded to his Leviathan," she said, "you will be bonded to her."

I turned my eyes towards the door and saw a bit of Ruth's orange haired head through the little door window. She had been peeking behind the small door glass. I felt she was confused and scared. That got me so angry. I was angry at Scarlet for not leaving me alone and I was angry at Ruth for being so nosey. But most of all, I was angry at myself. I cried.

"Please Scarlet, please don't do this. Please don't." I pleaded.

She silently turned and walked away from me.

"What now?" I asked her.

She paused for a moment and answered "Repent." Then she walked away.

Ruth made sure that my sister was gone before she got close to me.

She knelt down and slowly reached out her finger to tap my shoulder.

"What happened?" She asked.

I raised my head, still wiping the tears from my eyes, and gave her a sad smile.

"You're my whale."

3 THE DEVIL WEARS PEOPLE

My words:

Cold glass walls surround me now. I am condemned to suffer the worst of fates. My imprisonment is not of place but of will. My whole existence relies on the consciousness of another. I cannot fly. I cannot run. I lost my strength. I cannot influence the emotions of my jailor. Does she even know the power she holds over my entire life? I pray for mercy, but I will not find forgiveness unless I atone for my sin; the same sin that has freed me from the agony of living through every single emotion bred by humanity. I do not know which destiny is worse. Which torment should I choose?

I stared at the odd-nosed plump girl named Ruth as she nervously ate a granola bar. We'd gotten off the train and waited for her bus home. She kept avoiding looking at me. The fear and anxiety I felt from her led me to assume she was still in disbelief of the holy apparitions she'd seen. I explained to her that because she's my whale, I couldn't go anywhere or do anything without her. I told her about my siblings and of their ministries. I told her about my decision to resign from my ministry and that there was only one person in all of Creation who could help me quit. I asked her to come with me to meet him, and after making me promise I'd leave her alone if she did, she accepted. We would go after she got off from her job.

Ruth wasn't happy to be stuck with me at all. She looked like she wanted to jump off a bridge. I felt great sadness, and shame, and some anger coming from her, but mostly, I thought she just wanted to be left alone. Come to think of it, I think she just wanted me to leave her alone while she went to a public bathroom. But I just couldn't. I had to be with her all the time. I had to be with her while she ate her pepperoni slice at My Bro's Pizza, while she walked three blocks to get to her basement apartment, while she picked up her room and listened to glam metal rock god Duncan Blackheart, and while she worked as a ticket collector at a parking lot.

As far as whales go, I found Ruth to be quite boring. She kept quiet all the time. She avoided talking to people if she could. At one point, a man wanted to get his car out of the parking lot, but he said he paid the ticket to someone else before Ruth came in and he didn't want to pay again. I knew that he was lying, and I knew Ruth knew, too, but she punched his ticket and let him go without paying.

"It's not worth it." she said.

"You're like the worst parking ticket collector ever." I said.

"Whatever…" She answered while staring at the floor.

That's another thing. Ruth never looked me in the eyes when I spoke to her. She looked at the floor, she looked at the ceiling or a wall or whatever, but she never looked at me in the eyes. I began to think I made her uncomfortable since I was an angel, but she never looked at anyone in the eye. It seemed as if she was afraid of people.

After work, we took the F train to 2nd Avenue to find the one who could help me quit my ministry. We had to wait before crossing all the street corners because every time we tried to cross, the lights turned red and wouldn't change. The red lights gave me an uneasy feeling, like I was missing something. I decided to ignore the feeling and finish what I had to do already.

As we stood beside each other at one corner, Ruth asked me who the person we were going to visit was. I lied to her. I didn't want to unease her before she realized we were going to see Lucifer, the Devil. Nevertheless, she began to suspect when we arrived at his building, an abandoned brown-bricked four level complex; every window jammed with wooden boards. Only the main entrance door was open, and it creaked as Ruth pushed it in. The elevator was out of order, making us take the stairs. The place smelled as old as an antique store.

Being a prophet, Ruth felt these strange sensations about the place right away. She didn't know who we were about to deal with, but she felt something very wrong in the air, like the spirits roaming around her were being sucked by a powerful evil black hole entity.

"Don't be such a baby!" I said annoyed.

I had to push her upstairs to get to his apartment and once we got to his place, she knocked on the door once, before I stopped her.

"Just make sure you don't cross the door once he opens it." I told her.

"What, you want me to stay outside?"

"It's better that way. Trust me. You don't want to go inside this guy's crib."

"Why?"

"Gawd! You're so difficult sometimes, you know that?"

"I just want to know wha-"

The apartment door moved open before Ruth could finish her thought.

"I think I should warn youuuu…" I whispered.

That's when we saw the living room through the half opened door. Ed Gein, the dead nineteen-fifties serial killer sat at a small table wearing only a night robe and slippers. He held a glass with blood in it. The living room had a sofa with cushions made out of human butt cheeks. On the table, next to Ed's elbow and arm, there was a skull upside down filled with chicken soup. There was a small vest on the floor made out of a female torso and a belt made of many human nipples. The window shades were made out of knitted human lips. And there was a cluster of human skulls piled up at the corner of the apartment.

"Things may get a bit weird from here on." I said.

Of course, that wasn't really Ed Gein. That was just one of the many human aspects Lucifer wore. The Morning Star is a demon of a million faces. "Shape shifter chic" as my sister Goldie likes to say. Sometimes he'd be Genghis Khan, sometimes he'd be Jack the Ripper. He's an evil-themed drag queen, and he's pretty good at it, too. The only way you could tell it was him was by his black eyes. Eyes that are completely black mean they can never see the light of God. My sister Black is like that. That's the price she had to pay to see through the creepy dark places she goes to.

Ruth didn't know that, though. She saw the famous serial killer Ed Gein eating soup from a human skull. She stepped back and her mouth let out a low whimper where a scream was supposed to come out. Lucifer smiled at us politely.

"My sincere apologies for my appearance", he said, "I was just about to go for a bubble bath. Any of you ladies care for a drink?"

Ruth stormed away from the apartment and ran down the stairs. As I was bonded to her, my body got dragged down the stairs with her. I tried to hold on to the stair handles, but her whale powers were too strong. I couldn't stop her.

"Wait! WAIIIIT!" I yelled, but she wouldn't listen.

We went out the building door and she ran around the corner. I was right behind her screaming "Stop!", but she kept running. I tried to hold on to something, but I just couldn't. Finally, she stopped at a nearby alley, where she kneeled down and puked the pizza she ate at My Bro's.

"You're being such a drama queen!" I told her. "Those weren't really human body parts. It's an illusion. Come on! We need to go back!"

"I'm not going back!" She said, looking at the brick tiled wall in front of her.

"Hey, stop looking at the wall, Ruth! Didn't your mom ever tell you that is very rude not to look at people in the eyes when you're having a conversation?! Are you autistic? Will you look at me already?! Please! I have to talk to him! I need to stop being an angel to quit my ministry! He's the king of lies. He's the only one that can help me become someone else."

"Then you go!"

"You know I can't go anywhere without you! You're my whale!"

"Stop saying I'm your whale! You make me feel fat! First of all, I'm an orphan, so I'm sorry if it bothers you that I don't stare at you!" she yelled, "And second, I'm not autistic! And you- you- You didn't say he was the Devil!!!"

I wasn't getting through to her. I tried changing her emotions a bit, but I just couldn't affect her as long as she was my whale.

"Ruth, I need this." I pleaded. "You don't know how it is to live with my ministry. Imagine having all the feelings in the world in your mind at once. And you have to sort them all out and make sense of them! The pain is…I don't want it! Just… Please help me. I swear nothing will happen to you! Please…"

Ruth turned and looked at me with fear in her eyes. She must've remembered my episode on the train and felt pity, or maybe she thought this could help her get rid of me, but she finally managed to stand up and we walked back to the apartment building.

"This is crazy" Ruth uttered.

We stood at the opened apartment door and I held Ruth's hand to remind her she wasn't supposed to cross it. I pleaded my case to Lucifer and asked him to make me stop being an angel.

"I don't think you truly understand how this works." He responded. "Your ministry marks you apart from all Creation. Do you think God would give you a gift as powerful as control over emotions if He didn't know where to find you?"

Lucifer took one of the peeled human faces he had on his table.

"As long as you possess the gift," he explained, "your entire being is a beacon throughout the universe. To God, no matter whom or what I change you to, you would probably look…"

The Devil put the human face on like a Halloween mask. It looked sort of melted and floppy on him.

"… like this" He continued. "Pretty useless, don't you think?"

Ruth got nauseous again.

"Oh, my God! Oh, my God! Oh, my God!" she repeated nervously.

"It's impossible, then! I'm stuck with this ministry forever!" I cried frustrated.

"Oh, don't start crying on me now, child." Lucifer smiled. "There's always a way. What kind of Devil would I be if I couldn't grant your heart's desires? Get me someone, anyone, who will willingly accept your ministry. Be it angel, demon, or human, and I will transfer the gift."

I looked at Ruth and gave her a sad puppy look. Maybe she'd be interested...

"Don't even think about it." she said in a very rude tone.

"Who in their right mind would trade places with me?" I asked Lucifer.

The fallen angel barely heard my question. He took a whiff. Then he looked all around him. His deep black eyes shifted like a crazy person.

"Hmmm. Ladies" he finally said. "I'm afraid we have to cut this meeting short. We are not alone... It seems you are being... watched? I'm certain that we'll meet again, but if you ever do need me, don't forget my name. Off you go."

"What?!! Who's watching us? And how do we find-" I stopped my question right as the apartment door closed in front of us.

"Aaaaaaaah!!!" Ruth went nuts! "WE'RE BEING FOLLOWED! THEY'RE GOING TO KILL US!"

"What?!"

"He knows who they are! Ask him again! ASK HIM!"

Ruth opened the door again, but the apartment was empty. There was no furniture, no tables, no curtains, no Lucifer.

"Too late now." I said with a low voice.

I turned my look to Ruth. Her eyes and mouth were wide open as she looked at the empty room. She was terrified and confused and as much as I tried to hide it, I was pretty scared too.

....

Somehow, we were not alone. We took a bus back to Ruth' apartment and two guys got on after us. They wouldn't stop looking at Ruth and they were jabbering among themselves. Ruth held my hand tight.

"I think those guys are after us!" she whispered. "Those men have been looking at me weird since back at the stop-"

"Calm down. They're just making fun of your nose. I can feel them trying to hold their laughter."

"You think this is a joke?!" Ruth snapped at me. "We just had a lunch meeting with the Devil, who took the form of a serial killer that ate people and drank their blood in his lifetime. Not to mention we're being watched by only God knows who or what! And you're dissing my nose! Really?!"

"I'm not dissing your nose! I'm just saying these guys - Look, I'm sorry!" I lamented. "I didn't mean to put you through this. I'm really sorry. And I like your nose. I think it gives you personality."

"You really think so?" Ruth relaxed.

"Yes."

I lied to her again. I thought it would make her stop freaking out. I was right. We got off at our stop, but we still had a few blocks to walk.

"How will you know who will be the right person to take over your job?" my whale asked. I glanced at her.

"What do you mean 'the right person'?"

"I mean," she continued. "It has to be someone that can deal with the emotions of everyone in the world. All at the same time, and all the time. That's a huge responsibility. Not anyone can do that."

"I was kinda' just gonna pick whoever said 'yes' first"

"Really?! But that's-"

"Get off my back, Ruth! I know what I'm doing!"

"Clearly, you don't, Look, I'm just saying-"

"This is too much pressure! Leave me alone!"

I pushed Ruth and tried to run away from her, but I forgot for a moment that I was bonded to her, so I was right next to her running in the same place. It was pretty embarrassing. Then I sat on the ground and broke down in tears.

"This is Scarlet's fault!" I complained "Always pushing me around! Why can't she have my ministry?! Why can't I get her sword?! Why does Goldie get to make miracles and Evergreen gets to play with flowers?! Even

Black gets an easier job than mine! She takes care of the dead! They're dead! How hard can that be? They got the easy ministries and I get to keep painful emotions in check! It's just not fair! It's a very hard job and I'm sick of it! I just- I just want to be somebody else! Have you ever felt like that?"

Ruth sighted. "Come on, it's not that bad. Why are you so jealous of your sisters anyway?"

"Jealous?! Don't be stupid. I'm an angel! I can't be-" I stopped.

My eyes opened wide. "Oh, no!" I jumped from the floor.

"What?" Ruth asked.

I scratched my body all over. "Aaaaaaaah!" I scratched and scratched and scratched. "Get it off me! Get it off!!!" I screamed.

Ruth tried to hold me down.

"What?! What's going on?" She asked.

I kept scratching all over. I was jumping up and down. I was disgusted. I really freaked out. We weren't being watched from outside, but from within! Within me!

"Ewww! It's a demon!" I yelled at her, "It's a demon! Get it off me! I'm possessed!"

4 ANGELS AT PLAY

The first night after the Sao Paulo earthquake, White wandered through the destroyed city streets looking at people rebuilding their homes. All her siblings, except Violet, had performed their duties well and once again humanity would be able to pick up the pieces and move on. As with every other major disaster, White waited for all the other angels to leave before she took the time to observe and remember the senseless loss of human lives.

White looked at men and women in mourning, holding candles and pictures of fallen loved ones. Tears rolled down her cheeks as the angel stopped to get a grip.

"I hear you all." She lamented.

This time, the pain was too much to stomach. She thought maybe this was because Violet had left her duties unattended and the sorrow she and all these people felt had no boundary.

White stood at a street corner trying to focus. She saw a fifty-something year old woman who was leaving letters and many pictures of children who died in the earthquake at an improvised shrine in front of the gates of an elementary school. The woman was crying. The angel waited until the woman left before kneeling in front of the shrine with her face and hands on the ground.

White closed her eyes, raised one hand and whispered.

"Father, I pray to you as I always do when so many die by your will.

After all this time in your service, I have embraced my ministry. All life is precious to me. Unique, however small, whichever kind, I have come to know each and every one of your creations, as they were mine. As they were me."

A pair of beautiful feathery wings flourished out of White's back. Her outer glow grew more intensely.

"So I suffered in silence", she continued "that my sisters do not come to know my pain. I grieved for those who lost their lives. But I did it without ever questioning your judgment."

White opened both arms and her wings spread. She looked up at the sky. Her face expression was compassionate, almost messianic.

"Today I pray to you one last time, to ask not for guidance, but for answers. Things have always been according to your plan. Death has stained our hands in your Name for too long. It is not enough for me to trust these souls will be at Your side. I need to know... I just need to know, was there ever a purpose for them to have lived at all?"

White's compassion became serious determination.

"And what of those left behind by the deceased? How do they continue living without a piece of themselves? For all life is one unto You as You are in each and every one of us. Isn't that what life means after all? If I am to be, as I have always been, Your voice, let me know the answers so that I may proclaim them to the world. Let me serve you. Please."

The angel closed her eyes for a moment. She waited.

"Your silence, as dead as these people. So be it... So be it."

"Amen."

White stood up from the ground and wiped the tears from her face. She saw the Black Angel looking at her from the opposite corner of the street. Black Angel smiled excited and waved at her sister. White was horrified. She has always been terrified of her youngest sibling. Black Angel took a few steps forward, reaching out to White as if asking for her embrace.

White took a few steps back and whispered "Get away from me".

The angel of life spread her wings and took off to the skies, knowing her sister couldn't follow her where she was going. Black slowly lowered her arms with a sad and confused look on her face. She waved at her again, but not as effusively as before. The angel of death wondered why every time she tried to get close to White, she would stay clear from her. She began to suspect that her older sister did not love her.

....

At day break, Paolo, the young Brazilian environmentalist, reached the end of his long drive in his jeep to the Taipus de Fora beachhead on the Marau Peninsula. Wearing only ripped jean shorts, the bronzed-skinned Adonis drove from his apartment very early to catch the sunrise. He got off the jeep and ran barefoot and bare-chested towards the shoreline. He couldn't help his desire to dive in the water and feel the waves splashing against his body.

Paolo's footprints in the sand were shadowed by a female figured silhouette. The angel Evergreen had kept an eye on Paolo and she was fascinated by his beauty and his deep connection with nature.

The beach waves broke at Evergreen's feet, caressing them and turning into foam. Evergreen sat down on the sand and let the ocean water wet her thighs. The angel watched as Paolo dove in the water. She bit her lower lip.

"I shouldn't contemplate you," she thought, "but I follow your every step. You are human. I am… everything else."

Evergreen's toes played with the wet sand.

"But you are different. You watch. You care. You wish to worship all around you. Naked and relentless."

Paolo submerged into the water. Evergreen breathed deeply.

"Leave all your worldly pleasures behind." She continued, "I can give you something much better. Take it. Make it yours."

Paolo swooped out of the water. His wet head and hair splashed against the ocean.

"*Ah! Delicia!*" He said smiling. The angel smiled with him.

"Make me yours." Evergreen's legs moved in the sand as if dancing with the waves. She kept looking at Paolo from a distance.

"I'll embrace you with a force stronger than a thousand hurricanes... I will touch you with the tenderness of a single raindrop. I am nature and we belong together..."

Evergreen lied on the sand, her eyes facing the sky. The beach water touched her body completely. She was in ecstasy.

"I desire you..." She thought.

A confused Blue saw all of this from a distance. The cobalt angel had been up all night planning with Evergreen on Sao Paulo's restoration. He noticed her distant and uninterested in her work. When his sister disappeared on him, he worried about her very unusual conduct. He flew high with his laser-like energy wings and looked for her all over Brazil. Finding her on the beach fantasizing about a human was even more confusing to him. The truth was, he really did not care for Evergreen's sexual desires, but this was affecting their holy mission; there was a schedule to be followed.

Blue flew closer to Evergreen, still trying to keep his distance, and called her name many times, pretending not to know what she was doing to herself.

"Evergreen!" he yelled. "We need to get back to work."

Evergreen did not answer. This forced Blue to get closer to her. Blue didn't have any other choice but to walk up to her. His boots stood next to her head as he bended over her body. She was calm, almost asleep. Whatever it was that she was doing, she was already done. Blue's shadow covered Evergreen completely.

"*Delicia!*" said the green angel with much satisfaction.

"Evergreen!" Blue called again.

Evergreen opened her eyes and let out a scream. She jumped backwards, surprised and embarrassed to see her brother.

Blue sighed, "Sister, I truly think you need to get out more..."

....

Goldie, the angel of miracles, was bored. It was afternoon already and she had wasted another day watching her siblings do all the restoration work in Sao Paulo. Having nothing to do in Brazil, Goldie decided to try something she liked to do every time a disaster occurred and her talents weren't needed. It was a game she called *Guess Where*. The rules were simple: The angel had to close her eyes and fly with no direction around the world. Once she opened her eyes, she would have to guess where she ended up.

Guess Where had gotten Goldie in trouble quite a few times. One time in New York, Her eyes were closed when she bumped against a passenger airplane turbine and almost crashed it. She helped the pilot land the plane safely in the nearest river and then created some dead birds to make it seem that the animals had disrupted the engine. Goldie thought she got away with it, but her sister White caught on when all the news headlines read: "MIRACLE ON THE HUDSON RIVER". White forbade Goldie to play the game again.

Goldie was dozing off in Brazil. It was time for her to leave. The golden angel made sure nobody was looking. She closed her eyes before spreading her wings. "Guess where…" she said, and took off. In a matter of minutes, she felt she had travelled thousands of miles. In her mind, she'd probably flown around the world two or three times already, so she decided to land. The thrill of the surprise had her peeking a bit. Then, she opened her eyes completely.

The golden angel stood in the middle of a college campus. Many art students passed by her, carrying books and art materials. She saw signs that labeled the buildings around her by courses: "FINE ARTS, INDUSTRIAL DESIGN, ILLUSTRATION, GAME DESIGN", and so on. There was a group of students protesting at the college gates. They sang peacefully and handed out flyers to everyone that would pay them attention.

None of this gave Goldie a clue of where she was. That was until she noticed many same sex couples walking around holding hands, sometimes kissing. Young gay men and women expressing their sexuality freely could only mean she was either somewhere in Europe or…

"San Francisco!" she exclaimed excitedly.

Goldie got interested in one particular young student. A tall, thin, twenty-something Latino exited the Game Design building. He wore thick sixties style glasses, jeans and a white t-shirt with the phrase "THERE'S A MUTHA F@!%^KIN' SNAKE ON THA MUTHA F@!%^KIN' PLANE". His worn out jacket matched his brown sneakers.

The miracle angel loved that he smiled with no apparent reason. She followed him around and studied him. He seemed to be talking to himself and having a blast. Anyone who saw him would've thought he was a bit crazy. A human after Goldie's heart.

The golden angel snuck up on the student and tapped his right shoulder.

"Pssst. Hey, kid. What's ya name?"

The student turned his face to the right and the entire world around him changed. He was no longer at his art school. He now stood next to a wagon in what appeared as an early 1900's small town. The wagon was full of golden medicine bottles. There was a sign on the wagon that read: GOLDIE'S WONDER POTION CURES ALL. He felt he was trapped in an old Michael Jackson and Paul McCartney music video.

"Um, Hector." The young confused man said. "Did I just take a wrong turn somewhere? I swear I was in front of my school…"

Goldie posed in front of Hector as she showed him one of the bottles she held in her gloved hand with a used car salesman grin.

"Why you look like a fine young man with a good noodle on ya shoulders and all ya marbles in a row. May I interest you, Mistah Hector, in Goldie's Wonder Potion (otion, otion, otion…)? My friend, I say my friend, ya won't be findin' a better concoction in all Creation!"

Hector was confused. "Ok… well, what does it do?"

"'What does it do?' 'What does it do?!' Why what doesn't it do? Ever walked out to the park on a sunny day and all of a sudden a – a tiger falls from the sky to pounce? This, my friend, is the potion to prevent just that! It's the bee's knees. With it, you'll be sheltered from all feline attackers falling from the heavens! Lions! Panthers! Cheetahs! Kittens! Why even saber tooth tigers! Guaranteed a hundred-thousand percent!"

Hector had a skeptic look. "Hmmm, I don't think I have to worry about tigers falling from the sky. That's just impossible. But thanks anyway. I really need to figure out how to get back to class."

Goldie looked in disbelief at Hector walking away.

"Saaay, but everything is possible..." she responded with an eerie voice.

A huge fanged saber tooth tiger fell from the sky and attacked Hector with its huge claws. The sabre tooth roared at a shocked Hector.

"Aaaaaaaaah!!! Sonova bitch!!!" Hector screamed as he tried to fight off the tiger. The young student reached out his hand towards Goldie.

"Help me, lady!"

Goldie smiled at Hector from a distance. She played with the bottle to taunt him.

"Shoulda' bought the bottle, ya goon!" She said.

A bright white light appeared next to Goldie. The angel gulped when she heard a voice from the light.

"Stop playing around, Goldie. Unmake that tiger."

The angel White stood beside Goldie. She was clearly angry at her. Goldie made the tiger disappear. They were no longer at the small town, but back again at the art school. Hector stood up and ran for his life. Goldie lowered her head, not wanting to face her sister.

"That palooka didn't wanna buy my potion. He's all wet, see?" She whispered. White kept looking at Goldie with a stern attitude.

"I grow tired of pointing out the high cost of your miracles. Had that human died by your hands, the consequences would be dire for you"

"Aw! I didn't mean nothin' by it, sis. For a minute there... I lost myself... I-I'm cracking up like a worn out shoe!"

White saw that her sister was deeply upset. She gently lifted Goldie's chin with her fingers.

"I know, sister... I am not content with the way things are. But our sister Violet's negligence has set forth a chain of unstoppable events. Look..."

White and Goldie watched the students protesting at the college gate. They were no longer peaceful. The passion in their chanting increased to the point they fought each other.

"Everywhere you go," White continued, "humans and other living things are overwhelmed by strong unchecked feelings. Violet has let emotions run wild. Think of the graveness of this situation. On any given day, a human with a foul attitude can ruin the day for his or her closest peers. They, in turn can affect others. One of these people could be on the verge of desperation, craving a smile or an encouraging word to stop them from doing something drastic they cannot come back from. With no reassurance to hold on to, this person may go on to do something deranged like killing themselves or others. Now, multiply this spreading of devastating emotions throughout humanity a thousand fold. How many more people do you think will die?"

"Wowee!" Goldie exclaimed as she noticed that each person showed an extreme emotion: anger, sadness, fear, confusion, and so on. No one in the campus could control themselves. The fighting increased and as college security guards intervened, violence erupted and the scene became a riot.

"Where there are human emotions, there are human sins." White continued "And where there is potential for sin, our enemies come to sow the seeds of evil."

"Holy evil alliance, White!" Goldie's eyes opened wide before she punched the palm of her hand. "Sound the trumpets! Prepare for war!"

"Unfortunately, all of this must come to pass." White spoke with a defeated tone. "Everything happens for a reason. And everything must be as foretold. Come with me. There is something you must see."

White extended her hand to Goldie and spread her wings.

"Where we going?" Goldie asked as she took her sister's hand. White began to fly, taking Goldie with her. Goldie could have sworn she heard her sister say "Guess where…"

5 CHURCH ON SUNDAYS

Outside the universe, there was Hell. It was a place of great darkness untouched by the light of Creation. The darkness continuously sheltered what was mostly a desert made of ashes. There were some burned ruins, but what these buildings were originally, only God knew. It is there that horrible beasts that did not fit God's creation existed. This was the place where fallen angels were banished to. This was where they lived and thrived in darkness. The absence of light hurt them and reminded them of the grace ripped away from their hearts, leaving painful hollowness. Hell forever remained almost completely in the dark... Almost.

Deep in the center of the ash desert wastelands there was a dimming source of brightness. It was a small chapel made out of stones and wood. It had been moved there from Gallia since 339 CE and it was set there as a warning to all creatures of Hell. No demon was allowed to step inside a church. These holy places were protected by the light of Creation. Any demon that tried to step into the chapel would burn from the inside out.

But the Deadly Seven were not just "any demon". They were the worst of all Hell-born arch-demons. They did not fall from grace. They were the forefront of a dangerous new generation of demons inbred from the fallen angels that never saw or lived with God. Hell was all they ever knew. They did not feel the aching emptiness inside their souls that the fallen angels did. They just felt pure hate. To the Cardinal Ones, as they were called by their lesser demon servants, God was the only threat to their existence and therefore, He was the enemy that they had to vanquish. They got a kick out of desecrating what they could of His Creation. That is why they chose to personify the seven deadly sins: Pride, Wrath, Sloth, Gluttony, Lust, Greed and Envy.

The Deadly Seven chose to live just outside the small chapel in Hell's desert out of some sick sense of rebellion. Lesser demons were at awe that these seven would not be afraid to be so close to the chapel's burning light. They feared and served the Cardinal Ones, because when Lucifer was dethroned as ruler of Hell, they knew that if anyone could be successful in leading them in the war against God, it would be the Seven.

On Sundays, the Deadly Seven pissed and ate and had violent sex outside the chapel walls. They cannibalized on other demons, plotted against humanity and spat on God's name for fun. Sundays were also "tribute day". All the lesser goblins had to provide the arch-demons with freshly condemned human souls as offerings. These souls, however, had to satisfy the specific libidos of each of the Deadly Seven according to their respective cardinal sin, or else the lesser demons would suffer greatly at the hands of their masters.

Thousands of goblin demons arrived and kneeled down with their heads kissing the ground as they waited with their soul offerings for their lords. Seven thrones were set in line next to one another outside the chapel. The seven youngest of the lesser goblin demons stepped forward closer to the chapel thrones. They looked at each other with fear and sadness, knowing they were about to become sacrifice. One of them began to convulse and vomit green slime. A pale white hand clawed its way out of the shaking demon's mouth.

The demon's body stretched and tore and from its insides raised a chalk-white skinned man dressed in black. His face was ugly and his eyes were open wide, one wider than the other which - along with his long and thin French debonair mustache - made him look like a cliché movie villain. In fact, with his large black hat and long black coat, he looked like a villain from a German Expressionist film. A huge white gloved hand, the size of a car hovered a few feet over the top of the man's hat.

Greed was first to arrive. He moved his mouth to laugh and pronounce words, but no sound came from his mouth. He then opened his black trench coat, like an exhibitionist. The soundless words that Greed had pronounced appeared written inside his coat: *"BWAHAHAHAHA! I'M FIRST! ME! HAHAHAHA!"*

Greed moved with a cliché sinister walk that more likely caused laughter than intimidation. The giant white gloved hand followed and remained over him as he sat on his throne. The glove seemed to move in reflection to the Arch-demon's moods. The demon's eyes twitched fast and his fingers shook as he looked at the throne next to him. He put his legs on the other throne and then looked at the other five empty thrones. His eyes twitched again. The big floating gloved hand quickly rearranged six empty thrones in a circle around his throne where he sat impatiently. He talked again with no sound. He opened his black trench coat and new words showed written inside it:

"Where's my tribute? Where's my present? Gimme!"

From the crowd of thousands of kneeling goblin demons, one stood up and slowly walked towards Greed. This frail demon had long arms and legs, and his face and body was covered in badly sewn brown rags. He held seven bone-made boxes chained to his arms. The demon's name was Beggar.

Beggar opened the first box and from it, a glowing red shapeless fog flowed and slowly took the form of a sixty-something overweight business executive.

"Sire, Lord Greed, I am Beggar, Demon General and Grand Priest of the armies of Hell. We offer you the soul of Norton P. Knowles. In life, he was C.E.O. of a financial institution that stole all the money from his employees' retirement plans before bankrupting the company."

Greed yelled silently in excitement and opened his trench coat:

"Ooh! A Ceeh Eeh Oh! I love me those! Gimme!"

The giant gloved hand that floated over the Deadly Seven Demon moved its fingers in excitement, like a magician about to cast a spell.

Greed fed on the damned soul and its red light began to flicker. The soul of the C.E.O. suffered in agony as it dissipated. He was satisfied for about two seconds before turning his attention towards the demon priest. The Deadly Seven demon moved his lips to talk and opened his black trench coat with a new written message:

"What else?"

"We have thirteen-hundred more greedy souls-" Beggar continued before being interrupted by Greed talking silently and opening the coat again:

"That's it? Thirteen-hundred?! Bah! What about the Pope? I want the Pope!"

"We're working on it, sire, but-" Beggar responded.

The hovering white glove pulled Beggar closer to Greed's face. The villainous looking demon opened his mouth wide and yelled silently, with rage. He opened his trench coat, revealing new words:

"I WANT THE DAMNED POPE!!!"

Beggar breathed heavily and pissed himself. Greed let go of him, leaned back on his seat, and moved his lips with a bored look. He opened his trench coat:

"Another disappointing Sunday…"

The second of the sacrificial demons, convulsed and drooled green. He quickly exploded and Wrath took its place. Wrath looked like a Celtic barbarian. She was a tall, muscled-bound white beast twice the size of a bear standing. Her long black hair was tangled and unkempt. She wore the skin of dragons, chimeras and other creatures rejected from Creation that dwelled in Hell. A collar full of horns and fangs from several creatures she had killed adorned her neck, and at the center of it hung her own demonic horns. Her leather boots were broken, uncovering huge scaled reptile-like brown feet. She raised her huge blood stained battle-axe with her massive clawed hands.

Wrath looked at Greed and snarled. She quickly walked over to him and lifted him off the throne with one arm.

"OFF MY CHAIR NOW!"

Greed responded apologetic as he sweated cold. The words inside his opened trench coat read:

"Oh, is this your- I'm so sorry, my mistake, hah!"

Wrath threw Greed to the side and picked up her seat. She placed it a few feet away from the others and sat on it, placing her axe at her side.

"GET ON WITH IT!!!"

Beggar opened the second box and the glowing red ghost of a thirty-something woman appeared.

"Your excellence, this is Margarita Ramos, a housewife. She knifed her husband and three offspring after finding out he was unfaithful."

Wrath grunted. She picked up her axe and cut the soul in half. She gnawed on the housewife's soul like a dog would a bone.

"We also brought twenty thousand souls damned from anger." Beggar continued.

"RAAAH!!!"

Wrath kicked the demon away from her. Beggar fell to the ground. He nervously stood up and picked up the boxes it dropped.

The third sacrificial demon fell asleep while standing. The demon next to it poked it to wake it up, but its snore grew louder and louder. The demon's body turned to ashes and the wind blew it away, leaving the arch-demon Sloth standing and snoozing. Sloth dragged his feet towards his throne and plummeted on it.

Sloth looked like a skinny teenage slacker. He wore a stained t-shirt, pajama pants that he was too old to wear but didn't care to change, and flip flops that could barely contain his huge goat-like feet. He did not wear his horns because he forgot where he had left them and was too lazy to look for them. He wore a beanie hat so he didn't have to comb his long shaggy hair that covered his eyes; but even if the hair was removed, no one could ever tell what color his eyes were because he was always sleeping. "…hrm…" he would mumble, like talking in his sleep. "…hrm…"

Beggar opened the third box. A forty-eight year old man glowed red.

"Lord Sloth, this is Angelo Alfredo, a nobody. He could have been a great writer if he'd applied himself. Instead, he settled for being a mediocre part-time customer service representative and lived from his mother until he eventually committed suicide… Lord?"

Beggar stood closer in front of Sloth.

"Lord Sloth? Your offering…"

"…hrm…"

Wrath stood up from her throne and reached out to Sloth, shaking him violently.

"MAKE ME WAIT ANOTHER SECOND AND I WILL SHOVE MY AXE DOWN YOUR THROAT!" Wrath complained.

"…hrm…"

Sloth turned his head towards the red soul. The ghost slowly crumbled in small pieces that mixed with the black desert ash and faded.

"We have fifty-three hundred damned souls for you, sire." Said Beggar. "Fifty-three hundred souls of the lazy kind."

The fourth sacrificial demon began to rub its nipples with its fingers. It began caressing itself and then clawing its own skin, tearing chunks. Green slime gushed as it kept tearing itself up. Lust stepped away from the remains of the dead demon and sat on his throne.

Lust was a creepy sweaty overweight fifty-something bald man with Italian features that sported a big mustache on a hairy face that was not groomed. The little head hair he had on the sides over his ears was tied in a ponytail. He wore a stained dirty wife-beater that could not cover the hair foresting his chest and arms. The zipper on is blue shorts was open. For some perverted reason, he enjoyed wearing black leather high heel boots that every now and then he would tap the floor, when he'd reach his climax. Lust had a big bulky suitcase next to him. Parts of the suitcase moved as if there was a small child inside it. Lust opened the suitcase.

"Where are Papa's little helpers?"

Five goblin demons emerged from the suitcase. These creatures were altered to look like malformed midget women. They were dressed in diverse skimpy outfits; a nurse, a Girl Scout, a dominatrix, a maiden, and a kitty. The nurse dressed goblin gave Lust an I-pad. He talked to the I-pad as he typed.

"Papa like to chat. Hello, little girl… what… are you… wearing?"

As Lust proceeded to chat on his I-pad, Beggar opened the fourth box. The misty red soul of a twenty-three year old beautiful woman surged from it.

"I present to you, great Lust, with Natalie Marshall, a high school teacher. She is a nymphomaniac that slept with many of her students, giving them herpes."

"Papa like..." Lust slurred, barely containing his drool and keeping his attention to the I-pad screen.

"Ninety-one thousand lecherous souls for you, my master." Beggar continued.

The fifth sacrificial demon felt a rumble in its stomach. The creature felt a strong bellyache and fell on its knees where it began to puke green gunk and chunks of its own internal organs. It desperately gathered its vomited body parts while still suffering unstoppable nausea. The demon's body collapsed on itself and gave out one last barf before dying. Gluttony came out from the mouth of the demon's carcass.

Gluttony was short, thin, but with a muscle-cut body. He had Asian features and his hair was bright Sharpie yellow combed to the side. He wore a shocking pink colored headband with little boned horns coming out of it, and turquoise blue jogging sweater, pants, and white sneakers that would turn little lights on every time he took a step. He also held a jar full of water in one hand.

The skinny demon searched around him.

"What's for dinner?"

Beggar began to open the fifth box.

"Lord, Gluttony, we offer you-"

Gluttony took the box from the demon and lifted it face down over his head. He opened his mouth wide and took off the top from the box. The red condemned soul of an overweight eight year old fell right into the demon's mouth and he swallowed it whole. Gluttony threw away the empty chained box and turned his attention to an empty throne next to Lust.

"This my chair?"

The arch-demon did not wait for an answer from Lust and sat on the throne, where he drank some of the water in his jar.

"Sire" Beggar humbly spoke. "We have gathered eighty-five thousand ravenous souls for your satisfaction."

Gluttony turned his attention towards the leather cat attired goblin standing next to Lust's throne. The kitty dressed goblin feared Gluttony's look. Gluttony elbowed Lust.

"Hey, you gonna eat that?"

"Yeah...Papa gonna eat that..." Lust responded with a wicked smirk, still staring at the I-pad screen.

"Ugh! Don't play with your food!" Gluttony said repulsed.

The sixth sacrificial demon started to vibrate overwhelmingly. It screamed in pain as its body expanded and became to crystalize. Once the demon's entire corpse was made of pure crystal, it exploded in thousands of sharp shards. The shards stabbed and killed dozens of the lesser demons and from the green thick liquid that gushed from their bodies, Pride was formed.

Pride, the leader of the Deadly Seven, looked through his fancy shades at his elegant watch. He took his time to fix his expensive white suit and ivory shoes while attentively observing his reflection in one of the crystal shards. His tall athletic muscled cut black male body looked perfect. On Earth, he would easily be the most handsome supermodel ever, as it should be. He made sure to put on his golden demonic horn-shaped cufflinks before heading towards his throne where the other Cardinal Ones waited for him. As he sat on his throne, Pride made sure not to wrinkle his suit.

"Try to keep your bodily fluids to yourself this time", Pride said to Lust with disgust. "This suit is nothing you could afford."

Beggar, nervously stepped towards Pride. The demon priest opened the sixth box and a red mist leaked from it.

"Your Perfectness, to you we offer-"

Pride slapped the box top close. The red mist was drawn back into it.

"Take that garbage away from me." Pride complained. "If I wanted to eat poison I'd go to Burger Bob's. You may go now, Beggar. And do consider taking a shower now and then. Your presence is revolting."

Pride moved towards the center in front of his brethren.

"Gentlemen… and 'lady'," he continued while giving a taunting look to Wrath. "I believe we can begin our evening's celebrations. Due to prior commitments, Envy will not be joining us tonight. I have news from our mistress"

Wrath was furious. She leaped from her throne and raised her battle axe towards Pride.

"HOW DARE YOU SHOW YOURSELF, PRIDE?!" she screamed, "YOU EMBARASSED ME IN FRONT OF OUR MISTRESS!!! I AM NOT KNOWN TO FORGIVE!" She could easily grab and crush Pride's head with one hand if she wanted.

"Nor are you known for your wisdom either", Pride answered calmly. "You embarrassed yourself by suggesting that Neanderthal idea of raping and killing the angels or whatever barbaric nonsense you grunted. I, on the other hand, suggested a much more refined and flawless plan of attack. Envy was a nice touch, don't you think? It is quite clear I'm the only one with a brain in this realm. That is why you always end up doing as I say, don't you?"

Wrath grabbed Pride's suit and grinded her teeth.

"DON'T… TOUCH… THE SUIT…" said Pride while removing Wrath's arm from his suit.

"I ONLY FOLLOW MY MISTRESS, NOT YOU!"

"You won't object, then, if I tell you that your mistress has ordered you to fetch the angel Scarlet."

"SCARLET IS HERE?!"

"And causing a huge commotion, apparently. She's been killing goblin demons right and left since last night. She seems a bit… angry. I believe that is your specialty to exploit. Be a good foot soldier and go fetch her, won't you? I have much more important things to take care of."

Wrath took a step closer to Pride and looked down at him fiercely. Pride stared at her defiantly. After a moment, Wrath stepped back.

"I WILL DO THIS FOR MY MISTRESS, BUT WHEN I RETURN YOU WILL-"

"Wrath, do not waste our time with empty threats. You could not handle me on your best day and we both know it."

Wrath roared and swung her huge battle axe, missing Pride by an inch, and jamming it in the ground. Pride did not flinch. Wrath lifted her axe and stormed away.

Greed crept behind Pride with fingers rapidly moving against themselves and carefully tried to touch Pride's sunglasses. He pronounced a few silent words. A new sign inside his coat read:

"Would you look at those shades... I want me one of those..."

Pride slapped Greed's hand away.

"The shades stay on." Pride declared menacingly. "Always..."

Greed smiled and pulled away his fast moving fingers.

"Now that Wrath has Scarlet occupied", Pride continued, "We must go to Earth. Envy already awaits us. He appears to have succeeded in his task. Now it's up to us. We'll take out the angels first."

Gluttony didn't care about his mistress's orders or any of the other Cardinal Ones. He was hungry; really hungry. He turned and saw the seventh sacrificial demon a few feet away from him. He saw a hamburger with legs. He grabbed the small demon by the neck and dipped him inside the water jar he held.

"Riiieeek!" the doomed creature shrieked.

Gluttony took the creature out of the jar and rammed it up his mouth. His jaw and throat expanded to fit the creature entirely. He swallowed the goblin whole as if he were at a hot dog eating contest.

"Pay attention, Gluttony" Pride sighed.

Pride extended his arm and crackling energy flowed around it. The other Cardinal Ones stood around Pride in a circle and did the same as he did to release energy from their arms.

The combined energy concentrated at the same position in the air. Pride extended his other arm to reach out to the legion of worshipping goblin demons that kneeled on the ground. As he closed his fist, hundreds of the goblins randomly began to shake and drool as if they were having seizures. The goblins combusted one by one and their life essence drifted towards Pride's fist. They were feeding the present five of the Deadly Seven. At the same time, the five generated more energy. The concentrated energy became a portal. In a matter of minutes, all the goblin demons were dead.

The demons could see through the portal. They saw a sidewalk, a street, and a mailbox in front of a house. A man and his wife were arguing violently on the lawn. He had dragged her outside their home and hit her repeatedly. She kicked his crotch and clawed his face. He fell to the ground as she spit on him. Lust let out a slight moan in approval.

"Papa like it rough…"

The five arch-demons walked through the portal and found themselves at a suburban neighborhood somewhere in Oklahoma. Humans all around them behaved madly.

Pride stopped in front of a church and saw that the people coming out of it were all crying. Every last one of the church congregation wept passionately.

"We did this to Jesus! We killed him!" one person cried.

"We don't deserve to live!" another grieved.

Gluttony saw an old man laughing hysterically at the church goers. Tears came down his cheeks and his face turned red. He gasped for air, but kept laughing. He couldn't stop himself. The old man fell to the floor asphyxiated. Pride's smile barely registered.

"Can you taste it, Gluttony?" He asked. "Do you crave it, Lust? Human emotions... There is no control. Envy has done well."

Gluttony walked over to the old man's dead body and opened his mouth unnaturally wide. The bottom of his mouth reached just over his stomach. He swallowed the corpse whole like a python would a rat.

．．．．．．．．．．．．．

Wrath's anger intensified as she crossed Hell's desert. She pressed through an ash storm that almost blinded her. The arch-demon could barely breathe and she was sick of tasting so much ash in her mouth. She bit her lip hard and drew blood from it. Her tongue licked the blood. Its strong taste took over the dry nauseating taste of ash.

"Much better", she thought.

The Deadly demon saw a dim light far away. She knew that it could only come from an angel of God, so she stepped up her march towards it. Wrath climbed up a dune and stood at the top. She looked down at the angel Scarlet sitting on a rock resting. The red angel supported herself with her sword. Scarlet looked tired and sweaty. Her armor was dirty with black ash and green demon stains. The warrior angel was surrounded by piles of hundreds of dead demon bodies she had just defeated in battle. Most of them were missing limbs or heads.

The arch-demon Wrath was disappointed. She expected more from the legendary Scarlet than the weak thing she saw sitting on a rock. Still, her mistress demanded to see her and the assignment to bring the angel in fell unto her. The Cardinal One ran down the ash dune. As she got closer to the angel, Wrath felt Scarlet's anger and frustration. It was feeding her.

"SCARLET! FACE ME!" The demon screamed, raising her battle axe.

Scarlet did not move. She saw Wrath running towards her through the reflection in her sword. The reflection of the demon was distorted and unclear from all the ash in the air. Scarlet sighed. Wrath got close to the angel and swung her ax to decapitate her. Scarlet quickly ducked and turned around to block the axe with her sword. Wrath didn't see her stand and turn towards her. Scarlet grinned.

"Is my anger making you stronger, Wrath?" she asked. "Good. You will need the strength."

"HEAVEN WHORE!" Wrath shouted.

Scarlet's sword strokes were fast and precise. Wrath's axe swings were slower, but much more powerful. The angel could barely stop the axe with her sword. Sometimes she would have to move away from the demon to avoid her strike. Wrath pressed her axe using her body weight against her. Her body was three times the size of the angel. Scarlet relented and took several steps back. Her sword kept clashing again and again with the demon's axe.

"THIS IS THE GREAT SCARLET?!" the demon complained "THE TOM BOY WARRIOR ANGEL! YOU ARE NOTHING!!!"

Scarlet's angelic wings quickly grew out from her back. Her body elevated and hovered around Wrath. Wrath swung her axe repeatedly, but could not reach Scarlet. The angel attacked the demon with her sword, cutting her many times. Some of these cuts were deep. Wrath grew angrier and let out a frustrated howl.

"Tell me why there were thousands of demons in Brazil. An army like that should not be on Earth unless they were going to war."

Wrath stood still and laughed. Her laughter worried Scarlet more than any weapon she could throw at her.

"HAVE YOU NOT SEEN THAT WE ARE ALREADY AT WAR?!" DON'T YOU KNOW WHAT THAT PATHETIC BONEY CREATURE YOU CALL A SISTER HAS DONE?!"

Scarlet stopped. Her eyes opened wide and her face showed fear. Only then did she realize the real consequences of Violet's desertion of her duties.

"NOW YOU UNDERSTAND!" Wrath continued, "NOW YOU KNOW THAT AFTER ALL THESE CENTURIES TRAPPED IN HELL, WE HAVE A CHANCE TO CARRY OUT OUR REBELLION AGAINST GOD AND CREATION! AND WE OWE IT TO THAT SAD LITTLE THING YOU CALL VIOLET!"

"No!" Scarlet screamed as she savagely attacked Wrath with her sword. She stroke closer than ever to her face.

"There is still time! The damage can be undone!" She yelled.

Wrath blocked Scarlet's attacks and waited for the right time. She grabbed the angel by the ankle and did not let her go. The red angel tried to fly free, but the demon's grip on her leg was too strong. The Deadly Seven demon slammed her body against the ground. Scarlet lost her grasp on the sword and it fell a few feet away from her.

The demon jumped on the angel's body and savagely punched her again and again until she would not stand up. Finally, Wrath let Scarlet's body fall to the ground. She was barely conscious. She struggled to get up and reach her sword. Wrath simply walked up to her and hit her head with the end of her axe handle. The angel's body fell to the ground. Wrath stood next to Scarlet's still body. She held her axe while looking down on her.

"MY ENTIRE BEING WANTS TO CUT YOU AND FEED YOU TO GLUTTONY, BUT I MUST TAKE YOU TO MY MISTRESS NOW. MAYBE LATER…"

The demon dragged Scarlet through the ash desert with one arm; her axe and the angel's sword rested on her shoulder. The angel's body left a long linear trail in the ash that the winds slowly erased. Wrath never doubted that this would be the only outcome to her fight with the warrior angel. She could not wait to hand her over to her mistress so she could join her brothers on Earth and burn it all.

·············

There was a brown rat inside a hole in the floor of the dirty dark room. The room was full of trash and dead insects. The rat would not leave its hole in the ground until it was sure no one else was there. It waited silently, but it breathed hastily. It desperately wanted to crawl into the room already and find something to eat. But it didn't want to be hunted, so it waited. And when the room got really quiet, it waited some more.

The rodent crawled a short distance, and then it stopped. It smelled; it listened; nothing. The rat kept crawling. The rat found a days-old half eaten sandwich. The animal was too busy taking quick bites from the meat and moldy cheese to notice the figure lurking behind it.

Envy stuck his sharp index finger nail through the back of the rat's neck. The rat screeched and twitched for a few seconds, but it was already dead as the Deadly Seven demon kept piercing its neck with his long boney finger. The rat's head came off and blood began to squirt from its torn neck. Envy grabbed the headless rat's carcass putting his thumb on its neck to stop the blood from squirting out.

He had a skeletal and wrinkly body covered only by old black shorts. His malformed teeth looked like stalagmites in a cave with his lower fangs shaped like demon horns. His head was oddly shaped and almost entirely bold, except for a few strands of dry hair at the sides. He had bags under his big sick looking eyes. His brownish grey skin was dirty and tattooed with words and phrases all over his body: "your hair looks prettier than mine" "I want your job" "Envy" "Jealousy" "You cheated" "covet".

Envy held the dead rat with one hand and dipped his index finger in its neck. He turned on a light bulb that hung from the ceiling. With the lights on, the Arch-demon walked towards one of the walls stepping over the trash and dead bugs.

"They're all better than you." he chanted, "They all look down on you. You hate yourself. You will never be like them."

The scrawny demon was glad that Pride's spell to conceal his presence from Violet as he possessed her worked. It even kept him hidden from Scarlet when she confronted her sister. He reached out his bloody finger and began writing on the wall with the rodent's blood. He was in a trance, pronouncing the words he'd write on the walls as if taking dictation from himself.

The bloody letters on the walls read: "THIS IS SCARLET'S FAULT! ALWAYS PUSHING ME AROUND! WHY CAN'T SHE HAVE MY MINISTRY?! WHY CAN'T I GET HER SWORD?! WHY DOES GOLDIE GET TO MAKE MIRACLES AND EVERGREEN GETS TO PLAY WITH FLOWERS?! EVEN BLACK GETS AN EASIER JOB THAN MINE! SHE TAKES CARE OF THE DEAD! THEY'RE DEAD! HOW HARD CAN THAT BE? THEY GOT THE EASY MINISTRIES AND I GET TO KEEP PAINFUL EMOTIONS IN CHECK! AND IT'S JUST NOT FAIR! IT'S A VERY HARD JOB AND I'M SICK OF IT! I JUST- I JUST WANT TO BE SOMEBODY ELSE! HAVE YOU EVER FELT LIKE THAT?"

Envy stopped writing on the wall. He came off his trance momentarily and read the last question a few times. His face changed to sadness.

"Yes. Yes I have...It's my own little piece of hell". He answered before trying to restore his trance. "You'll never be as pretty as they are. You will always be an ugly fat whale-."

The Deadly Seven demon stood in the middle of the dirty room right underneath the flickering light bulb. He looked right up at it while holding his bloody rat. Violet had figured out she was possessed by him, but maybe he could still manage to regain control of her before she could exorcise him. He felt her struggling to free herself from him.

"Ewww! Can't you see?! It's a demon!" Envy laughed as he mimicked Violet mockingly. "I'm possessed!" Get it off me!" His face expression changed again.

"Make me." He said with a defiant and wicked grin on his face.

Envy was not going anywhere.

.

6 ¡EXORCISMO!

My heart is an endless void of sorrow. I suffer at the whim of demons of my own making; and they are legion. What need do I have for yet another, but the final shot from the gun to end my misery? What need?

Who ever heard of an angel possessed by a demon?! People get possessed! Pigs get possessed, not angels! What did that say about me as an angel?! How could I've let this happen?! How embarrassing! It had to be Envy! I knew it was him! He made me jealous of my sisters! The outcome of this deed could not be good at all! Demons are not supposed to possess angels! I had to get him off me! And I needed to do it fast because I felt I wouldn't be able to fight the demon inside me for much longer! I grabbed my whale by the shoulders and begged her to take me to see Father Anselmo.

"Who's Father Anselmo?" Ruth asked.

"He's like the only living demon exorcist left that I know. I mean, I'm sure there're others, but I don't know them." "Um...Never been to a catholic church before." she said, "Where do you know this guy from?"

So I told her...

Father Anselmo was a cranky old Spanish priest that served at St. Marks. That's where I met him before. Scarlet made me watch over him because he's got an important role to play in the End of Days. She said he was one of the last demon summoners left on Earth. That meant he could exorcise demons. But he was really depressed as he went through a massive crisis of faith. Scarlet didn't want him doing anything drastic like harming himself or others before he played his part in the Apocalypse.

The priest was such a dismal old grouch, I couldn't handle him. Most of the time I stood there in his room watching over him without letting him see me. It disgusted me to see him wearing nothing but his underwear and drinking bottles of Jack Daniels like it was Kool Aid. He smelled like old people, nicotine, and whiskey. I guessed he was sixty or seventy by the wrinkles on his face. His gray hair and the flabby skin that hung from everywhere you could imagine. He had this huge Spanish nose and this mean angry look all the time, like he had a demon horn stuck in his butt or something. And he kept saying "Joder!" which I know means something mean in Spanish.

I got tired of watching him lying on his bed all day. People that desperately needed him called him on the phone or knocked on his door. He just ignored them and kept drinking. I tried giving him the feeling of a little bliss for at least a few minutes, but all that did was make him remember happier times and it depressed him even more to see how he let his life go down the drain. There was so much regret in him...

I finally decided to cheat and take a peek into Father Anselmo's soul to see if I could fix whatever it was that bothered him. I opened a purple window over the priest's chest. Purple windows are a trick of mine. They let me see strong emotional images from the past, present, or future; they're visions of feelings that define or will define each person.

But with Father Anselmo, everything was wobbly. Out of all the priest's feelings, I could only make out the image of a really tall twenty-something-looking girl lying naked on a motel room bed. She was huge. Like seven feet tall. I think she suffered from gigantism. And I guessed her name was Melanie 'cause it was tattooed on her breast. She seemed sad, and Father Anselmo was sad too. I felt he wanted to help Melanie, but he didn't know how.

I kept looking at the huge sad girl, but I didn't notice there was a crack in the purple window until it was too late. The purple window glass shattered and a bunch of demon goblins clawed their way out, trying to escape the priest's soul. As it turned out, Father Anselmo trapped the demons he exorcised inside his soul. No wonder he was such a tool! He literally struggled against his own demons, all the time.

The demons grabbed me by the ankles and wrists. They tore through my shirt and pulled me towards them.

"LET US OUT, LITTLE ANGEL!" they yelled, "LET US OUT AND WE PROMISE YOU WON'T FEEL IT WHEN WE TEAR YOUR FEATHERS OUT!"

I was horrified, I just couldn't take it. I closed shut the purple window and ran away from Father Anselmo.

"You abandoned him?!" Ruth asked me.

"Shut up! I didn't abandon him!"

"Yes you did. You left him on his own with those demons–"

"Don't judge me! I-I got scared, okay? I've never been much for fighting demons and… well, they were already trapped inside Father Anselmo's soul. There was not much for me to do besides being there for him, which is probably what my sister Scarlet wanted me to do, but I just couldn't handle it. But he was still alive, right? He's pretty capable for an old fart"

"Please let him be okay" I kept telling myself, as we reached the old gothic cathedral in St. Marks.

It was one of those old churches with pointy spears and gloomy gothic designs, creepy gargoyles statues and all that. The place looked cool if you're into that spooky stuff, but I sincerely doubt God enjoys being worshipped at a place straight out of a Duncan Blackheart video. But that's just me.

Ruth knocked on the wooden door ring and a nice old lady let us in. My whale asked for Father Anselmo, but the old lady said he wasn't serving at St. Marks anymore. He'd been transferred to some island in the Caribbean called Santa Cristal. The lady asked Ruth to sit on a chair by the corner of the waiting room while she went to get his address. This was rough for me because they only had one chair and the lady didn't offer me one because she couldn't see me. I had to sit on the floor while we waited.

I took out my little purple pocket book and began to draw. Ruth stared at me for a while.

"Um…Can I see?"

I held my book tight to my chest. "Nooooo! It's personal."

"I just want to take a look at it."

"Don't make fun of me."

"I won't!"

I handed the pocket book to Ruth and she browsed through it. Then, she stopped at a random page and read a passage.

"There are no louder noises, no higher notes, no longer-lasting echoes, than the throes of their emotions. They are humanity. They speak…" she paused.

"Why are you smiling?"

"It's cool", she said. "You describe our emotions as sounds, almost like music."

"Yeah, I listen to feelings. It's hard to explain"

"I think it's… some of the words you use-"

"I like to write with feeling"

"I like it. But, um… How come you sound so different when you talk?"

"What do you mean?"

"If you truly are an angel, aren't you supposed be thousands of years old? How come you behave like you're in high school?"

"Okay, first of all I, like, resent that comment and stuff. Yes, I truly am an angel, but this is just how I want you to perceive me. Trust me, you couldn't deal with how an angel truly looks or sounds like."

"Okay, I get it, but… out of all the ways you could be perceived, why a school girl?"

"Shut uuup! I am so not a school girl!"

"Okay, whatever…" Ruth conceded as she turned her head away and back to my book.

We both fell silent for a moment. The conversation became a little awkward between us, so I tried to change the topic.

"There's some drawings after the middle..." I said.

Ruth skipped through the middle and took a look at some of my sketches. Then her face turned a bit serious.

"What?!"

"Nothing."

"Don't be such an ass."

"I'm not being- All you have here are little people with big heads hanging from the neck or cutting their wrists or shooting themselves in the head..."

"They're called chibbies!"

"But why are they killing themselves? Are you emo?"

That pissed me off! I stood up and yanked the book away from her.

"I. AM NOT. EMO!"

I walked as far away as I could from my whale, which wasn't more than a few feet.

"You're a stupid whale!"

"Hey! I swear to God, you call me whale again, I will punch your face!"

The old lady came in the room and looked at Ruth like she was crazy. The lady kept staring at Ruth as she gave her a piece of paper and spoke:

"He's at a church called San Felipito in the town of Ortega. He was removed from service here after... well, he attacked another priest. He was very violent, I have to say. I don't have a phone number, but here's the church address."

"Thank you."

"And, young lady... you are definitely not a whale."

"Ha!" I mockingly stuck my tongue out to Ruth.

Then a thought hit me: What if Father Anselmo was not okay? The church lady said he attacked another priest! What if the demons I saw in the purple window finally took control of him? I hoped the demons didn't get to him, but I was afraid. If something happened to that priest, Scarlet wouldn't let me hear the end of it.

....

I couldn't fly Ruth to Santa Cristal myself because my wings were useless, but I still got her a free plane ticket! I just made the lady at the airport feel compassion towards Ruth and she gave her a free employee air pass. The plane was full, so I had to sit on Ruth's lap. She was making fun of me because I got scared to fly by plane, but I've seen a lot of these things crash to know better!

Santa Cristal was a tropical sunny island with beautiful beaches and palm trees and humidity. It was located in the Caribbean, near the Antilles. There were luxurious houses and condos for rich people, but just across the street of these condos, there'd be poor houses that smelled like vomit and trash everywhere. Ruth said she heard that they built projects right next to rich people neighborhoods because they wanted the poor to look up to and "emulate" the rich people's lifestyle or whatever. All it got them was a lot of car-jackings and break-ins.

San Felipito's church was located in the middle of this poor dirty town called Ortega. There were chickens and iguanas all over the streets. The church seemed abandoned with paint scratched from the walls and a few broken windows. As Ruth opened the main door, it made an annoying screeching sound that echoed inside the church hall. We walked in and saw Father Anselmo, dressed in black pants and shirt with a white priest collar around his neck. He was talking to a young married couple. The priest was just finishing a counseling session with them. The couple looked to be in their thirties and a bit overweight. They both were sad and confused from the advice Father Anselmo gave them in a thick Spanish accent.

"What do you people want me to do?" He asked them. "It's been five years! I could tell you to pray all the Hail Mary's you want, but that doesn't change the fact that you guys can't have babies. Either the missus has dry eggs or the hubby has a lousy sperm count. Are you expecting any miracles here? Why don't you just adopt one of those African kids? It's worked so far for a lot of celebrities. Now, if that will be all, I have things to do."

Father Anselmo practically threw the couple out the door, passing right in front of Ruth and me without noticing us. When the couple left, he closed the door and loosened his priest collar. Ruth walked up to the priest. Back on the plane we had rehearsed what she'd say to convince him that I was there with them. I didn't want to let him see me right away because I didn't know how he'd react. My whale went up to the priest and introduced herself. She was stuttering and looking up to the ceiling

"Father, my name is-"

"I'm sorry. We're closed. Whatever they told you, I can't help. "

"But-"

"You should go now, and take that angel with you. This church hasn't been sanctified in ages and I can't vouch for her safety here."

"OMG! OMG! OMG! You can see me?!" I asked, covering my face with my shirt in embarrassment.

"And I also remember you, too. You were that good for nothing angel in my room that kept staring at me a few years back. Now, get going. I'm serious about what I said. You're not safe. I am a magnet for demons."

"But you peed yourself in bed!"

"So? I was drunk. You were the one that kept staring at me, you little pervert."

"I am so not a perv! I was like watching over you and stuff!"

"What, like a guardian angel? For me? Pheh! That'll be the day."

"It's true! I was watching you 'cause you're important in God's plan for-"

"Child, take it from me. God doesn't have a plan. He's just poking humanity with a stick. And his son... his son... Never mind. Both of you need to leave."

"This is so freaky!" I yelled, "How could you see me without me allowing it?"

"Being able to see demons and angels and other beings is part of my abilities." The priest explained.

If I'd known he was this powerful, maybe I'd have tried doing more to help him before- or maybe I'd still run away, I don't know. But this made things a lot easier for me to get rid of Envy. Maybe he could even help me find someone to take over my Ministry. Things were finally picking up!

"Wait, Father." I pleaded. "I got a demon inside me and I need you to get it off meeeeee"

"Hold on! You're possessed? That's just not possible!"

"I knooooooow! That's so messed uuuuup, right? I didn't know what else to do! You're so awesome at this exorcism thing, so if you could just-"

"This is not good at all. This means they're getting stronger. They don't fear God's boundaries anymore." Father Anselmo said really concerned.

"What does that mean?" Ruth asked.

"What do you think it means? It means they can come and raise Hell on Earth any time now and there's not a thing that we, or your angel friend here can do about it."

"Guys," I barged in "I'm sure my sister Scarlet will kick their butts back to Hell if that ever happened, she's badass like that, but I need your help now, Father! Pleaaaaaase!"

"I'm not exorcising you. I don't do that anymore."

"Whaaaat?! But-"

"I'm too old. I no longer have it in me to do that sort of thing. Now you girls run along-"

"No! You can't just- I need you- I-I can't..."

I was angry at Father Anselmo. I coveted his gift and felt that I was cursed with mine. And then I looked at Ruth, and I thought her mortal life was so simple and perfect and... Everything I saw turned red. I started... skipping, but I didn't want to skip. And then I looked at Ruth again and I thought that she was such an ugly girl. You could see she tried too hard the way she dressed. She wanted so hard to get attention. To be loved. But no one loved her. No one. And I let her know that. I told her!

"You are so pathetic, Ruth. You want people to like you, but look at that scythe you have for a nose!"

"What-what are you-?"

"You make me laugh! You make everyone laugh at you! That's what you were born to be. A pathetic little thing to make everyone laugh and feel better for themselves. But you'll never be like them!"

"Shut up!"

"You'll never be as pretty as they are. You will always be an ugly fat whale."

Ruth threw a pathetic punch at me. I caught it with one hand and twisted her wrist. She knelt in front of me crying and screaming in pain, but I wouldn't let go of her arm.

"Joder!" Father Anselmo interrupted.

He drew Ruth away from my grip, rolled up his sleeves and pulled me away from her. He started praying and hearing him pray hurt. It gave me a headache and my heart ached. He pushed me to the floor and got on top of me and looked at me straight in the eyes.

"Get out. Christ compels you." he said to me, but not really to me.

"Make me" I said with a wicked smile. Wait. Was that me?

He pressed his fingers against my chest and dug a hole like I was beach sand. It hurt soooooo much! I was so angry at him!

"Aaaaaaaargh! Make me, old drunk! You can't make me!" I screamed.

Father Anselmo pulled hard. My eyes glowed a red light and black blood came out from my mouth. He kept pulling what I thought was my heart. I got angrier, and scared. I was in pain and I kept seeing red. And I saw my heart coming out of me. It was grey and covered in bones and there were horns and... I realized that wasn't really my heart. Father Anselmo was pulling the demon Envy right out from me.

Envy held tight to me and screamed like a boy that didn't want to get his vaccine injection. The old priest grabbed Envy by the neck and yanked hard to choke him. Envy's head reached out from my body in pain. He should've burned instantly, us being inside a church, but since the place was no longer sanctified, Envy was safe to be there. Father Anselmo took a small glass bottle from his pocket and sprinkled holy water from it all over Envy and me. It was painful and soothing at the same time. Like getting menthol and alcohol poured on an open wound all at once.

The priest jerked Envy fast from out of my body, and I was in enough control to try to help Father Anselmo get him off me. The demon looked to the side and saw Ruth crying on the floor holding her wrist. He quickly leaped while reaching out his claws towards her.

"Remember me?!" he screamed.

Father Anselmo jumped on top of Envy and tried to push him to the floor while praying. The demon twisted and scratched under the priest to get free. Father Anselmo screamed in pain, but he kept pressing his body weight on the demon. He emptied the bottle of holy water on the demon's arms and part of his chest. His skin burned in cool looking black fire that turned into smelly smoke and ashes. Envy shrieked and vomited acid. The priest held him on the floor and slowly tried pulling Envy towards his chest, to trap him inside his own soul, but Envy wouldn't let him. He was too powerful. The demon scratched the priest's eyes and got loose from him. He quickly headed towards the main entrance of the church. Father Anselmo glanced at me.

"Don't let that little prick get away!" he yelled.

"Me?" I asked, "I just had a demon exorcised from me! Tell Ruth!" But Ruth was crying on the floor, holding her hurt wrist.

"JODER!" he snapped at me.

"Ohmygod! Okay!"

Truth is, the holes Father Anselmo dug in my body were closed and healed. I was pretty okay. I felt peachy actually. Like I just had a huge weight lifted off me.

I ran after Envy and threw myself on him, just before he could manage to reach the door. I got behind him and wrapped my arms around his scrawny stomach. I was so grossed out, but I held as tight as I could even though I felt he was very strong and he could've kept running with me on top of him and all. Ruth was on the floor and because I was bonded to her, I couldn't move away from her more than a few feet and neither could Envy as long as I held on to him. Ruth stood up and took a step towards me.

"Get him away from me!" She yelled.

As she took the step, so did Envy towards the church door.

"DON'T MOVE!" I screamed at Ruth.

Ruth stood still and even though I couldn't see her with my back towards her, I could feel she was pretty angry. I kept holding on to Envy with my wings spread while he kept struggling to get free from me.

"Um… What now?" I asked Father Anselmo.

The priest ran towards the church entrance and yelled "Don't let go of it! I will be back!" before he exited through the church door. We fell silent for a few moments. Even Envy stopped hissing. Ruth looked at the back of my head, and I looked at Envy's. It was all pretty stupid and kind of embarrassing.

"Let me go…" Envy said.

"As if!" I responded.

"I'm not talking to you." Envy's head turned and the corner of his eyes fixed at Ruth. "I would never lie to you. She doesn't like you. She's just using you."

"Hey! I'm right here!" I yelled at Envy.

"Violet, you said you liked my nose-" Ruth whispered.

"Really?! Are we getting into this now?! Can't you see I'm a bit busy trying not to let a demon escape out to the world?"

"You're a liar,"

"Oh, Ehm, Gee!!! I'm sorry, okayyyyyy?"

"No, you're not." Envy said smiling.

"You shut up!" I yelled at Envy.

"She doesn't like you, Ruth. She's not your friend. I know. I was inside her heart."

"Shut up! You are such a dick!"

Ruth took two steps towards the door. So did Envy.

"Stop it, Ruth! He's trying to make you move so he can get away!"

I could feel Ruth was really angry at me and I got scared.

"I really, really like you, Ruth! It's true! Please don't listen to him! Just stay still, please." I pleaded.

Ruth took another step. Envy smiled.

Father Anselmo came running through the door holding a huge green iguana by the neck and tail. The iguana moved its legs rapidly, trying to get away from the priest, but then it just stopped and waited, accepting its fate.

"You're too strong for me to kill you" said Father Anselmo, "But I'm not letting you free. Now either get in the iguana or I will hold you in my heart until I die and then I'll take you with me."

"NOOOO!" Envy screamed as Father Anselmo got close to him with the iguana.

The demon shrieked and shook violently. Father Anselmo prayed again. The priest placed the iguana next to the demon's face and chanted a few words in Latin: "Recessimus a Dei creatura unde venisti ad tenebras" or some cliché rambling like that. Envy opened his mouth and vomited black ooze on to the iguana. As Envy disappeared from under my arms, the reptile shook in Father Anselmo's arm pretty hard until the priest let him go. The iguana fell on the floor unconscious.

The priest kicked the comatose iguana to the side and sat on one of the church benches.

"Well, that's that." He said exhausted. "You got your exorcism. Don't forget to get rid of that lizard. As long as he remains trapped in that iguana, you'll be safe. Now, both of you get out. I think I have some wine left around here."

I looked at Ruth, but she avoided looking back at me. I walked up to her and tried my puppy look with her. This time I was sincere.

"I'm sorry that I hurt you. I really do like you. You're a good wha-friend. You're a pretty good friend. I admit your nose is a bit odd looking, but-"

"Shut it! We're not friends! Don't talk to me!" Ruth yelled as she gave me a mean look.

Father Anselmo pointed his index finger above us. Ruth and I turned our heads and saw the iguana on its back floating in the air. Its head winded around the neck and it breathed fast.

"Goddammit! Stop your bickering! There's a lizard levitating behind you!" Father Anselmo complained as he rushed towards the floating iguana. He took off his black belt and tied the buckle side to it and held the other side like a leash. It looked like he was holding an iguana shaped balloon.

"Here" He said, as he handed me the other end of the belt. "The demon is trying to gain control of the iguana's body." The old priest continued. "You better get him away from here before he does."

"Too late." The iguana spoke,

"Oh, that is so creepy! A talking iguana! But what do we do with it?" I asked.

"Kill it. Throw it off a bridge. I don't care. He's your problem now."

"Too late for everything, Priest." said the floating iguana. "The Deadly Seven are already here on Earth. Humans are easy prey to us now. The armies of Eve will join us soon enough and we will rape your world! All thanks to you, Violet"

"That's enough from you." Father Anselmo replied.

"The armies of Eve?" Ruth asked.

Father Anselmo walked over to me. He grabbed my arm like Scarlet does when she's mad at me. I always hated that!

"What did you do?!" The priest questioned angrily.

"Don't blame me! I didn't do anything!"

"Exactly…" The green iguana's eyes glowed as he smiled at me. "Yours is the first of the Seven Seals. You broke it. That means the end is coming!"

"I don't understand, Father. What's going on?" Ruth asked.

"I'm not sure either but… the Book of Revelations speaks of seven seals, each one guarded by an Archangel of God. When the seals break and the seven horns are sounded, the last war between Heaven and Hell will begin."

"I did NOT break any seal! I just, well, I kind of… oh crap, maybe just a little…"

"What do you MEAN maybe just a little?!" Ruth questioned.

"Look, don't be mad at me, okay? My sisters and me, each of us seven angels have a ministry to protect. But these ministries; life, death, miracles, free will, nature, progress, and emotions; these are like the seals that protect Creation from darkness and stuff. They are the only things that keep order in the world. If one ministry is unattended, well that's a broken seal right there, But the thing is, the chaos caused from the first broken seal would lead to the breaking of the other seals, one seal broken as result of the other. And if all seals break…"

"Joder! Your angel friend here just started the Apocalypse!"

"I'm sorryyyy! I figured I could quit really quick and have Lucifer deal with it or whatever before it became a thing."

"Seriously?! You were going to leave the end of the world in the hands of the Devil?! Do you know how messed up that is?!"

"Oh, you would've done the same! Leave me alone! This is too much stress for me! Now we have to make sure the other seals remain unbroken and find a way to fix my ministry!"

Ruth suggested finding Scarlet for help, but I couldn't feel her anywhere on Earth. I couldn't feel White or Goldie either. That left Evergreen, Blue, and Black Angel to reach and warn about the seals. But I didn't want to see Back Angel because I felt uneasy around her, so I only told them I could feel Evergreen and Blue in Brazil.

"Don't look at me. I am not getting dragged into this." Father Anselmo said as he led Ruth and me towards the church door.

"But, Father, if this is the end of times then you have a role to-"

"I don't have to do shit. This is on you, so you fix it! Besides, there's somewhere I need to be in a few hours. It's an important commitment."

"What can be more important than stopping the end of the world?!" Ruth asked.

"Believe me, you don't want to know. Good luck and let me know how it goes." Father Anselmo said as he slammed the door in our faces.

"Well, ok then, grumps! Me and Ruth-"

"Shut up, Violet!" Ruth interrupted looking angry at the cement tiled floor in front of the church. "I don't have a choice but to go with you to clean up this mess, but I need to say something first. You are- you are such an unbelievable jerk! I'm so sick of you! How could you forfeit your ministry knowing you'd cause the end of the world?! Are you really that selfish?! You-you go on and on about how nobody loves you and you have this huge burden given to you, and everybody's having fun but you, and this and that, but you're really messing with billions of souls and the whole universe and it's like nothing to you! You are an inconsiderate, egotistic... little... ditz! You really don't care about anyone but yourself! I really don't know how God could give this huge responsibility to a whiny little drama queen like you. Your sister Scarlet was right. You only make things worse for everybody."

I was shocked by what Ruth said. And she meant it, too. I could feel her resentment towards me. I tried to hold my tears, but it was kind of late for that. I felt so ashamed, I had to cry. I couldn't talk, I couldn't even say "I'm sorry". I just lowered my head and cried. Ruth stood silent for a moment and then she grabbed me tight with both arms.

"Let's go." She said. "And keep that thing away from me", referring to Envy. We were awkwardly silent during our flight to Brazil. I could feel the floating green iguana laughing.

I'm sorry! I'm sorry! I'm sorry! I'm sorry! I'm sorry! I'm sorry! I kept writing in my little book.

....

Ruth and I had to find Evergreen and Blue before things got worse. Ruth kept avoiding me during our trip, pretending she was asleep, but I still felt her anger. I felt really bad and I didn't know how to fix things between us, so I kind of pretended I was asleep too and, well, that was our flight.

The airport in Sao Paulo, where I felt my siblings were, was destroyed by the earthquake so we had to take a flight to another airport by the coast and take a bus from there. The bus driver told us we'd take the route through the coast highway because the earthquake had destroyed the other routes and it would be a four hour drive.

Envy slept all the way while still floating. I had to convince Ruth to hold on to the lizard's belt in public because no one could see me, but they'd freak out if they saw a floating iguana following Ruth around. Ruth was not happy about it. She felt disgusted and terrified to be near Envy. I could feel her distress, but there was nothing else we could do. People looked weird at Ruth for carrying what they thought was a lizard-shaped balloon. One kid kept trying to touch it, but Ruth shooed him away.

"I'm sorry that you have to carry Envy." I said. "And I'm sorry I made fun of your nose and called you my whale. I'm sorry I caused all this trouble to you and – and to the world. I don't deserve my ministry, but… we'll find someone who does. We'll find someone that can do what I can't and help us fix this."

Ruth said nothing. She just looked out the window. When I looked, I noticed everyone was acting all weird outside the bus. Obviously, it was because I quit my ministry and no one was keeping emotions in check. People were arguing and screaming and laughing and crying. They were going crazy. Then Ruth saw a cop shoot a taxi driver in the head. Everyone in the bus panicked, but I felt Ruth wasn't upset or sad for what she saw. She felt numb, indifferent. That scared me a little, but I couldn't dare to ask her why she felt that way.

The bus suddenly stopped. We were stuck in traffic. Ruth looked out the window and saw and endless line of empty abandoned cars all along the highway up to the valley where we were headed. The driver yelled at everyone to get off the bus, so we did. Ruth and I walked the highway up hill. We saw people around us fighting each other. There were folks running towards us scared and screaming and telling us to go back, but we kept walking. After a while, there was no one left at the highway but us. As we kept walking, the sounds of people screaming faded in the distance until there was only silence. That's when Ruth finally decided to talk to me.

"Violet, back at the church, what did Envy mean by armies of Eve" She asked,

"Who's Eve?"

"You know, Eve. As in 'Adam and...?' Ok, look. If I tell you the story you promise not to tell anyone."

"What story?"

I scratched my head and looked to both sides nervously.

"The story of how Adam and Eve got divorced... you promise?"

"Yeah, sure, I guess."

"First of all, I need to make clear these are only rumors, okay? This may not have happened the way I'm going to tell it."

"Okay,"

"Right, so, waaaay back in the beginning, God created the Earth and the skies and animals and plants and Adam and Eve and they lived in Eden and stuff, right? And He told them Eden was theirs and forbade them to eat the fruit of life, which of course they obviously did. Then when Adam and Eve got punished for it and got banished from the Garden of Eden. They were cast to live the rest of their days working for food, begat Cain and Abel, yadda, yadda, yadda. Sooooo... Fast-forward, many years later, Adam and Eve never grew old and they realized God made immortals. Adam thought there should be some reason they couldn't die. So he figured maybe they could get back on God's good side if they stayed on Earth to shepherd humanity whenever it would stray from His Plan. Like, if Lucifer tried to manipulate governments into doing evil things like going to war and stuff, they'd have to infiltrate the governments and make things right. It's like they were James Bond secret agent types for God and stuff."

"Huh."

"And you know, as far as immortal lives go, it wasn't that bad for them, but I guess after centuries together, they'd get tired of it and of each other or whatever. All I knew was that by the late nineteen hundreds, Adam and Eve couldn't stop arguing and hating each other. And then one night, Adam left a note and just walked out on Eve."

"What was in the note?" Ruth asked.

"How should I know?! I wasn't there! Thing is, not much time after that, Eve also disappeared for a while. That is, until she later showed up in Hell to challenge the Devil for control of his domain."

"Wait-What?!"

"Tell me about it! Eve really went and challenged Lucifer to a fight for control of Hell! Would you believe she actually won the duel? Since then, the demon hordes have been given only one mission by their new ruler Eve: to find Adam wherever he's hiding. Eve is the queen of Hell, and the Devil, the one we just talked to back in New York, he's been exiled to Earth for a long time now. Like since probably the beginning of the twentieth century. And it's been kept secret for a reason. You need to understand, nobody's happy about this. White says not even God…"

"But that doesn't make sense! How could Eve beat Lucifer? Isn't she human? She's the first woman-"

"Actually, that's not true. Eve's not the first woman. Adam is the first man, but Eve is really the second woman. Lilith came first."

"Oh, yeah. Lilith. I've read about her. Mother of demons and all that, right?"

"Oh, yes. She's really bad news. Evil in its purest form. At least that's what I hear. We don't talk about her much, but the little I've heard is not good at all. She's mean and manipulative and they say she eats spiders and vomits roaches and has an unquenchable thirst for blood and she loves to kill everyone and everything created by God and stuff."

"Wow. Is she alive too?"

"Lilith? I don't know. Maybe. If she is, she's probably somewhere in Hell having orgies with demons and snakes."

"Eww!"

"I tell you, she's evil!"

"Okay, so -um- Eve's in charge of Hell and she's been looking for Adam, but no one knows where he is?"

"He's a really good secret agent, I guess. And it makes sense that the first man to exist knows Earth well enough to find a place to hide from-"

Ruth stopped walking and that made me stop too. She pointed in front of me and I looked. There was a wall made of giant trees and bushes and weeds and flowers blocking the highway. There were huge yellow butterflies the size of cars flying over and around the wall. That wall could only be made by my sister Evergreen. I became afraid because it was the first thing I've ever seen she's done that's not supposed to be there. It wasn't natural.

I knew there was something really bad going on, and whatever it was, it got to my sister Evergreen. I swallowed and took a deep breath. Then I said to Ruth: "We need to go in there…".

7 MEET THE WEEPING QUEEN

Scarlet woke up with the sound of a woman crying. The warrior angel was confused as she lied on the ground, but this much she knew: she was no longer on Hell's ash desert fields. The floor felt smooth and cold. She instinctively reached out for her sword, but realized she was tied in heavy chains. She looked around and guessed she was in the throne room of Hell's citadel. The room was wide and… silver. Everything in the room, tables, lamps frames, walls, everything was silver. The crying woman's moans and sobs continued to vie for Scarlet's attention.

Wrath stood next to the chained angel, pointing her own sword at her face while resting her axe on her shoulder.

"MISTRESS…" she finally spoke. Scarlet followed the sound of the crying woman to the throne.

The Weeping Queen sat sideways on the throne, crying and sobbing. She ignored both the angel and her demon as she wiped the tears that kept coming from her eyes. Her face was pale white with swollen red eyes that showed she'd been crying for a long time. The Queen's hair was bleached blonde with pink highlights. She wore a long tight silver tunic that made her look like a silver statue. Her hands and bare feet were barely visible under the robe. She also wore a silver crown on her forehead and several silver chains around her neck to match.

"Leave us, Wrath." she sobbed "wait outside until I call you."

"THIS ONE IS DANGEROUS"

74

"I said wait outside! Go away!"

Wrath clenched her fist, trying to control her desire to decapitate the Weeping Queen. But she was the Mistress, she kept reminding herself, she was the Mistress of Hell. Wrath threw Scarlet's sword and it slid on the floor all the way towards the Queen's feet at the throne. She lifted her feet just in time to avoid getting cut by the sword.

"Brute!" the Queen screamed. Wrath ignored her, and left the throne room.

The Weeping Queen turned her face slightly towards Scarlet, trying to compose herself for a moment. Scarlet managed to take a look at the Queen. She recognized her, but she was still confused.

"Eve?" Scarlet asked.

"You-You wouldn't happen to know where my husband is, would you?" The Weeping Queen responded.

"No...I-"

Eve turned her head away and continued crying angrily.

"Will I ever see him again?!" she lamented. "I have - I have sent all of my demon hordes to Earth with one simple mission. All they have to do is find him. And have they done that? NO THEY HAVEN'T! BECAUSE THEY'RE ALL INCOMPETENT IDIOTS! ALL THEY WANT TO DO IS KILL AND DESTROY AND BE EVIL!"

"They are demons" Scarlet replied, "It is their nature to-"

"SHUT UP! They're cattle! That's what they are! They need leadership!"

Eve sprinted from her throne and kneeled beside Scarlet. She lifted and held the red angel's chin.

"You..." She continued, "I've seen you battle hundreds of demons all by yourself. They fear your name! They fear you! You could be the leader they need!"

Scarlet shifted her face towards the queen. She was astounded.

"Are you asking me to join Hell's army?!"

Eve moved her face closer to Scarlet's. "Find him for me! Find the First Man!"

"Why would I?" Scarlet asked in disbelief.

"If you find my husband for me, I promise Hell will forfeit the Apocalypse. Isn't that what you want? We will withdraw from Creation and surrender to God."

Scarlet hesitated. She briefly thought of all the billions of souls she would save by helping Eve. Then she thought of the price she would have to pay in exchange.

"No. I will not lose my soul for-"

"You stuck up armored bitch! I will find my husband with our without your help! I will destroy all of Creation if I have to! And you-you can rot for all I care! Wrath! WRATH!"

Wrath, followed by four demon goblins, rushed into the throne room.

"Throw her in the cavern!" Eve ordered. "Then you may join your brothers on Earth."

Wrath smiled. As soon as she got rid of the angel, she would be able to wreak havoc on Creation. She ordered the demons to pick up Scarlet. As they dragged her away, Eve lifted Scarlet's sword from the floor. Scarlet saw that Eve held on to the weapon with sorrow in her face. Eve burst into tears again.

"I-I will give you time to reconsider. Please help me…" Eve cried with a broken voice.

As she was taken away, Scarlet lowered her head with dread.

"Lord above, what is going on here?"

· · · · · · · · · · · · ·

Paolo rode his red bicycle back home from work. It had a bumper sticker pasted on the back of the seat that read: "RECYCLING IS THE TRUE CIRCLE OF LIFE". He liked the feeling of the wind against his face, but although he was tempted, he did not close his eyes or took his hands off from the bike handles. He was still upset because of the mess the construction workers were doing at Ibirapuera Park, and he lamented the senseless chopping of trees, but there was nothing he could do until he could rally people to protest at the site. That would have to wait until tomorrow. Today, it was his mother's birthday and he planned to make it special for her.

Paolo reached his neighborhood street, where the houses were all small and made out of wood and supported by cement blocks. He stopped at Mona's Bakery to pick up the cake he ordered the day before. The young man chained his bike to a nearby meter and noticed a small beagle puppy sitting in front of him. He petted the dog and ordered it to guard his bike. He went inside the bakery thinking he should get a treat for the dog, too.

The young man waited in line behind two old ladies that couldn't decide which type of cheese to get for the week, Swiss or American. The young fifteen year old boy behind the counter was Mona's boy, Nico. Paolo had played basketball with him once or twice and got a glance from him pleading for some kind of help with the old ladies. He was Nico's childhood hero, and as such he didn't want to disappoint him. Paolo wrapped his arms around the old ladies and with a lovely smile, he suggested they be adventurous and try the provolone. The old ladies were charmed and bought two pounds of the provolone. He kissed both ladies hands and escorted them to the door.

Nico got Paolo his cake. It was plain vanilla with white frosting, just like his mother liked it. The cake was decorated with green leaf-shaped drops and green letters that read: "HAPPY BIRTHDAY LORNA". It wasn't a big cake, so he was able to carry it on one hand. He bought a lose piece of bacon for the dog and promised Nico to hang with him in the weekend.

Paolo stepped out of the store and saw the beagle still sitting next to the bike. He was amused at the dog's obedience and wondered if it had an owner as he fed it the piece of bacon. He figured he was just a few houses away from his home, so he unchained the bike and continued on foot while dragging it with one hand and carrying the small cake with the other.

The young man noticed the puppy walking at his side looking up at him.

"Sorry, I'm out of bacon, my friend." Paolo smiled.

He looked behind him and saw seven dogs and four cats following him. As Paolo stopped, the animals stood still waiting for his next move. The young man was a little confused and scared. He kept walking and the animals followed. Six pigeons landed behind him and followed him too. Paolo stood still again and this time he was perplexed that these animals were after him without fighting each other or making a sound.

He tried to shoo them away, but they would not move. Paolo walked faster towards his house. He could hear the animals behind him increasing in numbers. At one point, he heard galloping behind him. Without stopping, he turned his head and took a peek. There were hundreds of animals marching behind him; dogs, cats, birds, rabbits, squirrels rats, insects.

Paolo dropped his bike and held on to his cake with both hands and close to his chest like it was a gun to defend himself with. When he turned around, he saw a beautiful naked woman standing close to him. Flowers and butterflies grew from her hair. Paolo swallowed hard at the sight of this woman. He fell madly in love and had an incredible erection at the same time.

"I've been watching you for a long time." said the naked woman.

"Who are you?"

The mysterious lady smiled at him silently.

"Lady, you're naked. People are going to see-"

"No one can see me unless I want them to. Right now, only you can see me."

"What do you want from me?"

The woman walked closer to Paolo and took a bit of the cake frosting with her finger. She licked her finger slowly and stared at Paolo intensely. Paolo looked at the animals around him. The dogs, cats, squirrels, insects, they were all mating in front of Paolo. Paolo looked back at the woman. She licked the last bit of frosting on her finger and smiled innocently.

"This is so strange." Paolo said.

"Strange? I think it's perfectly natural."

"Shouldn't we go have dinner or watch a movie first?"

"Are you hungry?"

"That's not the po- Look, this is a bit overwhelming for me. I need to process-"

"I understand. Take your time. I will be waiting for you behind those trees."

The beautiful naked woman walked towards the trees behind one of the houses. The animals followed. Paolo could not stop looking at her body.

"Good Lord! What am I doing?" He asked himself while running after her. "Hey! Wait!"

"Bring the cake." She said without looking back at him.

Paolo and the woman lied behind the trees and consummated their attraction repeatedly. Paolo was nervous, afraid to be discovered by someone, but the woman reassured him that no one would see either of them. Paolo noticed that the grass grew tall around them, and he could've sworn the trees moved to cover them from the street view. He grew uneasy with all the animals watching them.

"Are they bothering you?" the woman asked.

"Yes they are. Pretty much. I feel like I'm giving them a show."

The beautiful woman sighed and the animals dispersed. She turned around and sat on Paolo's hip.

"Again. Let's try something else."

"Can you at least give me your name?"

"You can call me Evergreen."

The demon Lust watched the couple from a branch up on a nearby tree. He petted one of his goblin helpers. The goblin wore a skimpy Girl Scout outfit. He felt pleasantly surprised at how easy it was for him to manipulate Evergreen's desires. Lust felt aroused by the notion of driving an Archangel to sin. He munched on the cookies he took from the goblin's Girl Scout cookie box.

"Evergreen and Paolo sitting in a tree." The Girl Scout goblin sang with a creepy voice. "K-I-S-S-I-N-G"

"More!" Lust moaned.

"More" Evergreen moaned.

"More?" Paolo asked. "But we've done it four times already. I could use a little break."

"I need you now." Evergreen pleaded.

Paolo stood up from the grass and put on his shirt and pants. Then he picked up the cake and walked towards his red bike.

"Maybe later, okay? I need to go now. My mother is waiting for me. Could I get your number?"

"PAPA WANT MORE!!!" Lust screamed.

Evergreen rose from the grass and stomped on the ground.

"I WILL NOT BE DENIED!"

The loud stomp created a crack on the earth that slithered towards the tree that stood next to Paolo. The tree's roots snapped open, and let go of their grip of the earth. The trunk fell towards Paolo. The young man looked up and froze. He dropped the cake and it smashed to pieces on the sidewalk. The tree smashed into his chest pinning him to the ground.

Evergreen took a few steps forward and then jumped on Paolo's trapped body. She continued forcing herself on him and began to breathe heavily. Paolo tried to yell but no voice came from his mouth, but gurgling sounds as he choked on his own blood. He couldn't breathe and slowly lost conscience, with Evergreen's beauty as the last thing that he saw before he stopped breathing altogether.

Evergreen kept making love to Paolo, ignoring his passing. Two small tornadoes, each about the size of a truck, began to form, one from next to Paolo's body and the other from a few yards away. The tornadoes clashed against each other as if they were dancing together. They slowly grew surpassing the nearby houses. The deafening sound of their winds against the concrete alerted the town's people too late.

As they kept growing, the tornadoes hit all the houses in the neighborhood and destroyed cars, lamp posts and signs. One of the tornadoes lifted Paolo's red bike in the air where it remained spinning until it landed on the pavement of a nearby highway. The two tornadoes merged into one bigger and terrible vortex. The terrified neighborhood people barely escaped with their lives, but a few of them were caught and thrown away at large distances by the winds.

Evergreen was about to be satisfied when she looked at Paolo's dead eyes. She screamed in horror and leapt off him. Lust smiled with heavy sweat.

As the tornado winds died, Evergreen crawled towards Paolo and ordered a hundred weeds to remove the tree from him. The weeds wrapped around the trunk and pushed it away. The naked angel kneeled beside Paolo and she had lost awareness of everything else around her. The weeds kept growing, becoming giant monster plants that enveloped the town. Branches became walls, bushes became labyrinths, and flowers became ceilings. Giant moths broke away from their cocoons and flew over the weeds, circling the area. Evergreen had turned the town into her own impenetrable green fort that failed to protect her from her own actions.

Lust was satisfied for the moment as he climbed down from the tree. He walked away followed by his pet goblin. The goblin sucked its fingers dry, turned around, and blew a kiss to Evergreen, before throwing the Girl Scout cookie box away.

The green angel felt her dead lover cold between her arms. He was limp. Motionless. She shook him and yelled at him "WAKE UP!", but he wouldn't make a sound. Not the sound of breathing. The devastating realization that she lost him forever, that she would live eternity without him, terrified her. She laid him on the ground, crying, praying to God and bargaining with the Devil for his recovery. She would do or give anything to have him back.

Leaves from the Princess tree grew from the ground cocooning him from the rest of the world. He was hers and hers alone. She touched his face and kissed him with wet kisses and her tears dropped on his dead eyelids. As her tears rolled down his cheeks, it looked like he was crying instead of her. His face was pale. His lips were blue. She caressed his cold chest hoping for a sign of life.

She looked around and screamed for help, but all she saw was grass and trees and yellow butterflies and all kinds of birds. There were turtles and dogs and horses and cats crying the heartbreaking cries of sad impotent animals. They were as impotent as her. For the first time in her life, she was overwhelmed by the sounds of nature. But there were no human beings anywhere to ask for help. She had scared them all away. Water, leaves, or honey would not be enough to bring him back. This was not a bee sting that could get better if you peed on it. Nature was not enough. Evergreen was not enough.

She called for her brother. He'd know what to do. If there wasn't a cure, he'd invent one. She called for her brother. There were only overgrown plants and mountains of rock and soil that echoed her calls. She called for her brother, her kind reliable brother that, all bickering aside, would always be there for her when she needed him most. She called for her brother to save her from the chaos of herself once more. She called for Blue… but there was no answer.

She knelt naked beside his motionless body, with her head resting on his chest, and cried inconsolably, deciding that nothing else mattered. Not her duties, not her siblings. Not humanity. She decided to let go.

All over the world hurricanes and earthquakes and droughts and floods would rise. Let them handle it themselves, she thought. Let them handle the plagues and ruined crops and antagonistic climates. She would stay with him until his flesh and bones decayed and go back to the earth where they came from.

There was a cold hand that touched her shoulder from behind. It wasn't his brother's. It was too skinny and cold.

"Evergreen" She heard her sister Violet say "We need your help, like, yesterday! The Deadly Seven are here and they're making people crazy. And they're here because I screwed up 'cause I abandoned my ministry and emotions all over the world are bonkers and that sort of kind of broke the first of the seven seals of the Apocalypse and I'm afraid the world is ending unless we stop iiiit? …Pleeease?"

Violet was standing behind Evergreen. Ruth watched in fear at all the eerie animals around them. Evergreen removed Violet's hand from her shoulder and kept looking at him.

"It's too late" The green angel said.

"What do you mean it's too late?" Violet asked right before her eyes opened wide and she looked at the place around her. The animals, the plants, the earth, nothing was natural. Not anymore.

"OMG! OMG! OMG! OMG! Sister, what-what did you do?"

"Leave me be."

"Who is that guy on the ground? Is he dead?"

Evergreen stood up from the ground and pushed Violet back

"LEAVE ME BE!" She yelled. Violet fell to the ground. Ruth ran towards Violet to help her up and pointed at the animals around them.

"I-I think we should go now, Violet" Ruth said.

The dogs and birds and horses and cats were acting strange, slowly closing in on the visitors, ready to attack.

Violet let go of Ruth's arm and walked towards Evergreen.

"But she's in pain. I feel her guilt and loneliness." she said, "I can help her. I can make her feel better. I just need to-"

Two large dogs jumped on top of Violet, pinning her to the ground. Their loud barking paralyzed the scared angel. One of them went for the kill opening its jaw wide to bite off Violet's face. The angel protected her face with her right arm, but the dog pressed its fangs into her elbow and forearm. Violet screamed in pain. Ruth took off one of her shoes and ran towards the dogs to try to shoo them away. She hit them hard with her shoe, but they ignored Ruth, focusing only on attacking Violet.

"Evergreen! Please stop! You're hurting her!" Ruth cried.

Evergreen turned her face slightly to the side. The dogs backed off from Violet but kept growling. Her arm was bleeding. Ruth took off her jacket and wrapped it tight around Violet's arm.

"If you don't go now I will not call them off again." Evergreen warned.

Ruth helped Violet up and

"Come on!" Ruth ordered Violet.

"But-"

"She's out of it! We have to go!"

They both ran away from the wild animals leaving the green angel alone with her dead lover.

"I can bring him back to life." Lucifer's voice uttered from behind Evergreen.

She looked back and saw the beagle puppy that Paolo fed before sitting a few feet away from her. The small canine's eyes were entirely black.

"What are you doing here?" Evergreen asked the creature.

"That is up to you. I am either here to pay my respects, or to make good of my end of our deal."

"What deal? There is no deal..."

"Like I said, you decide. Please, do not mind me. I will stay for a while." the dark-eyed puppy said, "take your time, and just listen to what I have to offer..."

Alone in the wilderness born from concrete, surrounded only by the animals and plants that echoed her pain, Evergreen mourned her dead lover in silence.

Out on the highway, Violet and Ruth ran for their lives. The purple angel stopped and wrapped her chest with both arms. Ruth saw the sadness in Violet's eyes and placed her hand on her shoulder.

"You okay?" Ruth asked.

"She broke her seal, Ruth." Violet cried, "She can't control her sorrow because of me! I did this!"

"We can still fix it, can't we?" the girl replied, "I mean it's still two out of seven seals. We still have time-"

"We have to find Blue. He will know what to do..."

"I really hope you're right"

"Me too"

Violet and Ruth ran back down the highway full of empty cars. They got back to the bus they'd come in, but saw it was empty.

"Do you know how to drive a bus?" Ruth asked.

"Why would I?"

"Okay, well, I think I saw a bike on the highway."

Ruth and the emo angel walked back up the highway hill and found a red bicycle on the pavement with a bumper sticker pasted on the back of the seat that read: "RECYCLING IS THE TRUE CIRCLE OF LIFE". Ruth pulled up the bike and mounted it. Violet sat on the handle and they rode down the highway hill.

. . . .

Blue sat on top of a bulldozer at Sao Paulo's Ibirapuera Park. He played with his floating holographic screens and calculated that Evergreen had been gone for twenty-nine hours, forty-seven minutes and twelve seconds. He was mad at her. He wasn't upset because she wanted to do disgusting things with that human. Her life was her own. He was her brother, but he wasn't obsessed with her. It wasn't an unnatural Donny and Marie type of relationship or anything like that. He just looked out for her as she always did for him.

The angel of progress was mad because he wanted to finish the Sao Paulo restoration job already. He could do it all by himself, but White had ordered them both to accomplish the task together. Besides, even though he would never admit it to his sister, he knew that his work was always better when they put their heads together. Technology and nature, like science and religion, could better manifest the wonders of Creation in unison than separately.

Evergreen and Blue had already started working on the idea of a statue in the middle of the park that people could watch up close by crossing a hovering bridge. The trick was to have a pocket of hot air constantly flowing under the bridge to keep it floating. Evergreen figured she could create an active geyser to provide the pressurized airflow. She told Blue she would need time to make sure the geyser would always supply the needed vapor, but before doing that, there was somewhere else she had to be. She promised him she'd be back soon.

Blue waited for his sister, counting minute after minute, feeling anxious and useless. He went over his proposed plans again and again;

looking for flaws that he knew would not be there because he'd executed his ideas perfectly, as he always did. His disappointment grew and he became disenchanted and detached with the work on the park in Brazil.

He jumped from the bulldozer and roamed through the park looking for a distraction. He saw a thin shaggy haired teenage boy with pajama pants and a grey t-shirt sitting on the grass playing a hand held video game. Blue took pride as he fondly remembered his portable creation and walked closer to the teenager. The young man was playing Castrator 3: Eunuch's Revenge, but he was struggling at to pass a boss level. The angel decided to do something he hasn't done since he last spoke to Leonardo da Vinci: he would reveal himself to a human.

"Look at youuu, you like the Castrator games, huh?"

"…hrm…"

The teenager ignored Blue and kept playing the handheld game his own way. The angel sat on the grass next to the young man. Blue noticed that he was feeling tired. He yawned a few times and felt his eyes heavy for a moment. He remembered that he needed to go back to his duties, but they seemed so overwhelming and complicated. The cobalt angel decided to take a break. He figured he was entitled to one anyway and he could always reschedule whatever project he needed to take care of. Besides, he reasoned there wasn't that much he'd be able to accomplish without his sister Evergreen. At that moment, he felt it didn't hurt to relax and maybe have a little fun. Just for a bit.

"You know, if you get close behind it and press B and down at the same time, you'll make it eat its own tail. It's pretty cool…"

"…hrm…uhuh…"

"Oh, just wait until you see number four. I mean, it's not in the market yet; it's not even invented yet, but trust me, it blows all the others away. I know the story already."

"…hrm… shhh… playin'…hrm"

"Sure. Right. Sorry."

Blue watched the game over the teenager's shoulder for a while. He kept thinking that the boy seemed familiar to him. He tried to look into the teen's eyes hidden under his hair. Then he leaped back as he realized who the boy was.

"Sloth! You dare show yourself on Earth, demon! ATTACK MODE!!!"

Blue's command activated his armor. Dozens of little blue lights sparkled as gears spun and metal plates shifted allowing several weapons to come out from underneath the armor.

"I will banish you in the name of God!"

"…hrm… wah-ever...hrm"

"Stand up and face me!"

"…hrm... wuh-bother...huh...too much work…hrm"

"You won't fight me?!"

"… busy... mhrm"

Sloth kept focused on his portable video game.

"This is so embarrassing. Now you're making me feel silly…"

Blue deactivated the weapons and sat next to the demon.

"No, no, you're doing it all wrong, sweetie. Hit A and then X…"

"hrm…"

"And after you finish the game, we will fight each other and I'll banish you to Hell."

"… hrm...wah-ever…hrm"

Blue launched his holographic screens around him and the demon.

"Hey, I could absolutely plug your game in my screens and I could join in if you'd like." Blue said. "My sound system is craaaaazyyyy!"

The demon kept playing. He did not care about the screens floating around him.

Time passed as Blue and Sloth played the video game together. Blue made a couch appear to make the experience more comfortable. Then, he increased the sound and improved the colors coming from the holographic screens.

At one point, the demon complained he couldn't concentrate with all the park construction noise around them, so Blue enclosed himself and Sloth inside a giant bright blue solid energy bubble. The bubble was sound proof and it protected them from mosquitoes and kept the temperature nice and cool. Not even Blue could see the world outside the bubble which freed him and the demon from any possible distractions. He was proud of his bright blue bubble and wondered why he hadn't thought of making one before. He found it relaxing.

Sloth did not thank him for the bubble. He just mumbled "…hrm…" and kept playing, but Blue didn't care. He didn't care about Evergreen anymore either. He just wanted to finish the game.

Some time had passed before Blue heard a knocking from outside the bubble. He chose to ignore it, but after a while of hearing the annoying echoes of the banging, he decided to see what the knocking was about. When he tried to stand up from the couch his legs and back hurt. He took a few steps, but felt a painful cramp behind his legs. He felt tired. His eyes were drowsy, so he only opened them half way. He felt like he'd just woken up.

Blue managed to reach one wall of the bubble and touched it to open a door through it. He scratched his hair and stuck his head through the door to look around. It was night time, but something was wrong. It was too dark. It took Blue a few seconds to realize there were no lights, not in the park or in the city. He could barely hear people screaming in the distance.

"Blueeee!" Blue heard the whiny voice of his scrawny insecure sister Violet calling him. He rolled his eyes and turned his face towards the voice. Violet and a young weird looking girl with a big nose stood a few feet away from him.

"Blue, where've you been?!" Violet yelled. "The world's going nuts without you! Two of the seals of the Apocalypse are broken and we need your help to fix it before we all die and we need you to talk to Evergreen 'cause she's gone bananas, but now all the lights have turned out and nothing's working and…"

Violet saw Blue take a few steps outside the door. Ruth turned her look away from Blue.

"Um…Why is he-" she whispered to Violet.

"Oh my God! Dude! What's wrong with you?! Put some pants on!" Violet yelled at Blue.

Blue looked down on his body and remembered he'd taken off his futuristic armor at some point to be more comfortable in the couch, and because angels do not wear underwear, he was wearing nothing underneath. He touched his face and noticed stubble on his chin and cheeks that felt like a beard. He looked at his wrist, but somehow he'd also taken off his wrist Mac.

"What time is it?" He asked.

"Almost midnight." Ruth answered.

"I couldn't have grown this beard so fast. What day is it?"

"It's Wednesday."

"Oh…"

Blue had spent six days on that couch playing video games with a demon. He'd neglected his duties as keeper of progress. When Blue stopped caring about the future, so did the rest of the world. There was no point in improving technology or maintaining it. Phone signals dropped, access to the internet was lost, cars broke down with no one to fix them, the power went out in major cities and small towns everywhere, and people just didn't care.

"Brother, we need to fix it, we need to fix your seal!" Violet begged.

"But…Nah, that's too much work. I got too much to do now-"

"What are you doing that's more important than saving Creation?"

"I've got this game I got to finish… I-"

"OH EHM GEEE!!! You did NOT just say you need to finish a video game!"

"…hrm…" A mumbling was heard from inside the blue bubble.

"What was that? Who's inside your blue spaceship?"

89

"Oh, it's … um... listen, Violet, I gotta go, darling."

"But we need you, brother! Evergreen will only listen to you. And you have to save your ministry!"

"Maybe tomorrow."

"But-"

"Bye"

Blue stepped back into his bright blue bubble and sealed the door behind him. Violet and Ruth looked at each other shocked and confused.

"Okay. That's three broken seals." Ruth broke the silence. "I'm starting to get a bit concerned now. Can't you reach any of your other siblings?"

Violet thought their last hope would be the Black Angel. Even though she dreaded talking to her creepy younger sister, she saw no other option but to reach out to her. Violet tried to sense Black's feelings to be able to locate her, but after trying a few times, she realized the angel was no longer on Earth. Neither was Scarlet, White, or Goldie. Violet and Ruth were alone and the world was ending right before their eyes.

"Oy…" Violet said as she slapped her forehead. She then looked at Ruth as they tried to figure out what to do next.

Blue walked inside the energy bubble and dropped his body on the couch next to the shaggy looking demon. He grabbed a game control and joined in the game. The demon Sloth turned his head to look at Blue next to him and then turned to face the floating screen again. If Sloth wasn't so lazy, he would probably savor his moment of victory. No more working. No more building towards the future. There was absolutely nothing to do in life other than munching on chips and playing video games.

8 SEASON IN THE ABYSS

Wrath led a small group of demons that included Beggar and four goblins that carried Scarlet towards a huge cavern somewhere in the black ash desert of Hell. Scarlet was chained from feet to neck, allowing her almost no movement. Once inside the cave, Wrath took off Scarlet's helmet from her head, knowing this would anger her more.

The warrior angel glanced at Wrath with hate in her eyes. As the goblins kept carrying her, the angel saw the bones of unnamed beasts encrusted on the walls. Beggar told Scarlet that the cave had been a place where monsters had come to die since before humanity. They had many shapes, forms and sizes. Some of them were reptilian in shape with rock-like black and gray scales and had many legs that crawled the walls like spiders. Others slithered like snakes with pointy hooks for limbs and long acid drooling tongues.

These creatures, shunned by God and banned from Creation, wandered aimlessly through Hell with no point to living; only waiting for death. A few of them had some intelligence, enough to comprehend they were living imperfections, rejects from a trial and error process by the Creator of the universe. They craved a death to free them from the misery they lived in, but even after death their spirits would still remain roaming aimlessly in the darkness.

"It is said that a traveler once came and tamed these dark beasts." Beggar continued. "He became their master and named them Leviathans. He also gave them a purpose, one that fed on their resentment and sense of abandonment. The traveler told the creatures that out there in Creation, there were beings blessed by God called men that lived brief lives and their souls would then cross the darkness before becoming one with God in eternal bliss. He ordered the monsters to hunt and destroy these souls as they passed through the darkness. Then the traveler left Hell to never return."

Scarlet had only known of the Leviathans through her sister Black. The Black Angel had single handedly fought these creatures for centuries. But Scarlet never imagined they were so many of them. Looking at all those skeletons in the cavern, she was at awe at her sister's bravery.

"What became of this traveler?" Scarlet asked Beggar.

"Who knows? No one ever knew who he was…" he replied.

"ENOUGH!!!" Wrath shouted as she knocked Beggar to the ground with one backslap.

The demon goblins dropped Scarlet's chained body near the edge of a rift on the ground the size of a football field. It was the mouth of an endless abyss.

"YOU WILL DIE FEEDING THE LEVIATHANS OR YOU WILL FALL INTO THE ABYSS" Wrath declared, throwing Scarlet's helmet off the edge of the cliff.

The Deadly Seven demon grabbed a goblin by the neck and pulled out its limbs one by one. The goblin screamed in agony.

"THIS SHOULD BE ENOUGH TO CALL THEM", she continued, as she dropped the goblin's torso on the ground. "SHOULD YOU SURVIVE THIS, COME LOOK FOR ME ON EARTH."

Wrath and Beggar walked away from Scarlet, who remained chained and kneeling on the floor. The other three goblin demons scattered to hide while Scarlet struggled to free herself from the chains. Scarlet felt a trembling on the ground and walls around her.

The monster skeletons began to rise, sucking up all the dirt and ashes around them. The ashes became uneven rock-hard skins for the creatures. Each one of them quickly took notice of Scarlet and slowly stepped towards her. The beasts began to group around Scarlet. One of them jumped on her and bit off her left cheek. Scarlet screamed and jerked her body to her side closer to the precipice.

The beast on top of her lost its grip, falling off her body and into the abyss. Scarlet dragged her body to the very end of the cliff, noticing that the beasts avoided getting closer to it. They managed to graze and bite Scarlet a few times, but they would not dare to move closer for the kill.

"Enough!" the red angel screamed. "If you want me, come and get me!"

Scarlet flipped her body face down, with her head hanging from the cliff. The warrior angel hesitated for a moment as she looked down at the endless pit. Then she looked back at the nameless beasts. Scarlet slowly pulled her body and slowly turned it feet first towards the rock face. By the time her stomach hanged from the edge, the rest of her body was hauled into the rift and she fell.

....

Darkness.

"Da dee dee da daaa" A high pitched squeaky female voice sang. The darkness faded as white light crept in. And there were two feet; two bloody feet hanging from a wall.

"Da dee da daaa… Oh, good- God is good, is God good- you are awake"

Scarlet was dizzy and confused. She was staring at two pale feet. She'd hit her head when she fell and tasted blood in her mouth. When she tried to move, she noticed the chains were loosened and her arms were free, but she felt a sharp pain on the back of her head and she couldn't move her left leg. She remained still and kept looking at the talking feet hanging from the wall. The bloody right foot scratched the left foot.

"You should rest. - hard days lie- How fares your head? That wound on your head looks bad —wink, wink- Would you like me to sing to you? Singing always makes things better. Da dee dee da daaa…"

Scarlet kept trying to move her leg, but she felt it pinned between two rocks.

"Singing… feet?" Scarlet asked, still confused.

"That's silly! —now we are three! - Feet do not sing! …Do they? I've been here so long that maybe… Regardless, my feet cannot sing -."

Scarlet managed to move her head and look up. The feet belonged to a pale bluish-skinned petite naked girl that hanged high on the cavern rock wall. Her black hair floated upwards and moved calmly as if floating underwater. Her eyes sockets were pink and her lips were bluish purple. She was stuck to the stone wall with a thick rock shaft nailed through her stomach. Lines of dry blood reached from her womb to her feet.

A small spider hung from a web line very close to the black haired girl's shoulder. The girl remained still for a moment, her eyes fixed on the spider. Her left leg unnaturally bent by the knee on a "V" shape with her foot facing up. The foot grabbed the spider and brought it close to her face. She quickly jerked her head towards her toes and snatched the spider with her teeth. She crunched the spider with her teeth and chewed on it before swallowing. The black haired girl noticed Scarlet was repulsed by what she just did.

"What are you?" Scarlet uttered.

"Oh, I apologize for the awful sight -boy or girl; girl or boy-" the girl said, "But I have not much of a choice of what I can eat here."

Scarlet slowly sat up. The pain in the back of her head prompted her to touch it and she felt the blood on her fingers. She yanked her left leg a few times until she managed to set it free from the two rocks pinning it. The angel managed to stand up and take off the rest of the chains that confined her, but her left ankle was twisted and she had to limp to get closer to the naked girl.

"Many blessings, you are well!" The girl smiled at Scarlet.

"Your feet…" said Scarlet "They do not touch the ground. You are… pure of heart, a saint. You are not supposed to be in Hell…"

"I did try so hard to tell them-he loves her, he loves me not, he loves her, he loves me not -, but these demons, they seemed so happy to have me here as some sort of ornament. Say, could I trouble you for a little help- God help me-?"

"You…you want me to… set you free?" Scarlet asked.

"Why yes, if you could. This place- you liven up the place- being here, like this, is all I've known most of my life- aaaah! Spiders!-, except for my brief time living… somewhere else. I have forgotten most of it by now, but I think I'm ready to return."

"Are you… well?"

"Oh, I am fine! - I HATE YOU! - Will you help me?"

"Will you not bleed to death if I pull it off?"

"Maybe. Perhaps I am already dead- no one coming for you-. But If I still live, I do not wish to spend my days nailed to a wall in a pit of Hell. It gets a bit boring and sticky. And, well, I am nailed to a wall in a pit of Hell, ha, ha! Hee! No. I would rather die. Would you not?"

"Of course."

Scarlet slowly paced closer to the black haired naked girl and lifted her arms to reach the rock shaft stuck through the girl's belly. She tried to pull it off, but her fall had left her too weak. She rested a moment and tried again. The rock shaft began to move and the girl screamed in pain.

"Keep at it, please!-I disgust you-Do not mind my pain!" she repeated.

Scarlet complied. The angel pulled the shaft a few times. Blood gushed from the girl and spilled over the dried blood all the way to the girl's feet. With each try she was able to move back a part of the shaft, but it became more painful to the girl. Scarlet stumbled back when the shaft finally loosened off, expecting the girl to fall on the floor. Instead, the girl's feet hovered a few inches over the ground.

Scarlet dropped the bloody rock shaft and kneeled at the naked girl's side. The angel stood up and they both looked at the girl's stomach. A circle shaped hole perforated the girl through her back. The naked girl got curious and immersed her arm through the hole in her torso. Scarlet could see her hand on the other side as she wiggled her fingers.

"Ugh!" Scarlet barely managed to say before throwing up in her mouth.

"I really hope this will heal --." said the naked girl. "It is a little windy by my innards, but other than that I am feeling fine. My feet are asleep, though."

"Then… let's get out of this place."

"The only way out is up through that hole you fell"

"Then, we have some climbing to do."

Scarlet took off her grey cape and wrapped it around the naked girl.

"What are you doing?" The girl asked.

"You are naked. You… should not walk like that in Hell."

"Naked? - make love to me - I do not understand."

"Aren't you cold?"

"I am a little, but-"

"Then hurry."

The warrior angel grabbed the drifting girl by the shoulder to support herself as she limped and the girl floated towards the wall of the chamber. She felt a small draft coming from one of the corners of the place and found a small cavity right above her head. With the floating girl's help, the red angel tried to ignore the pain from her leg as she ascended towards the rocky gap. Once they climbed up the abyss, they reached the top side of the cavern tunnels where the lighting was too dim to see farther than a few feet ahead; a faint blue glow came from the stone walls. The passageways became uncomfortably tight, forcing the angel and the girl to move one in front of the other, both supporting themselves against the walls. Scarlet still held on to the rock shaft in case she needed to defend herself in the absence of her sword.

After heading up the tunnels for hours, they reached the top of the cliff. Scarlet carefully scanned the area, but found no beasts around.

"I feel hunger" The black haired teenage girl whispered.

"It seems we are out of spiders." Scarlet joked.

"Perhaps you may share a bit of your blood."

"Are you mad?!"

"Just a bit.-not too long now- We could nip your finger so that I may suck on it."

"No! I will not give you my blood!"

"I am sorry. I did not mean to upset you with my request. I do hope you forgive me."

"We are almost out of the caverns anyway. Listen carefully, once you exit the caves, you must head west through the ash desert. There is a portal that will lead you back to Earth."

"What is a portal?"

"It is- it is a glowing watery widow. Trust me. You will know when you see it."

"Like a waterfall!"

"Sure. I guess."

"Are you not coming with me? - GET AWAY FROM ME! - Is it because I wanted to suck your blood?"

"No. I still have business in Hell. I am not leaving until I get my sword back."

"What is a sword? Could you at least bless me with the knowledge of my savior's name?"

"I'm Scarlet."

"I like your name, Scarlet. —stupid girl! - I am-"

"Shhh! Stay behind me. We are clear to move now."

Scarlet and the naked black haired girl hurried towards the entrance of the cavern. The angel felt the same ground trembling as before when the beasts awoke. Dirt and ash under her feet whirled and picked up. The unnamed beast skeletons raced after them. Scarlet turned around and raised the rock shaft.

"Keep moving!"

"What? But-"

"We won't make it! I will give you time! Go!"

"Very well. Thank you for all your help! - sad evil creature- You have truly been a friend to me and I sincerely hope-"

"GO!"

"Many blessings! Da dee dee da daaa…"

The black haired girl hovered through the cave entrance and vanished from the angel's sight. Scarlet walked fast towards the skeletons. She figured if she had a chance against the beasts it would be before their bones merged with the ashes.

Scarlet jumped towards the closest skeleton, the bones of a huge scorpion-like monster with a sharp boned tail. She stabbed the beast's skull repeatedly. Shards flew up and it seemed like the angel was picking on a huge chunk of ice with a big ice pick.

The scorpion creature attacked the angel with its sharp tail. After several tries, it managed to wound Scarlet's right arm, making her drop the rock shaft. Scarlet fell to the ground face up, trying to deal with her pain and the scorpion beast that came in for the kill. The angel timed the tail attacks and moved to the sides each time the tails stroke to avoid them. She waited until the creature's skull was almost on top of her and grabbed it, jerking it to the side just when the sharp bone tail stroke. The scorpion stabbed its own skull with its tail, dying instantly.

Scarlet moved away from the falling skeleton corpse, but was hit on her back by a snake bone tail and again on her wounded shoulder by a huge bone claw. Two more beasts were attacking her, their ash skin hardened already. The angel was cornered to a cavern wall and she saw twenty more beasts closing in on her. Scarlet saw the rock shaft lying on the floor near her. She quickly picked it up and stood her ground, ready to die fighting the unnamed beasts of Hell.

As the first bone claw of a bird-like bone creature swung for Scarlet, she deflected it with the rock shaft, but the shaft broke in pieces upon impact with the ash hardened skin of the beast.

"Great." Scarlet smiled.

Suddenly the bird creature's claw began to rot. It shrieked in pain. The rotting spread all over the creature's body turning everything to ashes and dust. All the other unnamed beasts panicked and ran away from Scarlet, but one by one they began to rot and turn to dust as well.

"Ashes to ashes. Dust to dust" Scarlet whispered in relief. "Sister

Black, have you come to my aid?"

The Black Angel walked in from the darkness of the cavern shadows. She smiled at Scarlet and reached out her arms to hug her. Scarlet knelt and buried Black in her arms.

"I am so glad to see you!" Scarlet cried.

"But how did you know I was here?"

The Black Angel pointed at the dead scorpion beast lying on the ground.

"Ha! I should have known all it takes is one death to get your attention." Scarlet replied. "I got lucky."

Scarlet noticed Black's face seemed tired.

"Are you alright?" She asked. The Black Angel smiled at Scarlet, but it was the smile a sick or exhausted person gives another when they cannot hide their condition.

"How many are dying on Earth? You seemed overworked..."

The Black Angel did not respond.

"Something's wrong with Creation, Isn't it? We need to figure it out and we need to find Violet. Wait here."

Scarlet stood up and headed towards the cavern entrance. Black Angel tugged Scarlet by the leg. Scarlet turned to her sister. The Black Angel pointed towards the Shadows in the cavern.

"I need to visit Eve's throne first. I will return once I get my sword back."

Scarlet turned and the Black Angel tugged her leg harder. She saw her sister pointing at the darkness with a sad look on her face. A tear rolled down her cheek and she breathed faster.

Scarlet bent in front of Black and wiped the tear from her cheek.

"Little sister, I'll be fine. I will return and we will go back to Earth. Whatever's going on, you and I will fix it together. We will save the world. I'll see you very soon."

The Black Angel nodded with a sad look on her face. Scarlet kissed

Black on her forehead, stood up and left the cavern. The Black Angel saw her sister walk away. Scarlet's words "I'll see you very soon" lingered in her head. The Black Angel sighed and nodded. She walked towards the cavern shadows and became part of the darkness.

....

When Lucifer fell from Heaven, it did not take him too long to gain reign over Hell and all its demons. His power was surpassed only by God, but it was his strategies and manipulations that led him to become the uncontested ruler of Hell for thousands of years. His first task was to build a temple-citadel in which to place his throne. He thought of building a tower, a majestic palace to rival Heaven's stronghold, but that seemed rather unoriginal to him. He wanted his throne to stand on a place where no single living or dead creature would doubt Lucifer's influence over Hell and Creation itself. But if a slug's point of view would greatly diverge from a shark's, and if a little Japanese school girl would view Hell quite differently from an African war lord, it would seem impossible to build a place universally recognized and revered for its power.

Lucifer needed to build his fortress from a generally common element. He chose to build it on fear. To achieve this, he covered the floors and walls of his castle with special mirrors able to reflect perception and suppressed horrors. Any creature would subconsciously design their own Hell from deep within their souls and see it become physically real in this place. Lucifer's throne would always be at the center of all. This was an ever-changing temple perfectly tailored for a being that could alter his shape to achieve his goals.

Scarlet knew the risk she took when she entered the Devil's citadel. It felt like walking into a nightmare that one could not escape from. She knew that none of what she saw was real as she walked the halls, but it still tortured her to see a place where mortals were unthinking slave units unwillingly serving their mistress. To Scarlet's view, walls and floors were made out of human beings whose bodies were used as mere blocks to be placed on top of one another as to shelter Lucifer's throne. Everywhere she looked, mortals were things, not persons. Some stood as living useless statues. Others were lined up in an endless pointless file, which started with the last person being born into the line and as the line progressed each person was closer to maturity and death. All of them seemed broken, heads down and dead stares, like they led meaningless purposeless lives. It was a place with no freedom, no self-sovereignty, and no dissension. Lucifer's will imposed over man was Scarlet's Hell.

Scarlet struggled to move up the levels of the citadel until she reached the throne room, now occupied by Eve. Sometimes she got lost walking through the human shaped halls, but she'd find her way back by following the sound of Eve's weeping. The cries of Eve for her lost husband would never stop. Scarlet encountered a few demon guards here and there, but she disposed of them quickly. She became more focused on her task of retrieving her sword as Eve's moans grew louder.

When Scarlet reached the throne room, her vision of Hell ceded to Eve's egotistical majesty. The floors and walls became silver as well as the stalagmite-like décor. The ceiling was made of thick glass, with a view of the void where condemned soils would fall from Creation. They looked like small blue stars falling from the night sky on to Eve's throne in the center of the room.

"Where is my sword, Eve?" Scarlet asked with a commanding voice.

Eve knelt and skulked behind her throne. She stood up, moved beside the throne and extended her arm to catch fallen souls with her hand. Once she amassed a few in her palm, her hand lit up on fire and she threw the burning souls at Scarlet as if they were fire balls.

"Do not talk to me like that!!!" Eve screamed.

Scarlet moved quickly to avoid the shower of burning souls coming at her. She could hear the souls screaming in agony as they smoldered to nothing. A few of the burning souls nicked Scarlet's armor. However, it was the ones that reached Scarlet's bare skin that hurt her most. As Eve kept throwing burning souls at the warrior angel, one of them hit Scarlet in the back of her hand. She felt the soul scorched her physically and emotionally. It was the agony of a mortal being ending its existence knowing there would be no redemption or second chances, only the knowledge of unfulfilled potential and wasted lifetime.

The angel rolled over the floor, holding her burned hand. She fought to keep the painful tears inside her as she launched herself towards Eve. She slapped the queen a few times and pinned her to the floor.

"Now" Scarlet grinned. "My sword, please."

"You should have joined me when I offered, Scarlet. Now, it appears I don't need you anymore."

Scarlet felt the pointy edge of her sword poking the back of her neck.

"Let her go." A familiar melodic voice ordered. The angel stood up and stepped away from Eve. Scarlet was stunned.

"White" she whispered, "What in God's name are you doing?"

White stood behind Scarlet pointing her sword at her. Goldie watched from a few feet away.

"Goldie?" Scarlet asked confused. "What are you doing here?"

"I'm here to perform a miracle!" Goldie announced excited. "It's the end of times, see?"

"White, what is going on? Are you two rebelling?" Scarlet asked in disbelief.

"Sister, this is how it has to be so no one else should ever suffer death." White replied.

"Is this what this is about?! You want everyone to live forever?! That is madness!"

"It is not. It is to be the new order of things."

"It is not God's will!"

"It is mine."

"No, it is not! This is not you, sister! I know you! Who has poisoned your soul?"

"It is God's disregard for humanity and life that has poisoned me! I cannot stand idle while He has us destroy cities and slay thousands in his name! All life is sacred! All life has purpose! I will-I will show you His way is wrong."

"I cannot let you do this!"

"That is why you must be stopped now."

Scarlet walked up to White, pressing the sword against her armor.

"Aim true, sister. You will need more than a sword to stop me."

"She'll need a miracle!" Goldie replied smiling.

The golden angel took off her top hat and, like a magician, moved the fingers of her gloved hand and held her hat in front of her with the other gloveless hand, showing the other two angels the hat's empty hole.

"Ladies and demons!" She voiced. "Preee-senting a one-time-only spectacle, the Am-ay-zing Goldie! I give you Goldie's Incredible Vanishing act!"

She aimed the hat's hole at Scarlet's armor. The ruby armor mutated into red fireworks with a variety of shapes that eventually decomposed into little red butterflies. The butterflies flew in swirls into Goldie's hat. Scarlet was left almost naked in her grey robes. She turned to Goldie, shocked.

"Raphael..." Scarlet pleaded.

"Maaaagic!" Goldie replied with a grin.

Scarlet moved towards Goldie with her raised fist.

"I do not believe in hat tricks!" she exclaimed.

Suddenly, Scarlet stopped cold and looked at the edge of her blade stabbing out from between her breasts. Blood gushed from her chest and mouth. Scarlet fell on her knees, still looking at Goldie. White pushed the sword further inside Scarlet's back.

"No!" Goldie screamed at White. "Whaddaya doin'?!"

"I do what is necessary, sister." White replied with tears rolling out her eyes.

"You're killin' her!" Goldie pleaded.

Scarlet fell lump on the floor. White knelt beside her, holding her hand and whispering to her.

"I am sorry Michael..."

"Gab-Gabriel...Who has poisoned your soul?" Scarlet uttered before drawing her last breath.

White cried and began praying. Goldie ran towards Scarlet and pushed White away from her.

"This ain't happenin'! This can't be happening! I can fix this! I just need ta- I can fix her!"

Goldie placed her hands on Scarlet's pale forehead.

"In the name of the Father and the Son and the Holy Spirit, come back! Live! Come on! Live! I'm healin' ya! I'm givin' you a miracle, see?!" Goldie turned her eyes towards White.

"Why won't ya let me bring'er back?!"

"I cannot"

"But it's your ministry! You are life!"

"She stood against us."

"SHE'S OUR SISTER!!! You said we would only stop her! Ya never said... Ya never..."

Eve stepped closer to White and Goldie.

"It is done now. Do you stand with us or do we have to stop you too?" Eve said as she signaled a few demon goblins to enter the throne room and circle around Goldie.

"When pigs fly..." Goldie uttered.

She glanced at one of the demons and winked at it. The demon turned into a huge pig with wings. Goldie ran towards the winged pig and mounted it. The pig took flight. A bright colorful rainbow sprung out of the swine's butt.

"When pigs fly!" Goldie yelled.

The flying pig broke the ceiling's thick glass and disappeared in the darkness, leaving only the rainbow trail left after the pig's passing.

"Go after her!" Eve screamed.

Legions of demon goblins crawled up the silver walls like cockroaches and left the citadel.

"Now we are going to have to kill her too, White!" Eve shrieked at White in anger.

"No." White answered with immense sadness as she kept playing with

Scarlet's red curls. "She cannot hurt us. Only the Black Angel, can stand against us, but that... has been taken care of."

"You mean-" Eve did not finish her question.

"With the fall of Michael, four Seals have been broken." White continued. "You know what that means."

"Then, we continue our plan. And you will help me find my husband..." Eve said.

"As promised..." White retorted, numb. One of the goblin demons approached Eve with its head lowered.

"Your Grace..."

"What now?!" Eve answered angrily.

"The red one, she- before she escaped the abyss... she freed her. A- And she has made her way to Creation!"

"NO!" Eve screamed and slapped the demon away.

"Freed who?" White asked.

"That bitch!" Eve bellowed in a tantrum.

"Freed who?" White asked again, lifting her eyes towards Eve with concern.

"LILLITH!" Eve replied screaming. "Your sister Scarlet has freed Lillith!"

"But that's impossible!!! Lillith died! I thought you-"

"Trust me, she lives; and she can easily ruin our deal now."

White smiled at Scarlet's dead face.

"Dear sister, even in death you do not stop making my life difficult."

She lifted Scarlet's body and carried her as her wings spread wide. Scarlet's blood stained White's pearl white dress.

"Deal with it." White commanded.

"Me?!" Eve asked incredulous. "What am I supposed to-"

"Deal with it or our agreement is off." White said as she flew away,

Scarlet's body in her arms, through the roof of the citadel.

"God dammit! GOD DAMMIT!" Eve cursed. She quickly stepped towards the throne and with her hands lit on fire, she burned all the small bluish souls that poured into the citadel.

"She's going to find him first!" she repeated over and over. "She's going to find him first!"

. . . .

White carried Scarlet's body in her arms as she flew hurriedly towards the abyss caverns. She knew that she'd never be able to remove the stains of Scarlet's blood from her white gown, but she wanted to be rid of her sister's body as quickly as possible. She also wanted to be done with the unavoidable encounter she was about to have.

The white angel stepped into the cavern's darkness, her aura being the only source of light in her path. She kept walking into the darkness until she felt she'd gone far enough. She made sure she was surrounded by darkness from all sides before carefully placing her sister's body on the ground. She heard sobs, like a little girl crying in silence, but after turning to all directions she couldn't tell where the sobs came from.

The Black Angel stood right next to Scarlet's body. She let herself drop on her knees and cried, letting out the agony of losing her sister and not fully understanding why. White stepped back and maintained her distance from her. She was terrified of the Black Angel and of what she would do after seeing Scarlet dead. The Black Angel looked up towards White. Her tears and sadness did not swathe the confusion she felt. Without pronouncing a single word, White knew her sister was questioning her. She wanted to know why.

"You-you will never understand why!" White screamed, her body trembling with fear. "You play a part in His plans. You deliver the dead! I am doing this so that no one else needs to see you. I am doing this to keep the promise made of eternal life! A new plan unfolds. Every piece of this new plan is slowly coming along. Unfortunately, some will have to be removed, but they will be the last. For then, no one will need to die. We will all live forever. All of us…"

The Black Angel stood up and took a step towards White. White jumped back and stretched her arm to stop her sister.

"DO NOT COME ANY CLOSER!!! STAY WHERE YOU ARE!!!"

The Black Angel stopped moving. White tried to compose herself. Her hands were still shaking.

"I will... build a new, better world out of the ashes of Creation. With Uriel's seal broken, it was... easy for me to deal with Jophiel and Zadkiel. The seals of nature and progress are shattered. But if I ever hoped to keep you out of my way, I needed a fourth seal to be broken. I chose Michael's because I knew she would never allow me to succeed while she drew breath."

The Black Angel closed her eyes and lowered her head.

"You are ashamed of me?!" White asked enraged. "You, the murderous arm of God! You, the killer of thousands of Egyptian firstborns! You, the reaper of the Bubonic Plague and the Holocaust! YOU ARE ASHAMED OF ME?!"

The Black Angel opened her eyes and stared at her sister with anger. White stepped back once more and swallowed hard.

"Four seals are broken. The Four Horsemen are coming. They will raze the Earth if you do not stop them. They are coming."

White spread her wings and flew over the Black Angel and Scarlet's body.

"You do not have a place in my new world. I will see to it. I hope yours will be the last necessary death to come."

With those words said, White took flight away from the darkness of the abyss and the cavern, leaving the Black Angel alone to mourn her fallen sister.

9 SCORNED

Hours passed like nothing to Eve as she cried on the throne in the silver room of the citadel in Hell. One of the worst ash storms in centuries was brewing outside. It was already impossible for demons to cross the gray wastelands. Ash storms brought toxic agony and death to anyone and anything that got caught in them. But Eve's wails were louder than the sound of the storm winds. Demons everywhere were terrified to hear her crying so loudly. That would always mean she was about to do something really stupid and dangerous (usually for the demons).

Eve cried, but she also listened. She searched for the voice in her head, the one that started it all. Even in Hell, after all these years, she could feel the first breath of life granted to her. She could still remember that unique and encompassing voice and the first words it uttered to her:

"Open your eyes" Eve was born from these words.

When she first opened her eyes, she was overwhelmed by intense white light. After a while, her eyes adjusted and she saw colors. She saw beauty.

"You are Eve" the voice continued, *"You are woman. God made you from the rib of your man. He is Adam."*

Eve stood up and looked around her. It was a garden. She saw flowers, green grass, fruitful trees, small cute squirrels and bright colorful butterflies. It was a sunny day and the sky was clear.

"Where am I?"

"You are in Eden."

"Eden" Eve thought with delight. She heard the sound of running water and followed it until she reached a river. She bent down and saw her reflection on the water and she realized she was beautiful. Eve had blue eyes and long golden hair with a gorgeous smile. And she loved her smile. She thought it was more beautiful than the flowers and the butterflies. She turned around and there was someone more stunning standing behind her.

The light that Eve saw when she first opened her eyes came from this person. Her face exuded compassion and peace. A single luminous white feather adorned her long flowing white hair and a bright white halo over her head. And she had gorgeous feathery white wings. Eve felt jealous and wondered how she could get wings like those.

"Are you God?"

"No. I am an angel. I am... White. I speak on His behalf. He created the world, the day and night, the oceans and land, and the beasts that roam it. God created man to rule over them in His name. He created Adam and He created you. He loves Adam and He wants him to be happy. God gave Lillith to Adam and it made him happy. He now wants to give him you."

"Wait. Who is this Lillith?"

"She is the first woman, made from the splinter bone of Adam's foot."

"But, if Adam already has a woman, why does he need another?"

"God stands to reason that if one woman makes Adam happy, more will make him even happier."

"How many women does God want to give Adam?"

"As many as the bones in Adam's body can spare."

Eve did not like that answer. She did not like the idea of being created out of someone's rib and much less to be a gift to a "man". And the thought of being one of many "women" whose sole purpose in life was to make Adam happy repulsed her. She felt threatened. She wanted a life of her own. She wanted to explore the garden and rule over it. Why should Adam get to rule in God's name? Why not her?

"Adam and Lillith are on the fields at the other side of that hill." White said, "Go to him and make him happy."

Eve saw White spread her wings and fly away to the sky. She did not take her eyes off the angel until she was completely out of sight. The woman turned her eyes towards the hill. She panicked and ran to the opposite direction. She found a cluster of trees that she thought would be a good hiding place. After climbing the tallest of the trees, she rested on a branch. Her heart beat fast and she felt a sense of dread to the point of making her nauseous. Desperate and scared, she began to cry.

"Why do you cry?" A voice hissed.

Eve opened her eyes and lifted her head. She saw a huge long golden snake slithering down the top of the tree towards her. Its eyes were entirely black. Eve moved back towards the tree shaft. Her eyes were opened wide in terror. The snake sat at the edge of the tree and smiled at Eve.

"Do not be afraid of this form. I gain nothing by harming you." said the serpent. The creature lifted its body until it stood erected. It grew arms and legs and its head mutated. Its scales receded into its skin as huge black feathered wings sprouted from its back. A tall dark haired angel with black wings hovered over the branch were Eve sat. None of the features of the snake remained, only its black eyes.

"Do you like me better now?" The dark angel asked.

"You are an angel of God!"

"Who I am does not matter, child, but who you will choose to be."

"Why are you here?"

"I am curious to see the only sad living thing in this paradise. You do know you are in Eden, correct?"

"Yes. I just…I am meant to be another lover to Adam"

"Hmmm. How utterly disappointing that is. I see in front of me a very special and wonderful being with so much potential. But of all the things you could be, of all the things you could do, you choose to be… a wife?"

"But it's not me! I do not want this! I do not want to be submitted to anyone. I do not wish my purpose to be making Adam happy."

"You must always take that which is meant to be rightfully yours.

What is it that you truly want?"

"I want the freedom to lead my own life!"

"Would you think, then, that Adam is in the way of that freedom?"

"Yes."

"Would you say that if he did not live in Eden, you would be free?"

"Yes."

"Then it stands to reason that to be free you must-"

"Take Adam's life..." Eve said with her eyes wide open with the sudden realization.

"You said it. Not me." The angel responded as he slowly floated over Eve. "Do let me know how it all turns out. I'll be around."

The dark angel smiled as he flew away from Eve. The woman felt elated and terrified at the same time. Freedom was at her grasp and maybe even the chance to rule over Eden. She climbed down from her tree and picked up a stick to draw her plans on the dirt. She could lure Adam to the river and hit his head with something hard before pushing his body to the water. She could hang his neck from a tree with a vine. She could start a fire and burn him to a crisp. She could push him to a ditch or bury him alive. All these thoughts came to Eve's creative mind one after the other. It became hard for her to decide, but in the end she settled for stabbing him repeatedly with a sharp object.

Eve waited until night time and headed towards the hill holding a sharp arrow shaped rock she had filed earlier in the day. She crept quietly up and down the grass filled hill and followed a trail that led her to a cave. Adam and Lillith slept close to each other next to a fire. She tip-toed over Lillith and bent over Adam. She put her hand over his chest and raised her arrow shaped rock. The way his hard chest felt made her stop. Eve looked at Adam's face and passed her fingers through his beard. She touched his rough hand. He also smelled good. Eve stared at Adam for a while.

He was perfect.

Adam woke up and sat up. He marveled at Eve's beauty.

"Who are you?" he asked.

"I am Eve." She answered while lowering the rock. "I am... a gift to you from God."

Adam smiled and gently touched her chin.

"You are so beautiful."

Adam reached his arm towards Lillith and shoved her gently.

"Lillith, wake up."

Lillith woke up and sat up next to Adam and Eve.

"I have good news." said Adam. "The Lord has blessed me with another wife."

"Yay!" Lillith rejoiced. "Now we are three!" She exclaimed while hugging Eve. "We can be sisters!"

Eve felt repulsed by Lillith and had to fight her urges to stab her eye with the arrow shaped rock. Adam joined in the hug and his face next to Eve's melted her. She let go of the rock and wrapped her arms around Adam. This felt good. It felt almost perfect, except for Lillith's embrace.

············

A week passed and Eve had happily settled into her new role of wife. Every day she woke up earlier than Lillith to find the juiciest fruits and fresh eggs to make Adam's breakfast. She bathed him in the river and slept close to him at night to keep him warm. The blond beauty tried to be with Adam as much time as possible.

Each evening, Adam offered sacrifices to God in gratitude for all the blessings He had been given such as life, the garden, and his wives. Adam taught Lillith and Eve how to talk to God. He made it clear that God should always come first in their lives. Eve held his hand tight when they prayed to God because she knew it was important to Adam.

Lillith noticed Eve behaved oddly around her. When Lillith cooked, she made sure there was enough for both Adam and Eve. When Eve cooked, there was never enough food for Lillith. Eve also avoided talking to Lillith except when she needed something from her. She gave Lillith too many orders and kept her as far away from Adam as she could. However, Lillith and Adam would always find time to be together. They would take long walks and talk about everything and laugh together. Eve did not like it when they were together. Adam never talked much to Eve, and he certainly did not laugh with her the way he did with Lillith. It tortured her to see him laugh with Lillith.

One day, after bathing Adam, Eve stayed in the river a while longer to clean herself. The dark angel stood at the shore staring at her emotionless. Eve saw the angel and lowered her head in shame, knowing already why he was there. The angel waited for Eve to get out of the water and they both sat down on the grass.

"What are you doing?" the dark angel asked.

"I…"

"You were supposed to gain your freedom."

"I am free."

"Really? You feed him and bathe him and keep him warm. It seems to me that you are his servant. Does that make you happy?"

"I am his wife. And yes, I am happy. I like being with him. Adam makes me happy."

"But you are not entirely happy, are you?"

"Lillith…"

"Ah, say no more. The other wife. The one that makes him laugh."

"Tell me angel, what does he see in her? She's so skinny and her hair is a mess. And her face is so plain! I on the other hand am so much more beautiful than her and yet…"

Eve hesitated briefly. Then continued.

"Every day, my hate for her grows. I would be in your debt if you'd slay her…"

"Oh, I'm afraid I cannot do that. Her soul is pure, and therefore, protected by God. I would feel His wrath upon me the very second a drop of her blood touched ground."

"What then?"

"There are much more satisfying ways to get what you want. Make

Adam forget her. Use your beauty. Make him look at you. Adam is a man. You are a woman. You have power over him that he will never comprehend."

"I do?"

"Child, Lillith was not blessed with your beautiful big breasts. Use them. You want Adam's undivided attention? Next time you get close to him, take his hand and place it on your breast. Then you will touch him between his legs, and have him touch you between yours."

"I don't understand."

"Trust me, you will have him so deep under your control, you will not care who he laughs with, and neither will he. Always remember, you are truly gifted, and those who have been more gifted than others, will go farther in life. That is, if they know how to use their gifts."

"Thank you, angel, I will try this."

"Hmmm. My advice does not come free, you know. There is a price."

"What is it that you want?"

"Oh, I will let you know…"

The angel picked a cherry from a tree and ate it as he walked away from Eve.

"Make me proud. I'll be around."

That night, Eve slept close to Adam in the cave. Lillith slept a few feet away from them. Eve woke up and began to caress Adam's chest. Adam opened his eyes and looked at Eve with curiosity. Eve took his hand, put it on her breast, and was about to reach between his legs, but she stopped. She figured it would be much better if she reached between his legs with her mouth. Eve kept her eyes looking at Adam's face at all times. She saw him squinting and moaning. She knew she had him. Adam was hers.

Every day, Adam and Eve would make love in the Garden of Eden. Adam barely remembered Lillith's name. They did not go for walks as they used to. One time, Adam tried to make love to Lillith, but it was awkward and uncomfortable. Lillith was disturbed and ran away. Since then, Adam and Eve were inseparable.

. . . .

The river waters flowed calmly as the dark angel wrapped his arms around Lillith's wet dead body and pressed her closer to him. His head and neck grew and mutated into a giant serpent. Eve remained still. The dark angel opened his mouth unnaturally wide and swallowed Lillith's corpse whole. His neck had extended like the body of an anaconda. Eve could see the shape of Lillith's body sliding inside the angel's neck. The dark angel moved his face closer to Eve's and winked at her.

"I could never kill this girl, but it does not mean you could not. Congratulations Eve, you are the first murderer in the history of mankind."

"Adam must never know of this. No one must ever know."

"That will be a bit difficult. God will know. I also foresee that the story of Adam, Eve, Lillith, and the children they begat, will be told from generation to generation. Everyone will know of what you just did until the end of time."

"Not if I change the story. Not if I hide the truth. No one must know of Lillith and if they do, it will only be in whispered blasphemous lies."

"Hmm. My admiration to you, if you can actually pull that off. Then again, you seem to be quite the over achiever. Not just killing one, but two."

"What do you mean?"

The dark angel winked at Eve. "Our deal is done. Nice doing business with you." he declared.

And with that, Eve was left alone in the river.

. . . .

That night, a thunder storm hit Eden for the first time. Rain poured uncompromisingly with winds so strong they knocked over some of the oldest trees. Bolts of lightning lashed the garden repeatedly, creating fires that spread with no control. The deafening sound of thunder was the most intimidating part for Eve as she desperately ran barefoot on the muddy grass looking for cover. She hurried between the trees and reached the river shore where she stepped inside the wild running waters.

"Help me, angel!" She yelled "Do not forsake me!"

The river waters grew rougher, the rain and thunder became more intense. Eve struggled not to lose her balance and kept as close to the shoreline as possible, but there was no sign of the dark angel.

"What have you done?!"

Eve recognized the melodic voice coming from behind her. She dreaded to turn her head and look at White. The angel drifted over Eve, moving her wings faster to make up for the strong wings. White seemed confused and dejected.

"I cannot feel her... What have you done?!" White asked, tears rolling down her cheek. "WHAT HAVE YOU DONE?!"

"I...I took her life."

"Why? Why would you do such a terrible thing?" White uttered, breathless.

Eve did not answer. White descended into the river until the flowing waters reached her knees. The angel stood face to face with Eve and looked at her with sorrow.

"You have tainted Eden! God is angry... He wants you to leave..."

"What about Adam?"

"He is to stay here with God. You are not to see him ever again"

"No!"

"I am sorry."

"NO!" Eve screamed pushing White back and heading towards land. White followed Eve.

"There is no other way, Eve."

Eve ran as fast as she could until she reached the other side of the forest and a single apple tree she had discovered earlier in the day. She picked up fallen apples from the ground and threw them at White. The angel seemed surprised that Eve would dare to throw fruits at her, but she kept tailing her. Eve held the last apple in her hand, but did not throw it. Instead, she held on to the apple and faced White.

"There is nothing I could say to you to make you understand!" cried Eve. "You have never loved! You may care for things, but you have never loved so deeply you would lose yourself! One day, you will love as I have! One day, you will find yourself doing things you thought you'd never do for love! On that day, you will remember me, and you will understand!"

White observed with sadness as Eve ran into the woods.

"I love life." The angel whispered.

Eve kept running under the storm towards the cave. She searched the caverns, but Adam was nowhere to be seen. She got back outside under the rain and yelled his name.

"Eve!" She heard Adam's voice calling for her, "Eve!"

Eve saw Adam running towards her from the woods. She kissed and embraced him.

"Are you well? Eve, are you well?"

"Yes."

"God is angry! We need to hide in the cave! We need to pray!"

"No! Adam, we need to leave Eden!"

"I do not understand. Why? We need to find Lillith!"

At that moment, Eve realized she still held the apple she did not throw at White back in the forest. She looked at the fruit in her hand and then at Adam's eyes. She did not want to lose him. Eve was about to do another thing she never thought she'd do for love.

"Adam" she said, "I have betrayed you..."

....

A few years into the second half of the nineteenth century, the sun was setting by the Plantation Hacienda house at the outskirts of the town of Ortega on the island of Santa Cristal. It was a spacious two story white house with a brick floored porch and wooden balcony all around the second floor. The house was surrounded by all manner of tropical trees such as mango and flamboyán. When the wind blew, a mix of flowers and fruit smells scented the house reminding Eve a little about her days with Adam in the Garden of Eden.

Eve chose to remain inside the white house. She wore a long corseted blue dress with ribbons. She closed the curtains, fired up a few lanterns and sat on the couch determined not to fall asleep as she waited for her husband's return. Adam had been out for weeks, secretly pushing for the island's emancipation of African slaves. He had Eve pay off the right politicians while he fought and killed a group of Lucifer's shadow spies. Adam sent Eve home and promised to return to her once the law had passed. The last letter he wrote to her cited some delays with the proceedings, but promised his safe return after three weeks.

The blonde woman heard the sound of fast galloping and rock-crunching wheels. She went upstairs and stood on the creaky balcony to get a better view of the black carriage coming towards the house. She looked forward to seeing Adam again and was determined to make love that night even if she had to get him drunk. When the carriage stopped right outside the house's main entrance, Eve went back inside and checked her makeup and breath in front of a mirror. She ran downstairs and saw the carriage tied to one brown horse, parked a few feet away from the main entrance. Eve greeted the driver, a young twenty-something African descendant named Jacinto. He was one of Adam's paid servants.

The carriage door remained closed, so Eve went ahead and opened it herself, realizing it was empty inside except for a basket of tropical fruits.

"Where is Adam?" Eve asked the driver.

"Ma'am Eva, Don Adan done say he need tah stay in the city few moh days. He send some fruit for ya."

"WHAT?!"

"Telled me to give ya this heah lettah", the driver said, extending his arm towards Eve and offering her a letter addressed to her.

"How could he-?! I am NOT waiting anymore!" Eve shouted as she snatched the letter from the driver's hand. She barely read it, knowing already what it said, and crumpled it before throwing it back at the driver's face.

"Take me to him!"

"B-but ma'am-"

Eve jumped up the driver's seat and whipped his face repeatedly with the horse's reins.

"TAKE ME TO HIM NOW, YOU GOOD FOR NOTHING WHELP!"

The driver relented and Eve closed the black carriage's door. The woman had had enough of Adam's obsession to please God as an Earth Agent. She thought they had already paid enough for their transgressions against the Lord. Not being allowed to return to Eden was punishment enough, but having to spend their immortality playing cloak and dagger games against Lucifer's shadow spies was daunting and stressful. Eve barely remembered the last time Adam touched her even to satisfy his needs, but the only person he seemed to want to please was God. She wanted her husband back.

Eve took off her long silk gloves and slapped them on her thighs. She looked out the carriage window, looking at the woods moving fast past her. She sighed and grabbed a banana out of the fruit basket next to her. As she peeled off the yellow fruit, she stuck her head out the window facing up at the driver as the wind hit her face.

"Driver, what is your name again?" She asked.

"Jacinto, ma'am. Jacinto."

"Jacinto, I know we started off on the wrong foot. Please forgive my rudeness."

"Oh, no, no, ma'am. I's live ta serve. You's let ol' Jacinto know what yah needs, ah done obey good. As mah wife Petra always say-"

"Yes. Yes, that is good to know. So hard to find good help these days. Would you mind going faster, Jacinto?"

"Right away, ma'am, right away."

Jacinto whipped the brown horse and held his reins tight. The carriage sped up through the tropic woods. Eve sat back and ate her banana as she wiped a drop of sweat from her forehead. She fixed her dress a bit and blew hard before sitting erect in upright position.

Once the carriage reached the town of Pueblito Cristal, Santa Cristal's capital at the time, Eve stormed into the Congress Hall where she expected

Adam to be. She practically kicked open the Mayor's office door, but neither Adam, the Mayor, or his secretary were there. Eve moved to the next office and then the next, finding a few workers, but none of them knew where her husband was. One of the office doors was locked. She banged on it loudly.

"Adam! ADAM!" She screamed. "I know you're there!" She continued slamming.

The door opened and a young tanned skinned black haired woman stood on the other side rushing to put back her dress on.

"I knew it! You harlot! Where is he?! Where is my husband?!"

"He's-"

"I will kill you! -ADAM!"

An obese fifty something bearded man, came from the room shirtless. He struggled to button his pants while walking fast towards Eve.

"Who are you?! Why are you looking for Don Adan here?"

"Mister Mayor…"

"Are you his wife, madam? Don Adan has not been seen in this town for weeks."

Eve felt a blow as she dreaded something worse than another infidelity from her husband was going on. Adam had abandoned Eve and he did not want to be found. Still in disbelief, she exited the building and stormed towards Jacinto.

"You told me he was here!"

"He was! Don Adan was heah when I's left!"

"Are you sure it was my husband who gave you the letter?!"

"I's-I's don't- It could'a been-"

Eve picked up a rock from the ground and threw it at Jacinto's head, knocking him off the carriage. As Jacinto lied on the floor, Eve ran towards him and kicked him repeatedly. Jacinto covered his bloodied head with his arms

"YOU UNBELIEVABLY DIMWITTED IDIOT!!!"

"I's sorry mah'm! I's sorry!"

"I WILL MAKE YOU TRULY SORRY!" she screamed, aiming her kicks at his stomach.

"Ooph! I'S SORRY! HE GONE NOW!"

She stopped hitting Jacinto and held her chest. She found it hard to breathe and felt a little dizzy. Jacinto struggled to stand up and tried to support her arms.

"He gone..." Jacinto repeated.

Eve searched the whole town for Adam that day and into the night until Jacinto persuaded her to go home get some rest. Upon her return to the Hacienda, Eve noticed someone had been in the master bedroom. She saw a small note lying on the table next to the mirror.

"Adam..." Eve whispered.

Eve read the note and her heart stopped as she sat on her bed, sweating cold. She tried to compose herself and think of her next move. The hand that held the note would not stop shaking.

. . . .

Over the next few years, Eve looked for her husband in all of Santa Cristal and the rest of the world. She travelled with Jacinto to Europe and Asia, trying to retrace all journeys she and her husband had ever made. Every night, Jacinto would hear Eve crying herself to sleep; sometimes the sobbing lasted the entire night.

On New Year's Eve of 1899, having found no sign of Adam for many years, Eve decided to return with Jacinto to Santa Cristal. The empty Hacienda house was occupied only by a few big wooden boxes. The woman, wearing only a long white sleeping gown, sat next to the window of her empty room and moved the curtains a bit to watch Jacinto come back to the house from an errand. Jacinto knocked on Eve's door.

"I's done got the things you ask foah, ma'am." He said in a low voice.

"Good." She responded, "Come sit with me. I would like for us to talk."

"I's better be on my way. My wife-"

"Jacinto, come sit with me. Do not make me ask you again."

The servant opened the door and entered the room holding iron chains and a brown bag full of candles.

"Jacinto, I need you to do something for me; something that will help me greatly in the search of my husband."

"Ma'am, maybe if yous considah-"

"Stop talking before you say something I will make you regret. You know I am a very dangerous person."

"Y-yes, ma'am." Jacinto answered with sweat drops rolling from his forehead.

"Do you know the difference between me and a stage magician?" asked Eve.

"… I's-"

Eve took the chains and bag from her servant and placed the candles around them while lighting them up.

"With me, once I make a person disappear, they will never be seen or heard from again. Knowing this, please let me know, how much do you want to see your wife Petra again?"

Jacinto kneeled. His breathing was heavy. His hands were shaking.

"Please…" Jacinto pleaded almost breathless.

Eve closed the curtain and pulled Jacinto towards her bosom in embrace.

"Such good help." Eve said to Jacinto, swirling the iron chains around Jacinto's body.

"In a few hours a new century will arrive."

．．．．．．．．．．．．．

The first time Eve set foot on the grounds of Lucifer's citadel, she was naked, her body bursting of bleeding cuts and black ash from Hell's desert. She was being dragged by four goblin demons ordered to escort her to Lucifer. As Eve crossed each level of the palace, visions of her most intimate horrors came to life around her. She feared rejection from Adam.

She feared failing him and losing him. She feared she lacked the power to protect him from God whom she thought was ultimately responsible for her and her husband's agony.

Eve was taken by the goblins to Lucifer's throne room where he waited for her, taken the form of the black winged dark angel Eve was familiar with. The Devil stared at Eve with curiosity.

"Eve, I am so impressed by you! You opened a doorway to Hell right at the stroke of midnight on the turn of the century to enhance the portal's power. Pointless, but impressive nonetheless. Good for you!"

He wiped some of the ashes from her forehead and kissed her.

"I have to say, I've missed our sessions so much, Eve." Lucifer declared, "The world has gotten so… complicated since back in the good old days. You were always such an amusing little thing. I am so happy that you are here, with me, instead of fighting my shadow spies out there on Earth. There are so many things we need to talk about. Where to begin?"

Lucifer caressed Eve's blonde hair "Ah, yes. Why are you here?"

"Angel, I have come to ask you to help me find Adam. Let me find him and live the rest of my days with him. In exchange, after one thousand years, I will offer my immortality to you. And I will give you my soul"

"One thou- You have got to be joking, child! After all these years, are you still so obsessed with that Neanderthal, you are willing to give your soul for him even if he has never loved you?"

"You said he would be mine!"

"I said you should fight to make him yours. Push away anything or anybody that gets in your way-"

"God. Adam loves God."

"I see…"

"But I can still make him love me!"

"Who are you trying to fool? Yourself? Keep at it then. It's funny to watch. Besides, your soul already belongs to me, Eve. Let me tell you a little secret, child. One day you will die. Do not be fooled by false promises of immorality by the Great Divine. YOU WILL DIE! And when you do…

123

What, you thought a nasty little piece of work like you had any chance of making it to the pearly gates? I have already set a special place for you at Lillith's side. I cannot wait to hear what you two will chat about."

"Lillith is still alive?" Eve asked surprised. "But I made sure I…"

"When it comes to me, do not ever believe everything you see…"

Lucifer smiled mockingly at Eve, his black eyes fixed at her and expecting her next words to plead for mercy.

"If you will not help me then I challenge you for the throne of Hell." Eve declared defiantly.

"…What?" Lucifer asked confused.

"Did you not hear me? I CHALLENGE LUCIFER IN A DUEL FOR THE THRONE OF HELL!"

The goblin demons present in the room stared at Lucifer in awe. Lucifer laughed hysterically.

"HAHAHAHA!!! A duel?! Have you ever seen a rat walk up to a human and scream 'I CHALLENGE YOU TO A DUEL FOR OWNERSHIP OF YOUR HOUSE'! I find it so bizarre."

"If you think the notion is absurd, then let us validate that thought for a moment. Accept my challenge and I promise you will lose. Are you not at least a bit curious to know why I am so certain I will beat you? And if you know me Angel, if you know my soul, you know you will not be disappointed."

Lucifer hesitated. He scanned Eve with his eyes, trying to find an angle.

"Ha. Very well, child. What are the terms of your challenge?"

"We fight until the first one yields. Any weapons or magic of our choosing is valid."

"Agreed. I suppose I can find a broom somewhere to smack you around." ·

"Let this fight be at the suicide pavilion. Let all demons and lost souls see us battle there."

"Oh, now you want to make your humiliation public, too? Hmmm, I guess the suicide pavilion is a fitting setting for your death. Agreed."

"If I win, Hell and all its demon hordes will be mine to command. If you win-"

"When I win" Lucifer interrupted, "You will not be allowed to be with or to see your beloved Adam again for all eternity."

"No! You cannot ask that of me!"

"As I said, I already own your soul. You do not have anything to bargain with. You play for my world, I play for yours. Accept this term or the duel is off…"

Eve fell silent for a moment; she barely managed to control her panic as she considered the price to pay if she failed against Lucifer.

"…Agreed"

The Devil smiled at Eve, his black eyes wide open.

"You always did know how to bring a smile to my face. Let us take this outside."

. . . .

Suicide Pavilion stood on the ruins of one of the buildings burned by God in the days before Creation. It was a field of cindered rubble that expanded thousands of miles to the horizon. Early in his reign, Lucifer chose the area as an eternal slaughterhouse for souls of the suicidal. Billions of tortured souls were perennially crucified, their naked bodies riddled with bloody open wounds from constant whipping and chained to rock hard posts. Most of these bodies were mutilated and their heads covered with old russet hay sacks. The crucified souls were arranged randomly because the ruins themselves were used to attach the souls. This made the place look like a labyrinth of people or like a crowd at a concert.

Millions of demons gathered around Lucifer and Eve as they faced each other in the Pavilion. Lucifer had changed to the form of conqueror Napoleon Bonaparte, black hair combed to the side and wearing a nineteen century French blue and white military uniform and black boots. His eyes remained black, as always. Eve was allowed to wear an iron armored suit. She had taken off her helmet for a better peripheral view.

Lucifer stretched his arm to the side and screamed "WEAPON!"

A demon crawled to him with reverence and handed him an old broom. Lucifer inspected the broom mockingly.

"Yes. Yes. This should be enough."

Another goblin handed two swords, an axe and a shield to Eve. Another one placed three loaded muskets and an iron mace at her feet.

"Do you know how to shoot an arrow?" Lucifer asked. "Give her a bow and arrows."

A goblin placed the arrows next to Eve and stepped back.

Eve dropped one of the swords, attached the shield to the arm that held a sword, strapped the bow and arrows to her back and picked up a musket.

"I am ready." She said defiantly.

"Let us begin, then." Lucifer replied.

He tapped the ground with the broom and a hole opened up in the ground around Eve, swallowing her whole. Eve's scream echoed from the hole. Lucifer began to walk away.

"And that is that. Who wants their punishment sentence reduced? I'm feeling merciful tonight."

A loud shot was heard from the whole in the ground. Eve had fired her musket from below. Lucifer turned around and stood a few feet in front of the hole. After a moment, Lucifer saw Eve's fingers holding on to the edge of the hole. She slowly crawled out of the hole and pointed her sword towards Lucifer.

"I do not yield." uttered Eve.

The Devil breathed fire blasts towards Eve. She managed to block the blasts with her shield, but was propelled back several feet and landed on her butt. One of the fire blasts hit her torso and she began to burn. The woman screamed in agony as she struggled to put off the flames on her smoldering body armor.

"Just yield, child. This is not as amusing as I thought it would be."

Eve shot an arrow at point blank range towards Lucifer's face. The arrow penetrated below his jaw and stuck out through the back of his head, in diagonal position. Lucifer seemed annoyed as he pulled the arrow from his face. When he looked back at Eve, she was not there. He looked around at the crucified souls, searching for her.

"You cannot hide from me, Eve. I will find you. I will burn through all of these souls to find you. I can do that too, you know."

The Devil waited a few moments for Eve to surrender. She did not come out from her hiding place.

"Have it your way." Lucifer grunted.

Lucifer breathed out huge fire blasts, burning a path through the crucified souls. As the souls burned, only ashes were left on the ground. He walked slowly looking for Eve and incinerating more souls. At one point, he found parts of Eve's body armor scattered on the ground. She had exchanged protection for stealth and speed.

Eve briefly came from behind a pile of rubble and ran in a line across the field. Lucifer caught her in the corner of his eye and threw fire blasts at her, missing by inches. Eve threw herself behind a group of souls tied together with heavy iron chains.

Lucifer concentrated his fire at the group of souls. The souls burned instantly, leaving ashes as expected. However, a burned human skeleton was also left tied with a rope to a heavy piece of rubble on the ground.

He stared at the crisped bones.

"Child. What a big disappointment you turned out to be."

Eve walked from behind a stone post where a soul was crucified.

"What did you do?!" Lucifer asked Eve, realizing the burned corpse was not hers.

She picked the scorched skull from the tied corpse and raised it towards Lucifer.

"Do you remember what you told me back at Eden, all those centuries ago, when I asked you to kill Lillith? This is- was Jacinto; a good servant and family man. His soul was pure, and therefore, protected by God.

Prepare to feel His wrath upon you."

Eve untied the rope and the burned corpse floated a few feet from the ground.

"Oh…OOOOOH! HAHAHAHAH! You sneaky bi-" Lucifer laughed in admiration.

A massive thunderous bolt stroke Lucifer. The sound was deafening. The huge crowd of demons scattered around in fear. Lucifer was on the floor, his black eyes and nose bleeding red. His body was skinned alive and he was malformed. Half of his body still had Napoleon's shape while the other mutated back to the form of the dark angel. Only one wing came out from his back and it was shattered.

Eve walked over to Lucifer's shaking body.

"Y-You are one little… bag of surprises…" He said smiling.

"And?"

"And…I yield"

"Thank you very much. I will spare your life, Angel. If you can manage, you can go live the rest of your eternity on Earth. I hear Paris is nice this time of year."

As Eve walked away from Lucifer, all the billions of demons knelt, head down, around her. She reached the citadel. The mirrors on the walls, ceilings and floors did not reflect her inner fears. They just projected her reflection as she passed through all its levels. Eve finally reached the silver throne room and looked at her new seat for a moment. She sat down, dropping her body with a tired slump.

Beggar, the high priest demon general that headed the tribute ritual for the Deadly Seven, humbly entered the throne room.

"What would you have us do, mistress?"

"All of you go and find me Adam. Find me the first man."

"B-but-"

Eve raised an angry look towards the demon.

"Your will, mistress. Your will." Beggar quickly responded as he retreated out of the throne room.

....

Hours passed like nothing to Eve as she cried at the throne in that silver room of the citadel in Hell. Hours became days. Days became years. Years became decades.

That night, the ash storm outside the citadel pressed harder and grew stronger. Eve wiped her tears before standing up and walking towards a silver cabinet at the far side of the room. She opened it and took out an old small wooden box from within. The wood was corroded and had a few dry blood stains on it. As she opened the box, Eve moved her face away disgusted by the stench. She then took out an old decayed skull from it.

"There may yet be need for you to serve me again" she said, holding the skull in her hand.

Eve put the skull back in the box. Tears began to fill her eyes again.

"I'm such a sentimental fool" She cried, cracking a slight smile.

The storm pressed on.

10 ROAD TRIPPING

It feels like the end of the world when everything around me slips out of control. The simplest things turn out to be so hard. I am overwhelmed. Amongst the chaos that is my life, I stop to ponder: My sister Scarlet is no more. I am not only alone, but truly lost. Every time I pray for her I ask God why it wasn't me that died instead. Until I get an answer, I feel my days have become stranger and will continue to be so.

I didn't know what they'd done to my sister Scarlet yet, but the moment she died, I suddenly felt so sad, but I didn't know why. Ruth and I were in a café at Ibirapuera Park. It was afternoon and we just ate feijoada, a stew of beans with beef and pork. The cook and the waitress were really nice people and they treated Ruth very warmly. There were a couple of construction workers eating at the tables. The feijoada was pretty good. Ruth ate most of it, but the bits she let me taste were really nice. Thank the Lord she's not a real whale, right?

We would've enjoyed the meal more if I hadn't fallen to the ground and convulsed from a sudden soul attack. Billions of voices pierced through my heart. I had to listen to them all as my nose and ears bled. This was one of the worst episodes I ever had. It wasn't a mix of different emotions like I've suffered before, but one single concentrated emotion: fear. I felt a hurtful sickness of fear straight from the heart of everyone all over the world at the same time. It was frightening.

Ruth grabbed my hand and moved my head face up while wiping my sweat and blood from my face.

"RUTH! RUUUTH!!!" I cried.

"I'm here!" Ruth answered, not letting go of my hand.

She stayed with me until my pain faded. I grabbed her shoulder and we looked at each other straight in the eyes. A historic first, if you've been paying attention to what I've said about Ruth's social skills.

"Suh-Something really bad just happened..." I managed to say.

Ruth helped me up from the floor of the café. She put my arm over her shoulder and we took a few steps. We kind of expected the people there to look at Ruth like she were a weirdo, but instead... instead we saw that everyone present were possessed, their eyes glowing red. They looked at us like they wanted to kill us. So we found ourselves throwing stools at them and moving tables and seats to block their path, and when we reached the door of the café, we ran for our lives.

It was difficult already to avoid stumbling through the earthquake rubble; we also had to get away from rabid possessed construction workers and park employees. Ruth held onto the floating iguana with just a few fingers. She felt the same disgust one gets when they hold someone else's dirty underwear.

The workers were growling and drooling and contorting themselves while simultaneously running really fast. Everywhere we'd go for help people would be just as bestial as the workers. To normal human eyes, people were either auditioning for a Zombie movie or just bonkers, but I could see the demon goblins on top of them, controlling them like puppets with some slimy web substance coming from their claws. The prophet Ruth saw them too.

I was so scared for Ruth. I really didn't know how to protect her from these crazy people. I mean, this was more Scarlet's thing. She'd probably jump on all of these people like a crazy person and swing her sword and slash each and every one of these demons. Sometimes Scarlet would bring me along so that I'd use my emotion mojo on people and help them break their possessions, but I never knew how to do that. To take them to an emotional place that'd make them strong enough to resist the demons...It was just too hard. But I could try, right? I'd try for Ruth.

"Ruth, stop. Running!" I told her.

"What?"

"Trust me! Just stand behind me!"

"Are you nuts?!"

"Trust me!"

Ruth stopped running under a bridge and so did I. I turned to face the coming horde of crazy folks. Ruth placed herself right behind me.

"What are you doing?" She asked.

"I got this. Wait."

I looked at all of the people running towards us. I reached into all of them at the same time. The trick was to amplify their feelings; fear, rage, sadness, confusion, whatever it was they were feeling at the moment. I needed to make those feelings grow strong enough to break the possessions. But all I got from people was fear. Everyone possessed, they were all really scared underneath. I tried my hardest. I really did, but I could still hear Scarlet in my mind nagging; claiming that I was doing something wrong. So I tried harder, and for a moment, I felt it work.

"Um.., Okay, Ruth?"

"Yeah?"

"Run! Run! Ruuun!"

Of course it didn't work! Why on Earth would I think I could pull off something stupid like that?! All I did was make them angrier, but it wasn't enough to break their demonic connections.

We ran as fast as we could, but the crazy possessed mob was catching up to us. I thought maybe if I'd find Scarlet or Black we could fix things, but I couldn't feel them on Earth. They were both... somewhere else.

"It's too late." The floating iguana hissed and pointed with its claw. "Just you watch. One by one, the seals will be broken. This world belongs to the demons now. When my brothers come for me, I will make sure both of you are flayed alive. I will have my brother Gluttony eat your... your... Aaaaaargh!"

Envy screamed in pain as it stretched sideways. The lizard's body was being pulled in opposite directions by an unseen force. Its scaly skin began to tear. Its bones and organs cracked and were pulverized. Ruth and I halted as we saw in awe how the creature kept stretching until it tore in half and fell flat on the floor in front of Ruth.

Ruth screamed and stepped back, but she tumbled against a rock and fell on her back. The fall pulled me towards her and I fell face down next to her. A male hand reached out to Ruth. She took the hand and stood up. As I stood up, I realized we were no longer in Brazil chased by a crowd of possessed park goers. Everything turned black around us. The air became damp and it was hard to see; we eventually figured out we were inside a cold dark cave.

"You ladies are welcomed for taking Envy out of your hands, by the way." A familiar voice spoke to us from what looked like a dead dragon's brownish grey decayed skeleton the size of a bear. Its eye sockets were entirely black. "Now, it's only been a week since our last encounter and you've already managed to let four seals to be broken."

"Lucifer!" I reacted, "No! Hey! It's three! It's my ministry and Evergreen's and Blue's"

"Really? And what do you call the legion of angry demon controlled crazies chasing you back there?"

"But that's impossible! My sister Scarlet's ministry-"

"Are you serious? Scarlet's seal is broken?" Ruth asked.

"Didn't you girls feel the jolt?"

"No! You're lying!" I yelled.

"Am I? What would you call the sudden massive wave of fear you just felt from every human being alive?"

"You're behind it somehow! You did this!"

"Do not try my patience!" the boney dragon growled, "It is obvious Violet can't handle her obligations, so find someone who can and I'll transfer her ministry onto them."

"I don't believe you!" I insisted. "You're just trying to scare us! Scarlet would never let her ministry fall. She would die first!"

"Interesting choice of words. Would you like to go to her? See her yourself?" Lucifer asked as he extended his paw towards the darkness behind us. Ruth and I turned around and we suddenly felt very cold. And there was nothing anywhere, just darkness.

Then we saw my sister Black. She was sitting on the floor crying. We couldn't hear her cry, but we could see her tears. Ruth kept her distance from her. She wasn't ready to meet her yet. But even though I found her a bit creepy, I kind of liked her and it broke my heart to see her so sad. I knelt next to her and put my hand on her shoulder.

"We don't have much time." said Lucifer. "I am not welcomed here."

"Sister, why are you crying?" I asked the Black Angel.

Black Angel pointed in front of her and that's when I saw Scarlet. She lied lifeless on the ground almost naked with a bloody hole in the middle of her chest. I cried too. I prayed with Black, holding her hand tight.

Ruth felt sad for us, but didn't know what to do. She kept her distance out of respect for Scarlet. Lucifer stood behind me and Black and whispered "My condolences."

Black Angel extended her hand towards Scarlet's corpse. I saw blue flames engulf the body. The flames rose tall and took the shape of my fallen sister. Scarlet's flame stood over her burning body. I felt a lot of anger and frustration from the flame. Then she looked at me, the blue fire face. I saw disappointment in her look. The feelings turned to pity. She pitied me. I felt so ashamed that I turned my eyes away. I knew I shouldn't have done that since the fires that consumed Scarlet began to die away. She was called into eternal rest and I missed the last few seconds I had to see her face to face before she faded.

I had never seen an angel die before.

Lucifer in the form of the dragon carcass approached Ruth.

"Come along, chubby one" he said to Ruth, "There are places you need to be if you're to get us out of this mess."

"Don't call me chubby." She said angrily.

"I only play with your insecurities." He responded with a grin.

I turned my eyes and searched for Black Angel, but she wasn't there.

She disappeared without saying goodbye.

"Where's my sister Black?" I asked.

"Trust me; she has her hands pretty full with what's coming. She's already gone to meet her destiny." Lucifer replied.

"Where is she?! I'm not leaving without my sister!" I demanded.

Lucifer exposed his fangs and looked at me irritated.

"You seem to forget who you're talking to." He growled at me. "I'm not here to play or do you any favors. Creation is moldering in front of your eyes and you seem content in being the spoiled little emo girl."

"I AM NOT EMO!" I yelled at Lucifer, (Yeah, I know. That was really stupid of me...)

Lucifer grabbed me by the neck with his huge bone claws and squeezed hard as he lifted me up with just one arm. I turned red and purple and my head was about to explode. I couldn't breathe and I really thought I was going to be killed by Satan. I peed myself a little. Ruth ran up to Lucifer and tried to hit him with pathetic girlie punches.

"Let her go!" She screamed "You're killing her!"

Lucifer laughed at Ruth.

"I know your type!" She continued "You're so brave with people weaker than you! You're a bully and a coward! I'm not afraid of you!"

The skeleton dragon was not happy at all. He lifted Ruth by her shirt with his free clawey hand. Suddenly, we were not in the dark place. It was day time and we were in a rocky desert. Red sand and rocks surrounded us and there with a few cactus around. It took me a bit to realize where we were, mostly because Lucifer was dragging both of us by the neck. Then he threw us over a dune. Ruth and I rolled all the way down. When we reached the bottom of the sand hill, Lucifer was waiting for us there and he pulled both of us up by the hair.

"Stop wasting my time." he said, "If I were you, I'd start running and wouldn't stop until I'd find the new vessel for your ministry." With those words, the Devil disappeared and left us stranded in the desert.

I looked at Ruth and shrugged. We were both confused. Who did

Lucifer expect us to meet in the middle of nowhere? I suggested trying to find the nearest payphone, but then we saw a peach colored RV moving on a road about fifty yards away from us. We ran like two crazy persons screaming at the camper. Maybe I was the crazy one because if the people in the RV heard or saw anything, it would've been Ruth and not me. But what was I supposed to do, stand there doing nothing while Ruth screamed her lungs out? I had to at least give her some support – not to mention I just couldn't be too far away from her.

Ruth and I managed to reach the road just before the RV truck passed us. We were shocked to see a car moving at all after my brother Blue's seal broke. We ran after it and yelled for help, but the vehicle kept driving away from us. Ruth got so red and started panting. She slowed down her pace until she couldn't run or walk anymore. I, of course, was stuck with her.

"Come on! They're driving away! Don't stop now!" I said to her.

"Stop…huff…bugging me!"

Suddenly, the RV stopped and went in reverse. It stopped right beside us. The signal lights in the front and back of the vehicle began to flicker on and off. I felt again the same strange sensation I had when we crossed the red lights in Second Avenue to visit Lucifer, but I just couldn't afford the time to think about it.

Two handsome men were in the RV. The driver was rugged black haired thirty something Middle Eastern looking guy with a goatee and thick eyebrows. He wore black sunglasses, a blue t-shirt with a drawing of Aquaman swimming towards you. He also had jeans, sneakers and a Cubs baseball cap. The passenger was a twenty something blue-eyed shaggy haired blonde surfer type. He sported tight black leather pants and a designer t-shirt. His shoes were black and had little silver chains that matched his wrist bracelets, a silver collar around his neck and a cool little skull shaped earring.

The driver seemed to be looking at me for a moment, but I couldn't really tell because of his sunglasses. He quickly turned his face to Ruth.

"Hi." He said to her. "You're lucky we passed by. I don't know if you heard, but all the cars in the area, probably the whole state of Nevada, are not working. Good thing I'm good with cars."

"What's wrong with your signal lights?"

"I don't know, they started acting up just now. Must be something with the battery…" He said, as he played with the lights switch next to the steering wheel. "Any way, are you okay? Do you need a ride or not?"

"Are you guys psychos or perverts?"

The driver smiled and looked at the passenger who also smiled. Then the driver looked back at Ruth.

"We're gay. Does that count?"

"No. I'm cool with that."

"Cool beans, then. You want to hop in?"

"Yes, please." Ruth answered with a smile.

And with that, Ruth and I got in the RV through a door in the back that the passenger opened. The signal lights went off as soon as we got in.

"There you go" said the driver, "fixed it."

The truck was huge on the inside. It had a tiny kitchen, a bed, dining table slash lounge for hanging out, and of course a small closet-sized bathroom. Ruth sat by the small table. The sun was setting and everything looked pretty and orangey.

"I'm Hassan, this is Steve" said the driver.

"I'm Ruth."

"Nice to meet you Ruth. That a New York accent?"

"I'm from Queens."

"See?" Hassan told Steve. "I'm great with accents."

"You never guessed mine…" Steve smiled and looked out the window.

"Alright, so Ruth, where to?"

"West?" Ruth responded as she looked at me with doubt.

"Whatever." I shrugged. I really didn't care. Things were so messed up already; I really doubted they could get worse.

"You really need to be careful out there." Steve commented. "Last news we heard on the radio were reports of riots all over the world. All of a sudden, everybody's going crazy. Did you hear about the church people up in Minnesota? Fifty people locked themselves inside the church for three days. When the cops arrived they found them all dead and they'd torn each other's faces out."

"Oh my God!" Ruth reacted.

"Tell her about that hospital thing in Hoboken." Hassan interjected.

"Oh, yeah." Steve continued, "Two days ago, out of nowhere, twelve mothers that had just given birth stormed the maternity ward and grabbed their babies before throwing themselves through the window glass, eight floors down. Just like that."

"No. Not 'just like that'." Hassan interrupted, "People have always done crazy shit. You just hear more of it now 'cause we got internet or whatnot. And they don't need much to drive themselves nuts. One day with no cell phone signal or no internet and they have to lynch someone."

"Come on, this is a little bigger than that" Steve responded, "What was it the other day- twenty-three zoos all over the country had animals escaping and attacking people. All at the same time. They had to put them all down. It's like the end of the world out there. How could folks not be scared?"

Ruth stared at me a bit worried.

"Listen, it's always been this way." Hassan argued, "Strange stuff always happens, but that's when you have to keep it together and deal with whatever it is that's happening. But then you see people going ape-shit and killing each other. People are sick. That's the way we're wired. There's no hope for us"

"You may be on to something there" Steve said, "There's gotta be something really wrong with me for wanting to be stuck with you in the middle of nowhere and listening to your pessimistic crap"

"It's the truth,"

"You want the truth? Your farts smell." Steve joked.

"You love the smell" Hassan smiled.

I sat next to Ruth, leaning my head against her shoulder and resting my legs on the table. Ruth elbowed me.

"Whaaat?!" I complained, as I moved my legs.

Ruth stared at Hassan's shirt.

"You like comics?" She asked him

"Me? Not really. But I like Aquaman. King of the Seven Seas and still finds the time to hang out with his super friends."

"I like Aquaman too…" Ruth said with like this schoolgirl admiration.

"There you go. She's beautiful AND smart." Hassan smiled, keeping his eyes on the road. I swear I saw Ruth blush!

"You are totally crushing on Hassan! OMG!" I whispered to her, giggling.

"Aaaaanyway, who wants some homemade cookies?" Steve interrupted as he opened a plastic container with cookies in it.

It was like this throughout our journey. Everything was just normal and fun. I knew that we should've both been on our way to find a new vessel for my ministry, but when I looked at Ruth and noticed her smiling; I thought it wouldn't hurt to take a short break from all the end-of-the-world craziness.

So I joined in and decided to have some 'me' time. I took out my little purple pocket book and doodled a chibbie of Ruth with a happy dreamy face and three little hearts floating around her head. Then I drew a muscular Hassan dressed as Aquaman with inflated chest and square chin and all, posing heroically. Ruth briefly turned her eyes towards me and I showed her the drawing to tease her. I also wrote "YOU DO KNOW HE'S GAY, RIGHT?" below the drawing. Ruth beamed with embarrassment and turned her face away from me.

"I feel weird." Ruth said to Steve.

"Are you allergic to chocolate?" He asked.

"No"

"Then it must be the little something Hassan put in the cookies." He smiled.

139

Ruth sat up laughing and shoved Hassan.

"Are you serious!?! Hahaha!"

"You're welcome, my lady." Hassan smirked.

"You guys!" Ruth laughed. "Give me another one!"

"Look out! It's the cookie monster!" Steve quipped, passing a cookie to Ruth.

"On the next Intervention…" Hassan said with a funny TV narrator voice.

"Pfft! Hahahahaha! Stop it! You're making me spit all over!" Ruth laughed.

From the way Steve glanced at Ruth, I think he noticed the way she stared at Hassan. But he didn't feel jealous, more like… amused.

"So, really, Ruth" Steve asked, "What is a New York girl doing all the way out here in Nevada?"

"It's kind of complicated. We're looking for help-"

"We?

"Well –um- I'm trying to help someone. She's got this really important job, but she kind of screwed it up? We need to find someone to take over and fix it."

"What kind of job?" Hassan asked.

"Um…"

"Make something up!" I told her.

"Oh she's uh… she works for the Government. It's… top secret stuff. I can't really say."

"Seriously?!" I shook my head.

Hassan raised his eyebrow, but kept his eyes on the road.

"Wouldn't want to have to kill us if you did, right?" Steve quipped.

"Ha. Right."

"So, this friend of yours-" Hassan began to query.

"She's not my friend…" Ruth quickly corrected him. I bumped her head with mine and stuck my tongue out to her.

"But it's one of those things that if I don't help out, a lot of people get the shaft."

"Sounds pretty serious." Hassan continued. "But where is this other person? The one that's not your friend."

"She's uh…"

"I'm in hiding." I improvised.

"She's in hiding" Ruth repeated.

"Hmmm. Well, Ok…"

We all fell silent for a moment. Ruth gave me a snappy look and I ignored her. She said I wasn't her friend anyway.

. . . .

That night Ruth, Hassan and Steve got high and stuff on the magic cookies. At three in the morning, Steve had to park the RV at the side of the road and they all went to sleep. The guys offered her the bed, but Ruth said she was fine on the inflatable mattress that they set on the floor space across them.

I was awake of course. Angels don't sleep. So I watched over Ruth and tried to ignore her heavy snoring. I looked at the full moon through the window. I thought about Scarlet and I cried. She was never mean to me. I mean she was strict, but that was because she wanted to make me better. She thought I could've done much more with myself. I never saw it, but I loved her for thinking it. I loved my sister and I never got to tell her that. I was also worried about White, Evergreen and Goldie and Blue, but mostly, I was really scared for Black. Only God (and apparently Lucifer) knew where she was and what was going on with her. They were all screwed because of me. If I'd only…

I suddenly felt so much hatred next to me. I turned my face and looked at Steve who was sleeping. Was he having a nightmare? Why was he so angry? He felt so- AND THEN HE OPENED HIS EYES AND WAS STARING AT ME! HE WAS LOOKING AT ME AND I FROZE! I DIDN'T KNOW WHAT TO DO! AAAAAAAH!!!

He just kept looking at me! I played possum (ok, I know that was unbelievably dumb. He either couldn't see me and I was being stupid or he already knew I was there and it was kind of pointless to be still anyway), but I managed to wiggle my big toe to touch Ruth. I practically stuck my whole toe in her thigh to give her a nudge, but she wouldn't even move. I looked back at Steve and he kept looking at me so creepy and I panicked. How could he see me? Did he drug Ruth on purpose? I stuck my toe even deeper in Ruth and my toe nail must have scratched her because she slapped my leg and mumbled "stop it". I pressed my toe again and she shifted her body to face me. She whispered vehemently at me in a low voice

"Cut it out!"

"He's looking at me now!" I whispered back.

"What- who?"

"Your boyfriend's boyfriend is looking at me now. Ohmygawd, he's so looking this way and-"

Ruth and I both looked at Steve who kept staring at me.

"Steve?" Ruth called softly. He remained still.

Ruth stood up from her mattress and slowly walked towards Steve.

"Steve?" She called again.

Then she got close to him and waved her hand in front of his eyes. He didn't flinch or moved his eyes or anything. Ruth went back to her mattress.

"He's asleep."

"But his eyes are open?"

"Some people do that."

"But-"

"Violet, you think if he'd actually seen you he wouldn't say something? Stop it already"

"But what about his hatred?"

"What?"

"I so felt his hatred and anger and stuff. I mean it's gone now, but it was so intense-"

"I dunno, maybe he had a nightmare. Stop bugging me."

"But-"

"Violet! Shut up and go to sleep!" Ruth quietly hissed.

"Angels don't sleep!"

"So what do you do?"

"We watch over you and pray for you."

"That's nice. Do that. Good night."

I finally gave up and let her go to sleep. I looked out the window, trying to ignore Steve's creepy I'm-looking-at-you-but-I'm-really-not-'cause-this-is-just-the-way-I-sleep eyes. However, as someone really smart once said, you can't out-troll a troll. That nasty hatred I felt from him was too much for one guy to have. And I should know. I looked at Steve and squinted at him. I turned my face away from him and quickly looked back. I turned my face again and quickly looked back. I did that for like four or five times.

"Yeah, you better keep your eyes on me" I whispered, "I'm watching you, buddy."

Steve opened his eyes wider. I quickly hid under Ruth's sheets and played possum again.

What?! Angels get scared too! Shut up!

11 AN A.D.D RIDDLED PRAYER

Late at night, as the worldwide black out continued, the silhouette of the Vatican looked like the shadow of a black wolf raising its head and howling under the moonlight. The distant roar of people rioting grew louder by the minute and Catholic Church staff members took their cue to gather whatever they thought was valuable and leave.

Pope Matthew I, an eighty year old sickly thin man, sat on the edge of his bed still wearing his grey pajamas. He wiped the sweat from his forehead and struggled to control his breathing. He was relieved the lights went out two days ago. That bought him some time. His panic attacks had increased since the week before and it was hard for him to hide his fear from everyone. He was scheduled to speak publicly about the Church's position on the recent climate disasters and riots erupting in many different regions of the world. He didn't have any answers to give; he couldn't even explain the reason for his panic attacks.

He stepped off his bed and took a sip of water from the glass on his night table. He managed to move a few steps ahead, but froze when he saw a strange man standing by the door of his chamber. The man's skin was paper white and wore a hat, trench coat, and shoes; everything black. Matthew thought the man looked like he came out of an old black and white movie. He noticed there was a huge white-gloved-hand-shaped balloon hovering over the man, but there was no string attached to it. The stranger moved closer to the Pope with a funny overacted pace, followed by the giant hand, like a cartoon of a man with a cloud over his head. The man eyed him from top to bottom, one eye wide open and the other almost closed. He opened his mouth and moved his lips, but no sound came out from his throat.

"Who are you?" Matthew asked.

The giant hand moved its fingers. Matthew stepped back, his fear coming back to him as he realized the hand was not a balloon. The stranger opened his black trench coat which revealed a written message. Matthew read it.

"Are you the Pope?"

"Yes..." Matthew answered with trepidation.

The stranger eyed him with disapproval and looked around the room. He lifted his index finger, signaling Matthew to wait. He opened his trench coat, and took out a white mitre with gold-laced borders. The stranger stretched his arm to Matthew, offering the pope hat to him, and moved his lips. Then, he opened his coat again:

"Put it on." written on the trench coat

"I-"

The old man's heart raced faster with fear. His face turned red.

"I need... I need to sit down"

The stranger's mouth opened wider and moved as if pronouncing words, but none were heard. His eyes glanced at the Pope intensely. He seemed angry. Writing appeared inside the opened trench coat:

"PUT IT ON!"

The stranger pressed the mitre against the Pope's chest. The old man grabbed it, threw it at the stranger's face and ran towards the door. Matthew made it to the hall and struggled to keep running. He was too nervous to focus, but he kept trying to pray to God for guidance. He kept trying, even though he thought his prayers fell to deaf ears. He felt a sharp pain on his chest and stumbled to the floor. Pope Matthew was suffering a heart attack as the stranger grabbed him from behind and put the mitre on his head. The stranger moved his lips with a smile on his face and opened his coat:

"Ha! Now you look like a Pope!"

Goldie and her winged pig crashed through one of the acrylic windows. The stranger saw a rainbow coming out of the flying swine's butt, which marked the trail of the pig's passage.

"MAMMON!" Goldie screamed. "I knew ya couldn't leave ya greedy paws off the Pope! You leave that man alone if ya don't want a good lickin' coming to ya!"

Greed frowned and held Matthew close to his chest as he screamed in silence. He opened his trench coat again, revealing his words:

"Get your own Pope, Goldie! This one's mine! MINE!"

"Popes ain't pets, see?!" Goldie responded as she dismounted her pig. "I can get you a gold fish, or a parrot, if ya ask nicely. How's about some sea monkeys?"

Greed moved his mouth with a skeptic look as he patted the Pope's mitre. The inside of his black trench coat showed new words:

"Sea monkeys don't wear funny Pope hats!"

Goldie took a glance at Pope Matthew and noticed he was unconscious and pale.

"See here! Ya bettah not've broken that Pope! And gimme back the glove ya stole from me while you're at it!" She yelled at Greed as she raised her fists and posed them in the style of an early twentieth century burly man fighter.

Greed looked at Matthew, shook him a bit to try to wake him up, and tossed him to the side. The Deadly Seven demon raised his fists and moved towards Goldie with his funny villain pace. The gloved hand floating over him closed into a giant fist. As Greed closed in on Goldie, he jerked his right arm, pretending to throw a punch. Goldie quickly blocked her right side. The giant floating fist punched her from the left side, sending her flying towards a wall. She landed on the floor and struggled to get up and face Greed again.

"A wise guy, eh?!" She said "Two can play that game!"

The angel placed her gloved hand near her lips and blew on the glove's thumb, inflating it like a balloon. The glove grew massive, the same size as the giant white gloved hand. One glove slapped the other glove. The other glove slapped it back, and both hands began to fight, holding each other with their fingers and having what seemed to be a lethal thumb wrestling duel.

Greed threw punches at Goldie, which she blocked and responded with a few blows of her own. The Pope lying on the floor caught the corner of her eye, and she knew she didn't have much time. She handed Greed a strong uppercut and two more punches in his stomach to leave him breathless. Greed fell to the floor and gasped for air as Goldie ran to pick up Matthew. She could not feel him breathing.

"Is there a doctor in tha house?!" Goldie yelled. "Ooh! Ooh! I am!"

Goldie took off her hat and a monkey with a funny red hat and two golden cymbals came out from it. The monkey hit the cymbals against each other two times and then proceeded to hit the unconscious Pope's chest with them, making the loud sound of the musical instrument.

"Clear!" yelled Goldie. "Clear!"

The giant white gloves were deep in a fierce rock paper scissor battle. Greed stood up from the floor and ran screaming towards Goldie. No sound came from his mouth. He opened his black trench coat again to reveal new words:

"GIVE ME BACK MY POPE!"

Goldie opened her pocket and took out the magic potion bottle she had offered the student back in San Francisco. She took off the tap and threw the golden liquid at Greed.

"AH, SHADDAP!" she screamed.

The potion liquid took the form of seven golden saber tooth tigers that savagely attacked Greed, tearing him to pieces. Greed screamed in silent agony as he bled black. His last movement before dying was to open his trench coat which showed only one word.

"Ow!"

Greed's bloody dead head rolled near Goldie's shoes.

Both floating giant gloves deflated and fell to the floor next to Goldie. She put both gloves on and smiled, then checked on Pope Matthew; he remained lifeless. The angel only had a few minutes to perform the miracle of resurrection, but that was something she could only do with the help and blessing of her sister White. Goldie had to decide between calling her sister and save the old man while risking capture from Eve's demonic legion, or let the Pope perish during the end of times, when he was needed most. The golden angel froze. She could not make up her mind. And in her desperation, she took off her hat, knelt down, joined hands, closed her eyes, and prayed:

"God. It's me. Goldie!" she declaimed. "I've been meanin' to pray to ya… Now, I'm not talkin' about ya typical prayer where ya put ya hands together and chant an old creed ya may not even know the meanin' of. I'm talkin' the kind that you're alone by yaself lyin' in bed and ya stare at the ceiling of ya room and ya can't sleep because ya worry about this huge problem that ya can't seem to be able to fix and you're drowning in the thought of it and all, see? And ya think of tha things ya didn't get to do in the day and the work ya still need to get done, and ya feel so sad for that guy with no food and no home ya saw on the street and ya wish you'dda had some change to spare for him, but instead ya made his life worse by ignorin' him, and then ya think of those who love ya, and ya feel so grateful to have 'em in ya life, and ya dream of buying a penthouse with a great view and rooms for everyone to live together and have teddy bears runnin' 'round and really wishin' happiness not just for you, but for all of 'em, and then it gets so quiet and ya hear your own heart beating and ya relax and every other thought dwindles away and it's only you, and ya feel good in the quiet and there's a moment of clarity when ya go AHA! And ya know what ya gotta do to fix your problem, and ya say thank you, 'cause ya don't think it was you who came up with the answer and ya have this feelin' that someone was right there next to ya listenin' to your rant 'bout work and teddy bears and all of that baloney.

"So what I'm tryin' ta say is I need your guidance. I'm in trouble, see? The whole world's in trouble! It's getting' tougher and tougher for me to keep it together."

She paused.

"Saaayyy, why haven't ya never talked to me, Lord? Why've I never been asked to perform a big miracle? I'm just an extra in this show that my sisters star in. *I coulda been a contender! I coulda been somebody!* All this time…Are You like the others, expectin' me to screw up again? Well, are ya?

"I try to help people, see? I try fixin' them right as rain! And I make You look fabulous while doing it. When You told White You needed a show stopper, I came up with the miracle of resurrection! The transmutation of endin' life to continue life anew through the re-incorporation of old souls into new corporeal- yadda, yadda, yadda, badda-bing, badda-boom, people back to life! Ta-daaa!!! I made everything a-okay and I did it all by myself, see?

"And Lord, I'm tellin' You all this 'cause-'cause I'm really tryin' to make things copacetic again…"

Goldie choked.

"God, I've… I murdered my sister. I am so sorry…I didn't mean to- But I guess I made it happen… White- I thought she was Your voice… When she asked me to do what I did… I thought You were- to hear You ask somethin' of me again… I thought I was servin' You…

"She's outta control, White I mean. I dunno what to do. I dunno what to do. I dunno what to do. I feel so lost. God, I helped kill Scarlet. She's the only one who coulda helped us. We never needed Scarlet more than now. She'd know what to do. Heck, she wouldn't a let things get this far, You know? With all the seals bein' broken left and right, I think mine is the only one in place. I'm tryin' so hard to hold on to my ministry; to keep the universe collected… but the demons are coming to Earth, see? With the Deadly Seven loose, Pride and his bad bunch are gonna make a mess of the humans.

"And Greed… I knew that stinkin' glove-stealin' Greed would make a grab for the Pope! So I came here to rescue him! *'They may take our freedom! But by golly, they won't never take our Pope!'* I say."

Goldie paused and pressed her hands harder against each other. Her lowered closed eyes showed sadness.

"Just tell me what to do. Tell me how You need me to fix things. I know I deserve to be punished for what I did to Scarlet. I'm prepared to face Your judgment, but please, just allow me the chance to help one more time. Please, let me be Your instrument again. Let me do Your work. How do I stop White? How do I stop her?"

Goldie stopped talking. She waited for any kind of sign keeping her eyes closed and hands joined, but after a while, all she heard was nothing but silence. Eventually, she relented and opened her eyes. Goldie found herself illuminated by a single ray of light that came through the broken acrylic window she came crashing in with her flying pig. It was a shade of violet.

"AHA!" She exclaimed, "Thank You!"

The golden angel stood up and put her black hat back on. She ran towards the winged pig, but suddenly stopped and ran back to the spot she had kneeled to pray.

"Oh, and I think the Pope is dead. I thought You should know."

"Aaa-men!"

12 ON THE ROAD AGAIN

I must confess I do not expect to succeed in saving Creation. My wings are tied heavily, but heavier still is my spirit. I cannot rise to what everyone expects of me. I do not know how. My heart bleeds dreading the thought that when it all ends, I will be judged by those I love, saddened by the truth they always knew; that I am a coward, that I never should have been granted my ministry, that people dear to me have mistakenly put their faith on me and died because of it, and that I did nothing to amend. I dread the pity in their eyes as they watch me lead their march into oblivion, not surprised, yet still disappointed. But what I dread the most is facing Ruth, my jailor, my only friend, and having to accept her very honest and condemning word. What if she is right about me?

There was a gas station at the side of the road where we stopped to fill the RV's tank and stack up on munchies and stuff. It wasn't like those derelict dirty old places ran by a creepy old toothless guy you'd see in horror movies. It actually looked nice and new and well lighted. Even though the mini-market was open and a generator powered everything, we didn't see anyone there manning the cash register. I guessed maybe the employees left in a rush because of the end of the world or whatever.

While Hassan filled up the tank, Steve, Ruth, and I went inside the store. Ruth went straight to the Hot Pockets, Doritos, and unhealthy sweets. Steve walked over to the fridge to get beer, juice and water.

"Gots da place to ourselves!" Steve quipped, "Don't tell me. You're a Smirnoff girl. Green apple?"

"I'm that obvious, huh?" Ruth responded.

"You're a bit of an open book. But that's cool. You're trustworthy."

"What else can you tell about me?" Ruth asked as she filled a small plastic bag with a bunch of buck fifty banana cupcakes.

"I know you like Hassan." Steve smiled.

"Busteeeeeeed!" I whispered to Ruth's ear.

She turned red. Her right foot tapped the floor anxiously, and not to anyone's surprise, she began to stare at the floor.

"I'm- I'm really sorry Steve. I would never-"

"Oh, no, honey! We're cool. I can't blame you. Guy's handsome as hell."

"But he's with you. I don't want you to feel-"

"Ruth, baby. It's all good. In fact, I think you should tell him."

"What?"

"I'm just saying. What's the point of having feelings for someone if you won't share them? Just let him know how you feel. But I'm warning you. Don't expect this to become a dirty degenerate threesome or whatever. Not gonna happen. God, I miss those…Are you into threesomes?"

"Um…"

"I'm just playing with you." Steve winked and smiled at Ruth as he gently touched the side of her face and guided her eyes towards him. "You're a really nice girl. Hassan will be flattered. I would."

Steve left a fifty dollar bill on the cash register counter and told Ruth the banana cupcakes were on him. As Steve left the mini-mart, I noticed Ruth was still a little nervous.

"That was pretty cool of him, wasn't it?" I said, "You okay?"

"I feel like shit…" she said breathing heavily.

"Why?"

"I am such an asshole!" Ruth said as she hit her forehead repeatedly.

"Hey, now! Stop that!"

I grabbed both of her wrists and stretched her arms down next to her legs.

"Stop. It." I repeated seriously.

A short plump curly haired brown skinned woman came out of the bathroom. I felt the lady was calm, but she seemed creepy to me for some reason. She wore thick glasses, a polo shirt with the gas station logo and a gold tag that read: "MONICA", matched with black pants and sneakers. Her big chubby head was really red, like her blood pressure was high or maybe she had some sort of rash. Her mouth was dirty with gray powder stains around her lips. She carried a green porcelain urn which she was capping up close to her chest.

"Can I help you?" She asked.

"Oh, no," Ruth replied "We just got a few snacks and some gas, my friends and me, but there's a fifty there on the counter and you can keep the change."

The gas station lady placed the urn next to the cash register and viewed the bill against the light.

"What did you guys get?" She asked.

"Um…Two six packs of Bud Light," Ruth answered "a large cranberry juice, and a water gallon. Thirty bucks in premium gas. And the cupcakes. Five."

"Okay" The lady uttered as she punched some buttons on the cash register and put the bill inside it. "Have a nice night."

Just as Ruth and I were at the door going out, we saw the lady opening the cap of the urn and taking a handful of gray slag that she put in her mouth.

"What are you eating?" Ruth asked the woman.

"My husband" She replied calmly as she kept consuming the powder.

"Are those his ashes?" Ruth asked shocked "Why are you eating your husband's ashes?"

"I miss him…"

"That is so messed up." I said to Ruth. "Let's just go."

"You do know this is your fault, right?" She replied. "You need to help her"

"Me?! I didn't do anything!"

"Look at her. She misses her husband. She can't cope because she can't control her feelings. I know you quit your ministry and all that, but can you at least help her?"

"Fine." I conceded.

Ruth and I moved closer to the lady. I opened a window to her soul, to see what was wrong with her. I saw memories of her staring at the urn crying. Then I saw a familiar demon's hand touching her belly. I closed the window.

"It was Gluttony! He did this, the rat bastard!" I said to Ruth,

"Gluttony?"

"Yeah, like Envy, one of the Deadly Seven Arch-demons. Sins related to eating are his thing. He twisted her tummy and turned her sorrow into hunger! The more she eats her husband, the more she misses him!"

"Can you fix it?" she asked

"Maybe, I don't know." I replied "I mean, it's not like we can put her on a grief diet."

"Monica, um, maybe you should give me the urn." Ruth said to the gas station employee.

"Why?!" Monica replied intently as she held the urn close to her chest "He's my man!"

Ruth reached for the urn.

"This is so wrong. Look just give me the-"

Monica slapped Ruth's hands and stepped back behind the counter. She started munching on the ashes like a desperate child whose candy has been taken away.

"Ow!" Ruth shouted.

"Drop it, Ruth. Let's just go" I said to her.

"No! Eating your husband is not kosher!"

Ruth actually climbed the counter to grab the woman's urn. I swear I'm not kidding! Her chest was half way over the counter, pressing against the surface and leaving her legs hanging with her feet flapping in the air. She grabbed the urn from the gas station lady and pulled it towards her, but Monica wouldn't let go of it. They both went at it like two wrestling Oompa Loompas on a sugar rush which would be pretty funny to watch if the employee hadn't taken an exacto from under the counter and cut Ruth's forearm.

"Aaaaah! What the hell?!" she yelled.

"AIIIIEEE!!! OHMYGOD!!! Ruth!" I flipped out.

Blood prattled from her arm, so Ruth let go of the woman and came down from the counter to put pressure on her wound. The urn fell to the floor and broke with the ashes spreading all over. Monica stooped down and gathered as much of the powder as she could. At that moment, Hassan and Steve came running into the store and quickly gathered around Ruth to tend her cut.

"What's going on? Ruth, are you okay?" Hassan asked.

I almost caught Hassan giving me an angry look, until I realized he was looking through me at the gas station lady getting up from behind me. She held up the knife with one hand and a handful of ash in the other from which she took a bite.

"Are you going to use that on me, too? Try it or put it down." Hassan remarked with a serious look.

The gas station lady licked the ash off her fingers as she lowered the blade and dropped it on the counter.

"I'm sorry, okay? I don't wanna go to jail. Is she alright?" She queried.

"What the Hell's wrong with you?!" Steve asked Monica.

Steve got a small first aid kit box from one of the aisle gondolas and after disinfecting the wound, he bandaged it.

"We're not paying for the first aid kit!" Steve yelled as he lead Ruth (and me) out of the store.

Hassan stayed a few more minutes inside the store. We could see him talking to the gas station lady through the glass. He left the store and joined us in the RV. When he got in, he passed by Ruth without saying a word. He sat at the passenger's seat and leaned his head back to sleep. Steve drove us away.

....

Things were quiet on the road for the rest of the day. Hassan took over driving the RV and Steve came a few times to the back by the bed where Ruth lied to check on her arm.

She sat on the bed, her legs stretched and her injured arm resting as she put on her headphones. I sat on the floor next to her with my legs crossed. I wrote a few lines in my little purple book and chewed on a Twizzler I got at the gas station.

"You- um...you could've helped me back there." Ruth said, her eyes fixed on the roof of the RV. "Don't think I didn't see you grinning"

"What?! I wasn't grinning!"

"Whatever, just forget it."

"Ruth... Why are you so angry?"

"I just...I wanted to help that lady. Maybe I went about it the wrong way, but at least I tried! You could've done more."

"I know...sorry. ...But that's not what I mean. I feel you angry all the time. You're annoyed at everything."

"I'll stop being angry when we find your replacement and I know the whole world is not ending."

"It's not that. Look how you went at it with the gas station lady. And back in Brazil, you acted kind of weird when you saw people beating each other up."

"So?"

"At the cave, you yelled at Lucifer... to his face! You wanna know how many mortals in the history of humanity have ever dared to do that? None! No, wait, four. Four!"

"..."

156

"I could help, you know. I could open a purple window to your soul and-"

"Don't even think about it! Like I'm going to let you peek into my private life. I don't know you. I don't trust you."

"Really?! I'm like, the freaking angel of emotions! Who else are you going to trust with your feelings?"

"Great job you've done so far…"

"Ok, you know what? I just wanted to be a friend to you and stuff, but whatever. Play it like that."

I went back to my writing and Ruth focused on her music for a while. Then I noticed she gave me a suspicious stare.

"Let me read your book." She requested.

"What?" I asked.

"Your purple book; I'll let you see my soul if you let me read it."

"No way!"

"Right. You want me to share my feelings with you, but you won't share yours with me. That seem fair to you?"

"It's not the same."

"How is it not the same, Violet? You don't feel comfortable sharing your personal stuff. I get it. Neither do I. So there."

Ruth turned her back against me and fixed the headphone in one of her ears.

"Alright. Here you go." I sighed as I softly slapped her back with my book.

"I was just making a point. I don't need to read your book."

"I know. I want you to."

Ruth sat back up to face me. She gave me a skeptical look.

"I'm serious. You don't have to let me see your soul or anything if you don't want to. But you're my friend and I'd like to, you know, share my stuff with you."

"Really?"

"Just don't make fun of it. And let me know what you think."

"Um… Okay" She said as she took the book with a bit of trepidation.

Ruth opened my purple book at the very first page and began to read:

In God's name, I am the guardian of the ministry of emotions. It is my duty to guide humanity's destiny through their sensations. My given name is Uriel, sixth of seven Archangels of peace proclaimed in the Pax Dei. It is hard for me to remember myself before I was granted my ministry. My form was Cherubim, a nameless winged dancer in the lower echelons of Heaven. Cherubim were not supposed to reach the higher spheres. We kept to the aerial gardens, where we ate fruit and tended to Jophiel's flora, or chatted by Zadkiel's prism fountains. We also frequented the gathering hall, where echoes of our harmonies and prayers resonated with the crystalized murals that hung like stalactites from its golden ceiling.

I remember there were so many of my form; we numbered in the hundreds of thousands, A Cherubim's main duty was heeding and cataloging every prayer from all corners of humanity. We were bestowed the responsibility of carefully choosing pleads that needed to be brought to God's attention for immediate holy intervention.

And we sang forever. Our melodies meshed in perfect harmony praising the Lord. We sang to His perfection, to the beauty of His light. We adored. We proclaimed. We thanked him for creating us and giving us the opportunity to dedicate every living second of our existence to remind ourselves that we were us because of Him, a God we were never meant to see, but feel. We saw God through the love we felt towards each other. We saw God through the wonders of Creation, perfection in experiment. But mostly, we saw God when we witnessed the clockwork efficiency of the Seven Lights, the Emissary Archangels.

These seven, above us all, were the will of God personified. They were, and always will be, the keepers of order on Heaven and on Earth. To see them act in His Name was always an honor and cause for rejoicing. They inspired us all to do our roles as best we could. And so, because of them, we would sing until our lungs gave out and our voices cracked.

The eternal truth by which we abided was that the Seven Lights were pure and immutable. They were always Gabriel and Metatron; forever Michael and Raphael; perpetually Jophiel and Zadkiel. They were infinitely Abaddon. And it was him, the angel of death, the one I praised the most. I was fascinated by the passion he showed in his work. He held a resolute bearing at the edge of darkness. His drive was only rivaled by Michael's, and his wisdom matched Gabriel's. I had pleaded to serve as Abaddon's aide. I wanted to shine his boots, to feed him, and sing to him. I hoped that maybe he'd even allow me to assist him with his ministry one day. I dreamed...

So it was very hard for me to accept that a day would come when that eternal truth would crumble. I lost my chanting voice the day Gabriel came to us and announced that Abaddon betrayed us, that a human was chosen to ascend and take his place, and that our dear brother Metatron was dead. I was shunned by all my siblings. They thought of me a follower of the greatest deceiver since Lucifer. I was the single drop rejected by the ocean.

My faith was shaken, not just in Heaven, but in myself. I spent my days alone, misunderstood and confused as to my purpose within the angelic hierarchy. I struggled every day as I tried to find a new dream to justify my existence. But I grew tired of being looked down upon and being gossiped about by other angels. Being Cherubim became a burden. I was more of a celestial ornament than angel. I pretended to listen to prayers and eeny meeny miny moed my way to choosing which would be answered. I stopped singing altogether at choir and just moved my mouth with fake mocking gestures.

I just didn't care anymore.

It was not long after when a calling of angels was ordered at the gathering hall to announce a successor to the ministry of emotions. The host of angels joined hands as we looked up at the six remaining of the Seven Lights. Gabriel, the white angel, hovered above us. Michael, Raphael, Jophiel, and Zadkiel were present at Gabriel's side. Azrael, the second Black Angel, reared silently and unseen behind them all. The angels below held each other's hands in expectation. Several of the Cherubim, our very best, were whispered among the hierarchy as possible candidates. "Amion's servitude: perennially impeccable" "Ennadel's voice: angelic among angels" "Isophie's courage, awe inspiring"

I did not feel the energetic eagerness of my siblings. I was sickened with blasphemous thoughts. I carefully joined the hands of both angels beside me to free myself from their hold and intended to take stealthy steps to leave my ranks and hide away in the gardens. I had no interest in knowing who would be the new Archangel. To me, they were no different than the rest of us.

"I speak for God..." I heard Gabriel's harmonious voice beckon. "The Verb has chosen. Blessed be the one to carry on with Metatron's work, the will of God sanctified upon emotions. For it is one of seven sacred seals that bind the universe. Blessed be the one to join the ranks of Archangels, for we are Emissaries of the Presence. Blessed be..."

Gabriel went on. I hesitated for a moment, enamored by her voice; her every word, a symphony of hope. For only the hopeful choose to live. I hesitated for a moment, but the moment went away, and I took more steps. The hall's gate was close to my reach. Suddenly, I heard the white angel utter the words that froze me where I stood and forever changed my destiny:

"You. Your name is Uriel. The ministry of emotions is yours."

The whole cast of angels fell silent. No whispers were heard in the hall. I shifted my eyes side to side and I saw the entire hierarchy looking at me. Cherubim are not good liars. They all seemed confused and disappointed. Even the Archangels could not hide their disbelief. Michael in particular, who seemed troubled as she turned her face to Gabriel.

"Uriel?" She whispered to her.

"It is God's will." Gabriel responded in a low murmur.

"Huh…"

Gabriel stared at me seriously as she extended her arms.

"Come join us" she said.

Every Cherubim in the hall stepped aside to allow a path between me and the Archangels. I thought I would never be able to move. I never knew how my wings opened and levitated me through the path. I did not have any other real choice. I found myself right in front of White, who raised her arm over my head and delivered a prayer. I closed my eyes.

Since then, my form has spiraled in descent. I walked alongside Archangels, keeping order in the universe in the name of our Lord, but I have never truly felt I belonged with them. They all measure my work with reproach and discontent. Except the Black Angel, who always smiles at me lovingly… as she probably does every living being in this universe. And poor Michael, she took it upon herself to lead my development, maybe out of some heroic compulsion, or just mere pity, but I barely manage to uphold an emotional balance on Earth. In truth, my heart has never really accepted this ministry. I lack the interest to learn the meaning and purpose of the spectrum of feelings. To me, love, faith, compassion, admiration, all of these are inevitably tied to disappointment and pain. This is the only real eternal truth I've ascertained in my days as guardian of emotions. At least, that is the only way I can be able to understand the workings of my ministry: if I love, I suffer.

I worry that even the angel of death seems to have a better, braver perspective of the purpose of emotions than I do. It is too bad she cannot talk; I would have asked her so much. Maybe even offer to trade ministries. I would gladly guide the dead, as I once dreamed I would alongside Abaddon. At this point, I fear I do a disservice to my ministry. Perhaps someone else should be chosen over me. But I could never resign my duty. Could I? If I ever faced this God that one cannot see but feel, I would ask Him why He chose me. Why me?

Ruth stopped reading and closed my purple book.

"What if she lied?" she queried, still staring at the book.

"What?" I asked confused.

"What if it was never you, Violet?"

"What are you talking about?"

"You said in your book, you never felt comfortable with your ministry; that you didn't feel you belong with the Archangels. You said White spoke for God. But He never, you know, He never actually ever showed up and said you were chosen for your ministry. What if White lied about it? What if God wanted someone else to take over your ministry, but White chose you so this- all of this would happen?"

"What?! No! How could you say-why would she-I would never-!" I screamed confused and angry.

I leaped from the floor and took the book from her and hit her on the head with it.

"You're just like all of them! You're an ass!"

"Ow! Violet, listen! I didn't mean anything by it! Just listen to me for a second! This whole mess we're in, it's been going downhill so fast that we're this close to see the world end. Evergreen and Blue are out, Black gone, Scarlet murdered. Yes, I admit I feel you're not the right person, or angel or whatever, to handle the ministry of emotions, but you definitely didn't kill your sister. I think White-"

"No! White would never kill!"

"I-look, I don't know, but if White was rebelling or something and wanted to destroy the world, she'd need a weak link to break the seals. I think she knew you were vulnerable. You said you were an outcast because of Abaddon. So she named you as Metatron's successor. I mean, who's going to question the voice of God?"

"But it doesn't make sense. Why would White want to end the world? And if she didn't speak for God, why didn't He do anything about it?"

"Beats me; but listen, maybe I'm wrong about all this, but we should avoid White until we make sure."

"Okay... That kind of makes sense, I guess. And hey...I wanted to let you know, I'm feeling my sister Black on Earth again, but I think she's in trouble, 'cause she seems pretty afraid. We should go to her."

"Okay, I'll tell the guys to take us. Where is she?"

"I think she's in the desert".

"Ok, so she's close."

"No. The Gobi desert. She's somewhere in China."

"China?! Uh...How are we going to get there? There're no airplanes or boats working. Look, let's just keep looking for your replacement and then we'll figure something out. I'll ask the guys to drop us off at the next town or whatever"

"Um... aren't you forgetting something?"

"What?"

"Hassan. Are you going to tell him?"

"What? Oh, that! Well, I dunno, should I? Does he-?"

"Do you really want me to tell you if he likes you?"

"No, yeah. He's with Steve. It doesn't matter."

"But I think you should still tell him. Steve's okay with it."

"Um...Okay, I'll let him know tonight when he stops driving. We're leaving tomorrow, so what the heck, right?"

"Right."

Ruth put on her earphones again and moved her feet to the beat of her music. I opened my book again, but I didn't feel like writing anymore. I scribbled *'What if she's right about me?'* and stared at the words for a while. Ruth tapped my shoulder and extended one of her headphones to me.

"Um… It's the new Duncan Blackheart album." she asked.

"Okay. Cool."

I got to bed and lied next to her. We listened to Duncan's awesome gothic tunes on her iPod for a bit. We both head banged to the heavy music beat. Not too hard, we're not savages or anything. We didn't get to share the deepest darkest secrets of her soul or whatever, but to me, it was a start.

. . . .

"Stay as far behind me as you can." Ruth asked me with a nervous voice.

Her hands were shaking as we opened the door out of the back of the RV. It was a really dark night except for the moonlight that allowed us to see our silhouettes moving. Hassan had parked the car on the side of the desert road again. The guys were sitting on the roof of the truck checking out the stars. Ruth held the handle of the little ladder at the side of the van, but froze before taking the first step up.

"I-I can't" she muttered.

"Oh my God, you're such a coward!" I murmured back.

Steve peered over the side of the van's roof and looked down at Ruth. He smiled and, with his index finger, he signaled Ruth to come up. She sighed and began to climb the ladder. I followed.

"Look at this girl come for more brownies!" Steve joked.

"Oh, too late for that, I'm afraid" Hassan replied "This guy here hogged them all. Come sit with me, sweetie."

As Ruth sat next to Hassan, Steve headed down the RV's ladder.

"That's a problem easily solved, my friends." He said "I got another batch by the counter. I'll be back, kids."

Steve gestured with his hands at Ruth, telling her to say what she needed to say. I giggled and Ruth blushed as she got comfortable next to Hassan and leaned her head on his shoulder. They looked so cute together! I could stare at them forever. They both glanced at the stars for a bit.

"How's the arm?" Hassan asked Ruth.

"Oh, it's fine. I'm fine."

"Sorry I haven't checked on you. I've been busy."

"That's ok. Um…Steve kept tabs. He's a great nurse."

"He's a great everything, that one."

"Yeah…"

"Are you okay?"

"Me?"

"You look jittery"

"I… um…"

Ruth stared at the sky, her leg shaking nervously.

"'Um…I need to…" Ruth improvised "There's a change of plans. I need to leave you guys at the next town we pass by."

"What for?"

"I gotta go somewhere… can't tell you."

"I understand. Your secret government thing… We'll miss you."

"No, Ruth!" I whispered to her. "You gotta look at him and say it!"

I placed my hands on Ruth's cheeks and steered her head to face Hassan.

"I… um… I have to tell you something" Ruth finally said to Hassan.

"You have a crush on me." He answered.

"You know?" Ruth asked as her face turned pink.

"By the way you act around me." He smiled "Your voice changes a bit and you turn your eyes away when you're around me. It's cute"

"This is embarrassing" She said, hiding her face in the palm of her hand.

"I can also see your friend there behind you, the angel," Hassan said calmly.

My jaw dropped. I froze. Ruth stepped back, almost stepping on my foot.

"You can see her?!" Ruth reacted surprised.

"What the-?! You can see me?!" I mumbled shocked.

"I can see and hear you perfectly, Violet, is it?"

"But-" Ruth tried to speak.

Hassan touched Ruth's chin gently.

"Hey, it's okay, Ruth. You and I have the same gift. We can see everything and everyone around us for what they truly are. She's the one you're trying to help, isn't she?"

"Yes. She's... She's the reason the world is messed up. She's in charge of-"

"The ministry of emotions, I know. I've heard you before."

"Well, um... she abandoned her ministry and the world is going to end because of it. We're thinking we can fix things by finding someone to take over her job"

Hassan stared at me weird; like he was studying me.

"Do you trust her?" He asked Ruth without taking his eyes off me.

"She's okay"

"What she can do...She's dangerous..." he replied.

"Hey, I'm right here, you know. No need to talk about me like I'm a child."

"She was punished by another angel. We're kind of stuck together. She can't do anything unless I allow her to"

"Shut uuuuup, Ruth!" I yelled.

"She could control emotions." Hassan continued "Humans, angels, demons; anyone with a heart, right? That's quite the power. And you haven't found anyone to give it to yet? You need to be very careful. This has to be someone you really trust"

"You could have it" Ruth told Hassan.

"Me? Thank you for the vote of confidence, but-" he responded.

"Whoa! Wait, hold on a second there." I interrupted, "Ruth, could I talk to you for a sec? Excuse us, Hassan"

I pulled Ruth to the side and argued in a low voice.

"Are you nuts?! I can't just give him my ministry!"

"Why not?"

"What do we really know about this guy?"

"I trust him. And, hey, didn't you say you'd give your ministry to the first person who said yes?"

"Yeah, but- I was wrong, okay? We need to know we're doing the right thing here, maybe-"

"Violet, this isn't a coincidence. Think about it, why else do you think Lucifer dumped us in the middle of the desert? He knew we'd find the right person here."

"Maybe..."

"Look, it's Hassan. He's cool. I can't think of anyone better to do this"

"Let me think about it."

"You're going to think about it... The world is crumbling around us and you're going to think about it!"

"Hey, don't pressure me, Ruth!"

"Ugh!"

Steve climbed the RV ladder holding a bag with brownies. He saw Ruth looking and talking to herself in the opposite direction of Hassan.

"Hey, who you're talking to like a crazy person?"

Hassan reached his arm to help Steve get on top of the RV's roof.

"Stevie, I need to show you something." Hassan told him, "But I need you to keep calm, I'll explain everything. Violet, could you please reveal yourself to Steve?"

I looked at Ruth and she nodded in approval, so I revealed myself to

Steve.

"Aaaah! How did- Who-?!" Steve screamed. "What's going on here?!"

"It's okay, man." Hassan said holding Steve's arm and trying to calm him down. "She's an angel. Remember those times I've told you I've been around? Well, I wasn't kidding."

"I don't understand…" Steve said nervously.

"It's okay. It's a little too much to take in, but… Angels, demons, they're all real. I know a little about them."

"But- how-?"

"I used to fight demons all my life. I was kind of good at it, too. But I went into hiding some time ago."

I shifted my stare at Hassan in shock.

"Adam?" I asked.

He returned a smile and nodded to me.

"OMG! OMG! OMG! OMG!" I yelled as I pointed my finger at him. "It's him!"

"Him who?" Ruth asked with a confused look.

"Ruth! He's Adam!"

She suddenly squeezed my hand as she realized who he was.

"*The* Adam?! The first man?!" Ruth screamed in disbelief.

"Adam?" Steve queried.

"I was getting to that." Hassan said.

Hassan held Steve's arm "My name is not Hassan, babe. It's Adam. And I'm… I'm really, really old."

Ruth tapped my shoulder.

"Violet, do you hear that?" She whispered.

I hadn't notice the distant snarling sounds all around us. The growling kept getting louder until it became deafening. As I turned my attention to the desert under the moon light, I noticed shadows moving and closing in.

The shadows took the form of disgusting looking demon goblins crawling in circles surrounding the van. I quickly held on to Ruth and I let out a yelp.

"Oh, God, are those-?" Ruth asked before swallowing hard.

"Demons!" I yelled and freaked.

I wasn't ready to fight them. I couldn't even handle just one, let alone hundreds of them.

"Oh, my God" Steve reacted horrified at the monsters gathering around the RV.

"Calm down, people, please. Let me handle this." Adam said to all of us.

A moment passed. Even though we expected the swarm of demons to jump on us none of them moved to attack us. They seemed to be waiting for something. Steve stared at Adam fearful and angry.

"I really wish I had more time to explain things…" Adam lamented.

"What is going on?" Steve asked panicked.

"My wife is coming." Adam said to Steve with sadness.

"You're married?" Steve uttered with a broken voice as he dropped the bag of brownies from his hand.

13 RESENTMENT

Eve was the only thing in Adam's mind. He could not stop yearning to lose his face between her breasts; to grab her from behind and press his body against hers. Every morning, he would wake up next to her in that cave at the heart of Eden, eager to touch her again, and touch her repeatedly, and have her touch him, until he was satisfied. The little time Adam and Eve would not spend together, he would fantasize of new things he'd like to try with her. He did not care for any smells other than Eve's. He did not care for colors other than Eve's golden locks. He did not care for other sounds besides Eve's moaning when he touched her. With the exception of God, whom he still loved above all things, everything else in Eden seemed uninteresting and distant; next to Eve, paradise was irrelevant.

"Adam!" He heard a weak broken voice cry in the distance. "Adam!"

Adam turned his head to see Lillith by the cherry trees. The skies were orange as dusk embraced the Garden of Eden. Lillith had convinced Adam to join him for a walk as they often used to in the past. She picked some fruits and a spot up on the hill where they could sit and watch the sunset together. Adam turned to Lillith, slowly realizing she was with him.

"Hmm? Did you say something?" he asked.

"I was saying- sigh! Never mind." she replied, annoyed "Let us hurry up the hill before we miss it."

"Miss what?"

"The sunset... I can see your heart is not in this today. You are thinking of her."

"I-"

"It is fine. Do you wish to go to her?"

"I am sorry"

Adam and Lillith stood silent for an awkward moment. Using her fingers, she played with some of the fruits she had picked.

"If you want, you can make love to me" she finally said.

"You? But, we have never-" he queried confused.

"I-I know I am not her, but... I want to try to please you..."

"Are you sure?"

Lillith shyly nodded and sat on the grass under the trees. Adam sat next to her and began to kiss her face. He caressed her thin legs, but she trembled when he reached her upper thigh.

"Lillith-" he uttered frustrated.

"I am sorry. Please tell me what to do" she replied

"Just- lie down."

Lillith lied down and Adam kissed her as he tried to position himself on top of her. He placed his hand on her undeveloped breasts, but felt her sweat. She was shaking nervously. Adam held her still and kept trying to kiss her. As he penetrated her, her moans seemed like out of tune shrieks to him. He found her face expressions off-putting and tried to think of Eve as he stared at the cherry tree behind them. Adam just wanted it to be over.

"I-I disgust you." Lillith whispered angrily.

"No. No, I-" Adam wavered, not being able to lie to her.

Lillith shoved Adam to the side and stood up. Adam grabbed her arm, but she pulled it away from him and ran away to the woods. He did not follow her. The first man would not see Lillith again for several days. She had not returned to the cave where they slept and his obsession with Eve made him think of her less and less each day that passed by.

One night, after making love to Eve at the cave, Adam decided to get some food. He returned to the cherry trees near the hill where he had last seen Lillith. He picked a cherry and thought of her as he nibbled the fruit. It had been a few weeks since he last saw her, and he wondered what had become of her.

As he continued his stroll, Adam heard gurgling sounds he thought were growling from some kind of small animal. He quietly followed the sounds behind the trees. Adam found Lillith with her knees bent on the grass. She looked pale and sweaty. Her eye sockets were black. The first man thought something else was different about her demeanor, but he couldn't quite figure out what. Lillith wiped her mouth and turned to Adam, backing away from him.

"Lillith! Are you alright? You are not well. Let me-" he said as he extended his arm to help her up.

Lillith slapped his arm away and kept her distance.

"GET AWAY FROM ME!" She shouted.

"Let me help you…"

"You have done enough! The angel told me! She told me everything!"

"You are not making any sense. Come back with me to the cave."

"No! You go back and stay with her!"

"Is this about Eve? Listen, I love you just as much as I do her. Nothing else matters. You are my wife."

"I HATE YOU!"

"Stop this nonsense! Do as I say!" Adam shouted.

Lillith stepped back away from Adam.

"Listen to me carefully. I never want to see you again!" she screamed, pointing at Adam. "Do not dare to follow me!"

Lillith vanished into the woods again, concealed by the darkness of the night. Adam felt confused and immensely sad. He worried about her and wanted her to be safe. He felt a great affection towards her that later in life he would compare to the love from brother to sister.

"I am sure she is fine." Eve reassured him back at the cave. "And you need to respect her wishes. Leave her to herself."

"She should be here with us." Adam replied worried. "What if she does not return?"

"Then you will be better off without her. Surely you do not need a wife that will turn on you like that for no reason"

"But she is my wife"

"I am your wife too; and I am feeling very neglected right now. Should I abandon you so you can miss me too?"

"Eve, please-"

"I am serious, Adam. You promised to get me some food and all you brought are some cherries and this undeserved concern for that selfish woman."

"I am sorry"

"You should be. Never mind; I lost my appetite. But no more talk of her, please. Come lie with me. I am cold."

Adam did as Eve requested and held her close to him. However, he kept thinking of Lillith; hurt by her words and haunted by her altered form. He regretted not going after her and thought of many things he should have said to her. The first man prayed to God to protect her from whatever illness she had and asked that she come back to him.

But that night, when he saw her stooping by the cherry trees, was the last time he would ever see her again.

．．．．．．．．．．．．．

It was morning when Adam kneeled at the river shore to pray to God. He had not stop praying since he last saw Lillith over a month ago. He searched for the right words to give thanks for all the blessings he has been given and to plead for Lillith's safety. Since he was created, Adam immediately felt God's warm presence whenever he prayed. Through prayer, the first man learned God's purpose for him and what He expected from him. However, lately his prayers have felt hollow, like he was speaking only to himself. Adam found himself alone to deal with his own dilemmas. God's absence worried him. Was the Lord angry at him? He kept praying.

Water from the river splashed Adam's face. Eve was in the river and kept wetting him playfully.

"How long will you keep praying?" she said "Come join me!"

"I am conflicted" he responded.

"You need to stop burdening God with your pitiful predicaments and enjoy the many gifts that He has given us. Get your mind off things. Look, let me get out of the water. I will show you something I got for you"

Eve stepped out of the river and walked past Adam. He kept his eyes on her while she reached a bulk of fruits covered in big leaves she had left on the ground. She took a single round red fruit and brought it to Adam. Adam held it in his palm as Eve sat next to him.

"I found a tree on the other side of the woods." she said "Just this single tree among the rest of the others. One of its kind, I think. Taste it."

Adam took a bite of the fruit. He liked it.

"I have never seen this before." he remarked "I must have missed it. What is its name?"

"How should I know? You are the "man". It is your place to name it, not mine"

Adam stared at the round fruit.

"Red Pear."

"Red Pear? Are you really going to name such a unique fruit as the red type of another? Please! Make up a new name!"

"…Apple"

"Apple?"

"Apple."

"I like Apple."

"Me too." Adam said as he took another bite.

Adam and Eve ate their fruit quietly for a while. Eve slid her hand under his. She had finally gotten Adam to stay with her without the lure of sex. They were husband and wife, sitting together at the river shore. She was happy.

Adam was not.

"You are right." He broke the silence.

"What do you mean?" she asked.

"I should not burden God with my problems. They are for me to solve. I need to-"

Adam let go of Eve's hand and stood up.

"I need to find her." he continued.

"Adam-"

"Will you come with me?"

"No."

"I will see you tonight." Adam uttered as he walked away from Eve.

Eve sat alone holding the bitten apple. The dark angel sat next to her and took the fruit from her.

"You know my price." He said, taking a bite from the fruit.

"I will gladly pay it." She spoke with ire in her voice.

"Good." the Devil said, handing over the apple back to her.

Eve was alone once more. She threw the fruit into the water. A single tear slowly rolled on her cheek. It was the first of many she would shed for Adam.

. . . .

Adam had spent the day looking for Lillith. He began his search by exploring a series of hidden caverns located close to the cherry trees. At the third cavern, he found burnt wood and ashes from a small fire. He also found other signs that someone had been living there, including something that disturbed him: drops of dry blood stains on the ground.

The first man went back to the forest tired and with no clue of where to go next. He climbed the tallest tree to get a greater view of the area and cried out Lillith's name a few times. As soon as he looked at the skies above him, he noticed a curtain of dark gray clouds with flashing white lights coming from them.

"Is that you, God?" he asked.

He climbed down from the tree and ran towards the gray clouds. As he got nearer, rain drops fell on him. The rain grew heavier as winds increased. Adam found himself stepping on muddy waters that ran on small streams across the land. Suddenly, he saw a flashing light hit a tree, followed by a loud explosive sound that scared Adam to fall back on his butt. The tree in front of him was on fire. Adam kneeled in front of it head down.

"Lord! Why are you angry with me?" he shouted. "What can I do to atone?"

Another loud thunder was heard. Adam was frightened. He began to pray, but he was too nervous to speak the words he needed. The strong winds knocked him to the ground again.

"Puh-please! Talk to me!" he screamed.

Afraid for his life and that of his wives, Adam managed to stand up and march against the currents towards his cave. He cried out Lillith's name a few times, He heard Eve's voice from afar, calling out to him.

"Eve!" Adam shouted, "Eve!"

Adam ran towards Eve from the woods. He noticed she held an apple in her hand. She kissed and embraced him.

"Are you well? Eve, are you well?"

"Yes."

"God is furious! We need to hide in the cave! We need to pray!"

"No! Adam, we need to leave Eden!"

"I do not understand. Why? We need to find Lillith!"

At that moment, Eve looked at the fruit in her hand and then at Adam's eyes.

"Adam" she said, "I have betrayed you…"

"What are you talking about?"

"God is angry at us because… this fruit, the apple, it was forbidden.

When I found the tree, an angel came to me and announced we were never to eat the sacred fruit from that tree or else we would suffer God's wrath."

"That doesn't make sense. Why would God create a fruit if He did not want us to eat it?"

"Ah…There was, there was a snake, but now I know it was a fallen angel. The snake, it told me we should eat the fruit for with it… w-we would gain incredible knowledge; knowledge equal to God's. I thought-"

"You thought wrong, woman!" Adam yelled, letting go of Eve's arms. "Who are we to attempt to steal such power from the Lord?! …But, I took a bite, and no knowledge came to me."

"Well, it takes time…"

"Are you lying to me, Eve?!"

"…No."

Adam paused.

"I did not know the fruit was forbidden!" he continued. "If I'd known, I would never have tasted it. I should let the Lord know-"

"I am sorry, Adam! God only cares that you ate the fruit. We must leave now!"

"Oh, Eve! Why would you disobey His will?"

"Please, I understand your anger towards me and I deserve any punishment you deem just, but we have to leave Eden together or we will die by God's hands."

"But maybe if we prayed for forgiveness-"

"There is no time! We must leave now!" Eve said, pulling Adam's arm.

Adam stopped.

"We need to find Lillith!" he declared.

"Lillith- she is no longer in Eden. I saw her today. I did not want to tell you this, but she was lying with the snake. I saw her!"

"Oh, no!"

"Yes. And…other unholy beasts. She lied with them all! She is to begat monsters for the snake! And-and she eats spiders and cockroaches!"

"Shut up! I cannot- I cannot take any more! She was my wife!"

"She is now the Devil's wife. I am sorry. She belongs to him now!"

"That snake will pay for this!"

Adam turned his face to the skies.

"GOD! WHY DID YOU NOT PROTECT HER?!"

A loud thunder roared. Fire spread through the Garden.

"Adam, we must go! Take my hand!"

Adam and Eve held hands as she led him against the thunderstorm. They headed south until Eden was no more. The first man fell on his knees and broke in tears. He could not contain the sorrow of losing God's grace. Eve held him tight to console him.

"We've got each other. That is enough." She would repeat in whispers.

After what seemed like endless days of travel, they reached barren desert lands. It was desolate and inhospitable, but the storm did not spread to that territory and they were still alive. They were both on their own, lost in a new dangerous world without God to protect them.

Adam couldn't help but look back. He walked alongside Eve across a desert valley. The sun burned his scalp and the sand underneath him scalded his bare feet. He was hungry, thirsty and very, very, tired. Everything felt wrong to him.

"God, please forgive me. Take me back." he whispered to himself over and over again making sure Eve could not hear his words.

Adam stopped to pick up a long, dry, leafless tree branch from the ground. He watched Eve happily strolling a few feet away from him, singing and smiling like nothing had happened. How could she sing when they just lost the grace of God? At times like this, Adam wished that he hadn't abandoned Lillith... While Eve continued singing, Adam became of a mind to hit her head repeatedly with his long branch. As he raised it once to clog her, he stopped, knowing she was all he had left in this life. Eve turned to Adam and pulled his free hand.

"Come, husband", she told him lovingly, "leave that silly thing where you found it. There is nothing left for us back there. We will find a new Eden or we will make one ourselves."

Adam dropped the branch and continued walking, but he could not stop looking back. His eyes searched for a place that was no longer there, no longer his. God had abandoned him. Eve held Adam's hand tighter and smiled. She gently caressed Adam's face and turned it towards her.

"I will make it up to you." she said.

But she never did, and from then on he would always be of a mind to hit her head repeatedly with that long, dry, leafless branch.

....

The island of Santa Cristal just before the twilight of the nineteenth century brought Adam and Eve's inner clashes to another level. They had been arguing all over Europe, Asia, and America and each time they visited a new place, things got worse between them.

After they had left Eden, the couple had managed to survive by learning how to farm and hunt. They begat Abel, and Seth and Lila, and Farrah, Gail, Ken, and Noel, and poor Cain, whom Adam had to lock away after he was marked by God; and many more daughters and sons. Their children spread across the world and multiplied. Families joined into tribes, which grew into nations. Adam and Eve witnessed the world change in front of their eyes. Even though the sons of their sons had heard of God and were raised to love and fear Him through the concept of religion, each coming generation relied a little less spiritually in the Lord than the previous. It was the dawn of a Godless civilization. This was a great concern to Adam who still loved God above all things and could not forget his days in Eden.

However, Adam was more worried about the fact that while he and his wife saw their children and descendants wither and die, they remained young and healthy. Adam and Eve were immortal, and because of this, he thought God still had a purpose for them. He just had to figure out what the purpose was. Adam never stopped praying, year after year, century after century, hoping to feel God's presence again and receive His forgiveness and guidance, but he never got it. Instead, Adam had come up with a course of action for himself. He had seen how Lucifer, the golden snake, had worked his influence over humanity through greed, deceit and betrayals. The Devil had been successful in leading the world away from the ways of God, from single individuals to entire governments. The first man thought that he and Eve should actively fight Lucifer at his own game, by infiltrating societies and swaying them into the light. Slight manipulations and larger espionage schemes became the basis of a cold unspoken war between Adam and Lucifer for the soul of humanity.

Eve was particularly good at deceit, and became an invaluable asset to Adam. She devised and executed plans to bring down corrupt officials. She created an intelligence network before there ever was an intelligence network, and gained access to historic documents which she forged to rewrite certain facts in their favor. Eve had amassed great power for her husband with the hope that when they'd win, he would turn his attention to her. However, as time passed, the war evolved and intensified, making Adam more obsessed with his mission. Eve felt she was less of a wife and more of an assistant to Adam's cause. She pleaded for him to retire and let God and the rest of humanity handle Lucifer. They could've lived happily enjoying their eternal youth just the two of them. But Adam wouldn't hear of it. Each day, new causes that commanded his attention commenced, and the first man had to be more focused to keep up with the Devil.

It was in Santa Cristal that Adam would turn the tide against Lucifer. The couple had travelled there to fight for the abolition of slavery in the island. The night after they arrived, they used their influences to get invited to a masquerade ball hosted by the island's Governor. The gala was held at the dignitary's mansion near the northern coast. The white manor was a marbled walled building lighted by candle lamps and chandeliers. The main ballroom was surrounded by many windows and four spiraled stairways at each corner. Outside, a row of horse carriages lined up in front of the tall main wooden doors where the invitees were greeted by a dark skinned door man.

Adam sported a black tuxedo and a white double faced Janus mask. Eve wore a scarlet sequined evening gown and a white feathered half mask with an elongated beak. The Governor, an obese bald sixty year old wearing a white suit and a sad clown mask, introduced them to legislators and other officials from the island. They were also introduced to important representatives from other countries, among them were three tall blonde Austrian delegates in black suits and red devil masks. As soon as they met,

Adam and Eve recognized them as agents of Lucifer. The three blonde men acknowledged the couple and inconspicuously stepped away towards the door.

"Stay and mingle with the crowd. See if you can find out who we need on our side to have our little laws approved." Adam told Eve. "I will deal with the Austrian representatives."

"No! Let them leave. Let's do what we're here for and be done with it. These fellows cannot do any harm now that we are on to them."

"You know things don't work like that."

"Because you are so obsessed with eradicating Lucifer's agents, you do not see there are other furtive ways to handle things."

"I don't have time for this."

"Or me. Not anymore. You need to decide if your meaningless quest to brown nose God is worth losing me."

Adam hugged Eve, pressing her face against his chest to shush her.

"We. Will talk. Later. Do as I say."

Eve let go of Adam's embrace and took a glass of wine from a waiter as she composed herself. She took a sip.

"Come back to me safe" Eve finally responded, "And please, not a stain to your shirt. It was hell to wash."

Adam took a sip from Eve's wine before following the Austrian men outside. Eve was left alone trying to compose herself and flashing fake smiles to nearby politicians.

As Adam reached the garden in front of the mansion, he saw the Austrian men hurrying off towards the gates. The first man took off his suit jacket and laid it next to the fountain. He looked around him and noticed a beehive up on a mango tree. A few bees buzzed around frantically.

"Gentlemen, I hope I didn't say anything to scare you away from this fine party. Would you care to stay a bit longer and chat at the balcony?"

The three tall individuals stopped on their tracks as they heard Adam's voice behind them. One of the men nodded at the other two and the three turned to face Adam.

"Our massster instructed usss not to engage you, firssst man." The Austrian hissed. "But I think he will be pleasssed to have your head tonight."

"Now, now. Play nice. I think we should all try to behave more civilized." Adam replied, "Let me extend my offer to you: Leave the men that you've possessed and flee this island, never to return, and I will let you live."

"Heh. Only you against the three of usss."

"I know, it does seem a bit unfair. However, do I need to remind you that while you take human vessels you suffer the same frailties as we do? When in Rome, and all that..."

Adam hummed, and his humming sound turned to a buzzing. Bees from all the many nearby beehives flew close to each other forming a cluster in mid-air. The buzzing of the bees was deafening. The insects relentlessly attacked the three men by engulfing them and stinging their faces. The Austrian men screeched unnatural shrieks of pain.

"And God said 'Let us make man in our image...'" Adam quoted with a preacher's inflection, "'and let him have dominion over every creeping thing that creepeth upon the earth'... I paraphrase a little. Point is; you need to leave the bodies of these poor men alone or feel the pain as they feed my pets with their faces."

"You would ssssacrifice thessse men to hurt ussss?" The Austrian screamed.

"The need of the many, my friend..."

The demons that possessed the Austrian men left their bodies and bolted. As soon as the goblins abandoned the human vessels, the Austrian men fell unconscious on the floor and the bees dispersed away. Adam approached the men and checked their pulse.

"They still live." A melodic voice uttered from behind him. When Adam turned around, he was blinded by an intensely bright white light.

"You..." Adam muffled, "I saw you once before..."

"When you came to life" the voice replied.

"The white angel…" Adam whispered as tears flowed from his eyes. He got on his knees and bowed to the angel, his face almost touching the dirt on ground. "Has He finally heeded my prayers? Is God-?"

"I do not speak for God, first man." The angel responded, "Please stand up."

Adam slowly stood up and faced White. She wore a luminous white gown. Her wings spread wide. Her halo lighted. His eyes took a few seconds to adjust to her light.

"Then why are you here?" He asked with a tone of disappointment.

"I am here to tell you what your heart already knows." White answered, 'And what God has allowed for you to never know. It is the truth of what happened at Eden. The truth about Eve-"

"I have forgiven Eve for giving me that apple to taste against God's will. It is the harshness of our penance that tortures me. I ate of the fruit that day, and I have prayed for His forgiveness each and every day since then. I have dedicated my life to gain His favor, but He-"

White placed her hand on Adam's shoulder.

"Adam, do you truly think God gives a damn about a fruit? He did not exile you, He exiled only Eve."

"…What?"

"You were supposed to stay in the Garden. Leaving Eden should have been her punishment, not yours."

A chill crawled up Adam's spine.

"What are you saying?"

"That day, before the storm hit Eden, Eve… murdered Lillith." White continued, "She lured her to the river and drowned her. That is what provoked God's wrath."

"No…I don't believe you! Eve loves me!"

"It is the truth."

"… All these years I thought-"

"That Lillith consorted with demons? That she became Lucifer's concubine? I have read the books. Eve was very… creative in her designs to ruin Lillith's reputation in the eyes of humanity…to say the least. No. Your wife took her life and when she was told to leave the Garden, she lied to you to make you go with her."

"W-why are you telling me this? Why now?"

"I tell you this now because the time for me to be idle while you waste your existence searching for answers to the wrong questions has passed. This is the time to make things right. Eve murdered innocent Lillith, but it was God who let the lie keep. All these years of prayer and He did not care to let you know that you were meant to stay at Eden; that you did not do anything wrong. God cares for you as much as He does for any in this world; not much at all. He does not care for your war against Lucifer, which you are fighting alone, by the way. He does not care for the fate of humanity. Mankind was born to die, as you and I will do someday, with no purpose but merely to amuse Him."

"But- His plan…" Adam said trying to regain control of his heavy breathing.

"His plan is that there is no plan. We just die."

Adam felt dizzy. He sat on the edge of the fountain. The angel sat next to him.

"He does not love you. He never did."

The first man sat silent, White moved closer to him.

"Adam, God lied to you since the moment you first drew breath." The angel advised, "He had you believe your life and that of your children were precious to Him, but in reality, your progenies die. They live brief lives searching for a reason for living, a higher purpose that only comes when they die and they become small offerings to the Lord. Imagine this Earth as the altar and humanity… each and every one of you, as nothing more than sacrificial lambs."

White spoke in a lower voice and closer to Adam's ear.

"We need to make things right. You and I can make a new plan. Together, we can take control of Creation."

"Are you mad?! How could we ever-"

"We can. I have taken steps to end this reality. It will not be easy, and many will suffer, but once we accomplish what needs to be done, we can re-make everything. Make things better. The universe will need a new Lord. I am an angel, I cannot rule. I can only guard humanity and, if you let me, I can speak for you. But you will be God to this new world where all will live forever, and we will all bow to you."

"Why me?"

"Because you are the first man. The first living being with a conscience to discern between good and evil, between life and death. All I need of you is to do what must be done. When the time comes, you must end God."

"NO!" Adam stood up from the fountain and stepped away from White.

"You fill me with evil thoughts and lies! Get away from me!" he continued.

"These are not lies." White replied, "I have no need to lie to you. See for yourself and take some time to think. I will wait for your decision. For now, there is one more truth that you should know. That day at the river of Eden, Lillith did not die alone."

Adam dropped on his knees and covered his ears, tormented.

"Get away from me!"

White fluttered her wings and flew away. Adam was left alone, his mind and heart lost in thoughts of what had been revealed to him. After a while, Jacinto, his assistant, ran towards him and helped him up.

"Don Adan! Don Adan, are ya well? What done happahn 'ere?"

"I...I am fine. Help these men on the ground. They need medical attention."

Adam began walking towards the gates.

"Please tell Eve I won't be joining her at the house tonight."

....

Heavy rains showered the northern part of the Island in the hours after the incident at the Governor's mansion. Adam reached the nearest town by foot and paid for a room where he slept for the rest of the night.

The next morning, the first man visited a chapel and waited for the few people present to leave. He lit a few candles and knelt before the altar. He closed his eyes and joined his hands. After a while, he stood up.

"All these years I suffered, asking myself what I did to push you away from me. All I wanted was to be with you. I fixated on knowing why you wouldn't listen to me, but she is right, isn't she? How does God not hear a prayer? How does God not forgive? ...Only if He does not love." Adam said before he stepped out of the chapel.

Adam remained in town for a few weeks, under the pretext of working on slave emancipation. He kept sending letters to Eve to have her wait for him at the Hacienda. All the while, he made preparations for a long journey and he did not want to be followed. On the day he was ready to leave, Adam had one last note he wrote to Eve. He decided to deliver it personally.

That night, upon Eve's return to the Hacienda, she noticed someone had been in the master bedroom. She saw a small note lying on the table next to the mirror.

"Adam..." Eve whispered.

Eve read the note and her heart stopped as she sat on her bed, sweating cold. She tried to compose herself and think of her next move. The hand that held the note would not stop shaking.

The note read: "I wasted an eternity believing your lies. You killed Lillith and our child."

14 DEATHMATCH

The very second the Black Angel set foot on the Gobi desert, she felt cold. The sun was about to set on that part of the world, and she could already see her breath as she took careful steps on the arid sand. It felt like walking barefoot on a mile-long iceberg. She knew she was too late to try to fix things. The Four Horsemen were already waiting for her and she could see them from afar. If these harbingers of oblivion were set free on Creation, it would mean the end of everything. The angel was sure she wasn't strong enough to stop them, not with the seals broken as they were, but maybe she could slow them down, delay the inevitable until... something- a miracle? - would present itself.

As the Black Angel got closer to the Horsemen, she realized they were not actually men riding horses, but repulsive half angel / half horse hybrids, their rotting flesh and decayed wings seemingly sown together by heavy rusty chains. The chains also restrained their bodies by binding arms, wings, and necks, limiting their movements. The rest of the chains lied on the ground, dead weight dragged by the four-legged monstrosities.

The Black Angel was sickened by the putrid sight and stench of the four creatures that stood in front of her in line next to each other. The white centaur, the skinniest and most ill-looking of the horsemen, corrupted all desert life in the area by releasing a grey poisoned air from his mouth. Every living thing in the vicinity became terminally ill.

"Thermo-nuclear Halitosis, dearie" said the naked white skinned

186

horseman to the Black Angel. "Pestilence of my own design. Megaloth am I." Megaloth said as sick plants and carcasses of insects and small rodents adorned his surroundings.

The red horseman, the biggest and strongest of the four, stomped on the ground and raised his arm pointing at the Black Angel. The angel felt pure hatred towards her own being and began to scratch her face intensely, drawing blood. She hallucinated with visions of uncontrollable violence; men and women murdering each other, whole countries destroyed.

"War is the alpha and the omega. War is the language. War is the song. I am Gothaku." The red horseman declared.

Black Angel closed her eyes and kneeled, pushing her arms against the ground. She opened her mouth to scream. Suddenly, she opened her eyes and stood up, wiping the blood and sweat from her face. She stared at Gothaku defiantly.

The angel felt a sharp pain in her stomach and lost her balance. Her pain increased a thousand fold, forcing her to rip open her dress under her chest. Her torso had divided and opened in half. A mouth with sharp teeth and a tongue had formed on her belly. The Black Angel turned her gaze towards the black creature and he looked back at her with sorrow. His face had no mouth. The pain in his eyes revealed that he did not mean to hurt her. She felt as if he didn't belong with the Horsemen.

The Black Angel used her hands to force the mouth on her belly shut. She joined the mouth's lips and held them together until they merged and disappeared within her stomach. After resting a few seconds, the angel buttoned her dress back on.

"Famine, the nameless is he." said the pale-green ghostly horseman in a weak raspy voice. "And you know me, little usurper. You know true Death. You know Abaddon."

Black Angel turned her eyes to Abaddon. She recognized his six arms and long boney fingers. She had indeed seen him before.

"Step away and you may yet live to see the end of things" Abaddon continued.

The Black Angel took a step towards the horsemen and with her foot, she traced a line in front of her. Gothaku stood in two legs, enraged.

"I want her chained!" He yelled.

"She belongs to me" Abaddon responded.

The Four Horsemen moved forward towards the Black Angel.

The Black Angel took a step back. Then another, as the Horsemen slowly advanced towards the line drawn in the cold sand. She turned around, increasing her pace and ran away as fast as she could from the Horsemen. The four of them kept moving forward until they crossed the line traced by the angel, where their legs wedged. The earth underneath began to slide within itself like quicksand. Hundreds of corpses reached up from under the ground, clutching and clawing the legs of the Horsemen. The rotting bodies belonged to men, women, and children from all races and all parts of the world.

"She has opened a dark tunnel" Abaddon explained unamused. "These are her armies of the dead; reanimated corpses without souls. This will only take a moment"

Abaddon stared at the hundreds of rising dead. His glance slowly made the corpses dry up, turning them to white salt. The salt of the dead spread across the parched plains in front of the four creatures, solidifying the ground underneath them. The Four Horsemen continued their march.

"Gothaku, bring her close to us" Abaddon ordered.

War picked up one of the heavy chains that were sown to his ribs. Each rusty link was the size of a truck tire. At the end of the chain, a sharp edged spike anchored it to the surface until War pulled it off. It took a lot of strength from the red rider to lift the chain and throw it at the Black Angel, The chain stretched, making a loud clacking sound as it reached the ground right next to the angel. The girl tumbled, but quickly stood up and kept running. Gothaku pulled back the chain and raised it again. He threw it back at the Black Angel and the spike penetrated her leg. She fell and cringed from the pain feeling her black blood gushing from her wound. She tried to pull off the spike from her leg, but the blade released tiny shards that sewed onto her.

The red centaur recalled the chain with one hard tug, dragging the Black Angel by the leg. War caught the angel with one hand and raised her by the pierced leg leaving her hanging head down. The little angel tried not to panic as she struggled to get free. War handed the angel to Death. The Ghost Horseman studied the Black Angel tilting his head close to her face.

"I never understood what God saw in you." Abaddon said.

Abaddon's ghost chains floated around him. One of the chains slithered through the air towards Black Angel's chest and buried itself within. At that same moment, War's rusty spiked chain released her leg and dropped to the ground where it anchored itself once again. The angel cried as the pain she felt from the ghost chains burned her soul. She felt her entire being ripped apart from within her.

"Come with us. I want you to see." The ghost horseman continued. "You should know what it means to be a true angel of death, I think."

Each one of the Four Horsemen renewed their stride and dragged their chains across the Gobi desert. The Black Angel hovered behind Abaddon, pulled by the ghost chain anchored inside her heart. She saw living desert animals or plants withering and perishing as the Horsemen passed nearby. The angel cried when she saw the spirits of these creatures decay and turn to nothing.

"Death from the Horsemen means nonexistence" Abaddon said, "Oblivion. That is the legacy the four riders intend to leave behind when we raze the world."

The sound of honking alerted the Black Angel. She turned to see a caravan of old cars and pickup trucks desert crossing up ahead of the creatures. Men drove the trucks while the women watched over their children playing at the back of the pickups. They were a group of about twenty, a big family, innocently singing along and making jokes as they headed towards a possible clan gathering. The males wore turquoise blue suits with golden corset belts with furry winter hats. The females wore long colorful dresses and the same furry hats as the men.

Black Angel needed to warn the humans in those vehicles and stir them away from the Horsemen. She pulled off the ghost chain from her soul. The act tore through many happy memories, ripping away the death angel's sense of security. She fought through the panic and wiped her tears from her face as she bolted, free from Abaddon's grip, towards the desert folk.

Night had already set when the angel sprinted as fast as she could to reach the cars. Fortunately for her, the creatures moved slowly, straining themselves a few steps at a time with their heavy chains. She slid and skipped down a dune and jumped sideways to avoid the chains that War would throw at her from time to time.

The Black Angel placed herself a few feet in front of the pickups and let herself be seen by the humans. The horrified driver of the first car instinctively turned the wheel all the way to the right and stepped on the breaks. The car behind it hit it from the side and the entire caravan stopped.

She crept towards the first car to warn them about the Horsemen. However, the people in the car freaked at the sight of the ghoulish looking girl and ran away from her. They screamed at the family from the other pickups and everyone left their cars, frightened by the apparition which they all kept calling "Oautu", a Chinese death wraith. The angel didn't mean for the fleeing humans to abandon their vehicles, but she was glad that at least they were running in the opposite direction of the four horsemen.

It was then that the Black Angel saw that one of the females that carried a small two year old stopped running and began to gnaw the arm of her small one. The child screamed in agony and confusion as it was being eaten alive, bite by bloody bite. Black Angel ran towards the mother and, with her touch, took away the life of the woman. She picked up the crying child from the dead female's arms and turned to search for other family members to hand over the kid. To her horror, the angel witnessed as the humans were tearing each other apart. They ripped away their clothes, revealing their bodies decomposing. Their skins showed greenish pus oozing from bursting blisters. They tried to tear each other's flesh trying to replace their own and keep alive.

The Black Angel thought it was too late for all of them; the riders were too close for them to escape. One by one, she took the lives of the twenty family members by touching each one of them. Her merciful touch released the spirits from their crumbling bodies. If the angel couldn't save these people's lives, she'd at least try to save their souls. Finally, she gently closed the eyelids of the crying child in her arms, and it stopped crying. Black Angel placed the dead child on the ground and stared at its cold pale face as she thought a quick prayer for the deceased family.

She felt the clopping of the four creatures behind her just as Abaddon's ghost chain stabbed and fixed itself through her back. The ghost chain stood like a rising serpent and lifted the weakened angel towards the pale green rider. He held slumped body in the palm of one of his six hands. Her head and limbs hung like a lifeless puppet in Abaddon's grasp. "You fail again" Abaddon said.

The ghost chain lifted the Black Angel, making her face the twenty spirits of the dead family. The angel saw that other ghost chains slithering from Death's pale skin picked, stabbed, and disintegrated the fleeting souls. The chain that held the angel released her, dropping her to the sand in front of Death. She was barely conscious enough to watch the last few remaining spirits disappear.

"You still think you can save them, Eshe." Abaddon declared. "After all this time, you are still so naïve."

. . . .

In the twilight of Ramses II's reign over Egypt, Eshe and Aziza went to bed without supper for yet another night. There was nothing to eat or drink in all of the empire ever since the waters of the river Nile became blood red, and a swarm of locusts made waste of the crops. If Eshe could talk, she would've suggested to her parents catching and cooking some of the frogs that plagued their country. After all, an old blind beggar she met told her frogs tasted like chicken. Then again, if her parents knew she'd consorted with a Jewish slave, she'd be punished for a lifetime. Esher's father had ordered the sisters not to go anywhere near the Jews. He said they were dangerous people, and the God they worshipped even more so.

The sisters lived a charmed life as daughters of the Pharaoh's personal physician. Before the plague, they got to run and play within the marbled lined walls and floors of the Pharaoh's palace, ate fresh food, dressed in the most delicate garments, and played with more dolls than they ever wanted.

Eshe was interested in learning. She enjoyed spending time with the court scribe, who taught her the history of her people and the pantheon of deities that watched over the Egyptian empire. Her favorite was Anubis, the jackal headed sentry of the afterlife, because she liked dogs. Sometimes the scribe would whisper to her tales from Jewish myths and the one God that favored and protected His people. The Jewish believed, the scribe said, that the one God would one day free His people from slavery. That made the eight year old sad, because she realized that the Jews did not like to be

191

slaves. Eshe was devoted to serve her older sister Aziza. She liked combing her hair and dressing her up. She let her eat from her food and even let her keep the prettiest dolls. She thought of herself as a slave to her sister and saw nothing wrong with that.

Things changed after Moses visited the court of Ramses II. The one God tortured Egypt with starvation and illness and for some reason the Egyptian gods did not answer their people's prayers. The citizens had now resorted to violence. Those who ventured outside their houses would risk being hurt by people rebelling against the Pharaoh for his decision not to free the Jews.

Eshe had not seen her father for days after he went out looking for their missing mother. The sisters were locked inside the house for their safety, but there was nothing to eat. The girls had checked the lower storage space under their floor only to find rotted food infected with rats and insects. Eshe tucked Aziza in emerald silk sheets and put out the fire next to her. The scary sounds of rioting from outside kept the older sister awake, but she had to try to get some rest. Aziza had become ill that night. She coughed blood and had a little trouble breathing. Eshe felt her sister's forehead burning up and wiped the sweat from her face.

"I should be tucking you in" said Aziza between coughs.

The girl smiled and shook her head. She pointed with her finger at her own eyes and then at Aziza.

"I know you watch over me, little sister." Aziza smiled. "I am fine. I-I wouldn't mind some water…"

Concerned for her sister's fever, Eshe decided to go look for water outside the house. Maybe she could find her father, too. The girl put on her sandals and tried to open the front door, but something jammed it from the other side. She pushed the table under a small crevice high on the wall and climbed her way through it. Once outside her home, the little girl saw soldiers trying to fight off a mob of Egyptian citizens. She had expected to see the Jews taking up arms, but none of them had left their dwellings. She wondered if her father was part of the mob, but she couldn't risk trying to find out.

The girl kept herself apart from the riot as much as she could by staying close to the walls of the houses. These were solid rock and dried mud brick walled households owned by Egyptian citizens, much like her family's place. She heard cries from inside a few of these houses.

When Eshe reached the poor hay roofed Jewish huts, a stench of dead animal caught her nose. All the doors of these houses were painted red. She touched one of the wet doors with her index finger and smelled blood. The girl struggled to conceal her fear and tried to focus on the task at hand. She ran through an alley towards a public well behind the houses. As she reached the well, she stopped at the sight of dead sheep corpses piled on each other. There were too many carcasses blocking her way to the well and the stench was unbearable. The Egyptian girl vomited and almost fainted, but she managed to gather the strength to walk fast away from the place. Eshe thought her father was right about the Jews. They were dangerous people, and they were dealing with some sort of evil witchery.

The eight year old ran back towards her house to check on her sister. She noticed a red clay basket as tall as her height blocking the door. She shoved it a few times until it fell in front of her, allowing a bit of space for her to open and squeeze through the door. Eshe did not hear her sister coughing and thought something was wrong. When she reached Aziza's bed, she saw a ghost of a pale twenty-something year old man with long black hair reaching his waist and eyes entirely black. His face had several ritual markings and he was wearing a rusty armor. He was a winged man with six arms. He caressed her sister's long black curls with his lengthy boney fingers. Eshe was paralyzed to see the armored man that had revealed himself to her.

"Come see." The ghost whispered to Eshe in a weak raspy voice.

Aziza trembled and tears rolled over her cheeks. She could not see the winged man next to her, but she dreaded a malevolent presence reaching for her soul.

"Eshe, I am scared" Aziza whispered.

Eshe stooped, facing the six-armed man to plead on behalf of her sister's life. She cried as she tried hard to enunciate words that she knew she could not speak. The pale visitor ignored the eight year old and with a touch of his finger, stopped Aziza's heart. Her eyes opened wide and became lifeless. Her skin became colorless. Frantic, Eshe quickly picked up a heavy clay vase from the table next to her and threw it at the man. The vase went through the armored spirit and broke upon impacting the wall. He turned his attention towards the young girl.

"The reckoning, it is not enough," the visitor whispered. "All of you must pay. I will kill you all, I think."

With unnatural speed, the winged apparition approached Eshe and penetrated her chest with one of his right hands. The tip of his fingers breached through the girl's back. She bled through her wounds as she took her last gasp. The Egyptian girl closed her eyes and the man quickly pulled away his hand.

Eshe collapsed and everything around her turned dark and silent.

"She's awake, She's alive, She is." Eshe heard a strange young male's voice in the darkness. Was this Anubis? she asked herself.

"She is dead, but she can hear us." Another voice responded. It sounded delicate and melodic. The girl guessed it may have come from Bast, the cat headed goddess.

"I do not think you want to bring her back."

"I do, but I do not feel the need for another angel of death. We can stop Abaddon ourselves"

"No, we cannot."

"Very well, Metatron. Lift her up. Let me talk to her... Eshe. Eshe, my name is... I am White. I speak for God-"

"No. I speak for God. I do." the other voice interrupted.

"Please let me do this... I – We speak on behalf of Him you call the one God. Your Pharaoh has not heeded the word of our Lord, and he keeps the chosen people of Israel captive. The one God has ordered Abaddon, the angel of death, to take the lives of all Egyptian first-borns. They cannot be saved. Your sister cannot be saved. For that, I am sorry. However, Abaddon has become mad, blood thirsty. He is going to commit genocide in Egypt. Every single human, both Egyptian and Jewish, will die if we do not stop him."

The voice stopped momentarily. Eshe kept concentrating, trying to hear the voice again.

"God has found favor in you." The voice went on, "You have been called upon to join us, but we cannot force you to do so. A choice stands before you. Keep your eyes closed and you will be free to join your sister and love her forever at the side of the Lord. You will know eternal bliss. Nothing will be held against you. Another will be chosen instead."

The melodic voice stopped briefly before continuing.

"Open your eyes and forever see darkness, never to see His face. You will bring death to the world, but only through the merciful will of God. You will be burdened with protecting the dead. You will guide their souls through the dark. And your name will be Azrael, the Black Angel."

Eshe thought about her sister and how much she wanted to be with her. It was always her dream that the sisters would be buried together, that their journey to the afterlife would be a bit less scary for both if they held hands in their travel. What would become of Aziza without her sister to serve her?

But if the voice spoke the truth, and the pale man with the rusty armor named Abaddon was about to kill everyone she ever knew, she had to do something to save them. If the one God needed her to stop the angel of death, there was no other choice for her. She needed to become a different kind of servant.

And Azrael opened her eyes...

The angel's eyes were completely black for the first time. She could see her dead white skin and the glowing purple halo that took form over her head. The halo brought her understanding. She was able to see any presence, living or dead, and open pathways through which God intended each soul to go through.

The Black Angel saw White and Gray, both angels of God, standing in front of her. Gray was a young bald brown skinned thin man. He wore a short gray shepherd robe and sandals. He supported himself with a long wooden staff. He seemed distracted talking to himself in low whispers. White looked divinely radiant, her glow almost blinding Azrael, but she appeared to be irritated and avoided looking directly at the Black Angel.

"It is done, Metatron, another angel of death." White uttered with disdain.

"God's will, Gabriel." Gray replied.

White turned her stare towards the Black Angel.

"Before you come with us, you need to do something about her" she said, pointing her finger somewhere behind the Black Angel.

Azrael turned her head and saw Aziza's spirit. As the older sister opened her mouth to speak, the Black Angel raised her index close to her lips to shush her. She smiled at her for the last time as she took her hand and opened a dark tunnel through the shadows.

It was after midnight when Abaddon placed himself right in the middle of the riot. He used all six of his limbs to pierce through soldiers and citizens alike. To the eyes of those present, a thick fog had descended around them, which was very uncommon in desert surroundings. The civilians thought of it as another sign from the one God. The Jews had to be freed. The riot had turned to a massacre. As bodies dropped on both sides of the conflict, people became more belligerent and killed each other savagely. White and Gray made their way towards the center of the rioters. Gray did his best to ease the humans' raging passions, but the revolt had gone out of control.

"Are you too weak to deal with these people, Gray?" White asked as she struggled to prolong the shortened lifespans of the gravely injured.

"I cannot handle these many angered souls at once." He responded.

White and Gray reached Abaddon and attacked him. As Gray held on to most of Abaddon's arms, White plunged her hands through the pale-green ghost's spectral torso. It began to solidify with living flesh forming around White's fingers.

"Live" White declared, looking at Abaddon in the eyes.

The death angel screamed. Abaddon snapped free from Gray's grip and slapped both angels away from him. The newly formed flesh inside him began to rot becoming a black clot of putrefying skin.

"If you do not yield, Abaddon, Michael will make you." White declared as she tried to stand back up.

"Let her come…" Abaddon whispered.

Abaddon stepped closer to White. He wrapped his long boney fingers around her neck.

"You have always been afraid of me." The death angel said. "As you can give life to me, I can bring death to you."

"It... is not.. God's will" White managed to speak.

Gray jumped on top of Abaddon's back, pulling to loosen up the arm that held White's neck. The death angel let go of White and used four of his arms to hold Gray's limbs and lift him from the ground.

"I am... tired of you!" The pale angel shrieked.

Abaddon spread his wings and carried Gray up in the air. He used his two free arms to hold his head and make him face the angel of death's eyes. Gray stared at Abaddon with sadness as he felt his body slowly solidifying to salt. The messenger angel used his final moments to mumble a prayer.

"Pray if you must" Abbadon growled. "Where you are going, no one will listen."

As soon as Gray froze completely into salt, the angel of death let go of his stiff corpse.

"Metatron!" White screamed as she watched Gray impact the ground and crumble into millions of grains.

She was still lying on the ground, when Abaddon swiftly landed with his legs arching over her body. He grabbed her by her robe and pulled her closer to him.

"You tell me, angel of life, if what I did to Metatron was not God's will." He said with a raspy voice.

Just as White opened her mouth in shock for what she'd witnessed, Abaddon retreated and let go of White. He was in pain. He felt something pushing out from his dead chest meat. The death angel held the rotten lump of skin tight with his six arms. He wailed in agony, no longer able to hold the throb. As he opened his arms, the Black Angel pushed her way out of Abaddon's rotten skin. She had opened a tunnel through his chest. The pale ghost grabbed Azrael by the back of her neck and slammed her against the dirt. The Black Angel struggled to get up, but Abaddon's rusty metallic boot pressed on her back, pushing her to the ground.

"You little… shit." Abaddon howled, weakened. "They chose you to replace me... I will make your time as angel of death a short one, I think"

"No" a strong female voice enounced.

A blade cut Abaddon's putrid chest from side to side. Abaddon stepped off the Black Angel and fell to the ground. He felt his chest bleeding black blood. The angel of death looked up behind him and saw Scarlet holding her sword. The red metallic plates on her armor protected her from Abaddon's putrid chest from side to side. Abaddon stepped off the Black Angel and fell to the ground. He felt his chest bleeding black blood. The angel of death looked up behind him and saw Scarlet holding her sword. The red metallic plates on her armor protected her from Abaddon's touch. She approached the six-armed angel and pushed him with her boot to turn him around and have him face her.

"You cannot…kill me" The wounded angel said with a low voice.

"I am not doing badly so far." Scarlet commanded as she pointed her steel at Abaddon's eyes. "Your lust for death has blinded you. You are no longer an angel of death but its shadow. I curse you Abaddon, in the name of God, to remain the rest of your existence in oblivion."

The warrior angel stepped back as ghostly green rusted chains rose from the earth and stabbed the death angel's body repeatedly; encrusting each link in his skin. Abaddon screamed as he slowly dissolved until he became part of the earth.

Black Angel managed to stand up, but she was still in pain. However, any ache she felt faded as she looked up and was astonished by Scarlet's strong presence. Everything about her new sister commanded attention from Azrael; Michael's chromium red armor, her long sword, her deep resolute blue eyes, her tough physique, the confident way she moved. At that moment, only one word crossed her mind as she stared at Scarlet: *Amazing!* This was the angel that the Black Angel would forever strive to emulate.

The warrior angel bent over and looked at the death angel's black eyes with curiosity.

"You are rather short for an angel of death." Scarlet stated, "Nice move with the dark tunnel."

The red angel saw White on the ground and rushed to her aid. She held the angel's arm and pulled her up.

"Sister, I-" Scarlet said.

White pushed Scarlet to the side and ran towards Gray's crumbled salt corpse. The angel of life sobbed for her brother as a blue fire silhouette of him rose from the ashes and quickly faded.

The red angel stared at White for a moment; then, she felt a tug on her boot. The Black Angel stood next to her pointing at the Egyptian rioters. Both angels could see a few goblin demons controlling the viciously revolted. Scarlet tightened the grip on her steel.

"Right." She said in a low tone.

The warrior angel quickly took care of the demons and dispersed the crowds. Black Angel assisted as much as she could; she led the spirits of the deceased away. Shortly after, the sun rose, and Ramses II ordered the release of the Jewish people.

Scarlet returned to White's side.

"He did nothing to stop it…" White said with a numb tone.

"To stare at Abaddon is to stare at death" Scarlet responded, "What could Gray have done?"

"I am not talking about Gray…" White interjected. "We must find another angel to take his ministry."

"Emotions" Scarlet assented. "But being God's emissary while carrying the burden of this ministry is too much for the inexperienced…"

"I will be the voice of God, then" White replied, "until a time when this angel proves capable of doing both tasks."

"Agreed."

White and Scarlet said a prayer for Gray. The Black Angel shyly stood beside them in reverence to the fallen angel.

"He is yours now." White said to Black coldly.

The angel of life wiped her tears and walked away. Scarlet followed, leaving the Black Angel alone next to a lifeless pile of salt.

....

The Four Horsemen had left the Black Angel for dead on the cold sand of the Gobi desert. She woke up a few feet from the caravan family's deceased bodies. She was too emotionally weak to walk. The pale creature's ghostly chain had torn open a wound in her soul. She noticed her hands shaking and couldn't stop the tears of sheer panic and desolation. The angel felt the task of delaying the Four Horsemen of the Apocalypse was impossible. Everything she could do to slow them down, she did, but it made no difference. She made no difference. The horsemen were just too powerful, Abaddon would prevail. He knew all of the Black Angel's tricks, having once been an angel of death himself. There was nothing she could try that he would not predict.

The Black Angel closed her fists until her hands stopped shaking. Panic, isolation, despair; these were the things the four riders wanted her to feel to keep her out of their way. She struggled with her feelings of abandonment, turning her fright into anger and hopelessness to resolve. The angel of death realized that she had made a mistake in fighting the Four Horsemen by herself. Fighting them face to face almost got her killed and if she died, so did the chances of Earth to survive. She needed to try an indirect approach. Azrael knelt and wrote four words on the sand with her index finger: "FAMINE, WAR, PESTILENCE, DEATH." She then stood up and invoked for help.

Through the years, there have been certain spirits whose bond to the affairs of the living have been stronger than the yearning to move on. These few have been called upon by the Black Angel, either as punishment or by need. Their existence is solely connected to the angel of death and therefore, much like their master; they will never see or feel the presence of God.

Opening a dark tunnel, the Black Angel summoned the spirit of a woman named Maria. She looked like a twenty-something Latino woman. Her long curly black hair reached her waist. She wore a stained white apron over a long light blue dress with white closures. Her dirty bare feet slowly dragged as she walked out the tunnel. Maria stood in front of the Black Angel and tilted her head. The red around her eyes showed she had been crying.

VIOLET DESCENDS

"Donde…"

The angel of death pointed at the corpses of the dead children in the caravan. Maria stared with horror and disbelief.

"Mis… hijos…" Maria mumbled repeatedly *"Donde estan mis hijos?"*

She leaned close to the dead bodies and lifted the smallest one, which she held close to her chest for a moment. Maria's spirit blinked in and out of existence sporadically, like a faulty bulb light turning on and off intermittently.

"DONDE ESTAN MIS HIJOS?!" She screamed, her cry mutating into a loud wail.

Maria's features became distorted the more her flickering increased; her eyes and mouth melted and became misshaped, her arms and hands grew long and disproportioned, her legs and feet atrophied, her hair took a life of its own . The ghost's dress tore to rags. She had become a wraith, a phantom known in many folk myths as *La Llorona*, the weeping woman, the restless spirit of a mother that spent her nights searching for her missing children. She turned her attention to the Black Angel.

The angel pointed at the first of the four words written in the sand: "FAMINE". Then, she guided the wraith in the direction the Four Horsemen had gone. La Llorona let out a loud shriek and glided through the air at great speed. Occasionally, she faded out of sight only to reappear farther away from the Black Angel.

The Four Horsemen had reached a small rural town in the outskirts of the mountains and its inhabitants already agonized from the calamities of their mere presence. Pestilence concocted a monstrous disease that gave consciousness to every internal organ in a person, making them function unconnectedly. People were unable to perform basic bodily functions like processing nutrients or even breathing. Those who didn't die were spared by Megaloth as a gift to his comrades. As War and Famine set out to dispose of the survivors, the riders heard a loud screech from a distance that caught their attention. La Llorona appeared from nowhere and flew hastily towards Famine. As she reached the horseman's face, she dug open his mouth and forced herself inside, making her way through his throat. The Nameless horseman choked, lost balance, and fell. Famine struggled to pull La Llorona's torn dress and legs from out of his mouth, but her body stretched and distorted even more.

The other Horsemen stared at Famine being attacked by the phantom mother. As War raised his chains to fight, Death signaled him to back off with his look.

"Be ready for Azrael…" Abaddon said.

A loud bang was heard. Gothaku felt pain and observed his forearm. He was dumbfounded to see a gunshot wound. Another shot was heard. The red horseman's shoulder exploded. The robust creature saw a dead man riding a lifeless, decomposing horse straight at him. The horse's rotted ribs were opened under its torso and a dead human hand hung from in between them.

The man riding the perished horse looked like a reanimated corpse. What was left of his dried skin was rotted, showing bits of his brownish bare bones. His empty eye sockets glowed red. He wore a decayed old western coffee colored cowboy suit that was covered in dust from the tip of his hat to the bottom of his leather boots. The star shaped badge on the side of his chest was all but concealed within his tattered coat. In life, his name was Murphy "Powder" Cain, and he was once a sheriff. Raised by the Black Angel, he had read one of the four words in the sand: WAR. The dead man stopped his horse several feet away from the Four Horsemen. He took out a second gun from his holster and pointed them at the riders.

"Evenin' fellers." Sheriff Murphy Cain said "Muh'fraid yah'all need to turn back where yah came from."

"War is inevitable!" War said enraged, wiping the blood from his gushing shoulder wound "War is finality!"

"Figgered yah'd say som' like that" the sheriff responded "Kee-yah!"

Both the undead cowboy and the red horseman galloped towards each other. War moved sluggish, slowed by his heavy restraints. He spun one of his chains in the air and hurled it towards the sheriff. The cowboy's horse moved around the chains. It quickly stepped off a dry tree trunk lying on the ground and jumped at Gothaku as the sheriff opened fire on War with both guns.

Meanwhile, Abaddon witnessed as Pestilence burst into flames. A young woman dressed in a 1600's Puritan black garment behind her and cast a spell on the white horseman. There was a metal scold bridle attached to her head and covering her mouth. Her entire body was lit on fire, but even though she felt the pain of the burn, she did not die.

With a hand gesture, Abaddon released the bridle and it fell off her face.

"Who are you?" Abaddon asked.

"My name is Fatima, sir." said the Puritan witch, "I have no quarrel with you, Horsemen, but my mistress made me read Pestilence's name in the sand. I cannot rest until he is vanquished."

"Aaaaargh!" Pestilence screamed "A bitch of a witch you are!"

"I have always found that the best way to deal with pestilence ridden bodies is to scorch them." Fatima replied with a grin.

Pestilence shook as much as he could to turn off the flames from his body. However, the more he moved, the bigger the flames grew. He turned towards Fatima.

"You may hurt me" Megaloth said. "But others much powerful than you have failed to slay me. I on the other hand…" he paused as he rasped his throat and spat on Fatima's face.

Pestilence's saliva hit the upper right side of Fatima's face. It quickly became a harsh yellow acid that sprouted worms. The maggots ate through the burning witch's face and skull.

"If that were only so." Fatima replied, wiping the acid spit from her face and boiling the worms with her fire. "I am immortal. I have been punished by my mistress to burn forever."

"Your mistress, where is she?" asked Abaddon.

"If I tell you, will you free me from my curse?" Fatima asked.

"It would not hurt your chances, I think." The pale rider responded.

"And will you make her suffer?"

"That I guarantee"

Fatima pointed with her index towards the horizon. It took a few seconds for the horseman of death to adjust his vision. He saw the Black

Angel standing still over a dune a hundred miles away, Her head was lowered, but her eyes looked straight ahead of her. She seemed to be in a trance.

"Ah, there you are." Abaddon said.

"She is summoning an agent to defeat you" Fatima continued.

"I see… Who could you send, little Eshe?" Abaddon laughed. "Who could you send that I cannot easily discard? You waste your time, I think."

Hundreds of miles away, Black Angel hesitated. She was angry at herself for what she was about to do. If Abaddon could predict everything she could do, then she had to do what no angel of death had done before. She doubted that what she was about to do could even be accomplished and it would take all of her strength to make it happen. She combined her power with ancient beckoning rituals only used by human mystics. It was an enchantment, and it required for the Black Angel to speak a name. With much effort, the angel of death struggled to pronounce it.

"…" she tried once,

"…Mh" she tried again as drops of black blood streamed out of her mouth.

The Black Angel became frustrated. She collected the blood from her lips and used it to write a word in the sand: "MICHAEL"

An excruciating scream was heard throughout Heaven. It was a rupturing; a tearing of what had once been an eternal and perfect union. It echoed on Earth, where most thought of it as the sound of loud thunder, or more like the shriek of a falling meteor. It echoed in Hell, where demons cringed and hid as best they could, because they recognized and feared the voice they heard. The Black Angel had summoned Scarlet, the warrior angel. She was not summoned through a dark tunnel, but pulled from Heaven, fallen, as Lucifer once did.

Scarlet's descent to the desert caused a loud bang sound and left a crater the size of a football field around her. She stood up, feeling the confusion and desperation of a child being born to the world. However, she was not being born; she was brought back from the dead. Scarlet's soul was ripped from eternal bliss, forever disconnected from God. Her armor was no longer ruby red, but pale rust red. Her face and hands showed cracks similar to a broken porcelain doll. The blue fire of the soul inside her turned bright red and escaped through the cracks on her skin.

The warrior angel breathed heavily. She could not stop looking at her hands and the monstrosity she had become; an undead angel. She turned her attention to Azrael.

"What... have you... done..."

Scarlet could not complete her question. The cracks on her face grew as she spoke. She touched her face and felt crystalized pieces of herself fall on her palm. Panic overcame her. The Black Angel pointed at the last of the four words in the sand, but Scarlet ignored it. The red angel stumbled towards the dead copses from the caravan and tore open the leg skin of one of the men's legs. She pulled out a bone from the leg and it made a crunching noise. Scarlet blew some of her inner red fire through her mouth into the bone. The bone altered into a massive sword. It was a blade forged from bone and red fire, and the undead angel was determined to use it on her new enemy, the Black Angel.

"Not... my.. mas-ter" She mumbled as the cracks on her face extended.

Scarlet hauled towards Black Angel and swung her sword at her. The angel of death raised her hand, her palm facing Scarlet. The undead angel's arm remained still, unable to finish her strike. Black Angel once again guided Scarlet towards the last of the four words; DEATH. The red angel was now bound to the word and knew she could not find peace until the horseman of death was destroyed.

Scarlet took some steps back from Black Angel. She spread her wings, which had turned black. As the wings fluttered, pieces of them crumbled to ash.

"Back... for you... Azra...el" Scarlet said to the Black Angel before she took off into the night.

As the Four Horsemen battled the servants of the Black Angel, Abbadon stared at Azrael a hundred miles away. He had witnessed the return of Scarlet and was no longer laughing.Scarlet flew down from the sky at great speed.

"Michael..." Abaddon uttered with fear in his voice.

She cut one of Abaddon's six arms and kicked his torso, tumbling him to the ground. Abaddon screeched. The red angel raised her sword again, and struck him. Then again, and again, and again. Scarlet attacked Abaddon with savage impulse and would not relent. He tried to defend himself, but could not stop her vicious blows.

The pale rider looked at the other Horsemen at his side. He saw Famine finally pulling La Llorona out of his trachea, ripping the wraith's shoulder off in the process. Sheriff Murphy Cain struggled to get free from the grip of War's heavy's chains. Pestilence and Fatima were at each other releasing and countering spells at one another. Abaddon smiled. The tide was already turning. He glanced at Scarlet's eyes and uttered a few words, even though he was not speaking to the undead warrior angel.

"It will only be a matter of time; I think" Abaddon said in his low raspy voice. "These pets of yours will not last long."

Black Angel stared at the small town. She knew her agents could only slow down the Horsemen of the Apocalypse for a short while. Even Scarlet with all her rage would not be able to keep Abaddon down for long. As the angel of death witnessed the battle taking place in that town, she prayed to God and pleaded for forgiveness for what she had done to Scarlet and offered her life to spare humanity from its fate.

Azrael had bought Creation a few hours at most, maybe a day. With Evergreen and Blue defeated, and Goldie nowhere to be found, she thought it was up to her sister Violet to stop White and try to fix whatever mess she had caused. She let the thought sink in: *it was up to Violet to save the world.*

The Black Angel shuddered and bent down to write in the sand:

"WE ARE DOOMED."

15 OH, HELL NO!

Scarlet, keeper of the light of freedom, I pray to you. Last night I thought I heard you scream in agony, but that could never be, as I know you now sit at the side of the Lord. And though I still wish you had stayed to shelter me, I know you deserve your gracious fate. Every breath you took in life, every drop of sweat and blood you spilled, you did to protect us all. There was never a greater believer or a fiercer warrior in Heaven. That is why I ask you now, my teacher, my sister, give me the courage and strength I will need to walk into the silver tower of tears. For if I falter, I fear not for myself, but for my jailor's soul as I drag her deeper into the chaos I have created. I am her prisoner as much as she is mine.

Ok, it was after midnight and it was pretty dark and we were all on the roof of the RV parked at the side of the road and we were fenced by thousands of demons on a radius extending many miles. At least as far as I could see under the moonlight, the legion of demons stretched to the horizon. I was really impressed with Ruth. She seemed calm for a human that was about to be chewed, digested and pooped by demons. I was scared to my knickers! I mean, they weren't attacking us or anything like that. They just stood there looking at us, waiting. But they're demons! Sooner or later they were going to rape us or something. It's what they do.

And on top of that, it turns out we've been hanging with Adam, the actual first man ever to live... ever. I'm serious. All this time Eve's been using her demons to search for him all over the world and he was road tripping with his beau Steve. But now that Eve had found us, Steve wasn't too happy to know he's been hanging with a married man. It doesn't take a ministry of emotions to tell Steve felt super angry and betrayed by Adam. The silence between Adam and his lover made Ruth and I feel uncomfortable.

"I know we should like, leave you guys to talk things out," I said to them, trying to break the ice, "But we're kind of surrounded by a ginormous army of demons right nooowww?"

"Shut uuuup!" Ruth said embarrassed.

"I'm just saying"

"I swear to you, we've been separated for years. Centuries…" Adam said to Steve.

Steve stepped back away from Adam. The first man grabbed Steve's hand.

"Don't leave, love. Please"

"Where the hell am I going to leave, Hassan? -or Adam or whatever your name is- We're surrounded by these…things!"

As the guys kept trying to work things out, I noticed some movement at an area a few feet away from us, so I pulled Ruth's shoulder pointing at some demons that looked like they were pushing each other.

"Look!" I yelled,

Demons were moving to the side and making space for a crack on the earth to open. The crack widened to a crater as Hellfire and lava burst from it.

A tall skinny demon rose from the fiery chasm and stood among the goblin demons who revered his presence. He only wore tattered rags and kind of moved slow, like an old man.

"I am Beggar, high priest general of Hell's army. Our search for you, first man, is done with. This nonsense can finally be over."

The demon signaled two goblins to grab Adam, but as they climbed to the van, he kicked their heads against each other, cracking their skulls. Both demons dropped dead on the ground.

"Look around!" Beggar shouted at Adam, "I could throw thousands of them at you! My mistress will have you tonight!"

The demon goblins around the van piled up against each other and began to shake and bang on the vehicle. The RV wobbled and tilted slightly on its side. Ruth lost her balance and fell face down on the roof. Of course, me being tied to her, I began to slip too, but I held on to the edge of the van and grabbed Ruth's arm to help her stand back up.

"Oh my Gawd, are you okay?!" I panicked as I held her close to me.

"I'm fine, I just-" she replied. "Stop grabbing me so hard!"

"Are you sure?" I asked.

Ruth ignored me and glanced at Adam. He gave her a reassuring look.

"No more games." Beggar said.

Or at least that's what I thought he said. I couldn't hear him with the huge rumbling sound coming from the ground beneath us. The demons around us backed away from the RV as huge fire geysers exploded all over the place. The fire spread around us. As the desert swallowed the van and us with it, I had a sinking feeling, like literally; like when you're on a roller coaster and it's dropping down?

We sank really fast and the only thing we could see was fire and dirt for a while. I looked up and saw hundreds of the demon goblins crawling after us down the crater walls. Then, we hit the bottom and the land that stopped the fall shook a bit as a loud bang sounded off. There were more demons waiting for us there. The field around us was littered with piles of rubble from old burned down buildings and it was really dusty. No, not dusty. There was black ash everywhere. I quickly remembered how Scarlet used to describe to me the times she would journey to the underworld.

Beggar had moved our RV to Hell!

"OMG! We're in Hell! We're all gonna die here aren't we?!" I cried, holding on to dear life from the girl.

"Are you serious?! We're really in Hell?!" Ruth panicked.

"Wait!" I shushed Ruth, "Did you feel that?"

"What?"

"Despair. I feel despair coming from over there!" I pointed. "No, hold on! It's Hatred! No! Sadness! It's coming from… that side over there! Wait, no- I'm confused!"

"Violet, what are you talking about?"

"I-this place is full of faint emotions. I can feel them one second and then they're gone."

"I like to call them ghost emotions." A female voice declared. Ruth, Steve, Adam and I turned around and saw her. "You must be feeling the last sparks of billions of them before they fade to oblivion. Welcome to the place the human soul comes to die."

A woman holding a sword stood next to Beggar.

"Eve" Adam whispered.

I had never seen Eve in my life. She and Adam were way before my time. She was blonde and very pretty and she wore a sparkly silver laced bodysuit with bare shoulders and a thin silky see-through cloak. The outfit seemed proper for an 80's Disco dancer.

I saw that Eve held Scarlet's sword in her right hand. How could she have it? Did she kill Scarlet? She swung it and pointed it directly at Adam. There was anger and resentment inside her, but she also felt dread and… love for Adam? No, it was much more intense than that. And she appeared to have been crying a lot. Her eye sockets were red and there were tears in her eyes. Beggar kept as close to Eve as possible; his only feeling was fear, which I guess kept him loyal and eager to obey his mistress's commands to the letter.

Another flow of strong emotions overcame me. I could feel a lot of anger and bitterness coming from Adam. It was too much for me, like when you're in a dark room for a while and then someone turns on the switch and you have to cringe your eyes.

Then I realized something.

"Pssst!" I whispered to Ruth, "Hey, that night when we were sleeping in the RV. Those powerful emotions I felt. I thought they came from Steve, but…" I pointed at Adam with my thumb and pouted. "I don't think Adam likes his wife that much…."

"Shhh! Not now!" Ruth murmured, keeping her attention at Eve.

The first man leaned his face close to Steve.

"I'll get you out of this, Steve" Adam told his lover.

"Steve?!" Eve's voice was loud.

"IT'S ADAM AND EVE, NOT ADAM AND STEVE!!!", She hollered; her scary yell echoing for a brief moment..

"You got me, Eve." Adam said, "I'm right where you want me; in Hell. Let him and the girl go and we'll talk this through."

"Get down from that van or he dies. I will not repeat myself again!" She answered.

Adam let go of Steve's hand, climbed down the RV and took a step in Eve's direction.

Under Beggar's command, the demon goblins surrounding us stepped aside to leave a clear path between the van and Eve. Adam walked between the demons and stopped in front of Eve and Beggar. As he stood close to her, the demons closed back their ranks on us.

"Beggar" Eve beckoned, "I need some time alone with my husband. I don't want to be disturbed."

Eve took Adam's hand and they left with a small escort of nine or ten demons through the burnt buildings and over a rocky dune. I lost sight of them as they descended to the other side of it.

The demon Beggar remained silent as he observed us for a bit. He tilted his head curiously like he was studying Steve.

"Humph! Because of you, my mistress has been in tears for decades. Under her rule, she derailed us from our war against Heaven and made us search for your lover at all corners of Creation." Beggar spoke to Steve. "Now that she has what she wants, you are inconsequential. You can die now and your friends with you."

"You won't get away with this, you rat bastard!" I yelled.

I pretended not to notice Ruth looking at me funny. I think she was embarrassed.

The demon goblins resumed the violent shaking of the RV. Ruth, Steve, and I held on to the roof's edge until the vehicle fell on its side. As we stood up from the ground, I placed myself between the humans and the demons closing in. I was about to take on an entire demon horde on my own.

"Stay behind me! I'll uh-I'll fight them off and stuff!" I said to my friends.

"You already tried this back at the park. Let's just-" Ruth pleaded.

"Hey, a little faith here, please!"

"Do you even know how to do this?"

I focused and reached out to the group of demons, trying to connect with their feelings of fear. I tried to magnify these feelings in hopes of scaring them away. And it worked for like a second there. The ugly critters stood still, overwhelmed by fear, but, the feeling was fleeting and dissipated quickly as they regained their senses and closed in on me and the humans.

"I don't understand!" I complained, "I swear this used to work when Scarlet was around! I need..."

I suddenly realized what was missing from my days with Scarlet and why I couldn't sway the demons around us or back at the park in Brazil. When it came to demons, I needed more than just altering feelings, I needed to bend their will.

"I need Scarlet's sword..." I declared.

I gave Ruth a dreadful look. Ruth pulled Steve by the shirt and bolted.

"Move it!" My friend screamed.

We all sprinted, but where can you hide from demons if you're in Hell, right? Several demons blocked our way and two of them jumped on top of the tilted RV behind us. Steve tried to fight off one of the demons that had jumped him, but two more goblins grabbed and subdued him easily. The group of demons dragged an unconscious and wounded Steve away. He bled from the chest and arms.

"We bring hisss head to the Queen. She will like it..." One of the goblins said.

Ruth picked up a piece of rubble and hit another demon on its head. The demon turned towards her and grabbed her face with its hand. Her cheeks bled with the demon's claws stabbing though.

"Now, you die firssst, fin nose." The demon hissed.

"Stop it!" I screamed.

I don't know what came over me. I just didn't want to see Ruth hurt and stuff. I jumped on the demon and hit its head repeatedly. I tore out one of the goblin's horns and managed to push it away from Ruth. She was stunned as she stared at me fighting demons. Then I threw a weak lame punch at the demon closest to me. I really didn't know what I was doing. The goblin laughed and pushed me to the ground with one slap.

"Pluck the little shit" said one of the demons. "Every lasssst feather…"

Three demons squatted around me and pierced my torso and limbs with their claws. I screeched and cried in pain.

"No! Violeeet!!" Ruth screamed.

She tried to shove the demons away from me, but they kept clawing at me relentless. One of the demons grabbed Ruth by the hair and slammed her head against the ground. Ruth bled from her forehead and was dizzy, but managed to crawl towards me and hold my hand.

"Ssslit their throatsss" a demon said.

Ruth and I were lying on the ground, bleeding next to each other. I really thought we were going to die. Ruth was dragged into this nightmare that I caused and I cursed myself for it. And she was going to die and it was going to hurt a lot before she did. I prayed a little and mumbled a lot because I was crying hard and sometimes when you cry hard, you can't even understand the words you try to say. Then you feel a little stupid and you laugh a little, which comes out awkward because people take that in a bad way.

"Tell me you are not laughing, you ass!" Ruth asked angrily.

See?

It was then when I wiped the blood from my face and opened my eyes wide to look up at the dark skies. Hell's firmaments were black with some stormy gray clouds flashing with lightning. I felt someone descending…

and I felt relieved.

"Ruth… I can feel her…" I uttered.

"Who?"

"I can feel her… She's coming for me…"

. . . .

The Nevada desert sun burned bright the previous afternoon. Adam was about to step out from the gas station mini-market where Ruth was attacked by Monica just a few moments before. He was the only one left there from the group after they had all gone back to the RV. The first man heard Monica speak to him.

"The time for revelations is at hand" Monica said with a sweet melodic voice.

He stopped in front of the door and turned around to face her.

"You need to stop that shit. Possession just looks creepy on you." He said to her.

"I apologize if I've upset you." Monica responded "This is the only way I can reach you without revealing my presence to Violet"

"But how the Hell did she find me, anyway?"

"That I do not know."

"Doesn't matter. What do you want?"

"Eve grows impatient."

"She can wait. Keep her busy"

"Adam, it is time"

"I'm not ready. I need more time."

"Adam-"

"Don't you dare tell her where I am!"

"I know you fear for your lover, but sooner or later, she will know. Better now that she does not suspect of him, than if she finds out for herself. And believe me, she will find out."

Adam clenched his fist.

"If she gets to him-" He voiced.

"Not if you know she's coming. Not if you plan ahead..." Monica interrupted.

Adam stood silent pondering Monica's words.

"Get it over with, then. You bring her to me tonight. Midnight. I don't want to be bothered until then."

"As you wish..."

"And promise me- promise that no matter what happens, you will look after him."

"It will be done."

Adam turned away from Monica and opened the door.

"You should do something angelic for once." Adam said as he was about to leave, "Keep that girl from licking off her husband from the floor."

Monica waited for Adam to be gone. She kneeled down next to her husband's ashes and passed her finger through them, raising it to her eye level.

"I am truly sorry for your loss." The melodic voice whispered through Monica's lips.

Suddenly, Monica snapped out of what seemed like a trance and found herself on her knees and staring at her finger covered in ash. Confused, she placed her finger in her mouth and sucked it dry. Then she gathered the rest of the ashes from the floor to eat them.

"I miss you so much..." she whispered to the ashes she couldn't stop from consuming.

. . . .

Hell's skies became brighter than the brightest noon as light from the sky blinded the group of demons that were about to kill Ruth, Steve, and me. The skin of the goblins holding Steve began to burn in flames from the light.

"The light of life burns passionately." A melodic voice echoed from the clouds. It was my sister White.

The other demons let me and Ruth go and ran. We covered our eyes as White descended to Hell. She hovered between Steve and the remaining demons, which scattered away in fear.

"This human is under my protection. If you value your lives, stay away." she said.

I was disappointed because I really thought she had come to save me. I kind of thought I would be important to her, right? But then again, she never spoke that much to me before; I don't know why I thought she'd care about me. Either way, by helping Steve, she saved Ruth and me, so it worked out. White approached Steve and touched his forehead. She murmured a prayer and completely cured his wounds. Then, she led him towards us. My sister bent to heal Ruth's head wound. She turned to me, wiped the blood from my face and held my hand, but she did not heal me.

"Sister, what have they done to you?" White lamented.

"Ouchie…" I mumbled.

"Aren't you going to cure her?!" Ruth asked White desperately.

"I can heal humans with ease." White responded, "But the fate of angels lie solely in the hands of God"

White combed my hair with her fingers. I think maybe that was the first time she was ever nice to me.

"Violet, What are you doing here?" White asked me intrigued. "Tell me how you managed to find Adam"

"It was-" I began to speak.

"Violet, don't." Ruth spoke softly. "It doesn't matter now." She raised her voice to White, "We need to help Violet!"

"We will…" White responded dryly.

The white angel lifted me by the hand and whispered to my ear.

"You will feel less pain now." She said to me.

Ruth placed my arm around her neck to help me walk. White turned to

Steve.

"My light will keep the demons at bay. I can protect all of you. Steven, stay close to me." she ordered.

"I Just- I can't be here. Can take me away from here?" Steve asked. He seemed a little off.

"I am afraid your part is not complete yet." White replied. "Please be patient."

White's light surrounded us as we stayed next to the tilted van. Beggar was mad. He stood as close to the light facing White and he kept yelling orders to kill us. Many demons tried to cross the light, but their skin would light on fire. The imps remained at a close distance watching us.

"We are safe for the moment." White said, "I will not be long until Adam turns the tide."

"Adam?" I asked, "He's the one you're trusting to save us?"

"You can leave and take your chances with the demons." White replied.

"Just stay put Violet." Ruth said to me as she sat on a rock on the ground.

So... What to do to kill a little time in Hell? I took out my ipod and offered Ruth one of the head phones.

"Duncan Blackheart? I've got Putrid Souls, Carved Your Name on My Open Veins, and the one he released after that." I let her know.

"Really?!" she asked, rolling her eyes.

"Well, it's not like we have anything better to do."

"I'm good here watching for demons not to kill me. Thank you."

I blew the hair on my forehead and sat next to Ruth, trying to ignore all those ghostly emotions that were bugging me. I took a look at poor Steve, who remained standing close to White and seemed to be in a trance staring at the demons surrounding us. His fingers moved quickly and he tapped the ground with his right foot. The feelings of immense sadness and betrayal that I got from him let me know he was not okay.

"I gotta... I need to..." He mumbled.

I eased his pain a bit, enough that he could handle it, but not be numb to it. He turned to face me, searching for some angelic wisdom, I guessed. I couldn't come up with anything.

"I'm so sorry." I said.

"Please tell him I'll always love him, but I don't want any part of this. It's just-"

Steve ran off as fast as he could from White's light and through a gap between some demons. He took everyone by surprise including the demons he passed by. He managed to reach a clearing before Beggar gave the order to capture him.

"We got to get him back!" Ruth yelled.

"Agreed" White replied

My sister spread her wings and flew after Steve and the demons that followed him. Problem was, she took her light with her and Ruth and I could not fly!

"Sister, wait!" I yelled. "WAIT!"

White abandoned us and didn't even bother to look back. Beggar turned towards us and ordered a bunch of goblins after us. We ran the opposite way 'cause there was only two demons in our way. I handled them easily by changing their feelings of rage into self-doubt and confusion, but Ruth and I were really scared. We were alone in Hell, followed by a legion of demons and I was limping and holding on to Ruth 'cause I was still hurting. A demon grabbed Ruth's leg, but I kicked him away. We kept running until Ruth turned really red and her breath became heavy. She was doing the best she could, but she couldn't carry herself and much less me, anymore. She stumbled and we both fell, the demons were almost on top of us. We stared at each other.

"I'm suh-sorry" she said panting.

"It's okay. ...I love you." I said to her and I gave her my bravest smile as we were about to die.

"Liar..." Ruth replied showing sadness in her eyes.

Ruth and I closed our eyes and held hands. We could smell the stench of the demons about to reach us, I heard them snarling and slobbering really close to us. And then... Then, a bunch of big ugly dragons attacked the demons.

What?!

They sure looked like dragons to me. Big gray scaly winged fangy clawed things; different shapes and stuff. These creatures came from everywhere. Some crawled from under the ground and swallowed demons standing over them; others flew in and picked up demons like eagles hunting mice. The beasts fiercely overcame the demons in battle, tearing goblin heads off and eating out their chests and stuff.

"Leviathans!" Beggar yelled.

Under Beggar's command, the goblin demons fought back by ganging up in groups of three to five to kill off the beasts one at a time. Two serpent-like creatures with feathered wings attacked the demons that corralled Ruth and I, allowing us get away. I stood up and pulled Ruth by the arm.

"Come on!" I yelled.

"I c-can't" Ruth cried. "I can't"

"What are you talking about?!"

"I can't handle-"

I kneeled down to Ruth's level. I held her face with both my hands.

"Don't give up, please. We'll carry each other. We can do this."

Ruth took a deep breath and stood up. We wrapped our arms around each other with our shoulders close together and did our fastest limping.

The winged snakes followed us, but not to attack us or anything, I guess to make sure we were okay? It seemed that way, 'cause as other demons tried to approach us, the beasts bit them or strangled their necks with their tails. Three goblin demons managed to hold one of the flying snakes while a fourth tore its head off. The other creature lashed at the demons, but was overcome by dozens of other goblins that grabbed and pulled it, ripping its body in different sections.

I felt really sad for the flying snakes, but Ruth and I managed to sneak away from the demons. Up ahead, I saw a bunch of burned ruins with many naked people chained to the rubble.

"Let's hide there!" I told Ruth.

We entered the ruins and got lost quickly in a labyrinth of naked bleeding chained people. They had brown cloth bags on their heads, all of them, and I could feel they'd been suffering for a long time. It was that same desolation, that deep sorrow that I've felt when I've wanted to kill myself. I could relate.

We took a few corners to get deeper into the maze and make sure we'd lost the demons following us. Everything became really quiet, so we stopped for Ruth to rest.

"This place scares me" Ruth said. "Who are all these people?"

"Well, we're in Hell, you know. So..." I answered. "They're broken spirits. These people have all committed suicide and now they're stuck forever with the emotion of that last moment of despair"

"Oh, God..." Ruth said.

She cautiously got close to one of the dammed, a naked skinny young male, and stared at him for a moment. I saw her arm reaching out to his covered face and I grabbed it just in time.

"What do you think you're doing?!" I yelled. "You looking for someone?!"

"I-um..."

"'I-um' No! You just can't peak under their sacks! There's a reason their faces are covered! Jeez!"

"Can't you, um, help them?"

"I bet I could, but I don't know if I should."

"What do you mean?"

"These mortals have been judged, you know. It's God's will?"

"But that's not fair. I think...okay, these people chose to take their own lives... but, to get to that point...to think that the only option is to kill yourself, you gotta, um, you gotta be at a pretty low point. I think what these people really need is help, not to be judged or punished. I mean… then what's the point in believing? if God won't be there to help when you're truly lost?"

"It's like people say: God helps those who help themselves"

"What?"

"God will show you the way, but you gotta be willing to take a step, you know. He can't carry you."

"Is that what they taught you in Cherubim school?"

"You don't need to get sarcastic with me!"

"Sorry. Look, all I'm saying is…um, when you're thinking of killing yourself, you don't feel like… taking any steps. Your mind is not able to make any choices at all. You only reach out for someone, anyone, for help. And these are the people that get condemned to this horrible torture in Hell? Why? What makes them so evil to deserve this?"

"I don't know, Ruth. I understand what you're saying, but… there is a reason why we were all created. I know it's hard, I've been there. Things can sometimes get so awful and stuff, you just want to give up. But to end our own lives, that's very selfish and cowardly. It's not up to us to decide when we die. That's up to God."

"God's a dick."

"What did you say?!"

"Nothing."

"Did you just say God's a dick?! That is so mean! Not to mention blasphemous and stuff!"

"Sorry, but- Violet, you've never SEEN God, before. Have you? You wrote in your book about Him being a God you "feel". What does that mean, exactly?"

"God is everything, You feel him through every loving emotion we get from each other and-"

"Be honest, You are the angel of emotions. Have you EVER, felt God?"

"Well, sure yeah, you know, when I pray and stuff-"

"I'm serious"

"Okay, No, but I-"

"No. You're the angel of emotions and you've never felt the presence of God. That makes me feel so much safer!"

"You are so not questioning the existence of God in front of an angel!"

"No... I wouldn't... um, but I'm not sure He pays attention to us."

"Ruth, just because I haven't-"

"Whatever, let's keep moving. We really need to find Steve and Adam and get back home."

I wanted to hit her head with a brick so hard, but she was right. We had to find a way out of Hell and that conversation wasn't going anywhere anyway. That kind of discussion never does.

"Eve took Adam that way" I said as I pointed towards a huge silver tower in the horizon. "Maybe we should check that place out."

"Man, It's so... far away." Ruth commented.

"I know" I replied as I pulled her by the arm "but if we keep going through the naked people maze, I think we'll be safe."

"Right... I hope Steve is okay."

"White will find him."

"I don't trust her."

"Yeah, but for some reason she seemed eager to protect him, so I guess we could trust her to do that."

"If we get to Adam, he could find Steve."

"I guess."

It took us about an entire day walking, but Ruth and I had finally made it through the creepy naked people labyrinth. As we neared the gates of the silver citadel, we heard the loud noises of a battle between demons and leviathans. We stayed at a safe distance from the fight and hid behind a burnt wall erected near the rubble of an old destroyed building. I stood by the side of the wall and took a peek. Lucifer's citadel- I mean, Eve's citadel stood at the end of a long valley passage way where goblins and beasts were going at each other. It was a very fraught space in the valley within a cracked black coal-like rocky mountain.

Debris from the place falling all around us as a huge scaly black multi-headed Hydra the size of a skyscraper kept slamming on it. We could hear the loud thumping sound it made every time it pushed the tower with its massive body, trying to knock it down.

A jizzillion demons and leviathans brawled in front of the entrance like a scene out of a Tolkien novel. They looked like when you step on an anthill and all the ants run around crazy aimlessly for a while. There were corpses everywhere. We kept staring at the demon hordes fighting leviathans for a while, with no idea what to do. It was scary and disgusting to see these uglies rip each other to pieces.

"You mean to tell me we need to get in there with that dragon tearing the whole thing down?!" I asked. "This place is not gonna be standing for long!"

"I know, but... we have to get to Adam!" Ruth insisted.

"Are you still crushing on Adam?!"

"Um..."

"He's like your great great great great great great great great great-"

"I get it..."

"Great great great great great great great great grandfather!"

"Shut up!"

"You are so gross. Anyway, couldn't we just wait until they stop fighting?" I suggested,

"Really? Like these monsters are simply going to stop killing each other!" Ruth snapped at me.

"Well, let me know when you find a way in without getting us killed." I said, as I opened my purple book and penned a few ideas.

"Um...You should put that book away." Ruth spoke to me, staring at the silver tower close in front of us. "Not. A time. To write!"

"I wasn't writiiiing." I replied. "Just scribbling a few thoughs I don't want to slip away."

"Just… let's just do this already."

"Well… we could kill a demon and bathe ourselves in its blood so the others will think we're one of them, you know, from the smell"

"That's zombies, Violet…Also, ew!"

We sprinted towards the gates. They'd been forced open as a whole wave of monsters had pushed against each other through them. It was still a problem getting into the silver tower as the main entrance was guarded by demons. We had to circle around it to see if we could find another way to get in. Ruth turned my attention to the carcass of a weird beaked gray scabbed dragon a few feet away from us. It was the size of a horse and had chicken-like legs and wings instead of arms.

"Look at that one!" She whispered wide-eyed.

"That's a weird looking chicken dragon" I said.

"It's not a chicken dragon. Um… It's a wyvern" Ruth corrected me,

"A what?"

"It's like a dragon, but smaller and it only has two legs."

I gave Ruth a skeptic glance.

"I-um, I read a lot of books…" she said, "Anyway, we could use it as cover to sneak in."

"Like that is gonna work?!"

"I don't know, I think… I want to try it."

"Oh, my God! This is crazy!"

Ruth ignored me as she went down towards the dead chicken dragon. We picked up the heavy carcass and fit both of us underneath it. From time to time, we kept still if we saw anyone or anything coming at us, but the demons were too busy fighting to ever notice. It took some maneuvering, but we slowly moved around the tower. As we kept getting closer to the castle walls, I started to feel uneasy. The place really bugged me out.

Eventually, we followed a few long crack lines on the walls that met at a small orifice at the base by the side of the tower.

"Wait, Ruth!" I said, grabbing her arm, "This place feels weird to me."

"What do you mean?" she asked.

"I-I can't describe it. It's- It just feels wrong to be here. I think this is a really bad place."

"Um… We still have to go in. I'm not turning back."

"I know… Just be careful, is all I'm saying"

At that moment I looked up to the sky as a huge white flash briefly lighted Hell's darkness. I felt like I was in one of those haunted house horror movies when lightning stroke just before the stupid kids got in? Only like, ten million times more. We ditched the dragon chicken carcass and got down on our knees, crawling through the opening into the silver citadel.

．．．．．．．．．．．．．

The journey through the wastelands of Hell was short. The demons that escorted Adam and Eve joined another army that protected Eve's silver palace in Hell. As they entered the gates, Adam whistled a strange tune and his wife remained in awkward silence. They reached the top of the citadel through a dark passageway known only to Eve. The murky hall led to a silver-lined room with a single round window at its ceiling right above Eve's throne. The first man saw blue energy flowing through the oval window down towards the throne. The blue fire lighted the room's silver walls and floor.

"Okay. Now what?" He asked Eve indifferently.

"This is our throne. I'll have one made for you, of course, but we can rule over Earth from here."

Eve stepped closer to Adam and hugged him hard as she let her cries out. Adam stood still. He looked annoyed. He patted her back condescendingly.

"Right, so…" Adam mumbled.

Eve stepped back and stared at Adam's eyes with hurtful

disappointment.

"Of all the thoughts I had of you with other women, I never imagined-" Eve told Adam.

"You don't get to talk about him. This is between you and me. Will you let them go now, please?" he asked her.

"There's still time. Do you think-? Maybe we could start over. I can make you… love me again"

"You can't."

"Why? Is it because of him?"

"You can't make me love you again because that implies that I'd loved you before. I never did."

"Don't say that. I felt your love-"

"You felt me lusting for you, nothing more."

"There was a time before all this, before your war against Lucifer, before you ran out on me; when we built the world together. We were happy. Can't you see?! Earth is ours! God doesn't rule there! We do! Why do you think He never answered your prayers? Wherever He is, it's not there."

"God abandoned me before we even left Eden," Adam replied with bitterness, "but I was never happy with you. To be with you always felt wrong in my heart. Now I know why. I was trapped within your lie. You took me away from Eden."

"Who cares about some damned garden?! I gave you the world! We have travelled to many amazing undiscovered places- magical places! - and you want to go back to that stupid shitty piece of overrated lawn?! Humankind is our legacy! They are my gift to you! You can have as many sons and daughters as you want! And we can rule over them together! Just come back to me!"

Adam smiled condescendingly and returned to his whistling. Eve tried to compose herself.

"Why are you acting as if you have a choice?" She asked. "You know I won't let you leave me."

"Take a look outside" He told her.

The first man made a long whistle sound. Eve felt a tremor as outside the citadel the ground beneath the demons shook. Eve ran towards one of the silver walls of the throne room. The silver became liquid and receded, leaving a glass with a view of the area outside the palace gates. The Queen gasped as she saw many holes cracking open on the lands and demon goblins slipping and falling into the craters. Adam stood beside her as they witnessed huge monsters that surged from the ground, clawing their way up the holes, and dismembering demons that got in their way. The reptilian-like creatures with gray scales resembled the physique of dragons, basilisk, wyverns, and other distorted beasts of myth.

"Leviathans!" She yelled. "You're controlling them!"

"We have an understanding." Adam said to the Queen.

"You're the traveller?!" Eve queried, "You're the one from the stories, the one who tamed the leviathans?"

"I stumbled into a dragon in England back in the eleventh century. I got curious. Turns out I could break them as much as any beast of Earth. Let's not sweat the details. What I need you to understand is that I have an army of my own and you need to surrender Hell to me before the hydra outside topples this place. That's the one with the seven heads in case you didn't know."

"I will have your boyfriend and those girls killed!" She said.

"That won't happen either. I ordered my leviathans to protect them. And just as a safeguard, I left Steve in good hands."

"White? You are working with the angel White?! That double-crossing winged whore!"

"Good. You're catching on."

Adam grabbed Eve by both arms and squeezed them hard.

"Now let me show you a tune I wrote just for you."

Adam pressed his cheek against Eve's and hummed an odd sound to her ear. Eve felt a sharp pain on her abdomen and pushed Adam away. She began to cough hard and spit drops of blood.

"What did you do to me?!" she yelled.

"My friends come in many sizes. Back at that island, when I realized you betrayed me, I sent you a present. A fruit basket. I really hoped you'd eat one of the fruits. Just a bite would be enough. You took in hundreds, probably thousands of Leviathan eggs that leached into your stomach all these years. I just told them to hatch."

"Gahck- urrgh!" Eve grunted as she held her stomach and began to sweat profusely.

"You can't begin to imagine how long I have wanted to end you, Eve" Adam said with joyful relief. "How patient I've been, how much planning I put into this moment. You know, me looking into your eyes as your life slips away."

"Please…" Eve barely spoke.

"Hell belongs to me now." Adam said coldly. "One throne is enough for me. You can stay over there by my feet."

The pain forced Eve to bend on her knees. Adam looked down at Eve with contempt as he sat on the throne.

"You've lived long enough. This is for Lillith and our child you killed."

"Wait! She's not-gah-she's not dead! P-please don't kill me! Please!"

"Stop lying!"

"I swear! Lillith's alive! –gah!- It was Lucifer! He kept her alive all these years! I saw her! I saw her!"

"Where is she?" Adam asked astounded.

"I will bring her to you…"

16 GIRL MEETS WORLD

Lillith found a cavern near the cherry forest of Eden where she decided to stay after her fall out with Adam. Every night, she kept warm without her husband, by sitting close to a small fire she lighted with a few branches. Her back rested against the cavern wall with her legs crossed as she rubbed her small belly with both her hands. Lillith couldn't get past her last encounter with Adam a few weeks back. She felt too embarrassed after he saw her vomiting in the forest. The first woman felt bad for cursing at him, but as confused as she was about the changes in her body, she knew it was his fault that she suffered the aches she felt in her belly. She looked feeble. She bled every once in a while and lost a lot of weight and skin color. It was hard for her to sleep in a comfortable position and she had noticeable bags under her eyes.

"You are going to lose that baby if you do not take care of yourself" the golden snake in the garden said to Lillith.

Lillith turned her eyes to her left and saw the snake curled up next to her, its tail wagging randomly.

"Did I not tell you to go away?" She grumbled.

"It is a free garden" The snake replied. "You know, you used to be such a happy little thing."

"I am sorry. I should not take my discomfort on you. This- what is happening to me, I-"

"Yes, I can imagine it can get a bit scary. And I guess things have not been easy for you at all since Eve's arrival to Eden, have they?"

"No."

"Wouldn't you like things to be the way they were before? Between you and Adam, I mean?"

"Yes, very much. But Adam is very happy with her and… I am content if he is happy."

"Your child, once it is born. It will need a father. Does Adam even know of his progeny?"

"I will manage with my child. Somehow I will."

"It doesn't have to be this way. I could help you. I can make her go away. Adam will beg you to be back with him. It will be just the two of you living in Eden forever."

"That is terrible! Eve is my sister! I would never-"

"Oh, do not tell me the thought has not crossed your mind. How much of a 'sister' has she really been to you? All she ever cared for is taking Adam away from you. She is a vine that grows wild around your husband and needs to be weeded out. I could make it happen. In return, I only ask for-"

"My soul? Will you try to barter for my soul yet again?"

"Heh. I guess my fetish precedes my reputation. However, I was thinking of something a little more tangible…"

"You-you want my baby."

"Small nuisance that it is, I am actually doing you a favor. I could help you make all that pain you feel go away."

"Snake, as much as I wish the illness this baby causes me would disappear, I could not give my child away. I trust in God there is a reason all these things are happening to me, and I will do my part in the Lord's plan to raise this new person inside me. It is the path given to me and I will see it through."

"You are a stupid fool to have faith in God."

"And you are a sad evil creature, wasting your time hurting others."

"Your child will be mine."

"You will have to kill me first. There is nothing here for you. No deals for you to make. And I am really sorry, but I have to ask you to leave this place."

"I will see you again." The snake replied livid.

The golden snake slithered away into the darkness of the night. Lillith was left alone in the cold cavern as the fire in front of her began to dim out. The snake's words rang true in her mind. Her child will need a father. Lillith thought that it was her obligation to her baby to make sure Adam was a part of its life. She decided to meet him and let him know of the child. Maybe he could forgive her and let her be his wife again for the sake of their unborn. If Adam did not desire her, she would work on herself to have him want her. She was resolute to do anything in her power to make this happen. Would Eve help? Her blonde sister was so beautiful, she thought. Maybe Eve could help her become more attractive in Adam's eyes.

The next day, Lillith reached the hill where she saw Eve siting on the grass and combing her long perfect hair. She slowly walked towards her and shyly sat down next to her. Eve had not seen her in months, and quickly noticed how sickly and misshapen Lillith's body was.

"What are you doing here? I thought you left us." Eve said coldly. "You look appalling; more than usual, anyway."

"I know I cannot make Adam happy." Lillith said with a broken voice. "You are the better wife."

"I am the only wife."

"What do you mean?"

"The most important duty of a wife is to please her husband. That is something you cannot do."

"I agree…Would you teach me?"

"Teach you? Ha! You think you can please Adam with that scrawny body of yours?"

Lillith stared at the ground ashamed and tried to hold her tears as she made annoying sniffing sounds.

"Ugh! Stop that!" said Eve, "Very well! Come. Let us go to the river. I will teach you there."

Lillith felt so much joy, she couldn't help but hug Eve. Eve was disgusted, but still she took Lillith by the hand. When they reached the river shore, they both saw the dark angel standing in the middle of the stream.

"Do you know that… angel?" Lillith asked.

"Yes, he taught me all I know. Let us practice with him."

"Eve, listen to me! He is evil! We should leave!"

"Shut your mouth. Do not embarrass me in front of him."

Eve led Lillith in the river towards the dark angel. Lillith stopped mid-way.

"No!"

Lillith moved away from Eve and the dark angel and headed back towards the river shore. Eve swiftly caught up to Lillith and wrapped her forearm around Lillith's neck as she pulled her down to the river water. The girl took some water in through her mouth and nostrils. She managed to lift her head momentarily and gasped.

"Sister…please!" She begged Eve.

The blonde woman tightened her grip on the girl and pushed her face down to the water again. Lillith's throat quickly filled with liquid. She struggled to lose herself from Eve's grip. She could see Eve's face through the bubbly water and saw her wide eyed rage. Eve looked back at Lillith's face. The girl was in shock. Then, as Lillith stopped struggling, her face showed expressions of sadness and disappointment until she drowned.

…………..

Deep in the bowels of Hell, the golden anaconda slithered through a dusty fissure of Hell's murky abyss. The crack lead to a small natural cavity with its walls sealed except for several pocket orifices used by leviathans as grounding nests. Only one entrance existed which was the fissure at the center of the chamber's ceiling. Many beasts crawled around to witness the coming of Lucifer, but would not dare to get closer to the powerful dark prince. After reaching the empty chamber at the end of the hole, the snake coughed up Lillith's cold wet naked body on the uneven rocky floor. However, Lucifer noticed that Lillith's body did not touch the ground. It hovered a few inches above it.

"Huh. I supposed I should not be surprised." he uttered as its body grew limbs and took human form.

The dark angel spread his black feathery wings and stiffened them enough to use them to cut pieces of rocks from the walls. He pressed the rocks with his palms and made chains from them. When he was done, he kneeled next to Lillith and tied her to the ground. He then placed his fingers on her chest. Lillith convulsed. She opened her eyes and gasped for air, spitting water in strong coughs.

"You need rest." Lucifer warned. "Hard days lie ahead of you"

"Where am I?" Lillith asked alarmed.

"You are not in Eden anymore" he said. "I found us a very private place that no one may disturb us. I call it home. You may call it Hell."

Lillith wiggled her toes and then shook her body frantically, realizing she was floating. She tried futilely to free herself from the chains.

"What is happening to me?!"

"Bear with me. This is all new to me too." said the dark angel, "I believe your soul is too pure and blessed for you to touch unholy ground."

"My soul?"

"You are free of sin. Evil cannot touch you. That is the theory, at least. Believe me, I shall put it through the test."

"Those things-" She said frightfully, pointing at the leviathans.

"Do not mind them. They will not dare to hurt you-" Lucifer said and turned his attention towards the beasts. He stomped the ground which created a loud sound.

"NOT WHILE I AM HERE!" he hollered.

The creatures scattered back to holes on the ground, walls and ceiling of the cavernous chamber. The angel stared back at Lillith.

"Now, back to the matter at hand." he continued, "You have no idea how much I have gone through to get my hands on this baby."

"My child will never be yours! I trust in God that Adam-"

"Dear Lillith, Adam thinks you dead. I made sure Eve and every angel in Creation believed she murdered you. There is no one coming for you. Not Adam, not God."

"I will pray-"

"You are welcome to try. He will not hear you. He never does. You can trust me on that."

The angel placed his hand on Lillith's abdomen.

"A strong kick. Good. Just a few months more…"

"Why are doing all of this?"

Lucifer stood up and flapped his wings which lifted him up towards the ceiling exit.

"The question should be: why would God allow for me to do all of this?" he remarked.

"Please don't leave me here alone!" Lillith pleaded.

"I will return soon with some food. Make yourself at home, but not too much."

"Please!"

The dark angel ignored Lillith's cries as he exited the chamber.

Lillith struggled to move her head and scanned the room around her. She tried to move to one of the stone walls, stretching her chains as much as she could. However, as she neared the wall, two leviathans peeked out from one of the pocket holes and tried to bite her with their long fangs. Lillith retreated to the opposite corner. She felt a sharp pain in her torso and feared she'd hurt her unborn child.

The pregnant girl held her hands close together and prayed; doing her best to focus, as Adam had taught her. However, after a trying for a while, she could not feel His presence. Her prayers became yelps of despair and her faith slowly ebbed away in tears.

VIOLET DESCENDS

Lucifer pinned Lillith close to the ground trying not to harm the creature inside her huge belly. Some months had passed since her incarceration began. Lillith was paler than usual, and she sweated rivers. So much so, that her arm would sometimes slip from the Devil's grip, but the chains still restrained her to the ground.

"Hold still! This will only take a moment!" He told her.

"Aaaaaaiieee!" she screamed, "Leave me alone! It is my baby! MINE!"

"I will kill this baby if you do not hold still!"

"Aaaaaaargh!" Lillith shouted in pain.

The naked girl managed to slip her wrist free and scratched Lucifer's face with her nails.

"Stupid girl! We will do this the hard way, then!"

The dark angel grew claws from his fingers and used them to carve Lillith's lower abdomen open.

"NYAAAARRRGH!!!" The echoes of Lillith's agonizing scream bounced through every cavity of the caverns.

The Devil pulled out the baby and cut the umbilical cord. The baby in Lucifer's arms let a few whimpers out and then began to cry. The last thing Lillith was able to see was her child's eyes before falling unconscious.

Lillith woke up a few days later. She saw the dark angel staring right at her, his head tilted to the side as he studied her. Lillith was disoriented and it took her time to realize she was not chained anymore. With Lucifer directly in front of her, she could not tell if he was standing or floating over her.

"You look good on my wall." Lucifer smiled.

Lillith glanced down at her torso. A thick rock shaft nailed her body to the stone wall through her abdomen.

"NOOOO!" She screamed in desperation. "PUT ME DOWN!"

"I believe we are done." Lucifer told her, "I recognize these past few months have not been easy for you. But you delivered a very healthy child.

Good job."

"Please! My baby! GIVE ME BACK MY BABY!"

"MY baby is doing fine and sleeping right now, so I would appreciate it if you lowered your voice."

"Please let me go. Please." Lillith cried, broken.

"Now that you are useless to me, I thought of letting you go. I would have killed you if I could, but…I have grown accustomed to your wailing. You liven up the place."

"PLEASE!!!"

"Keep praying. See where it has gotten you this far. Keep being a good girl and maybe one day I will tell you the sex of the kid."

The dark angel flew up towards the hole in the ceiling. He stared at Lillith one last time and winked at her as he was about to exit through the crevice.

"God, please help me…" Lillith uttered with a weak voice.

The trapped girl suffocated. Her mind was racing with a million thoughts about her child, of Adam, and of herself. She kept trying to pull the shaft off from her belly until her palms bled.

"GOD, HELP MEEEEE!" She yelled.

No one replied for many centuries to come.

Lillith prayed.

Lillith waited.

Lillith sobbed.

Lillith hungered.

Lillith screamed.

Lillith self-pitied.

Lillith suffered.

Until eventually, Lillith snapped.

…………..

"Da dee dee da daaa…" Lillith sang as she stared at the beautiful blue flowers that blossomed in the garden in front of her. A small black squirrel sprinted through the grass trying to fit in its mouth any little thing it found and spitting out whatever it could not digest. Lillith lost herself in the clear open sky as the sun began to set and the bright live colors that meshed naturally in layers heralded the night on this untouched place. She marveled at the sight of the lake's quiet water that lied beyond at the horizon. The boney girl beamed with happiness at the thought that after millennia trapped in Hell, she had finally returned home. She had returned. And the garden was exactly as the little flashes of her fragmented memory allowed her to remember. She was so close…

"Too bad" Lillith sighed.

Too bad she could only enjoy the world through the hard glass window of the small white room she was locked in. The room was part of a tall gray building with long neon white lighted hallways and many doors that led to small rooms just like hers. There were others like her, other people trapped in that place. She tried talking to them, but gave up after they ignored her or became edgy when they heard her high pitched voice. The man named Doctor called it a hospital, but she knew what it was. It was a prison, just like that chamber in Hell where Lucifer had taken her, but at least they let her see the world a little through the window. At least they let her see the sunset as she sat on a wheelchair wearing a blue patient gown. A male nurse came to her room and had her swallow pills that made her sleepy.

"People of this world-singing feet-" she mumbled in a daze to the nurse as she tried to stay awake, "they do not like to see me naked"

The nurse led Lillith to the bed next to them and helped her lie down. As she fell unconscious, the frail looking patient tried to make sense of everything that happened to her since Scarlet freed her from Lucifer's captivity.

Lillith had followed the warrior angel's instructions; when she reached the desert above the caverns, she hovered west, her feet never touching unholy ground. She looked for a magic waterfall that would take her to another world. When she reached the glowing waterfall, she saw two small goblin demons guarding it. She hid behind a dune and waited, hoping they would eventually go away. When the demons finally left their post, they moved towards her direction. Lillith panicked, not knowing where to hide from the demons. Luckily, a gust of wind blew around from her area; picking up ash quickly and blinding the demons to her position as they covered their eyes. She waited quietly for them to pass by her. The girl's entire body was dirty with layers of desert residue from the wind as she stepped through the portal.

The first thing that the immortal girl noticed was her feet touching the soils of Creation, but she was once again lost in darkness. She had treaded into a subway tunnel, which she thought to be similar to the abyss caverns.

"NO! Not again! – happy little thing –" she yelled in panic , "I will not be trapped again!"

Hoping to find a way out, she walked along the tracks. Her legs were too weak for her to run, so she could not help but drag her feet across the tunnel. She stopped when she saw a rat crawling and tip toed behind until she got close enough to catch. The girl took a voracious bite out of the creature and then another, unable to contain her hunger anymore. This was the first thing she ate since Scarlet freed her from the rock shaft that Lucifer stuck through her stomach. The bits of rat fell out of her open belly.

"I hope this does not mean I will always be hungry."

"Oh, my God!" she heard a male voice shout behind her. "What are you?!"

Lillith turned and saw a man wearing an old brown coat, torn shirt and dirty jeans. He kept looking at her horrified, like she was some sort of monster.

"Many blessings!" Lillith said, after she swallowed the piece of rat meat in her mouth. "Eden. I look for Eden. Can you help?"

The man did not respond to her greeting. He did not understand what she had spoken. To him, Lillith's voice was like a shriek speaking an alien tongue. Coupled with the fact that she was naked, there was a hole that reached through her torso, her entire body was dirtied with black slag, and she held a dead rat she was eating, the man let out a yelp and ran in the opposite direction.

Lillith was confused as she continued to feast on her rat. She kept running until she stopped at the awe inspiring sight of a station platform. It was an open and spacious chamber where Lillith's voice echoed. A few homeless people sat at benches or stood around like zombies waiting for something. Excited to see so many new brothers and sisters she could meet, she climbed up to the platform.

"Can any of you lead me to Eden?" Lillith asked the group.

Everyone present kept their distance from the dirty naked girl with a dead animal in her hand begging them for help, and making jumbled screeches. Lillith watched curiously as some of them walked up the exit stairs and disappeared into the ceiling as other different people walked down from it. The naked girl stood in front of the stairs staring at them for a while. She then took a step, and then another. She remembered how some of her brothers and sisters held on to the handrail and she followed their example. As she kept going up, she stepped on a piece of paper that her foot kept dragging. She reached the end of the stairs and took off the flyer from her foot. She threw it to the side, thinking it may be a kind of weird leaf. If she could read and understand the language, she would realize it was a notice that all subway trains were out of service due to the world wide black out.

On the next level of the station, she saw a wide empty space and more stairs, but this time, sunlight beamed from outside. Her eyes cringed as she walked up the stairs and reached the street. She covered her eyes until they adapted to the light. The girl was astounded at the sight of the tall buildings around her. She wandered around with no direction; her face kept looking up at the curious designs of these sleek concrete mountains. There were a lot of individuals walking around her. She heard many loud voices that mixed with each other like the buzzing of bees. The noises around her confused her. Not looking where she was going, she stumbled into a large man, who pushed her back.

"Watch it!" He yelled as he marched away.

Lillith immediately noticed the violence around her. People argued with each other. Some actually hurt others physically, as they broke things or set them on fire. The dirty skinny girl couldn't understand why everyone was so aggressive; she did not understand that she had walked into a street riot. She just knew something was wrong. The violence reminded her of that day with Eve at the river and she zoned out momentarily until someone clogged her head. The blow dropped her to the ground and blood dripped over her face. Three teenagers gathered around her and kicked her repeatedly. She had offered them the rest of the dead rat she held and repeatedly asked them if she had done something wrong.

Two armed officers came running and tried to arrest the kids, but they ran away. One of the officers kneeled next to Lillith and spoke to her as he looked at the void in her stomach astonished, but she couldn't understand his words. She thought the men would harm her as the teens did, so she threw the rat at the officer and tried to escape both of them. The officers chased the naked girl and finally grabbed her between the two of them, pinning her to the ground. The officers carried her by foot to the nearest hospital.

After the effects of the drugs they gave her were all but gone, Lillith got up from bed and sat next to the window. They had cleaned the ashes away from her body and struggled with her to make her keep the itchy bandages that tightened her stomach and the light blue garment on. Eventually, she relented, thinking of it as a small price to pay for the tasty food they'd bring her daily.

"Any moment now" she thought as she waited for the orderlies that fetched her breakfast.

Lillith heard an increasing uproar outside, followed by screams. The girl moved slowly towards the door and listened through it before opening it. Nurses hurried the patients back to their rooms and instructed them to stay inside. They looked scared and some of the patients seemed nervous. Suddenly, the floor shook. Lillith held on to the door for support. Staff and patients alike panicked as a monster sped through the halls, bouncing off the walls and making deafening roars.

The beast was nothing like Lillith had seen before, and she had seen many differently shaped monstrosities during her time in Hell. Like the leviathans, its body was made out of Hell's ashes, but this one was shapeless, struggling to keep a form as close to human as possible. When it failed to keep a form, the beast's ashes swirled like a moving tornado propelling itself from side to side. Only a decayed brownish skull hovering over the ashes remained consistently solid. As the creature sprung from one wall to another, it left black stains behind it. The monster made loud unintelligible sounds to almost everyone on the floor, but Lillith understood him perfectly.

"LILLITH!" the monster called, "LILLITH!"

Lillith ran across the hall away, as far from the monster as her feeble legs allowed her. However, when the creature pushed one of the patients against the wall and almost asphyxiated him with a shower of cinders, Lillith decided to confront the monster before someone would get hurt on account of her.

"What do you want with me?!" she yelled to get its attention.

The monster let go of the patient and pursued Lillith through the hall and down the emergency stairway. They reached the basement parking level, where she hid and moved between parked cars, hoping to gain some distance from it. She saw the opening of the building and made it outside where she kept running in the middle of the deserted street. The skull and ash beast moved faster. It smacked moving vehicles in its path to the side.

Lillith forced her legs to run faster, but as she turned a corner, her ankle twisted and she fell on a sidewalk. The beast caught up with her, lifting her up in a whirlwind and trapping her within its cyclonic torso. It bounced off the hospital building wall, leaving a black stain behind and propelling itself to the sky.

"Let go of me, you monster!" Lillith yelled, trying to speak over the loud swoosh sound of the spiraling air being.

"Not a monstah" The creature replied.

"Where are you taking me?"

"You need be back ta Hell." the monster said.

"No! I am not going back!-eat spiders-I will not!" Lillith yelled as she struggled to get lose. "Do you know what Lucifer did to me?! He-he stole my baby! He stole my child and pinned me to a wall in a cave!"

"Sorry, ma'am. So sorry"

"-boy or girl, girl or boy- Only Lucifer knows where my baby is!"

"But Lucifer ain't in Hell no moah. Eve is da mistress"

"Eve?! Oh, no!-He loves her, he loves me not- Do you speak the truth?!"

"I does. She da queen of Hell."

"It was her! She killed me! I beg you! Do not take me to her, please!"

"I don' have no choice. She got a hold o' mah soul."

Lillith squirmed to break free from the creature, but she could not get a grip of the ash swirling around her. The girl stretched out her arm trying to cross the black whirlwind, but the rapid moving specks made a small cut in her hand. Desperation overwhelmed the girl as tears rolled down her eyes and a whimper escaped her.

"Please don' cry no more ma'am." the monster pleaded "You gone break mah heart"

Though she remained trapped in the center, Lillith tried to calm down and kept searching for a way out from within the beast's grasp.

"Is…Is Adam with her?" Lillith asked dreading to hear the answer.

"No. He hidin' somewheah" the monster replied, "Mistress been lookin' foah Don Adan decades now."

"I should have told him… I should have let him know…"

"Ma'am. I will pray foah you to see you chil' again"

"Thank you, monster."

"Not a monstah." the minion of Hell responded with echoing growls. "Jus' a slave"

17 UGLY INSIDE

Please stop! I'll do anything you want! Just stop! STOP IT!

Please!

Why are you doing this to me! Stop laughing!

"Ruth! Ruth! I'm right here!"

No more! I can't take this anymore! It hurts so much!

DON'T LAUGH AT ME! I WISH YOU WERE DEAD!

I HATE YOU!

"Ruth!"

LEAVE ME ALONE!

....

"Ruth! Gimme your hand!" I yelled as I stretched my arm, trying to grasp hers.

We were back at the same subway train we were on the day we met. I was only two seats away from her. She was on her fours in the floor at the center of the car. I tried to grab her, but her arms were so sweaty; they slipped my grip every time I got close to her. She'd slip, and then she'd be pulled further away from me. Like there was someone or something dragging her away. It's so hard to describe where we were. We kept shifting places every moment.

"Ruth! I'm right here! Can't you see me?!" I called.

We were in an alley, It was dark, except for a dim light coming from a street post lamp. Walls were dirty and riddled with graffiti. The place smelled awful from the garbage spread all over and I'm sure there was a dead rat lying somewhere. Ruth lied on the pavement, curled up in fetal position. Something really bad happened there.

"Ruth! listen to me!" I pleaded.

We were inside a hallway. A bell rang. Was this a school? Students came and went in a hurry, bumping into each other. The noise was too much. Everybody laughed so loud and some were gossiping-and they all talked about –

"Ruth! Please get up!" I yelled, "Try to fight this! Don't let yourself die!"

I saw her sinking into the concrete floor like it was quicksand. I couldn't move my legs. I thought-I was sinking, too. But I kept reaching out to her,

"I don't know if I can do this!" I cried. "I don't know if I can help you! You need to get up!"

We were in a room. It was a big bedroom with a few bunk beds. I thought maybe it was the orphanage Ruth was raised when she was a kid. Four little girls were sitting on the floor playing with dolls. They ignored Ruth as they laughed with each other. God! Ruth was crying and they ignored her, like she didn't exist! She was almost completely swallowed by the wooden-lined floor. I could only see her face and part of her torso. I stretched my body as far as I could until it hurt, but I was still inches away from reaching her. Ruth sank completely into the ground. The wooden floors and bedroom walls turned into mirrors.

"RUTH!" I shouted.

I was no longer sinking. I stood up and looked around me. I was inside a house of mirrors with distorted images of myself. Ruth stood at my side in some of the reflections. I saw Scarlet next to me in others. White, Abaddon, Azrael, Evergreen, Blue, Goldie, and my Cherubim brethren, they all appeared reflected, too. But, I kept looking to my sides and I was alone in the room. I walked over to one of Ruth's reflections and touched the mirror with my fingertips.

"Can you hear me? Are you okay?" I asked.

I got no answer. Ruth's reflection stood silent looking at me with pity. They all did. I closed my eyes and let myself lean on the mirror in front of me, my forehead resting on the glass as I slid down on my knees.

"I'm really sorry. I'm sorry I couldn't reach you." I cried. "I'm so sorry I failed you."

"Violet, what are you guys doing here?!" A male voice spoke from behind me. It was Adam.

I opened my eyes and all the reflections were gone. Except for Adam's that stood behind me. He carried Ruth's unconscious body.

"Ruth!" I wept as I stood up and touched her hand to know she was really there.

"Is she okay?"

"No, she's not! Do you know what this place is?" Adam shouted at me. "How could you let her come here?!"

"I-we needed to find you-" I managed to respond, still shocked by his attitude.

"Find me for what?! This no place for Ruth to be! This is a soul torture chamber! It makes you relive your most painful memories over and over! What did you think this would do to her?!"

"I-I didn't-"

"You're useless, you know that? You can't even look after her." Adam said as he carefully placed Ruth on the floor.

I didn't say anything. He was right. Adam gently tapped Ruth's face to wake her.

"Hey" he said, "Can you walk?"

"I'm okay..." Ruth mumbled as she struggled to sit up.

I quickly moved over to her and hugged her.

"I thought you were..." I said relieved.

"I'm fine." she replied, "Just-let go of me, please."

"Oh, sorry" I said as I removed my arms from her shoulders.

"No. it's okay. I just need- I need some space to breathe." She said

"I thought we got separated!" I noted.

"You left me."

"But didn't you hear me? I was right there reaching out to you-"

"You were laughing at me! That's what you were doing!" She snapped at me.

"No I didn't! I was so not laughing at you!" I replied. "It's this place! Look what it did to us! It made our fears real! It-"

"I don't want to talk about it, please…"

We both fell in awkward silent for a moment.

"Where's Steve?" Adam inquired.

"He…" Ruth tried to answer, her voice choked, "White went after him, but-"

Adam's face changed. He looked fearful and worried. The first man touched the edge of one of the mirrors and pulled it open like a door with his fingers. There was a huge room behind it. Everything was made out of silver. A silver throne was placed right below an oval window in the ceiling. There was blue fire flowing from the sky through the window and right to the throne. Those were souls, I thought.

Eve knelt at the side of the chair. She was coughing heavily. I thought I saw blood in her hands. Scarlet's sword rested on the seat. For a moment, I thought Eve would try to pick it up, but it was Adam who did.

"Wait. What's going on here?" I asked.

Adam ignored me and grabbed Eve by the arm.

"You're coming with me." He told her coldly.

Adam led us through the same door we came in, but when we went through it we were outside at the front steps of the silver tower. Legions of demon goblins and leviathan monsters were not fighting anymore. The goblins, the dragons, the Hydra, even the demon Beggar were all there. They all stared at us and waited. They stared at Adam.

"Oh, no…" I whispered to Ruth as I realized what was going on. "This is not good."

"What?" she asked.

"Adam, please don't do this!" I begged.

Ruth pulled me aside.

"Violet, be quiet!" she ordered with a lowered voice.

"But this is wrong!"

"He's getting us out of here!"

"That is so NOT what is happening here, Ruth!"

Suddenly, the skies where lighted white and I was so relieved to feel the presence of my sister White, but she came down from the skies carrying a bloodied clawed up body. She laid it at the bottom of the steps and backed away from it.

"Adam" White lamented as she bowed remorsefully before him, "I was too late…"

"No!" Adam yelled.

"Oh my God! Steve!" I yelled.

Ruth let out her tears and placed her hand on Adam's shoulder. The first man went down the steps and held Steve's corpse. Sobbing, he wiped his dead lover's face, trying to clean ash away, and kissed his forehead.

"Good bye, love…" he whispered, "We won't see each other again."

I sensed immense sadness coming from him that quickly turned to that wild anger and resentment I'd recognized before from him. That scared me a lot.

"You couldn't save him either, could you?" He muttered, grinding his teeth.

"I-I have failed you" White declared.

"I am not talking to you." He replied to White.

Adam gently placed Steve's body down. His expression changed to total anger as he stood up and went back up the steps, forcefully pulling Eve next to himself.

"I think most of you already know what's about to happen." Adam yelled out loud to the beasts. "You feel a change in the air. Let's make it official."

The first man pushed Eve forward. She stumbled in the steps, but managed to regain her balance.

"Adam…" Eve uttered, "If you kill me-cough!- you will not know where she is…"

"Go on" he said to her.

"… I yield the throne of Hell-gah-cough!-I yield the throne to Adam."

"Thank you" Adam said, before slowly sliding Scarlet's blade through her back and out her stomach. Then he softly pulled it back.

Eve bled through her torso and mouth as she turned to look at Adam's eyes one last time. Her being immortal and all, any other blade that would struck her wouldn't have killed her , but this was Scarlet's sword. Tears rolled down the Weeping Queen's eyes. I was right with her, feeling what she felt in those last moments of her life. When most people die, they're usually fearful; but Eve, Eve only felt pure uncontrollable love for Adam until her very end.

As Eve's body hit the ground, all the demons bowed down to Adam.

"We await your command, master" Beggar declared.

"Adam!!! What are you doing?!" I yelled desperately.

I turned towards White.

"Sister! You can't let this happen!" I pleaded.

"I stand in service to Adam" White answered.

"WHAT?!" I shouted confused.

Adam stretched out his arm to Ruth. She took his hand.

"You know what I feel right now, don't you?" He asked her.

"Yes." Ruth replied.

"They've taken someone from you, too."

"Yes."

"I can see it in your eyes."

"Ruth, don't listen to him!" I interjected

She didn't even look at me.

"I want you to see, Ruth." Adam went on, "Steve's only sin was to love me and he paid for it with his life. This is what happens to those who put their faith in God. No matter how good you try to be; no matter how... obedient, you struggle to become... See for yourself. You try to build a little paradise. Just try to make the world a better place. See where it gets you. The savages come and do whatever they want. They rape, they steal, they kill, While we... we suffer and we die. This is the world we live in. This is the garden He created for us. To survive, you have to step over your brother. You have to be a complete asshole. You can say that all the evil on Earth is not God's fault; that it is humanity's choice to behave like damned pigs. And that may be true, but isn't it also true that He has done nothing-nothing!-to stop it, even though it's in His power to change things?! Don't you think that's evil? The problem, Ruth, is that while the Creator will not take responsibility for His Creation; while God lets every sin go unpunished in this world, there will never be any hope for the pure of heart. Somebody has to do something about this and if I'm the one to do it, so be it."

Adam took a step forward and raised Scarlet's bloodied steel as he addressed the multitude of demons and beasts.

"My orders are simple. We invade Creation. We destroy it. The Seven Lights are down. Heaven's Archangels have already been defeated. There is no one to stop us; no one but God Himself. And if God does not want to get his hands dirty. I am going to make Him. We are taking everything from Him!"

As the demons roared, Adam turned to Ruth.

"I want you to come with me. You can see the new world I'll build. A world where none of the sons of bitches like Eve or anyone who has ever hurt you will be allowed to exist. You don't have to suffer anymore. I promise you that."

"Don't listen to him, Ruth! He's totally using you!" I interrupted as I ran towards Adam and tried to push him away from Ruth.

"White, control your sister." Adam ordered.

White raised her wings and her light glowed intensely. I became blind for a moment and fell to the ground disoriented. White grabbed me by the hair and pulled me up. She twisted my arm behind my back.

"You're a traitor! I hate you!" I yowled.

"Violet, I knew you were destined to fail when I chose you for your ministry." White revealed, "Now that you have played your part, be silent or I will burn you!"

"Ruth! Can't you see what he's doing?!" I called to my jailor, "He just wants you to keep me under your control! Just let me go. We can stop this!"

"How?"

"… We'll figure something out. I know we can!"

"Well I don't think so, Violet. Really. And even if we could, I-I don't think I want to…" Ruth responded wiping the tears from her eyes. "Adam is right. I'm tired of… hating everyone. I'm tired of always being… so afraid! If he can do a better job than God, then… then I think he should try."

"But that's insane! What he's talking about- that's like, total rebellion against Heaven! Ruth, this is-this is the end of the world! A lot of people are going to die!"

"She's telling the truth" Adam confirmed, "I won't lie to you. It's going to get gruesome. Do you understand the price we're about to pay to make things better?"

"You're not paying jack, you hypocrite!" I yelled at Adam, "It's humanity that gets screwed!"

"…I understand." Ruth answered Adam.

"Ruth!" I yelled in disbelief. "Please!"

Adam turned his attention to the demons and pointed Scarlet's sword at Beggar.

"You, what's your name?" He called.

"Beggar, master" The demon replied.

"Let them know we're leaving. It's time to open the Gates of Hell."

Beggar smiled and raised his fist.

"At last!" Beggar declared, "Earth will fall!"

All the other goblin demons let out a singularly scary inhuman roar. They joined together with the Leviathans as the beasts let them mount them. Adam, Ruth, White, and I stepped up on a big litter made of leviathan bones that a bunch of demons straddled on two dragons. The litter resembled one of those platforms that fat kings would sit on while people carried it from underneath. It had a cedar chair that Adam ordered torn out and thrown away. He'd rather stand while being carried, I guessed. The first man ordered some goblins to place Steve's body on the litter too. White did not let go of me. She stood behind me and made sure to hold her grip on my arms behind my back. Adam and Ruth stood in front with their backs to us.

The Gates of Hell were at the other end of the naked people labyrinth Ruth and I had crossed a day before by foot, but we quickly reached them at the speed that the beasts and demons moved. The Gates themselves were a series of scary skull-shaped stone-made arches the size of tall buildings, all lined up and extending for miles. Underneath each arch there was nothing but air and black dust. I thought maybe we were at the wrong place 'cause they didn't really look like actual gates and they just led to more of Hell's ash deserts extending across them on the other side. But then Beggar gave an order and group of goblin demons stepped away from the legion's ranks. Each one of them stood underneath each arch.

"White" Adam called.

White let go of my arm and whispered to my ear, "Stay" Then she spread her wings and hovered above the gates. She let the light from her halo burn bright and caused each of the demons underneath the gates to light on fire. As the flames consumed the goblin demons, they turned into some kind of red squiggly watery plasma-like energy that spread into the spaces underneath the arches that contained them.

"Burn it all" Adam ordered as he pointed Scarlet's blade at the gates.

Adam gave an order and then he whistled a weird tune that the monsters reacted to. Masses of demons and beasts crossed through the red fires at the Gates of Hell. They were crossing on to Creation. They were invading Earth.

Our litter crossed the fire gates and we were in New York, over Union Square, where I often liked to come to write. It was night time and everything was dark because of the world wide black out. Suddenly, I got hit by a surge of strong emotions from people all over the world. Raw mixed feelings of sadness, fear, happiness, anger flowed through me as every human in Creation reacted to the reality of the end of the world. Adam's demon army attacked people and tore down buildings. I heard screaming sounds mixing with huge banging and roaring and stuff breaking. It got terrifying and confusing. I would have fainted if White wasn't holding me.

"Each one of the gates we crossed leads to a different location on Earth." White said to me with a heavy heart, "All over the world, demons are creating havoc. I can already feel... People are already dying. The final judgment has begun."

"I don't understand you! You're supposed to protect those lives! Why are you doing this?!" I asked.

"Stupid child!" She replied, "Don't you know I feel each and every one of these lives as they go? Don't you know how it tears me apart? But this is how things must be for Adam to take over Creation. Adam has to force God into taking action. Only then will he be able to face Him, and... end Him..."

White did not finish her sentence. I stared at Adam and already knew the rest of it.

"... With Scarlet's sword?" I muttered with a cracked voice.

White nodded.

I became nauseous and a bit dizzy. The idea that this was all going on seemed so unreal to me. None of my siblings were ready to defend the world from our enemies. I made them emotionally weak when I abandoned my ministry. I blamed myself for everything.

I glanced at Ruth and noticed that she briefly looked back at me too, from time to time. She looked a bit scared. I could tell.

"Ruth, don't let them do this." I pleaded with a low voice.

"I trust Adam" She said dryly.

"But why?! He doesn't even know you! He doesn't know what you've been through!"

"And you don't either!" Ruth glanced at me angry.

She struggled so much to look me in the eyes. But she really tried.

"You think you know what I feel?!" she continued, "You think you know me?! Juh-just because we've been together for a few weeks?! You don't even have a clue! My whole life I-I've lived my whole life being ignored or laughed at! People either pitied or mistreated me, like some sort of animal! Like a freak! Making me wish I was dead!!! Do you even know how that feels? To be regarded as less than human? Not knowing what I ever did to deserve being treated like that? Realizing that-that I've always been punished just for being alive... for being born! I don't want to live in this world anymore. Adam is right, Violet. People are cruel. They're bad! I gave them so many chances... Let them die..."

"I don't believe you mean that! This is not you-"

"Shut up! How could you even say this is who I am or not?"

"Because I know you're a really good person-"

"WELL, I'M NOT!" Ruth yelled.

Ruth stepped closer to me and took my hand. She placed it on her chest and cried; her face turned red.

"You don't believe me?! Here! See for yourself!"

"What? Ruth, you don't need to-"

"Go ahead. Look into my heart..."

Ruth pressed my hand deeper into her chest.

"I don't need to do this" I said to her, "I know you're hurting, but-"

"I said go ahead! Do it!"

So I did.

I stared into Ruth's eyes, and saw through her tears. I saw through her skin and into her heart. I opened a purple window and stared at her bare soul.

·············

I don't want to get up... I don't want to go to work... Not today, not ever...

I'm so sick of-of trying so hard... of screwing up again.

There were days back at school... there were days when it felt worse than usual. It was one of those days. I held on to my books hard 'cause I couldn't stop my hands from shaking. Never looked anybody in the eyes... Blocked out their taunting. It was just me, walking through the busy hallways. I could hear them laughing. Making fun of my looks. Calling me names. That's what I hated most.

Ruth. My name is Ruth.

I was the girl the boys didn't mind pushing around as if I were another boy. I was the one they all ganged up to throw snowballs at my face, always aiming for my nose. I had no friends- I never had any friends. I had people like Jodi, who pretended to be my friend to get something from me, or help the other kids embarrass me in front of everyone. I was the one they cornered at school and reached under my skirt...touching me, while I got my school stuff broken. They said I should be thankful, that no guy would ever want to be with me. And I believed them.

Sometimes I tried to fight back. When I couldn't take any more of the abuse, I'd see red. I'd scratch their faces with my nails, or try to bite them, or ram my head into them like I was a goat. They treated me like an animal, I would act like one. It didn't always work.

I met Rob that day after school. He was one of the freshmen; a tall and skinny, with a curly red mop for hair and a thick pair of glasses. I saw three guys push him face down into the school trash bin. I waited until they left and stared at the trash bin for a couple of minutes. He didn't come out. I got worried and walked over to help him out.

"Um... Are you okay?" I asked him as I reached my hand out to him.

Rob didn't take my hand. He got out of the trash container on his own and avoided looking at me, trying to hide his tears from me. I wanted to tell him it was okay, but I froze. I didn't know how to. Then I lost my chance when Rob just took off. I cried for him that night, because I knew how he felt; hopeless… angry.

Every day at school, I would stare at Rob and hoped that he'd stare back at me. I guess he noticed because he eventually smiled back at me. We began to hang together a lot. When we'd see the guys who threw him in the trash bin, we'd run and hide. Rob told me they weren't from school. They just liked to follow him and mess him up some times. So, most of the time, we kept close, mostly at the library, and away from everyone else as much as we could.

I loved to listen to him. He taught me a lot about angels. I shared his excitement. I mean, I've always been a geek, but it was more than that. I felt his passion and I experienced it through him. He made me forget about… me. Every day I wished there was something I were as passionate about as he was about angels. That is what I loved the most about him.

One day he was standing in front of the library with a book in his hands. He seemed happy. He pulled me by the hand and we sat at one of the tables. He opened the book and showed me some pictures on it. It was a book about angels.

"This is the one I was looking for. It finally got here." he said, "I'm going to do a paper on this. You'll see."

I stared at him, glowing as he showed me through the different casts of angels and their missions.

"These here, these seven are the most important ones." He went on, "The Archangels; Gabriel, Michael, Raphael, these three are there in all the versions. And then the other four; Abaddon, Metatron, Jophiel and Zadkiel. Sometimes the names change on the last four, depending on the source, but I think- I think I'm going to do my paper on these seven. This book is referenced a lot by the other ones I have. I think I'm good. The Archangels, also known as the warriors of light, have often been represented by different colors- Um… Is this boring you, Ruth?"

"Oh, no. I think it's- it's great… I – Sometimes I have these dreams…This is um- so weird. I - last night I dreamt an angel came to visit me." I told him.

"Really?! Wow, I'm so jealous!" he beamed.

"She looked so pale and sad. She was crying. When I asked her why, she said: *"You're my whale."*

"*'You're my whale'.*" He repeated, "So weird…"

"I know… It's- it's dumb."

"No, it's not." He said, "It's got to mean something. These dreams always do…"

He paused.

"I need to tell you something." Rob said to me, "Not here, though. Could we meet after school? Can I…Could I walk you home today?"

I stood waiting at the bus stop in front of the school. Some girls passed by and called me names… made fun of me. He never came. It started raining and I walked myself home. I stepped fast, trying not to get wet and as I turned a corner three blocks away, I saw him.

He was coming to see me, but they grabbed him. Those assholes took him to an alley and they pushed him against the trash cans. They tore his shirt. All three of them kicked him around and called him names. They had baseball bats. They used them repeatedly, pounding his head again and again.

I felt his pain, every blow he took, as if every hit was being done to me. I ran towards one of them and tried to pull them away, but he punched my face and knocked me down to a puddle of dirty water. The smell of sewer made me nauseous. I felt my cheekbone bruising up. They kept hitting and laughing at Rob.

"Please! He can't breathe!" I begged. "Why are you doing this to him?! Stop it!"

I tried to get up, but I slipped in the puddle. They laughed and came over to me. And they… They began to hit me… Rob tried to move, but he was too hurt. They kept kicking and beating me. I heard the cracking sound of my glasses being stepped on by one of them. I tried to cover my face but they held my arms and bloodied my face. As I got hit near my ear, I began to see black and all I could hear was a deafening ringing. I closed my eyes, trying to focus, and when I opened them again, I looked up at the guys. I saw three demons crouching over their shoulders. They were demons. They pulled some slimy strings attached to these guys. Every move our abusers made, every word they spoke, they weren't in control. These monsters were, and they were going to kill us.

"Please, leave me alone!" I begged the demons.

"I can't hear you!" one of the guys shouted as he slapped my face.

"LEAVE ME ALONE!!!" I yelled.

They pushed me back to the puddle and I landed face down.

"Please stop!" I screamed, "I'll do anything you want! Just stop! STOP IT!"

The same guy pulled me by the hair and lifted my head.

"If you want us to stop, you have to whack him good." He said, placing his bat in front of me.

"NO!"

"We will kill you. You know we will."

"I WISH YOU WERE DEAD!" I screamed, "I HATE YOU!"

"Choose" One of the demons spoke through the guy he controlled.

Rob looked into my eyes. He saw the fear, the frustration, the anger. He knew I was broken… And he-he just smiled to soothe me. He already knew what I chose to do. My only thought was that I didn't want to die. I stared at him and then I felt so ashamed I had to turn my eyes away from him.

I picked up the bat. I let out a scream and then… I stroke him again and again.

When Rob stopped moving I dropped the bloody bat and I ran. I knew he was dead, I just knew.

It was later at night in my room, that I'd see him again. Rob stood in front of my bed, staring right at me. His skin was translucent. I could see his veins coming through his bruises. His head was bloodied. And his eyes... they looked dead. I called his name a few times but he didn't respond. I stared into his eyes and I saw...

I was in my bed and he was gone. I didn't have a black eye or any bruises anymore. I couldn't sleep that night or for many nights after that. I transferred to another school and stayed away from people as much as I could. I mostly kept to myself. I began to hear voices, see faces, where there were not. But none of them were him. None of them were ever Rob. I never saw him again. I didn't even get to hear what he needed to say to me. And I never got to say how sorry I was. Not a day goes by - God, it's been so long...

My dreams came back, but they were different. I saw buildings crumble and... and people dying. I saw how the world burned. Every single person, everyone who's ever hurt me; everyone died. I witnessed how it all ended and my only thought was "this is happening, this is real". And I was ashamed of myself because... because I knew I should have felt something, anything; but instead, I was numb to all of it. I just didn't care.

I tried, don't get me wrong. I tried telling people about my dreams. I put up a blog. I'd try to talk to folks at the park. No one would listen. People thought of me as crazy. I thought of them as dead. As they frowned at me, I'd turn my gaze away from them. I avoided staring at their dead eyes because I knew that if I did, I'd be dragged into their world, like I was dragged into Rob's, and I just couldn't handle it. I hated them so much for what they did to me and for what they made me do... If people thought of me as an ugly freak, then that is what I'd be, inside and out.

I don't want to get up... I don't want to go to work... Not today, not ever... I don't want to see myself in the mirror. I don't want him to see me. I'm so tired.

I just want it all to end...

18 RISE OF THE CHERUBIM

The great hall of Heaven was overcrowded as all Cherubim were present for an emergency gathering. Buzzing among the floating ivory cloth attired angels echoed through the hanging crystal murals. Their worried whispers quieted down when Amion, senior server and white-haired eldest of the Cherubim, slowly walked up towards the main altar and stood in front of it. His old wings felt heavy as he tried to convey the grave news.

"Brothers and sisters" He began, "The seven seals are broken. The Gates of Hell are open...As I speak, the armies of Hell are moving towards Creation. I am afraid...I am afraid the end of days is here."

Many gasps were heard among the Cherubim. Some of the angels held hands in solidarity. Someone in the crowd exclaimed "Oh, no!"

Fariphel, a thin hazel-eyed librarian raised his hand.

"Surely the Seven Lights will restore the seals and push the demon forces back."

"Praised be the Holy Seven!" Ennadel, the long blond haired chorus leader declared, "We must sing to their glory!"

"Brother Ennadel," Isophie, a curly-haired brunette angel interrupted, "All due respect to your remarkably talented voice, can you not see this is not the time for singing?"

"Isophie is right. We cannot account for the well-being of the Archangels" Amion continued, "Reports are disquieting at best. You all know the fate of the late Scarlet. Torn from the side of God and denied her eternal rest. Poor Michael, she has left a void in her ministry. Demonic possessions are increasing all over the world. The will of the people to fight for their beliefs is broken. Freedom slowly degenerates into slavery of the soul as humanity bends to the whims of Hell.

"On Earth, Jophiel has created some sort of barrier or stronghold to isolate herself from the world. Evergreen is in mourning. And she has let the planet's fauna and flora fall in unnatural disorder. There are snow storms freezing desert areas. Large scale earthquakes and super-storms are shattering entire countries. Oceans have risen, devastating the shores. House pets savagely attack their masters. Plagues spread at an alarming rate not seen since the days of Moses in Egypt. Plant life is growing unbound and scattering, destroying infrastructures everywhere.

"Zadkiel, the blue angel, has left mankind in disarray. All means of communications and transportation are disabled. There is no electrical power to light humanity in these times of darkness. Without Earth's technology to help coordinate and defend it, humans are easy prey for demons. Blue has also secluded himself, only God knows why.

"We also know that with the seals broken, the Four Horsemen have set foot upon the world. The Black Angel, Azrael, is doing everything she can to keep them at bay. But facing the riders by herself has taken a toll on the angel of death. The ministry of death is unattended. There is no one to guide the spirits of the recently departed. They are becoming restless, turning into phantoms, and haunting the living. And if Azrael falters, the Horsemen will ruin all of Creation, with no remorse and no one to stop them.

"And then there is Raphael… We believe she may have killed the Pope."

"God help us!!!" Fariphel interrupted, "The head of the Catholic Church? *That* Pope?"

"To be fair" Amion responded, "Her seal, the ministry of miracles, is the only unbroken of the seals. Because of this, the rules that define the boundaries of Creation, what humans call the laws of physics, are still in effect. Reality holds for now. That means the Archangel has stayed true to the mission. It is very possible this may all be a huge misunderstanding."

"See, brothers and sisters? Praised be the Seven Lights!" Ennadel exclaimed, "No matter how dreadful things may get, their faith in God is unwavering! They are the example we should all be blessed to follow!"

Amion paused. He could not conceal the distressed look on his face. He shook his head. He cleared his throat.

"Ahem...Well... We are not sure what to make of our reports. It seems... for reasons unknown to us, White has... rebelled against the Lord. Gabriel has now joined the legions of Hell."

"Dear God!" Ubim, a four armed harp musician exclaimed. "But she speaks for the Lord! How will we know what to do?"

The news disconcerted all present at the hall. Whispering among the angels morphed into loud undiscerning arguments. Amion needed a few moments to calm down the crowd.

"...What of Uriel?" Isophie asked.

"She remains imprisoned with the human, in penitence for abandoning the ministry of emotions and basically causing everything that I have just described to you." Amion answered.

The angels fell silent for a moment.

"They should have picked Amion." One of them mumbled.

"You asked how we will know what to do." Amion continued. "We must always pray to God for illumination. There is no denying in the power of prayer... But there is also an old human saying that goes: when adrift, pray to the Lord and row for shore... I cannot tell you what to do, but I will tell you what I am going to do. In these dire times I am not about to remain idle and let the forces of darkness extinguish the light of Creation. We are angels. Our form is Cherubim. We are the guardians of Heaven and of Earth. We are the protectors of all that God created and saw as good."

The excitement in Amion's voice increased.

"But never forget our most sacred duty. We are messengers of God. And at this moment, it is clear to me that the message that we must deliver to these servants of evil is this: 'How dare you?! How dare you tarnish that which was perfectly made by God, our Lord and Savior?!'" Amion proclaimed with a harsh voice while stomping his foot on the floor.

"Brothers and sisters, I will tell you what I am going to do. I AM GOING TO FIGHT! I am going to show them that angels are a thing to dread, too! With the Lord on my side I will walk through the valley of the shadow of death and I will fear no evil! I am going to spend every drop of my blood and sweat to drive these demons back to Hell where they belong!"

Amion turned towards behind the altar and picked up a golden warrior helmet from a decorative armor in the back of the hall.

"I will be at Michael's armory. I cannot impose, but those who would join me willingly are very welcomed and have my eternal gratitude." He said, as he put on the helmet and spread his wings to fly out through the huge main doors.

Isophie was shocked by Amion's words. She looked around as the rustling sounds of many wings fluttering became louder echoed in the hall. No word was said, but serious stares permeated the room. These were the determined faces of guardian angels about to take action.

"AMEN!" one angel yelled.

"Amen!" Isophie found herself saying in kneejerk reaction upon hearing the word.

"AMEN!" the Cherubim crowd rumbled repeatedly with their battlecry as they all stormed out from the hall and took flight after Amion.

·············

Adam's army of demons did not waste time making their presence felt on Earth. Demons and leviathans plagued from the smallest towns to the largest cities. Dragons breathed fire to buildings that burned and crumbled. Men and women were being possessed by goblins and forced to commit atrocities against each other. Terror spread as a demonic spell made the skies red and blood rained over humanity. The influence of evil tainted any meager attempt by men to fight back.

Beggar stood atop the rubble in the middle of a ruined New York City street, deeply satisfied with the mayhem he saw around him. At last he'd witnessed Creation's demise, a dream he thought would never come to be under Eve's reign and her sick obsession with finding Adam. But the new master, he did not waste any time or resources. This was a lord the demon priest would truly and gladly pledge himself to. Hell's empire would finally expand beyond the ash deserts of obscurity to storm the Earth and eventually the Gates of Heaven.

Beggar was about to give a new order to his minions when he felt a faint tap in the upper back of his head. He turned around, but there was no one behind him. There was a single small green grape lying on the concrete. The rag clothed demon looked up and saw a flock of armed Cherub angels, numbering in the hundreds of thousands, descending from the skies. The winged beauties wore gold armor and handled short swords and shields.

"Back to Hell, demons!" A delicate high pitched voiced was heard. "Humanity is under the protection of the angels!" It was the voice of Amion, leading the angelic convoy.

Beggar seemed confused. Was this all the opposition that Heaven had sent? Was the war against Creation already won?

"Kill them all" he commanded with a tone of disappointment in his hoarse voice.

The ground trembled and buildings shook as hordes demons collided with the angelic fleet. The Cherubim warriors swung their swords and pushed their shields forward. They trusted their instincts as they braved into the battle zone. In their minds and in their hearts, they knew they had to persevere, because they were the last line of defense against the obliteration of all that is. Faith and prayer was all the strength they needed. God was with them. They were His instruments of peace and no demon goblin could stand against the power of the All Mighty. This was the fire that burned within the Cherubim hearts.

However, there was a great difference between the glory that motivated the angels' spirits and the outcome they expected and the events that actually transpired. What followed was a massacre unlike any described in prophecies. Wings were torn from backs; heads decapitated and mounted on pikes; halos taken as trophies; harps were shoved up angelic behinds; corpses tied and dragged from the tails of roaming dragons. As hard as the Cherubs prayed for God's deliverance, their enemies mopped the streets with their blood even harder. The morbid scene was a mess of severed limbs, bloodied feathers, and crushed fruits spread all over lower Manhattan. All the demons seemed to be enjoying themselves slaughtering the angels, finally letting out centuries of bottled hate against the self-proclaimed guardians of Creation.

Amion's old broken body was half buried face up in the street pavement. He could only move his eyes sideways to scan for any survivors. He heard the soothing sound of Ennadel's singing voice and turned his gaze a few feet away to his left. The angel lied on the ground with broken wings and punctured chest as he chanted a sad melody that made Amion's eyes tear up. Beggar's scaly foot stepped on Ennadel's face, bursting his head like a crushed melon. The demon kept his stride oblivious of the angelic voice he had silenced. His attention was focused on finding Amion. When he did, Beggar stood next to the Cherub and lowered his head to look at him in the eyes.

"Hello, Amion" the demon priest said to the Cherub elder with a hoarse yet cheery voice. "It is really good to see you. How is the fight for salvation working out for you today?"

"Beggar…you… will not… win…" Amion struggled to speak.

"We will not win? Is that what you tell yourself to cover the fact that you just led thousands of angels to their demise? It must have been you. Who else would they have listened to? You must have given one of your famous sermons to rile them up, didn't you?"

"…Our cause… is right…Given… the chance…I would-urgh!- I… would not hesitate to do this… again."

"Yes, you fool. I do not doubt that you would. Make the most of your last few seconds of life. See if your prayers get answered. Farewell."

With those words, Beggar continued his march. Amion was left alone wondering why God had not aided them in battle. If the Cherubim were not fated to save Creation, then who was? The Lord must have a plan, unless, he thought, could it be that there is no plan? Could it be that… there is no God?

"What have I done?" He uttered over and over again until he drew his last breath.

The angel Fariphel was one of the very few survivors that ran for their lives. As an army of demons ambushed the angels, the hazel-eyed angel pushed his brothers towards the goblin demons and bought himself time to run away. Fariphel stretched his leg to trip a fellow angel and stepped on her as he ran to escape, instead of answering her cries for help. But the selfish Cherub did not look back when two goblin demons ate the other angel alive.

Pride of the deadly Seven, still looking sharp with his pristine suit and expensive sunglasses, didn't bother with the torture of angels as he did not take pleasure out of it. He turned his attention instead towards the hazel-eyed Cherub and smiled.

．．．．．．．．．．．．．．

Lillith was disturbed by the appalling sight happening before her eyes. As the slave Jacinto elevated and flew above the demon torn city buildings, he transported her within the dusty ash winds that composed his body. The meek girl cringed as she witnessed the butchering of angels from high above. And with no one to stop the demon army, she had accepted her fate and waited for the slave to take her to the queen in charge of the demons.

"Jacinto – I feel hunger-" she called, "why has Eve released her demons upon the world?"

"I done not know, but…" Jacinto stopped himself. "urrgh!"

He felt dizzy. The ashes that had aligned to form a semblance of a body around his skull began to dissipate. Jacinto was losing himself.

"Done… feel her nooo mooore…Sheee…deaaaad" he slurred.

"Eve is dead?!" Lillith asked, "You are not well? -we nick your finger-"

"Tryyyy…hooold… maaaake… youuuu… saaaafe" He managed to say.

"Jacinto!!!" Lillith screamed.

Her body rapidly fell as she stretched her hands wildly, trying to hold on to something. Jacinto's ash body became a dust cloud that dove into the roof of a building. His skull crushed to pieces against a wall while Lillith fell close to the edge of the roof. The remaining black ash stained the roof floor and covered Lillith almost completely. After a few moments to recuperate, Lillith managed to stand up and limp over to the remains of Jacinto's skull. She picked up one of the cranium pieces and closed her eyes, praying to entrust his soul to God.

Lillith staggered down the pitch-dark stairs of the hundred and twenty-eight level building. The petrifying boom sounds and death screams coming from outside the structure became louder the further down she went. It took her almost six hours to reach the street. When she finally stepped out of the building, her knees gave out as she saw armies of demons piling up hundreds of angel and human corpses on the side of streets. She hid behind one of the cadaver mounds, waiting for the demons to go away. The girl felt her patient robe being tugged. When she looked down she saw a hand reaching out to her from the body pile. The hand jerked fast, like asking for help. Lillith pulled the hand hard a few times, each time revealing more of the body the hand belonged to, until with one final yank, she managed to free a female angel from the dune of bodies. The female angel took a few moments to catch her breath.

"Thank you, human" The curly haired angel spoke. "I am the angel Isophie, form of Cherubim."

"Many blessings!-dusty tap-I am Lillith!" She replied with a friendly smile.

"Lillith?!" the angel yelled alarmed.

Isophie quickly pulled a short sword that was stuck in a dead angel's torso and pointed it at Lillith.

"Spider eater! Demon mistress!" Isophie screamed. "You will not rape me!"

"Shhh! The demons will hear us!" the girl replied. "I do not wish to rape you!-suck your blood-"

"But you are Lillith! You begat with demons! Why else would you be here but to foresee the destruction of humanity?!"

"Why do people say such mean things about me? —eat leviathan dung-I barely escaped from imprisonment in Hell and I see that it has followed me here!"

"You lie" Isophie kept her blade pointed at Lillith.

Isophie looked over Lillith's shoulder and signaled with her finger to shush. She waived the sword to lead Lillith back behind the corpses pile. As they both hid and remained silent, a group of demon goblins scavenged the area and paved the way for something big that was coming. The girl and the angel felt the ground shake a little with the coming of two dragons that buoyed Adam's bone-made litter. When Lillith saw the immense creatures she let out a squeak forcing Isophie to cover her mouth with her free hand.

The goblins ignored the high-pitched sound as they kept pushing bodies out of the way.

"Hurry! Make way for the massster!" one yelled, "He isss coming!"

Lillith saw Adam on the litter. She had not seen him since during the days of her pregnancy at the Garden. He seemed thinner with a couple of wrinkles under his eyes, but other than that, he was as handsome as ever. The angel White stood at his side. She looked distressed and it was clear she had been crying.

"It is true what Amion said" Isophie sadly confirmed. "Gabriel has betrayed us…"

There was another weak looking purple angel and a young woman that Lillith didn't recognize. They sat behind Adam, facing each other in some sort of trance as the angel pressed her hand on the big nosed girl's chest.

"I do not recognize those two -Devil kept my baby-"

"That is Uriel, Archangel of emotions." Isophie whispered, "That girl must be her living prison. I cannot tell if they are rebelling too."

Lillith and Isophie witnessed as Violet suddenly pushed Ruth off the litter. She then pulled Ruth by the arm as they both ran out of site through some alleys.

"Bring them back, White" Adam ordered. "I don't want Ruth hurt, but we can't have her freeing Violet from her control."

White flew low after Violet and Ruth, leaving Adam alone on the litter.

Lillith stood away from the hide out and took a step.

"I must speak to Adam!-belly hole-I have to make him stop!"

"Wait!" Isophie warned as she grabbed Lillith's shoulder and pointed at the opposite direction of Adam's litter. Six of the Seven Deadly demons marched straight towards Adam. Pride, Gluttony, Wrath, Sloth and Lust were there. Greed was not present. Envy marched with them, but he was not the same demon that was trapped in an iguana. Lucifer had killed him before dropping Ruth and Violet in Nevada. This new demon wore a blood stained white tunic. He had a dirty face and red eyes. His wings withered to black ash as two small horns grew from his head and through a cracked and luminous red lighted halo. He took slow steps and wobbled having hooves for feet.

"I believe it is time the Deadly Seven, Arch-demons of Hell, were introduced to our new ruler" The demon Pride demanded.

"I agree." Adam spoke.

The present six of the Deadly Seven Arch-demons encountered Adam's transport their attention to the leviathans that carried the litter that Adam, White, Ruth and I were on.

"Adam? The first man?" Pride asked, "Under what rock did your wife finally find you? By the look of things, it seems she has paid the price for it."

"You could say that she has." Adam replied, "I see only six of you. Don't the infamous Deadly Seven know how to count?"

"We are... short staffed for the moment." Pride muttered annoyed. "But on to business... We are here to pledge ourselves to you."

As he said those words, the six Arch-demons kneeled and bowed their heads. Pride made sure to pull Envy's head down.

"Asmodeus, Lord of Lust." Pride announced, "Lethanus, Lord of Envy, Beelzebub, Lord of Gluttony, Amon, Lady Wrath, Belphegor, Lord of Sloth, and I, Mephistopheles, Lord of Pride, bow to serve you... master."

"Mephistopheles..." Adam repeated, "I'm not sure that's who you really are, Pride."

"Either way, what is in a name, when I have sworn myself to you?"

Adam paused.

"Fair enough, I guess." the First Man went on, "I need you to spread and lead my demons all over the world. Be as loud and messy as you can."

"It is what we do" Pride boasted.

Adam nodded and the beasts that carried the bone-made litter moved away from the Arch-demons.

"He seems to be a man with a plan, don't you think?" Pride uttered.

"ENOUGH TALK!" Wrath yelled,

"Agreed." Pride replied, "We have a world to kill... And can someone please find Greed for me?"

After the Deadly Seven left Adam, Lillith pulled her arm off Isophie's grasp.

"I must speak to Adam now." She said, with her eyes already fixed on the first man.

"No tricks or I will cut your head off."

"I will stop him - leggy shadows- He will listen to me!"

Lillith sprinted before finishing her response to Isophie. She crossed the street and shouted Adam's name a couple of times. She got captured and thrown face down to the street by two demons that were about to slice her neck.

"Wait! Don't kill her. Bring her here." Adam ordered the demons.

The first man still recognized the voice of his first wife after all these centuries. But she looked sickly and even thinner than he remembered her, if such thing would be possible. He noticed she wore a light blue patient robe and her torso was heavily bandaged. She was dirty with what he immediately understood was Hell's black ash. He whistled a tune that made the dragons lie low enough for him to get off his litter and walk awkwardly towards Lillith. He kept a cautious distance.

"Lillith?" Adam asked shocked, "You're alive..."

Lillith approached Adam and gave him a hug, but found it was not reciprocated.

"Many blessings, Adam! —slit her throat off - I have longed so much to see you again!"

"What happened to you?" Adam asked shocked.

"I was pregnant and then Eve killed me and I was dead. —sister please-

But then I was not and I was trapped in Hell. And I gave birth -push! push hard- but Lucifer took our baby. And I was still trapped. Then my friend Scarlet freed me –keep moving!- and I escaped Hell and came to Earth to look for you so you could help me find our child, but I got confused and lost because I have never been to Earth –uptown, downtown-. Some people took me to a hospital place and then a slave that was not a monster came for me. He was a kind soul–you gone break mah heart- but he had to take me to my sister Eve, who was the Queen of Hell until you killed her and took over and led the demons here to kill the angels. Why are you ending the world?"

"Our child is alive?"

"Maybe. Perhaps. I do not know. We should ask Lucifer. Could you please stop destroying Creation and help me find it? -boy or girl; girl or boy-"

"Lillith I- I am not going to stop. Everything that happened to you, to us; this is all God's fault. He did not protect us. He let all of this happen to us and I am going to make Him pay. I am doing this for us."

"But… I do not understand. I am here! We are together now! We can find our child and-"

"You need to find a place to hide."

Lillith looked confused as she took a few steps back.

"He loves her, he loves me not, he loves her, he loves me not" she mumbled.

Adam began to walk back to his dragon carried litter. Lillith frowned and followed Adam. She tapped his shoulder.

"Wait. Just you wait." The weak looking girl said, "Please help me understand. -if you see something, say something- You say God is at fault for all the bad things that have happened to us. But when I was in Hell – dark and scary- All those years I was in Hell, I did the only thing I could to keep myself alive. I did what you taught me. I prayed to God. I gave my heart to Him as you once did – Our Father who art in Heaven-. I asked only that one day I could see you again and I could tell you about our child –give me back my baby!- And… The way I see it, God has answered my many prayers. After all this time, I kept alive because of Him and He has made it possible for our paths to cross –I disgust you- We are alive you and I, nothing else matters. We are alive and together once again by the grace of God... And now that we are together you push me aside and tell me you are going to kill the world and punish God and you are doing it for us? ...I do not understand. You do not need to do this evil thing anymore. God has answered our prayers! I am here! We can be together! – do not touch me!-"

Adam turned his back to Lillith as he returned to his bone-made litter

"God never answered my prayers." He said bitterly, "I'm sorry, Lillith"

"Then you are lying! –he is evil-" Lillith cried, "You are not doing this for us! I do not know why you are doing all of this, but it is not because of us! –I am the only wife- But I still love you and because of that, I will find our child... and I will stop you!"

"You can't"

Lillith ran away from Adam and the demons. She headed in the same direction that Violet and Ruth went. The goblins began to pursue her, but Adam called them back.

"Let her go!" He yelled, "I will kill anyone who touches her. Just-just let her go."

Adam pondered on the words uttered by Lillith. His heart was heavy. Could she be right? Could he have lost himself in his quest to seek justice from God? No. God is the enemy. That is the true reason and his motivation.

"She's crazy" He told himself. "She's gone mad"

One more thing to blame on God, Adam thought as he gave the order to continue his demonic rampage on New York City.

19 LAST MINUTE RUNAROUND

I don't believe there was ever a time that Cherubim were trained to do anything other than sing and pray; much less fight. Cherubim didn't know how to use swords; they played little harps and ate grapes and berries and stuff (We ate a lot of fruit). So you know that things were really bad when the Gates of Heaven opened to release a platoon of golden armored munchkins upon the world. It didn't take long to hear the screeching cries of my fellow angels being butchered by goblin demons. They tried hard. They did their best to protect Creation from Adam's forces in the absence of the Seven Lights, but if their best was slap-fighting while screaming "stop iiiiit!" like little girls, there just wasn't much hope for humanity. And listen, you don't bring fruits to a war with demons. You just don't, okay?

At least I was spared having to witness all the bloodshed and having to channel the feelings of the fallen angels. While all of this was happening, I was reeling from peeking into Ruth's soul. Whenever I get to open a window to someone's heart, the feelings of the rest of humanity fade out just for a bit as I sort of merge with the emotional memories of whomever I'm with at the time and stuff.

After I closed the soul window, Ruth and I were back at Adam's dragon bone litter, facing each other in silence and teary eyed. For a moment, we were still too focused on each other to realize what was going on around us. Ruth felt ashamed and afraid of me because she knew that I knew everything about her. And I was so overwhelmed by the feelings of remorse and loneliness in Ruth's soul that it took me a bit to recover. I had so many questions for her. I didn't know where to start.

"You knew... you knew this- meeting me, the end of the world- you knew this was all going to happen?" I managed to ask, my voice still trembling. "Is that why you were so afraid of me when we met at the subway?"

"...I had seen it in my dreams." she replied, "When I –um- when we met, I knew that everything I've dreamt was real and that it was going to happen... I just... I knew there was nothing we could ever do to stop it."

"But why didn't you tell me any of this before?"

"It wouldn't have mattered, don't you see? All of it was supposed to happen anyway!"

"And Rob-"

"I don't want to talk about him!"

"But you have to."

"I DON'T WANT TO!"

"Those guys that attacked you were possessed by demons. It wasn't your fault. You-"

"Yes it was! I could've tried to do something, I could've... The only person in this world that actually cared about me and I threw him under the bus to save myself! I let him down."

"I know the feeling..."

I thought about Scarlet and all the other angels and how I'd failed them all for being such a coward. Feelings of dread and despair overcame me. It became hard for me to breathe as I couldn't control my emotions.

"Are you okay?" Ruth asked.

"No." I responded.

That's when I realized these feelings that were drowning me were not coming from me, but from White. She had been standing next to Adam, the first man, a few feet away from us. I felt as if I was waking from a dream as I began to focus on their voices. They were arguing.

"You did not have to slay them! They were not a real threat to us!"

White cried.

"You should've told me they'd try something." Adam replied aloofly.

"I did not realize they would dare!"

"What's going on?" I interrupted.

Ruth pulled my shirt hard and as I turned to look back at her, she pointed at thousands of dead angels piled up on each other all around us. The dragons that carried Adam's litter could barely make way through the bloodied flesh cluttered streets. I fell on my knees and let out a scream. I caught White's attention, but Adam kept looking forward. Ruth wrapped her arms around me.

"I am so sorry..." she said.

"Violet, be silent." White told me.

"YOU DID THIS! HOW COULD YOU LET THIS HAPPEN?!!!" I shrieked at her,

White came towards me and clutched my shoulder. I slipped from White's hold and ran towards Ruth. I wrapped my arms around her and hugged her tight before throwing us off the boney litter. I wasn't thinking; I was desperate.

As we fell to the ground, I heard Adam order White to get us back. I pulled Ruth's arm, trying to get away, but she pulled me back.

"What are you doing?!" Ruth asked.

"I can't be here!" I yelled crying. "I just can't be here!"

Ruth stared at me for a moment. She saw White coming towards us and looked back at me.

"Please!" I pleaded.

Ruth began to move and I held her hand as we ran towards some back alleyways. We could barely keep ahead of White as we crossed a few blocks. We reached the end of the stretch alley strip and we looked at each other while White hovered towards us.

"Ruth, you gotta let me go." I said to her. "You gotta let me try to fix things."

"I... I can't." she whispered. "There is nothing to fix. At least with Adam-"

"Adam is evil! Look what he did to my people! That's what he's going to do to humanity!"

"He will make things better."

I held Ruth's hand tight. I fought and failed to keep my tears from rolling down my face. Ruth stared at the floor to avoid engaging my eyes. I held her face and had her stare at me.

"Please, look at me" I begged.

At that moment White arrived, wings spread and all glowing and stuff.

"The time for petty games is over." She said sternly, "It is time for both of you to come back to Adam. Uriel, if you are to live, you must learn your place."

"Or what?!" I yelled, "You'll kill me like you did Scarlet?! I know it was you, wasn't it?!"

White's eyes glowed as her rage began to show through. I got a bit scared. Ruth stood between us.

"Look, she just needs some time to deal with things. Just give us as few minutes." Ruth told her.

"You do not have a few minutes, nor does this world." White declared.

"Sister, I know all of this is hard for you." I said, "I know you feel frustrated. I know it must be tough for you to see lives come and go with no apparent reason, but that reason belongs to God alone. It's not too late for you. We can rebuild this world and-"

"Silence! Do not mistake my tears for weakness. While it is true I did not intend for the Cherubim to meet their doom, everything else is going as I foresaw. Stop wasting our time and come with me."

"I hate you!" I yelled, "I'm not coming with you! And you're not my sister anymore!"

I made a signal with my eyes to Ruth and we both tried to sprint around White, but she caught me by the neck and threw me to the ground.

My ex-sister was pulling me back up by the shirt when a weird petite girl in a patient robe that I'd never seen in my life called White. I felt a lot of compassion coming from her; the kind I'd only felt from saints.

"White! You leave that angel alone! -Feet do not sing!-" the girl shouted with a squeaky voice.

"Lillith?" White asked, turning towards her in disbelief, "You live?!"

I didn't know how that human girl could see us, but I wasn't staying to find out. White's moment of puzzlement was enough for me and Ruth to take off. We ran as fast as we could, but White was already on our tails. Suddenly a curly-haired Cherub jumped on her and hit her repeatedly with a short blade. I knew her from the Cherubim chorus. Her name escaped me at first, but it was her curls that reminded me. I always liked her hair.

"Isophie!" I screamed.

"Run, Uriel" she shouted. "I cannot hold her for too long!"

"You cannot hold me at all, Isophie!" White exclaimed as she melted the little blade with her light, forcing her to throw it away. "Your weapon is a toy to me!"

The girl in the patient robe jumped on White's back and pulled on her wings while Isophie wrestled with her. White grabbed Isophie's wings and lighted them on fire them with the blinding white hot beam coming from her hands.

"Aaaargh!" Isophie shrieked in pain.

"Nooo!" I shouted scared.

"Run!" she yelled again even with the pain of her wings on fire. I looked at Isophie's eyes. She was sweaty and looked weak. Her wings were burned to a crisp with little flames still charring in a few parts. Isophie stared at me with a look that told me that even though she held on to dear life, she knew she didn't have much longer left. But she had bought me seconds.

I pulled Ruth by the arm and we sprinted. We ran for a couple of more blocks, scudding through scattered angel corpses and burning buildings and cars until Ruth had to catch her breath. We managed to avoid encountering a few demons we saw in our way and White was briefly out of our sight, but all of this running around was getting us nowhere. I had to do something before White caught up to us. I tried to think what Scarlet would do, but she'd just run straight to White and kick her ass. That would never fly with me. I was never that awesome. I needed to figure out another way. I couldn't afford to hide behind anyone else. I needed to deal with things my way.

"I'm sorry, Ruth, but I need to do this." I said to her before hollering; "Lucifer!"

"What are you doing?!" she asked.

"Lucifeeer!" I called again.

I pushed Ruth towards the next block corner. She was too confused to react. When we curved around the corner, the walls around us turned to tall barb wired fences. The street pavement became a grassy field. Piles of dead angels were no longer angels but humans dressed in stripped prisoner uniforms. We were no longer in New York City, but in a concentration camp somewhere in 1939 Germany.

....

The camp was quiet at night. Ruth and I stood in shock at the horrific scene that surrounded us. Even though I knew none of it was really real, I couldn't help but feel so sad to see the dead faces of so many people. Ruth shut her eyes and covered her face with her hands.

"What did you do?!" she asked alarmed.

A Nazi military jeep parked next to us. There was no one driving it. At the back seat sat Adolf Hitler with black eyes (who was really you know who). He stepped out of the car and stared at a petrified Ruth.

"Tsk! I forgot you are Jewish. My apologies." Lucifer said.

"Violet, what the hell?!" Ruth yelled at me.

"Hey, it's not like I get to pick who he's going to dress up as." I said awkwardly to her before tuning my attention to Lucifer. "You said I could call you when I had someone to take over my ministry. I have chosen Ruth."

"What?!" Ruth yelled.

"This will not make any difference in the outcome of things." Lucifer sighed, "Do you willingly accept the burden and responsibilities of the ministry of emotions?" not-really-Hitler asked her.

"NO!" Ruth shouted.

Lucifer sighed again. I bet he rolled his black eyes too.

"Just a moment, please." I requested from the Devil. "I know you think I'm giving you the runaround, but there's a point to all this I swear!"

I pulled Ruth to the side and moved my face closer to hers.

"Listen, I know you want this world to end because people have been awful to you-"

"It's more than that." Ruth interrupted, "I'm not just whining about my life. Adam is right. Humankind is evil and God doesn't care. They treat each other like animals, not just me."

"Well, fine. You think you're right about that? Then take my ministry and feel what they feel, everyone in this world. You're about to let Adam take over Creation, I think it's fair to listen to their emotions if you're about to kill them all."

"I don't need to be fair to anyone…"

"But you need to be fair to yourself. You need to see for yourself if humanity is worth saving. You're probably right. Maybe they're all bad. But if you don't know for sure, you can't let Adam end this world. Trust me, if you don't see for yourself, you will spend the rest of your life torturing yourself, not knowing if you made the right decision. Ruth, you don't know what it is to have all these deaths on your conscience. The Cherubim died because of me. Because I was a coward! I know how guilty you feel about Rob, Imagine that a hundred thousand times! I have to live with that for the rest of my existence, but if you let the people of this world die… that will be on you. You gotta make sure before you do it, please. I promise I won't be on your ass again and stuff. That's all I ask."

Ruth pondered my request for almost a minute.

"Will it hurt?" she asked.

"It will at first. But I can, like, guide you through it?" I said, hoping to sound convincing.

",,Okay"

Lucifer placed the palm of his hand on my chest and his other on Ruth's.

"You got your wish, Uriel. You are no longer the guardian of humanity's emotions. The ministry now belongs to Ruth."

The change was so quick and painless for me. There was silence, I felt that bubbly vacuum quiet you get when you go inside the water of a pool or the beach. Submerging in quiet. Like the sounds of the world going on mute. Like that, but with emotions. Having the burden taken away from me felt every bit as soothing as I thought it would be. Being able to just breathe my own thoughts so clear; to hear my own emotions again, this was something I hadn't done since my days as Cherub. I didn't want to go back to my ministry, ever.

But then I turned to look at poor Ruth. She was on the ground convulsing. A little foam drooled from her mouth. She held her chest and cradled herself to an embryonic position, just like I used to do whenever I had one of my emotion seizures. I remembered when she held my hand back at that dining place in Brazil. It felt good to have her next to me as I rode out the pain. I wanted to do the same for her now, so I quickly bent next to her and held her in my arms repeating "It's okay. I'm here with you" over and over again to her ear.

"Ruth. Ruth!" I called, "You need to breathe. What do you feel?"

"I can't –I can't take this!" she cried.

"You gotta try, please."

"I...there's fear... confusion... desperation... so much... loneliness." Ruth continued.

"I know, but I need to know what do *you* feel? Can you feel your own emotions?" I asked.

"I can't... I can't tell my emotions- um- from anyone else's. They're all-"

"The same, right? That's because everything that you feel, all that fear and resentment, all that loneliness, every emotion you feel that you think sets you apart from humanity, everybody feels the same way. Everyone. We all feel rejected, insecure and stuff. We all feel bullied by others and betrayed. You can't tell the difference between your emotions and everybody else's because we all feel like, the exact same thing. It's what we choose to do with that feeling that defines each person and stuff. You want to end this world because you think people are evil, but the thing is that you feel that *you* are evil, because of what happened to Rob, and you can't cope with it.'

"I am evil! I killed him! I chose to-"

"You said Rob appeared to you as a ghost, right?"

"Yes"

"That means his soul is restless. He needs fixing. The seal of death is broken, so I bet you that people's spirits are all loose and stuff. He could be back in this world. I need you to do something for me. I want you to focus and find him, please. You can so do that."

"No! I don't want to…" Ruth cried.

"I know it hurts Ruth, but if you want to make up for what you say you owe him, this is your chance. Rob's in agony. You can fix him. Just think for Rob and how you feel for him. Remember how good he made you feel about yourself. Are you breathing?"

"…I am."

Ruth closed her eyes. I kept holding her hands.

"He's… here. He's here" she said.

"Really?" I asked. "I don't-"

Suddenly the Nazi jeep parked next to us went nuts. The vehicle's engine turned on and off and on again while the lights flicked and the honk kept sounding. Confused, I looked at Lucifer.

"I can assure you, this is not my doing." He declared.

"Oh, God, He never left me. He was always with me…" Ruth said.

"Wait, listen! I get it now!" I suddenly realized, "When we went to see Lucifer the first time. The street lights went red every time we tried to cross and… Lucifer said we were being followed. I thought he meant Envy, but… And when we met Adam at the desert, the lights on the RV went nuts! And… at the silver tower in Hell, there was lightning just right before we went in. I think that was Rob!"

"He was trying-um- he was trying to protect us…" Ruth concluded. "From Lucifer, from Adam, from the citadel…"

"Ah, there you are." Lucifer said as he pointed to his right, "Reveal yourself to us now."

Rob's see-through reddish ghostly form appeared at the spot where old black eyes had pointed. I wondered why we weren't able to see him with us before. I mean, I guess Ruth may have blocked him out unconsciously, out of guilt or trauma or whatever, but did she also block him from Lucifer and me? From everyone we'd encountered? I'd have to ask my sister Black. As much as I thought they were cool, I was never really an expert on ghosts.

When Ruth saw Rob, she trembled and stepped back.

"Ruth, it's okay." I said, "You need to help him out."

"I c-can't- I-um-wait" she stopped herself, "He's desperate… I feel… He needs to tell me something"

"I don't think he'll be able to talk." I guessed, "You gotta listen to his emotions. Listen. What do you hear?"

"I- love… He loves me. He… he wants me to know he loves me and… he needs to know…"

Ruth fell on her knees. She began to cry.

"Are you okay?! What's going on?" I asked her.

"That afternoon… after school… He wanted to ask me to the prom…" Ruth sobbed.

"Oh my God! Oh my God! Oh my God! That is so romantic!"

"Is this the reason why you have wasted my time? Are we done?" Lucifer asked annoyed. "I have places to be."

"Wait! Just hold on a second, please?" I begged anti-Semitic-face, "I swear there's a point to this!"

"I am not so sure. You've seem to make things up as you go along during this entire ordeal."

"Just trust me! Pleeeaaaase!"

"Be silent child. You are annoying beyond belief. -Sigh!- Do whatever it is you're trying to achieve here and be done with it."

"Ruth?" I turned my attention back to her. "The man asked you a question."

"…Yes" she whispered.

Rob moved closer to Ruth and wiped a tear from her eye as he smiled at her. She smiled back. He held her hand. His ghostly reddish color became bluish. He seemed happy and then he became more and more see-through until he faded away. But then he faded back in existence. His face was frozen in that same smile he had, but he kept disappearing and coming back.

"What's going on?" Ruth asked.

"You did it." I said to her "He's at peace. Rob is ready to finally move on. I think for someone as good as him, Heaven is where he'd go. But the thing is; he can't. The seal of death is broken. Like everyone else, his spirit can't move from this Earth. He's stuck. If you let Adam end this world, Rob, and millions of others will never find peace."

Ruth watched Rob dissolve in and out of existence for a moment.

"Can you help him?" she finally asked.

"Maybe? We can try." I said, "We need to repair the seals; starting with mine."

"Take it back! Take back your ministry, please!"

"Lucifer," I sought from the dark angel, "I want my ministry back, please,"

"Are you certain about this?" the Devil queried, "You know you are free to run away where you want and no one could ever find you. This is what you wanted all along."

"I don't want to hide anymore" I replied, very surprised that I actually believed what I was saying, "I accept the responsibility. I accept the gift."

Lucifer touched our chests again and suddenly everything went loud again. It took me a few seconds to get back in control of the shower of emotions that ran through me. But I could handle it. No matter how much I knew it would hurt. I always could.

I turned to Ruth and helped her stand up from her knees.

"Please let me go." I pleaded,

We stared at each other for a few moments. I looked straight into her eyes. She didn't avoid looking back at mine this time. By the uncertain look on her eyes, I wasn't sure if she was going to say yes, but I really hoped she would.

"Someone comes." Lucifer interrupted. "I'm afraid our time is up"

The Nazi Devil waved goodbye with his fingers and took a few steps back as he slowly disappeared in front of your eyes.

"Don't go!" I yelled, "Don't leave us here!"

I strode towards Lucifer and tried to catch him, but it was too late. Lucifer was nowhere to be seen. And it was right at the moment when I turned back to face Ruth, that I felt my right shoulder burn with the touch of a hot hand pulling me back. It was White's hand glowing with fiery bright light. As she pulled my body down to the ground, Ruth was pulled towards me 'cause we were still connected. I saw our surroundings changing as I fell. It was as if we fell from the Nazi concentration camp to the same alley of the street block in New York City we were before. I hit the pavement sidewalk, butt first. Ruth ran towards me to make sure I was okay.

White was there, standing right in front of us, wings spread and glowing, really, really mad. She grabbed both of us, Ruth by her waist and me by the neck, took off to the sky. She flew so fast, we reached an altitude of like, thousands of miles in seconds.

"Stupid girl!" my ex-sister yelled to Ruth. "You are lucky Adam wants you unharmed! And as for you, Violet…"

White closed her hand around my neck and the light that exuded around it grew hotter and so blinding, I closed my eyes and screamed in pain. She released a weird beam that burned me, but not on the outside. My eyes and mouth glowed with the white light that scorched me from the inside out. I lost all control of my body. All I could see was bright white light everywhere, but I couldn't turn away. It hurt so much. It felt like I watched my soul being stripped apart from my body, and I couldn't do anything about it.

"Violet!" Ruth cried to me. She reached out and tried to touch me, but my hot skin burned her fingers.

I could barely hear Ruth's voice the more I got consumed by the white light inside me.

"Feel the breath of life as it consumes everything that you once were and renews it within the fire of a new being." White announced,

"Stop it! You're killing her!" I heard Ruth shout.

"Her form will not die. Nonetheless, what will go on living will not be her essence, but that of another more… submissive entity." White responded.

"No!" Ruth screamed as she scratched and punched White as hard as she could, but my sister didn't even feel a tickle.

"Be still!" White commanded.

But Ruth's struggle paid off. The traitor angel lost her grip on me and I slipped from her hand as I dropped down the sky. Ruth followed me because the pull of our connection was stronger than White's hold on her. We fell fast towards the Earth. Ruth was spinning and it was hard for her to tell which way was up or down, but once our bond pulled her closer to me she tried to wrap her arms around me, but my skin was too hot for her, so she held on to my shoe.

"Violet! Wake up! I release you! Do you hear me? I release you!" She yelled.

I couldn't hear her. I couldn't hear anything at all. The world around me faded away… and with the white light inside me consuming my entire self, I was fading away too.

·············

So this is what I saw in my mind or whatever as my soul burned from the inside out: I was trapped in a maze of wavy white light. I struggled to find my way through many walls of white fire that surrounded me. But it wasn't really a maze. I was lost inside someone else. I could already feel this other person-thing growing around me. Another heart beating and fighting to push mine away. It wasn't like I could actually see it, but I felt it and it hurt bad. There was no way of punching this thing born within me. It was not that kind of fight. It took my memories and created… something else from them. As if my life was my little purple book all filled up with written milestones; the first time I heard a Duncan Blackheart song, or Tasting Feijoada at that café in Sao Paulo; all this stuff written on my little book, and then having someone with a magic eraser wipe them out and re-write new strange alien stuff.

I fought by keeping my memories from burning. I did my best to hold on to my emotions. I loved Ruth. She was my friend and even though I made fun of her and called her names, she was always there by my side to help me with my many messes. I held on to that. I also held on to the need to stop White and Adam and the demons. And I thought that Scarlet and the Cherubim shouldn't have died in vain. And the rest of the world, I had to save it, too. I had to hold on. I had to live.

I prayed to God.

I took the time to try to listen to myself until I reached a calm moment. I could feel my own voice talking; only it was me and it wasn't? Was that God? It had to be! So I kept praying because it was the only thing I could do. And God prayed too, and we were both praying together. I got lost in our prayers, not knowing which words were His and which were mine. It was all mostly gibberish, but what mattered was the feeling; the emotion. Was this what some people called speaking in tongues? I don't know. It made me feel focused and connected. It happened so quick I couldn't make sense of any of it. But it was in that moment of clarity that God told me what I needed to do.

I stopped seeing the white lighted walls as a trap. It was my space, my heart. God was there inside me and He helped me fight that new person-thing that was growing inside me by embracing it. Instead of trying not to change and stay myself all insecure and scared, I changed into this other person, but I was in control. I determined what it was that I wanted to change into. And it was me, but without my doubts. The white lighted walls around me became purple because that is how I want them to know me, and I was able to break the new growing pumping heart thingie away. It had to be Him! It had to be God that came to my help. He was there. I couldn't see Him, but I really felt Him. I wasn't scared anymore.

I felt very clearly what I had to do to save Creation.

I slowly woke up and I felt the wind rushing up my face as I quickly fell towards the burning NYC skyscrapers. My memories of my experience with God began to disappear, leaving only my plan to stop the end of the world. And as I strained to remember my holy experience, I didn't know why I had thoughts of my sister Goldie.

No time to think about that. I heard Ruth screaming above me. She was terrified and her panic overwhelmed her to the point that her heart was about to give out. I stared at my hands and they felt different. I felt stronger. I was stronger. I felt I could do anything I wanted. I felt free. I spread my fluffy feathery white Cherub-like wings. I had my wings again. I was me again and it felt awesome! I flew towards my friend and caught her in the air. She quickly wrapped herself around me.

"Oh, my God, you're flying!" she yelled excited.

"Thank you so much for freeing me!" I replied "We have to fix the seals, but we need to get Scarlet's sword for that!"

"Violet, she's coming!" Ruth shouted in my ear as she pointed behind me.

I turned my head and saw White speeding towards us. I was never faster than her, or anyone for that matter, but I had to be this time. Carrying Ruth, I went back down so fast that I bet you wouldn't be able to see me going past you. I swooshed through the streets and turned every corner. White followed us closely.

I found Adam's dragon bone litter. His back was facing us, so he didn't know we were coming towards him at first. We headed straight towards him and we were so close to get him, but he turned around and spotted us and gave an order to his demons. The goblins bulked against each other forming a barrier between us and Adam. I tried to go higher to avoid them, but they grabbed my leg and pulled me towards them and to the ground. I held tight to Ruth with one arm to protect her and punched and kicked and winged (it's like hitting someone with your wing? same as tailing. I mean if you had a tail you'd know what I'm talking about) my way through an ocean of demons. I was stronger this time, so it was harder for the demon goblins to get me, but I still needed to get Ruth to safety.

"Hold on tight!" I told my human friend as I spread my wings to push the demons and make space to take flight again.

I managed to free ourselves from the demons, and didn't waste time getting to Adam. He was holding Scarlet's sword and was ready to use it on me, but I was faster than him. I pushed him out of his boney litter and he fell to the street. He lost his grasp on the blade and it landed a few feet away from him. I held him tight and he couldn't move, 'cause I was stronger than him.

"Get the sword!" I said to Ruth.

"Get out of my way, Violet" Adam told me calmly.

"I'm not letting you kill God!" I told him, "I don't know why you're so angry at Him, but I can fix you. I can make you better."

I used my gift on Adam. I tried to influence his feelings, but for some reason I couldn't turn his hatred around. That awful bitterness I had felt from him at the RV... It was literally seared to his soul. Just like -like the kind of people that have smoked so much in their life that the stench becomes part of them. They sweat nicotine and stuff; like that, but with bitterness. Adam was immortal. He'd been around so long, and he had resented God for so long, his hatred had become him. Add to that the fact that he lost his lover Steve and you get an ugly hatred machine of a man.

"You cannot change what I feel." He said, "Get out of my way."

I'd never seen anything like it before. The shock of seeing what the first man had become dumbfounded me and I released my grip for a moment. That was all he needed to slip away from me. I was still a bit confused when I heard Ruth's voice calling to me.

"Violet! I got it!"

Ruth ran towards me with the sword, but as I rushed to meet her, I got hit hard by my torso. White had caught up to us and had pushed me so hard she knocked me down to the street. I lost my balance and everything was spinning as I fell. I couldn't tell where Ruth was anymore, I had White on top of me, her light glowing so close to my eyes I had to squint. She thumped me hard. I was face up underneath her, trying to get loose, but she was too strong for me and stuff. She already bloodied my face with a few slaps. Then she grabbed me by the hair and kept banging my head against the ground.

"How did you manage to overcome the new life I breathed into you?!" White asked. "No matter. Understand: You will not succeed! You cannot stop me!"

"I will stop you!" I yelled. "I will find a way to- ow! I will fight y-owww! I will-OW! STOP HITTING ME SO HARD!"

"You will never be as strong as me. You will never be as fast. You will always lose against me." she declared. "That is why I chose you, Uriel. You are no threat to me. You never were."

And she was right. She was just too strong for me, even in my free form. White wrapped her hands around my throat and squeezed. Her eyes filled up with tears, warm drops fell on my face. That's how I knew the angel of life really meant to kill me.

"I could have saved you." she lamented, "You could have lived."

It was then that I saw a change in White's ivory glow. It was no longer completely white. There was a shimmer growing, like a sun rise. It was a sparkle of gold.

My sister Goldie, riding what looked like a winged swine, flew towards White from behind at a ridiculously fast speed. She crashed the flying pig into White's back. It made a cracking sound as it shattered in many pieces of shard glass. Some of them stuck on as the white angel screamed in pain and let go of me. Goldie quickly grabbed White's arm and lifted her up, then threw her hard against the street pavement. White looked up and both angels faced each other.

"Raphael…" White barely spoke.

"I've been practicin' a new act just for you." Goldie responded,

"You cannot hope to defeat me!" White yelled, "I am life! I am everything!"

288

Goldie lifted White by her pearly dress and pulled her closer.

"You're mad as a monkey on a trike, is what you are!" Goldie said, "Ya used me to kill Michael!"

She headbutt White and my ex-sister fell back dizzy. White touched her forehead and felt blood drops on her fingers, Goldie smirked and took off her black top hat as if saluting her. She revealed a small iron anvil on her bare head. She was always goofy like that.

White clenched her fists and a white hot light burst blasted Goldie a few feet back, impacting through a wall of a building behind her. Goldie's clothes were in flames. She stood up and wiped the fire and dust from her golden suit. It looked perfectly clean.

"You are too late!" White shouted, "Look around you! This is the end of Creation! Adam and I are about to start everything anew!"

"Is that so? Well that is a show you are goin' to miss." Goldie replied,

A giant black haired bulky soft rock dropped on White. The weight of the mass buried her below her chest in the street leaving only her arm and the top of her torso visible. White had not realized what had happened until she looked up over the black boulder and saw it was actually the butt of a giant ape that was sitting on her.

"TA-DAAAH!" Goldie "King Kong just sat on you! How's that for a show stopper!"

"Violet!" she called, "I got this broad on the ropes! Go do your emo angel thing!"

"I am not emo!" I yelled back.

"Beat it, kid!" She shouted as she raised both her fists and moved her legs around, like one of those old school boxers.

White was already freeing herself from under the giant gorilla while my sister was thinking of the next trick she would bring from her sleeve. The thing with Goldie is that the more she manifests gifts from her ministry of miracles, like giant apes appearing from out of nowhere or whatever, the more bonkers reality becomes. I had to move fast before the universe turned crazier than it already was. I was still a bit disoriented from White's hits, but I still looked for Ruth. She was nowhere to be seen. I felt much fear coming from her, and I was afraid Adam had taken her.

I followed the trail of Ruth's emotions as I flew over the demon riddled streets until I found Ruth holding the sword close to her chest as she ran from a group of demons. I dove to rescue her, but then I felt a sharp cut to the side of my torso that knocked me down to the ground. I passed out for a second and then I woke up to the left of my abdomen bleeding. I felt my body being dragged. I felt dizzy. I was losing a lot of blood and I couldn't move my wings. I glanced around me and saw the Deadly Seven demon Wrath pulling me by the legs. I was lucky she only grazed me with her axe, but it still hurt a lot. Wrath stopped in front of the two dragons that carried Adam's litter and she bowed in reverence to him. I saw the first man holding Ruth tight by the arm with one hand and Scarlet's blade with the other.

"VIOLET!!!" Ruth yelled.

"I'm okay…" I lied.

Wrath kicked the wound in my torso and I screamed in agony. Ruth turned her eyes away crying.

"Thank you for your service Wrath." Adam said, "I'll take it from here. Call your brothers back, though. With White fighting the golden angel, I don't want any more surprises."

"HURRRH! I WILL TEAR THIS ANGEL TO SHREDS…" Wrath spoke grinding her teeth.

"Sure. Go nuts." Adam responded with a jaded demeanor.

"No!" Ruth yelled struggling to get lose from Adam, "You can't do this!"

Adam pushed Ruth back. She landed on her butt at the center of the litter.

"I'm done trying to reason with you." Adam told her, "I don't want to hurt you, but I will if you try to stop me."

As Wrath raised her axe to strike me with the killing blow, Ruth and I stared at each other. I tried to smile; tried to be brave so she wouldn't suffer much for me. But I already felt her sadness. I felt it turn to desperation, and then rage.

Ruth quickly stood up and let out a scream as she ran head first towards Adam. She buried her head in his stomach as she tackled him out of the litter. They both fell to the street, Ruth on top of the first man. Adam lost his grip on the sword and it slid over the pavement straight to my hand. I was able to grab it just as Wrath swung her axe towards me. Scarlet's steel was too heavy for me and it was pretty hard to handle. I had to lift it with both hands to block the demon's axe. When both weapons clashed, a loud clanking resonated across the city. I was still lying on the street with Wrath standing over me when I awkwardly swung the sword again. I was able to stab the demon's leg; not too deep, but enough to get her off from me. I struggled to get up, using the blade to support myself.

Ruth threw herself at him again, using her weight to pin him to the ground and biting his nose.

"Get off me!" Adam yelled pissed as he slapped her and pushed her to the side.

I froze. It was hard for me to choose what to do. I only had one chance to use Scarlet's sword, but I didn't want to leave Ruth all by herself. I had to decide quickly what to do, and I already felt Wrath and a horde of demon goblins closing in from behind.

The first man stood up and took a step towards me.

"Get me that sword!" Adam yelled at Wrath.

Ruth, still on the ground, yanked his leg and held on to it.

"Go save him!" Ruth yelled, "Please!"

I took off to the sky as fast as I could with the sword in hand. I hated to leave Ruth alone, but the whole universe needed saving. My body ached a lot and the heavy weapon I carried pulled my arms down. I flew over the highest skyscraper and kept going. As I almost reached some clouds, I let my wings hover me and I used my remaining strength to raise the sword with both arms. Then I thought of Scarlet's teachings, and that trick we used to do together every time we dealt with a human tragedy. She'd use her sword to bend the will of demons while I made them afraid. Then I'd reach the humans and helped them be brave enough to face adversity and feel compassion towards each other.

I had to do better than that. I had to take back my ministry.

I've always said I could listen to emotions. I could also speak to them. I just never had anything worth to tell them.

This time, I had something to say.

20 APOCALYPSE NUMB

At the height I had flown, all the sounds of the destruction going on were distant. I hovered by the clouds, caressed by wind currents that helped me be calmed and focused. I took a breath, closed my eyes, and extended my reach.

I touched humanity all over the world. I made sure to sense every soul that lived - like Ruth, who still laid wounded on the street- and let them feel that, as ever, they were not alone, God was with them. Everything would be okay. I pushed my reach further and touched every single demon loose in Creation. I felt the Seven Deadly, and Abaddon with the rest of the Four Horsemen, and Adam, and my traitor sister Gabriel. I reminded them of the Presence; I let their dark hearts feel the truth that lay deep within each of them: Reckoning was coming. Then I reached out to the angels, to the handful that were still barely alive after the onslaught - like Isophie whose wings were lit on fire by White's light - I thanked them for their sacrifice and let them soothe their pain with hope. God had not abandoned them. Help was coming.

And I touched the Archangels, the fallen defenders of Creation. To them I conveyed a simple message: Listen.

As I spoke to my siblings, I felt my voice was mine, but it was not really me doing the talking. To my sister Goldie, who faced the wrath of White alone, I said "Let her come to me. Keep the boundaries of reality safe. Protect the seal of miracles."

When I said those words, I remembered why I thought of Goldie when I prayed before. God explained to me how her ministry of miracles works. It's like God's emergency override to all the other ministries in case one of us rebelled or, you know, if we couldn't perform our duties for some reason. Goldie can tap into all of the seals and change how they function if needed. But the thing is, if too many crazy miracles were done; that would cause a chain reaction that could end up undoing all the good work God did in seven days.

Goldie finally understood the importance of her role in Creation. My golden sister stopped trying to turn reality into a vaudeville show and undid all her magic wonders, like the huge gorilla, and the giant golden sock 'em robot, and the pigeons that danced like the Rockettes, and a building-sized anvil she had used to fight White. All of it was gone. The proverbial genie was back inside the bottle. She tipped her hat, stepped aside from Gabriel, and let her fly off. My golden sister saw a tilted bench by the sidewalk. She fixed it and laid on it.

"Break a leg, Violet..." she said with a smile.

To my sister Evergreen, who blamed herself for the death of her human lover, and to my Brother Blue, who became incapable of doing anything other than play video games, I said "The time for mourning and procrastination is over. You have been deceived by the Deadly Seven. They are loose upon the world and must be stopped. Reclaim the seals of nature and progress and send the demons back to Hell."

To my sister Black, who was weakened and exhausted by the onslaught of the Four Horsemen at the Gobi desert in China, I said "This is not the end. They cannot defeat you. God is with you. Drive them back. Reclaim the seal of death. The spirits wait for you."

All of this I felt through the emotions that flowed through me. The connection was deeper and clearer than I have ever felt before. More than just getting an earshot of their feelings, I could feel them taking action motivated through their emotions. People everywhere were taking back control of their lives, and instead of succumbing to their basest impulses; they strove towards the light by helping each other and re-establishing order. But this connection, this oneness with the world was interrupted by White's arms wrapped around my chest, pulling me down back to the earth.

She had flown at great speed away from Goldie and caught up to me high up in the air. With her weight pulling against me, I could not keep Scarlet's sword raised.

"WHAT DO YOU THINK YOU ARE DOING?!!!" she yelled as we both fell rapidly.

"You are such a liar!" I shouted "It was never you that spoke for God! It was Gray, wasn't he?! All this time you said you served as His voice! You've never felt His presence! Not once! He speaks through my ministry!"

"BE SILENT!" White shrieked enraged, "I WILL END YOU!"

We both felt the impact on the street as we crashed into it. I saw my surroundings and recognized a big golden Earth shrine to the other side of the lane, which told me we had fallen to the area in the city by 59 Street called Columbus Circle. As with most of the buildings everywhere by that point, the ones surrounding the circling road were scorched. Everything around us was fire, ashes, and smoke. It seemed the demons were bent on making the cliché line "Hell on Earth" a reality.

White was on top of me, her hands around my neck. I calmly gathered the last of my strength to lift Scarlet's sword and placed it close to her face, but I wasn't going to cut her.

To my ex-sister White I said: "Gabriel, you abused the ministry of life, murdered your sister Michael, and rebelled against our Lord. You are no longer the angel of life. Live the rest of your existence as a human and for the first time, feel closeness to mortality."

White stood up wide-eyed, stepped back and laughed.

"You cannot punish me! You do not have the power or the authority!"

A single feather slipped out from White's wings; then another; then another. White turned to grab hold of her wings.

"NOOOO!"

No matter how much she struggled to hold on to them, the feathers in White's wings flaked away. She looked like a tree shedding leaves in autumn. Her outer glow went away as she fell on her knees and cried bitterly.

I still laid motionless on the street for a while. I breathed deep as I tried to push my elbows down and boost my chest up. I gave up after a few tries and rested my head. I felt a pain on my back so sharp that I couldn't focus on moving my limbs.

"Your wing is broken-eat the spoils-" I heard a squeaky voice say.

The barefoot human with the hospital patient garment I saw earlier stood next to me with her face looking directly at mine.

"You... why did you help me fight White when she was after me?"

"She was being bad. I did not like that –love me forever- I stayed with the other Cherubim, Isophie, because she could barely move with her burned wings, but after the angel stabbed her many times, she passed away and then I saw you two falling from the sky and I came here."

"White...?" I asked instinctively as the girl helped me sit up. "She... stabbed Isophie?!"

"No! The other angel! –beg me! beg me!- " she replied, "the one that became bad!"

I thought of poor Isophie and tears came to my eyes. Another senseless death caused by Gabriel. I couldn't let Isophie's sacrifice be for nothing. I had to keep fighting.

"I saw her run away crying, the pretty one. You did something to her, did you?" the girl asked.

"Who...are you?"

"I am Lillith! -suck your bones dry- Many blessings! Who are you?"

"Violet... Are you... the first woman?"

"I am. I am her. I was trapped in Hell for a long time, but now I am here. Please do not believe the mean things they say about me. –leave her alone! - It is all lies, I swear."

Lillith interrupted herself as she saw a little spider crawling on the concrete. She caught it between the toes of her right foot and brought it up to her mouth like a flexible sideshow contortionist and chewed on the spider.

"Mostly all lies. I-(munch, munch, munch) - I try to be good."

"I know.., I feel so much love in you…"

"I am just happy to be alive."

"Oh my God! Ruth!" I snapped with sudden realization,

With Lillith's help I managed to stand up and pick up Scarlet's sword. I was in a lot of freaking pain. Like she pointed out, my left wing was broken and practically hanging loose from my back.

"I have to get to Ruth!" I whispered.

That's when I felt a hard blow on my face that knocked me again to the ground. My left cheek was bruised and bloodied. When I was able to lift my head up, I saw thousands of goblin demons crawling and climbing on top of each other, They had circled the area just like they did with the RV back in Nevada. Some of them mounted the Leviathan beasts that roared fiercely at me. Lillith and I were trapped, but even with my broken wing I was ready to take them all, The demon Beggar stepped in front of them, holding a long wooden cane that he'd hit me with. He still wore his dirty torn rags and weird seventies tubed boots, This time around, he had two big brown ragged bags full of coins hanging from his back. Beggar grabbed me by the neck and squeezed hard.

"I will have your power! Give it to me!!!"

"Let me go!"

"BEGGAR, ENOUGH!" a low toned male voice yelled from behind us.

Beggar stepped back and lowered his head.

When I turned around, I saw the demon Pride leaning against the light post posing like a male model.

"I do apologize, Violet, is it? We needed a new Greed. Beggar was there. I improvised." Pride said, "Not my best work. I admit."

The rest of the Deadly Seven stood behind him, with the zeal of barely controlled beasts that wanted to eat me already. I recognized the angel Fariphel among them, but there was something different about him. He smirked at me wickedly, knowing it shocked me to see he'd become one of them.

"The other angel!" Lillith yelled agitated while pointing at Fariphel. "The one that killed Isophie!- rip my eyes out- He is evil!"

"Be quiet, you." Pride said to Lillith while fixing his hair. "He goes by Lethanus now, or Lord Envy"

"Fariphel... You killed Isophie?! You are so going to pay!" I uttered as I stared angry at him.

"And who will do that? You?" Envy laughed. "You were always the shame of the Pax Dei! Even Amion said many times your only gift was to fade within the celestial chorus. You could never take me! But now- Now I am even more powerful-"

"Don't oversell yourself, you talking piece of trash," Pride interrupted, "We all know you joined our merry band because you're a coward, so keep your mouth shut and let the grownups talk."

Pride took two slow steps closer towards me and fixed the sleeves of his suit before opening his arms to gloat.

"Now, there you are, all weakened with a nasty injured wing." he said to me, "And here we are, a horde of thousands of disgustingly hungry wild demons and... the Seven Deadly Sins; evil incarnate, all powerful, all glorious. How do you think this will all turn out?"

Pride walked over to me and extended his hand.

"You gave it your best." he said, "No need to be ashamed. Now, hand over the sword... please."

The goblins were the first to attack me. I was stronger than them, I could take it. They piled on top of me like ants on a sugar cube while I bent and kept my head low and the sword close to my chest. They pulled my hair and my wings and scratched and bit my skin, but I resisted. The problem was protecting Lillith, crouching behind me. Luckily, the little demons were only interested in getting Scarlet's sword.

Pride kept staring at me with curiosity, until he got bored, I guess, and then he nodded at the rest of the Deadly Seven to move towards me. They were the ones I was really afraid of. I had to exorcise myself to beat one, let alone all seven of them at the same time would be too much for me. Hell's entire realm was ganging up against me. I had nowhere to run and I couldn't fly. But I still held on to the sword. I just had to buy a little more time. I needed to stand against them for just a few moments until…

A flash of golden light blinded the goblin demon horde. The light shifted and spun like it was coming from a disco ball. The sound of a bass and drum beat came from nowhere.

"Ladieees and Gents! May I have your attention, please!" My sister Goldie stood on top of the golden round Earth monument as she took off her hat and saluted, "Preeesenting, for one night only and back because YOU demanded it! The bringers of justice and awesomeness; the defenders of Creation and guardians of humanity; WE ARE THE SEVEN LIGHTS!"

The Black Angel was the second of my brethren to arrive. She came through a dark tunnel that took form by the subway station next to the mall. Thousands of undead people followed her in single file, including her agents, a zombie cowboy with his zombie horse (I'm serious), and an ugly scary wraith that looked like a disproportioned woman with an old grandma dress. My heart skipped a beat as I saw Scarlet among the dead. I didn't know she'd been brought back by the Black Angel. Her armor was different and her skin cracked like a broken porcelain doll. I could see her soul fire, not blue, but red. She was angry, but, as always, willing to play her part in God's plan.

The wind currents became stronger. Over by the statue in the middle of the round road, vines began to grow around the statue. The vines moved like tentacles that grabbed and crushed a few demon goblins that got in their haphazard way. My sister Evergreen stood behind the crazy octopus vine. She no longer had butterflies and flowers growing from her head. She sported a scorpion tail and sharp bear claws, a lion's head with long fangs. She was ready to fight and looked the part.

Then I looked up at the sky as many red laser lights pointed at the Seven Deadly's foreheads or chests. Blue hovered in his metal plated battle armor above the digital sign that told time and the weather on one of the nearby buildings. Dozens of flying robotic spheres moved in zig zag in the air with cylinders coming out of them as that fired lasers at the demons.

"Targets locked. Vibrational Ionic Plasma cannons ready." an automated female voice informed.

"Thank youuuuuuu!" Blue sang as he kept pushing hologram buttons from a blue screen that floated around him. "I call them VIP's. Bear with me now. These babies are prototype military hunter drones fresh from the oven, but they should do their job right if you guys so much as make a move."

"I count only five…" the demon Pride said, bored.

Goldie no longer stood on top of the earth monument. In a blink of an eye, she appeared right next to me.

"A little help here, sis…" Goldie whispered to me with a wink and a nudge.

I kind of stole a little from Pride, but I had to improvise, too, right? I turned my attention to Lillith and pointed Scarlet's sword at her.

"Oh! Um… Please do not kill me! –Kill me now!- I will be good." she said

"Noooo! Hey, I'm not going to kill youuuu." I said smiling, "Lillith, you've been through an eternity trapped in Hell and still remain merciful and nurturing. God needs you to be an angel now. He needs you to watch over all living things in Creation. If you accept it, the ministry of life is yours, and your name will be Ricadel."

"I will be whatever God wants me to be." Lillith replied without hesitation, "I just want to be of help."

Lillith's bloody bandages around her torso unwrapped themselves and swirled all over her body. Wings made out of solid light that looked like luminescent panels, beamed from her back. She began to exude an intense white glow; her bandages expanded and formed a white dress, similar to my ex-sister White's, but with blood stains all over and a hole that revealed a huge void she had instead of her belly. The bandages also formed beautiful pearled sandals around the new angel's feet, but she quickly took them off. I guess she was uncomfortable in them.

"I feel… different." she said, touching her head. "Calmer. Ricadel… That is a pretty name,"

I took a quick look at Envy and he gulped. Even as powerful as he was as a Deadly Seven demon and as injured as I was, I felt Fariphel's fear. I couldn't help but smile. Just a bit, you know. Envy tried to run away, but

Wrath grabbed him by the arm.

"RAAAH!" she groaned, "TRY TO RUN AND I WILL BITE YOUR HEAD OFF!!!"

I felt that all eyes were on me from everyone in the stand-off. All the seals had been restored except for Scarlet's. But the ministry of free will could only be claimed one way; by fighting for it. Even Pride, who always wore his high class shades, stared in my direction. I had Scarlet's sword, but did I have the guts to use it?

"Say the word, sister…" Evergreen said to me.

I glanced at the undead Scarlet, who looked back at me.

"Ready?" I imagined she'd ask me as she smiled at me.

"No" I smiled back.

She nodded with approval.

"For Scarlet" I declared.

And I raised her sword.

·············

When Evergreen felt Violet's call to arms in the town on the coast of Brazil, she looked at her dead lover Paolo's face one last time. She kissed his forehead and had the animals dig a hole in the ground to bury him. Wildflowers quickly grew over the burial site to protect it. The green angel tore down the green wall made of giant trees, bushes, weeds and flowers that protected her from the world. As the seal of nature was reclaimed, animals stopped attacking humans, and overgrown plants receded. Natural disasters like earthquakes and tsunamis stopped altogether.

Evergreen joined Blue at Ibirapuera Park in Sao Paulo just as he destroyed the luminous blue bubble where he lived for more than a week. He quickly brought back technology, transportation and communications all over the world. Efforts began immediately to evacuate large cities and towns to prevent more lives lost from the demon attacks. Humanity was no longer defenseless. The seal of progress was restored.

"You look good in futuristic battle armor." Evergreen said to Blue in a playful manner. "Have I ever told you that?"

"And you should see the cobalt speedo's I got myself, baby doll." He responded.

"Captain Commando is no more?"

"I'll leave that kind of thing to your hippie folk from now on. So... New York?"

Evergreen hesitated. Her face expression abruptly turned serious.

"New York." Evergreen said with a grave tone.

"I'm really sorry about your lover. Are you okay?"

"...I will be once I break Lust's neck."

"That's my girl. I got dibs on sleepy dwarf."

On the other side of the world, the battle at the Gobi desert against the Four Horsemen continued. The Black Angel heeded the message from Violet and felt her strength come back to her. The angel of death ran towards the small town where the horsemen battled her agents. She noticed that Abaddon was missing one limb, cut by the undead Scarlet's bone sword. She also realized that Fatima was no longer with them. She had betrayed them and escaped with Abaddon's severed hand. That made the Black Angel mad, but she would have to deal with Fatima later. She took Fatima's place and fought Pestilence. Her renewed force spread to her agents Murphy "Powder" Cain, La Llorona, and Scarlet. They increased the fierceness of their blows and kept fighting with no cessation. The Four Horsemen found themselves stepping back and losing ground.

"The seals..." Abaddon uttered with a worried tone. "They are being reclaimed!"

"..." the Black Angel grinned.

For the first time, Black Angel spread her ragged black feathery wings and levitated a few feet above the earth. With four seals restored to order, it was enough for her to stop the Horsemen. She opened a tunnel, the biggest one she'd ever made. It was a tunnel that led straight to the bottomless dungeons where the horsemen were trapped before they were freed. The chains attached to the skin of the Horsemen were pulled by the tunnel like a magnet. In turn, the horsemen themselves were drawn towards the tunnel. One by one they lost their grip on the soil they stood as the chains that wrapped around them dragged them to the abyss.

Azrael stared into the sad eyes of the horseman Famine as he was pulled into the tunnel, and she felt a familiarity she couldn't comprehend. Her attention shifted to Pestilence and War being pulled to the tunnel. Both of them pointlessly clawed the surface trying to anchor their bodies to our world. The last horseman to resist was Death. Abaddon had more hands to hold on to the ground, so he used them all.

"I will come back and end you first, I think." He told the Black Angel, "I will come back for you."

Abaddon let go of himself and was quickly swept into the dark tunnel. It was enough for the Black Angel to close shut the dark tunnel with the four seals already secured. She stuck out her tongue in mocking tone as she waived Abaddon goodbye. The dark tunnel closed, with a rusty metal gate that rose from the sand to cover it. Four round iron seals lined up in the center of the gates spun until they locked. The tunnel descended into the earth.

Taking only a moment to rest, the angel of death reclaimed her ministry, restoring the seal of death. She opened a tunnel to lead her agents and all the restless spirits around the world to New York. They all followed the Black Angel in a long single file, silently marching towards war.

....

When all my siblings answered my call and came to the city to defend Creation, literally all hell broke loose. Don't get me wrong, I was happy to see Blue and Evergreen back in control of their ministries, and I felt relieved that the Black Angel wasn't squashed by the Four Horsemen, but things were about to get a lot messier for all of us. But in a way, it sort of all felt right; I mean, all of us fighting together.

Have you ever seen an action movie where so much fighting is going on, you can't understand what you're looking at or where to focus your attention? This was like, ten times that. So many different epic battles happened in a matter of seconds, and then, opponents switched and other epic battles took place. Columbus Circle served as the battlefield of the Armageddon. Its round road connected 59 Street with 8th and Broadway Avenues. At the center of the circle there's a nice little plaza with a statue of Christopher Columbus. There's a mall to the west with entrances to the subway station at both sides of the street. There are many trees to the east, where Central Park begins. The rest of the streets expand to the north and south of the circle. It'd be a really nice place to hang out for a bit; if it wasn't decimated by arch-demons and dragons and goblins or whatever.

Everywhere I looked; demon goblins and leviathans faced spirits and zombies that fought under my sister Black's lead. There was a zombie cowboy on a dead horse - I kid you not - shooting goblins left and right. Some of Hell's armies struggled to get lose from Evergreen's moving overgrown jade vines. Leviathans were being fired at by Blue's VIP spheres. He kept to the skies shooting dragons from his high tech armor beam shooting thingamajig. At one point I saw Evergreen making it hail over Wrath. The big muscly demon got really mad and cut through the fast falling ice chips with wild swings of her axe. She tore and lifted up the big golden round-shaped monument near an entrance of the subway station. Wrath threw the whole thing at Evergreen, and it almost got her if Blue hadn't pulled her out of the way just in time. And then there was Goldie, she was popping all over the place, helping us out here and there by doing small miracles like, if she saw one of us cornered by too many demons, she'd turn some of them into Mexican sombreros or whatever. The trick for her was not to go too wild with her miracles so that reality wouldn't unravel.

I found myself pulling my head away from Gluttony's distorted mouth as he lifted me up and tried to swallow me whole. I cut his tongue with Scarlet's sword and got out, only to stumble and fall face down on the street because Lust was "playing" with my foot. As the two Arch-demons ganged up on me, the White Angel released a blinding flash of hot light that charred their skins. Lust and Gluttony had to step back and let me go to avoid getting burned alive. , I was amazed how Ricadel, my new white angel sister, seemed to be at home with her new ministry powers.

"You leave my sister alone!" Ricadel yelled at them.

"Thank you" I said to her while standing up from the ground.

"You are very welcome!" Ricadel replied. "Because we are sisters now, true?"

"I think so, sure."

Ricadel hugged me. The hug felt a bit awkward for me at first, but then it kind of felt nice. But we were kind of in the middle of the Apocalypse and I had to get back to the fight. We separated and I set my sight on Envy, I saw him hiding by the subway escalator at the sidewalk in front of the mall. I ran after him as he quickly made his way down to the station toll.

"Yeah, you better run!" I yelled at him while waving my sister's blade at him.

Envy jumped over the toll steel bar and turned around to face me. He reached his open palm to me and chanted.

"I'm not as powerful as you. Not as smart. Not as brave."

"Lame! That trick is not gonna work on me again, Fariphel!" I yelled as I jumped over the toll. "And the other Envy did it so much better than you!"

"My name is Lethanus!!!" he shouted angry while he turned to run again.

Envy headed towards some stairs that reached the train platform. I had to catch him before I'd lose him in the tunnels. I jumped on his back and dropped him to the floor with my weight. I landed on top of him and punched his face hard. I was so mad at him.

"This is for Isophie, you coward!" I yelled relentless, "I'll teach you to kick someone when they're down!"

His face made me mad. I was so enraged, I wanted to kill him. I made him bleed and hurt. He begged me to stop, but I kept hitting him. I couldn't control my anger.

Wait, I'm the angel of emotions and I couldn't control my anger?!

"Wrath!" I yelled.

"Ha! You fell for it!" Envy smirked.

I turned around too late. Wrath stood behind me and smacked my head with her axe. I fell down hard. Scarlet's sword landed a few feet away from me. My fingers touched the blood on the back of my head.

"HUHRRRAAAH!!!"

Her scream echoed on the walls and into my head as I tried to get a grip of myself. My body wobbled while I tried to crawl away from her. Envy kicked me to the floor and laughed at me, but Wrath smacked him, knocking him down.

"OUT OF MY WAY, WORM!"

Wrath played me and was about to take my life as trophy. She raised her axe to strike me. I closed my eyes. But as the axe came down at me, I heard a loud thud sound.

"YOU!" Wrath yelled.

I opened my eyes and saw Scarlet blocking the demon's axe with a red fiery sword made of bones. She'd been watching over me, just like when she was alive. Watching them clash their blades from up close was too much for me. They went at it like crazy.

"Got…this…" she said to me with a creepy hoarse voice and made a gesture with her head for me to leave.

I saw a small crack rip through her mouth when she said those words. That's when I noticed her face and body was cracking up all over. When she turned her attention back at Wrath, I knew I needed to crawl away from both of them as fast as I could. Maybe Envy thought of the same thing, because he took off as soon as they began to fight. I managed to drag myself to a corner of the wall where I rested the broken wing on my back.

Wrath rocked her axe with all her strength at Scarlet's side, but my zombie sister blocked in time. The axe had stuck halfway inside the sword. Scarlet yanked the axe from the barbaric arch-demon and threw both arms to the side.

"No…more…weapons…" she told Wrath.

My undead sister raised her arms to fight. Her fists were not completely closed because her fingers were cracking a bit too, so she left them dangling. Wrath closed her massive fists and quickly flew the first punch on Scarlet's face, The hit sounded like when you break a glass jar. I saw chunks of her face spread away. That scared me a lot, but Scarlet was not fazed. She stood still and twisted her face back towards Wrath. The parts of her face that were broken showed a scary red flame. Wrath punched her again from underneath the chin, breaking off what was left of her mouth. Then she punched Scarlet's chest, I couldn't take it anymore.

"Scarleeeet!" I cried.

"I WILL BREAK YOU TO MILLIONS OF PIECES!!!" The angry demon screamed.

Wrath kept pounding on my sister. She lifted her up and slammed her against the ground. But Scarlet never made a sound. She stood up and shook her head from side to side, shaking off little pieces of her face that hung from her.

"My... turn..."

Scarlet didn't even finish saying those words when I saw her right arm buried inside Wrath abdomen. Wrath let out a painful scream as Scarlet pulled out some innards from her body. Her other arm was already clawing inside the demon's chest. My sister was digging and into Wrath's body at a supernatural speed. She was so fast; I never actually saw when her arms moved at all. All I could see was guts and blood gushing out of the demon as if she was being shredded by a chainsaw. Wrath wailed and tried to push her away. I got nauseous and turned my eyes away.

Moments later the screams stopped, but I just couldn't bear to look. I felt a tap on my shoulder.

"You...alright...?" Scarlet uttered.

I peeked a bit behind my broken sister and saw a blood pool of body parts on the floor as well as blood splattered all over the walls.

"Jeeze, Scarlet! What did you do?"

"We had...history..."

Scarlet stretched her arm to help me up. I took it.

"I'm getting my butt handed to me every time." I said ashamed.

"Doing...fine..."

I couldn't help staring at her broken face.

"You look-"

"...dead..."

"Ha! ... right... um... Hey, I need to- I just want you to know. I'm, uh, really really sorry for everything and..."

I couldn't hold my tears. Scarlet put her dry blood stained hand on my shoulder.

"I-I killed you…" I cried.

"No…Gabriel… only her…" she spoke, "Need…to fight…"

"I will, I promise."

"I…know…"

We hugged. It felt like embracing a cold statue. But this was my sister and I loved her so much, and I felt so lucky to be able to see her again.

Suddenly, Scarlet backed away from me, her arms still locked with mine. I followed her eyes looking down at her chest and saw the edge of her sword (not the fiery boney one, but the one I had) sticking out. The demon Pride held it from behind her and pushed it in a bit more.

"NOOO!!!" I yelled.

"Ashes to ashes" Pride said.

The cracks in Scarlet's body grew rapidly and she pieces of her fell off fast. I felt her arms crash and crumble in mine until only pieces of her glass-like skin remained around on the floor.

"See, this is why I needed you to give me the sword." Pride told me, "Having it lying around with no care. Something so important as this powerful relic should not be discarded so easily."

I lashed at him with my awkward punches. He didn't feel any of them, but I kept trying.

"Pride! You killed my sister, you rat bastard!"

"Oh, if I could only take credit for that… She was already done for. She played her part well, I admit. I have no more need for her."

As I kept making a fool of myself by trying to fight him, the demon grabbed both my wrists with one hand and pulled me closer to him. He pointed the sword to my face.

"WATCH. THE SUIT."

. . . .

Columbus Circle was a mess of loud gunfire noises and beasts roaring that resonated in asymmetric rhythm with the popping bright flashes of Blue's flying sphere cannons. Gluttony consumed a large amount of the spirits that crossed his path, until the wraith la Llorona forced his mouth wide open and pulled most of the sprits free from his belly. She dug deeper into his supernatural digestive system looking for her children.

"*DONDE ESTAN MIS HIJOS??*" she wailed.

"Lady, they're not in there, I can tell you that much!" Gluttony cried.

La Llorona made her way out from the Deadly Seven demon's mouth. She stared at him for a moment with disgust. She sniffed and passed her finger over the holes that were her nose to wipe off the stench. The wraith flew away from Gluttony to continue the search for her children elsewhere in the battlefield.

'What?!" Gluttony yelled, grabbing his belly in pain, "Come back! Let me eat you properly!"

Losing all the spirits made Gluttony very hungry. Nothing a good meal couldn't fix, he figured. He looked to his side and saw the zombie cowboy riding his horse as he laid waste of the army of goblin demons.

"So hungry, I could eat…a horse" Gluttony said smiling.

Sheriff Murphy "Powder" Cain shot his guns repeatedly, making a path through the horde of demons while his horse galloped through the monsters. Suddenly, the horse stopped abruptly, and the zombie sheriff was thrown off a few feet away. Cain landed on three demon goblins that quickly tried to kill him, but he blew them all away with his two pistols. The zombie cowboy searched for his horse among the ocean of demons.

"What inna hell's wrong with ya, girl?!" he hollered, "Where are ya, now?"

"Eeeeiiihaaahhheeee!!!" the horse neighed.

Powder Cain followed the cries of his horse and pushed the demons out of his way until he saw Gluttony, his mouth abnormally extended, eating his horse with one swallow. The undead horse was half way inside him already.

"Ya ain't eatin' mah horse, ya spooky-bellied sumabitch!" Cain shouted.

The undead cowboy saw red as he shot and punched and kicked his way through the demons between him and his horse. He reached Gluttony and triggered his guns again and again emptying his rusty lead bullets on his abdomen. The pain in Gluttony's stomach was unbearable and he dropped to the pavement, trying not to vomit. The arch-demon finally relented and regurgitated Cain's horse. Powder Cain mounted his horse again.

"Ya be thankful ah don' mess with a fellah when he's down." the undead sheriff said, "Bettah not let me see yah again, ya hear?!"

The zombie cowboy rode his horse away while Gluttony held his belly and rolled on the ground. He waited a few minutes to recuperate and stood back up.

Black Angel stood beneath the tall Christopher Columbus statue in the middle of the circle plaza as she continued coordinating the fight of her army of restless spirits against the goblin demons. Gluttony saw her from a distance and figured if the Cherubim he ate were delicious; an Archangel should be an exquisite meal. He walked a few steps towards the angel of death, but Beggar, the demon Greed, stood in his way.

"Hold it." Greed said, holding him by the arm, "That little girl over there fought the Four Horsemen of the Apocalypse to a standstill. I am not that needy to try to take on her. I hope you are not that ravenous."

Gluttony stared at the Black Angel for a moment and changed his mind.

"There's gotta be something to eat around here…" he said to himself as he wandered away.

Evergreen made her way through the battlefield by stepping over corpses of the fallen demons. Every dead demon left behind her path bared a new flower or insect born from small seeds and eggs that dropped from her hair. The angel of nature was focused on finding only one demon, but she knew she didn't have to look for him when she could make him come to her. She stopped by the entrance to Central Park and leaned next to a tree. The green angel slowly moved her body in a sensual manner. She caressed her body and played with the tree with movements that resembled a professional pole dancer. It wasn't too long before Lust took notice and sat by the grass to stare at her. Three of Lusts little goblin slaves sat with him.

"Papa likes it slow." he requested with heavy breathing, "Yesss"

Lust drooled with mad ecstasy. Evergreen continued her seductive dance. One of the helpers, the one dressed as a Girl Scout, felt a bite on its leg. The demon saw a small mouse gnawing at it. As it tried to shake the animal off, the goblin felt another bite; it was a big rat this time. Another rat took a bite, and then another. The lesser demon was being attacked by rats. It looked at her master and the other two helpers. The helpers were already dead under a pile of frenzied rodents. As the Girl Scout goblin tried to stand up, one of its legs broke after the rats had ate its knee. The demon struggled to crawl over to its master, but the rats swarmed on top of its entire body to finish it off.

The angel of nature did not stop dancing and the arch-demon remained seated. He was too busy admiring her to notice he was completely covered by rats that were eating him alive. Evergreen had silently called upon all the rats that lived in sewers, basements, and subway tunnels of New York City. The critters left their valuable trash treasures, with the promise of a banquet waiting for them at the park. Thousands of dirty rodents gathered with hunger and ripped out the flesh of the Deadly Seven lord. A few of them sneaked inside his body through his mouth to eat him from the inside out. Shortly after, Evergreen stopped her dance to check on her work. When she saw that Lust became an empty carcass of gnawed flesh and bones, she stepped on his bloody skull which cracked under her feet.

Blue witnessed the whole thing from the sky. He saw the rats dispersing and his sister walk away from Lust's chewed body.

"By God, woman!" he exclaimed, "Darling, remind me never to cross you."

The blue angel had shot down almost all flying Leviathans. With the skies clear, his attention shifted to Sloth. He set up several alarms on his luminescent floating screens to wake him up in case he felt tired or fell asleep when he got too close to the Deadly Seven Demon. He located the Deadly Seven loafer resting on a bench by the park side walk. Blue set his battle armor on stealth mode and carefully hovered downwards to approach the demon. Once he found himself at a safe distance and a clear position to fire, the cobalt angel locked and loaded all the built-in fire arms in his armor. The clicking sound of the weapons woke up Sloth, who seemed surprised to see Blue.

"hrmm..."

"Hrmm yourself", Blue replied.

Blue opened fire. He threw everything he had at the demonic slacker. The demon's flesh became riddled with holes. His corpse remained motionless for a moment, until a low wind current knocked it to the side. The Archangel deactivated the guns in his armor.

"Well, that was anticlimactic..." Blue declared a bit disappointed.

"Hrmm-" Sloth slurred as he stood right next to the angel.

"Eeeeeeek!" Blue jumped on his toes surprised.

DEEEEEET DEEEEEET DEEEEET DEEEEET DEEEET DEEEEEET DEEEEEET DEEEEET DEEEEET DEEEET

Blue woke up from his slumber with the sound of the alarm. He had fallen asleep on the bench where he found Sloth.

"Mother flower!" he cussed, "He got me!"

The blue angel set up his alarms again to wake him up in case he felt tired or fell asleep when he got too close to the Deadly Seven Demon. He reset his tracking devices and renewed his search.

He found Sloth looking through the garbage of a trashcan. Blue quickly reloaded his guns and fired many rounds. After the dust settled, the angel of progress searched the area near the trashcan for the demon, but couldn't find him. He turned around and faced the direction where the rest of the demon army battled his siblings. Blue saw that all of the demon goblins' faces were identical to Sloth's. Even the Archangels looked like Sloth. Suddenly, every single one of them slurred at the same time:

"HRMM"

DEEEEEET DEEEEEET DEEEEET DEEEEET DEEEET DEEEEEET DEEEEEET DEEEEET DEEEEET DEEEET

Blue woke up from his slumber with the sound of the alarm. He had fallen asleep again near the trashcan.

"AAAAAAAH!!!!! That's it!" he yelled, "Gloves are off, you little pest!"

....

There was no one at the train station I could call for help. If I concentrated, I could have one of my siblings feel worried about me and want to look for me, but that was kind of hard to do when Pride held my arms tight and aimed Scarlet's steel to my face. Trying to kick him with my legs proved to be pointless.

"Stop resisting." He ordered me.

"I'm not gonna let you use my sister's sword!" I told him.

"I am not going to use it. You are."

"Wait, what?"

The Deadly Seven leader lowered his shades revealing his eyes to me. They were entirely black. He let go of me and handed the sword back to me.

"Lucifer?! You're Pride?!"

"A necessary guise given the circumstances. When Eve expelled me from Hell, I needed a way to return inconspicuous at my whim. Believe me, serving under her rule was unbearable at best."

"But you didn't have to do that to Scarlet!"

Lucifer/Pride turned me around facing the wall and slammed me against it. I could barely breathe with the pressure he applied.

"OW! Stop iiiit!" I yelled

"You are such an annoying creature. If you wish to help your human friend, HOLD STILL!"

"Okay! Okay!"

Lucifer patched up my broken wing with some weird long brown bandages with old language gibberish written on them. I immediately felt better and was able to flutter my wings.

"It still needs healing, but it will hold while you do what you need to do" he said.

He shifted me back and we were face to face.

"I'll be honest with you. I never truly believed you would be able to handle your ministry, much less Scarlet's sword. Somehow, you have turned the tide and there is a chance to save Creation. But none of your efforts will matter if you do not defeat Adam. He has the means to undo everything."

"How?"

"He corrupted his God given gift to dominate over beasts to control the Leviathans. They were not meant to roam the Earth, but Adam has led them here. Those creatures were created for a world long gone before this one was conceived. Some of them have the destructive power to raze this planet ten times over."

"Oy!"

"You cannot-"

Lucifer was interrupted by a loud roaring rumble and a tremor that shook me to my knees even though the dark angel remained standing unfazed. I instinctively held on to him until the quakes passed. Pieces of the subway station's ceiling crumbled almost on top of us as the walls cracked. I remembered, when I was in Hell, how the hydra monster almost destroyed Lucifer's tower. This felt a jizillion times worse.

"He's here. You need to finish this. Take the sword. By all means, do not let him take it from you."

"What about my siblings? If the Deadly Seven-"

"I own the Deadly Seven. I will take care of those monkeys."

"Why are you doing this? Why help me?"

Lucifer smirked, "I am your guardian angel."

I carried the sword to my shoulder and made my way through the rubble towards the stairs. I stopped cold and ran back to Lucifer.

"That was a joke, right? 'Cause it would really suck if the Devil was really my guardian ang-"

"LEAVE NOW!!!" he yelled at me with scary ferocity.

"Alright! Okay! I'm leaving!"

I ran back up to the street level and stopped cold with what I saw. Columbus Circle was like, literally crushed by what looked like a massive dark gray rocky endless tower wall thing that had landed on the whole area. Like a giant hammer just hit New York City. The few buildings left standing after the fight with the Seven Deadly Demons were decimated. I knew this thing's reach covered many blocks but I couldn't see how high up in the sky it went. Demons and beasts everywhere were crushed underneath the tower. Even the remaining members of the Deadly Seven were knocked out.

My heart skipped a beat when I saw my siblings down on the ground unconscious, most likely by the shock wave this thing must have created when it landed. Only Ricadel, the White Angel, was awake, and she was gathering my sisters and brother to safety, laying them close to each other by the mall entrance, God bless her. I ran over to them.

Blue's armor was damaged, with little sparks popping up on its conjunctures. A few spirits gathered around Black, waiting for her to wake up. Evergreen's arm was injured, and it was wrapped by a piece of cloth from the White Angel's dress to stop the bleeding. Goldie blabbered some nonsense while unconscious.

"Hey, are you okay?!" I asked Ricadel.

The White Angel hugged me tight. A tear rolled down her eye.

"Thank the Lord you are well, Violet! I couldn't find you and I thought-"

"I'm okay, really. Listen, we need to wake them up. We can't let the ministries go bonkers again. Or... wait. Wait, we can just wake Goldie up. Just her will be enough."

We sat Goldie up and slightly tapped her face, then shook her up a bit, until she opened her eyes.

"Heeey! What's the big idea, shakin' me like that?!" she queried annoyed, shoving me off.

"I'm sorry Goldie, but we need your help." I replied, "The others are down, and if you don't take over their ministries for them, the seals of Creation are going to break again!"

"All of 'em?! Oh, I dunno know if I can pull off-"

"Yes, you can! You're Goldie! You wanted to run the show? The stage is yours! Now get to it! I have to go stop that...thing, whatever it is."

"The stage is mine..." Goldie's eyes lit bright and her smile widened.

"Yeah... um, don't go too crazy now. No laser shooting dinosaurs or whatever, please."

"Laser shootin' dinosaurs? Pshaw! Whaddaya think, I'm an amateur? Imma real artist, see?"

"Okay, well... White, please take care of our siblings."

I held Scarlet's blade tight, looked up at the gray tower and spread my wings.

"Here goes-"

"Violet?" the White Angel held my hand, "If you see Adam? Please tell him... Tell him I pray for him."

I felt the sadness in Ricadel's soul. The downside to loving so much, like she did, is that you suffer equally as much when you get hurt. I kissed her forehead.

"Okay."

I took flight. I sped upwards as fast as my wings could take me. I went up, trying to find a top to the thing I was going to fight. I couldn't. It kept extending towards space. So I gave up trying to reach its high point and just flew back down towards the city. I rushed straight towards it to fight it, figuring maybe I could topple it. I swung the sword and hit it as hard as I could with it.

"Aaaaaaah!" I yelled as I stroke it again and again.

Nothing happened. I didn't even dent it. I felt like a complete idiot. Suddenly, a huge ball of fire hit the tower too close to where I was hovering. One of my wings caught a little fire at the tip, but it went away when I fluttered it, Two more fire balls passed right by me. I got scared and squealed. When I turned around, I saw the two dragons that carried Adam's litter breathing fire at me. Adam stood on the litter holding Ruth in front of me with a blade to her neck.

"Ruth!" I yelled. "Leave her alone!"

I could tell Ruth had been crying, but otherwise she seemed unharmed.

"What do you think you're doing?" He asked me.

"I'm going to stop it!"

"Do you even know what it is? I call it Ktulu. A creature so immense, it's too big to cross over to our world without leveling all of the northern east coast. What you are seeing extends all the way across Manhattan, Queens, and beyond. And that's just one leg. It's got hundreds. All I need to do is have the beast cross here in its entirety."

"I won't let you!"

"How? How can you possibly think you can stop this?"

That was kind of a good question. I really didn't know how to stop that creature from crossing over.

"Look, this is between us now. Just leave Ruth out of this, please."

"I will, I promise, but you need to give me the sword first."

"No!"

"Don't give him the sword, Violet!" Ruth yelled.

"I wish Steve were here to slap some sense into you! What do you think he'd say about what you're doing?"

The first man hesitated, his eyes showed me the pain I knew he felt for losing his lover. But the moment passed quickly, and his eyes went back to their normal dead-like way.

"I do this for him and for all of us cursed with living in this cesspool of a world that God created." he uttered. "I am killing God. This is going to happen."

Adam tightened the blade against her neck and it went in the skin just a bit. A thin stream of blood came out.

"Aaah!" Ruth cried.

"Stop! Please! Okay!" I yelled.

"You know I will kill her" Adam declared. "But give me the sword and I promise nothing will happen to her."

"Don't let him win!" Ruth cried to me as tears rolled down her eyes.

"I-I can't let him hurt you." I said to her with sadness, "I couldn't live with it."

I looked at Scarlet's sword for a moment and said "I'm sorry"

I extended the arm that held the blade towards Adam and slowly flew closer to him.

"No!" Ruth yelled.

Just when I was about to hand over the sword to Adam, I looked at Ruth's eyes. She saw in mine that I just couldn't let anything happen to her, even if it meant damning the world. She stared back at me sad.

"You know in what part of Hell I'll be at." Ruth said

Ruth pressed Adam's blade harder inside her neck and slit it from side to side, Blood gushed from her neck as Adam released the blade in kneejerk reaction. She slipped away from his grasp and tumbled out of the litter, falling rapidly thousands of miles towards the city.

"RUTH!" I called. "NOOOO!"

As Ruth fell, everything around me went silent. I could not hear any sounds, but the echoes of my scream. I could not hear any other emotions but the fast beating of my heart and the ever slowing pace of Ruth's. I dropped as fast as I could after her, forcing my wings to burn with the friction if necessary. I had to catch her. I could still save her. Luckily, I was able to grab on to her boot, and then the rest of her body. I carried her down and laid her on the street, holding her neck to stop the bleeding. But it didn't take. Ruth stared at me and I felt her confusion and sadness. She lied on the street facing me as she held the bloodied short blade with both hands. She gave me the same reassuring lying smile I gave her before when I thought I was going to die.

"Suh-save..." she mumbled.

I cried for her, because I didn't know what to do to save her. Then she stopped breathing.

"I can't-I can't feel you, Ruth!" I cried, "I can't feel you!"

Ruth committed suicide to save the world. She held on to the blade that killed her until the very end. That was her, telling me what I had to do. I still held on to Scarlet's sword, and I wasn't going to let it go. I stood up and looked up at the sky. Adam and his dragons were flying straight at me, breathing balls of fire my way.

I took off and flew straight at him, raising the blade to strike. As we were about to collide, I spun to the side and beheaded one of the two dragons with a quick clean swoosh of the sword. The weight of the dead dragon pulled the other dragon with it and derailed Adam's litter. When the other dragon tried to stabilize its flight, I tore open its belly with my sister's weapon. Adam slipped and plunged head first towards the earth.

I flew after him, trying to reach him. We locked glances and I saw he wasn't scared to fall. He knew he would survive it. Still, I thought the impact would get messy; and I was right. When the first man hit the ground all the bones in his body broke. He spewed bubbly streams of blood from his mouth. But he wasn't fazed by the pain. His eyes were still the same. I still felt that resounding old resentment he carried. It was Adam's hatred that called the huge creature to our world. As long as he lived, that monster was going to cross over and Adam would win. There was only one thing to do. If Scarlet's sword was powerful enough to kill Eve, it should be good enough for Adam. So I raised my sister's blade and I stopped mid-air.

"Oh yeah, um. Ricadel says she prays for you." I said.

"Hunh..w-who-?" he asked.

Then I struck the sword between Adam's eyes, killing him instantly.

As soon as the first man passed away, the leviathan beasts all over the city shrieked and scattered away. I figured their connection to Adam broke, and they were all confused and scared. The surviving armies of demon goblins were disoriented too. With no leader to follow, they all followed Beggar and the other Deadly Seven goons that survived while they retreated to the portal gates back to Hell. Meanwhile, Kutululu, or whatever its name was, slowly ascended to space until it was out of sight and completely gone from Creation.

I ran back a couple of blocks to find Ruth. When I reached her I cleaned up the blood off her face and hair as much as I could and sat on my knees next to her to cry for what little was left of the night. In the morning, my siblings found me sleeping with my head laid on Ruth's chest. They gathered around me as the White Angel tapped my shoulder.

"Violet." she said, "Angels do not sleep. Wake up, sister. Your siblings are all well. You saved Creation. You saved us all!"

I woke up and wished everything was all a bad dream. I just wanted Ruth and me to be back at that RV on the road, listening to Duncan Blackheart's gloomy gothic tunes.

Ruth and I saved the world, but it didn't matter to me. None of it mattered. My best friend was dead.

21 ...AND STUFF

A beautiful white haired woman woke up on a blue inflatable mattress at one of many shelters where hundreds of thousands of refugees were evacuated the previous night from the east coast of the United States. She didn't know exactly where she was, or how long she had slept, but the warm sunlight led her to believe the day was still within the hours of the morning. Her memories of the previous night were a haze, and when she thought about it, there was not much she could remember of her life at all.

"Nice dress" a man next to her told her.

The woman looked at her dirty white dress. It was a bloody mess. She wiggled her toes as she noticed she lost her sandals.

"Probably somebody stole your shoes while you were asleep." the man said.

When the lady turned to look at the man talking to her, she was shocked to see he had no arms.

"It's okay, you can stare" the man said, "It's my sexy chest hair, isn't it? Women can't help themselves."

"I'm sorry" she apologized.

"Sorry for what? I'm the best foot guitar player in the world!"

The woman smiled.

"You seem to have a positive perspective on life." she noted.

"Life is about lemons and lemonade, lady. You work with what God gives you. I ain't sittin' around with my arms crossed doing nothing and whining. Life's too short for that shit."

"Don't you want to live forever?"

"Live forever? Sounds pretty boring, if ya ask me. Where's the challenge in that? No. The idea- the idea is to do as much as you can while you roll with the punches life throws at you, before your time's up. Sure, there are times when you fall into despair, it ain't never easy, but what can you do? Comes with the territory. Trick is not staying down too long. You get up, wipe off your shoulder, and move on. That's why my shirt is so dirty, see? I can't reach my shoulders with my elbows. HA!"

The woman laughed as the man with no arms tried to reach his shoulder with his elbow.

"Who are you?" the lady asked.

"Oh, many things. A guitarist and song writer, a cook, someday I'd like to be a father... I dunno, maybe I could be the man of your dreams. You seem to be in mine a lot!" he half-joked.

"Right..." The white haired woman rolled her eyes and smirked.

"By the way, I'm Melvin. What's your name?"

"Gabriel"

"Gabrielle?"

"No, Gabriel."

"Isn't that a man's name?"

"That's my name."

"Okay, Gabriel. Let's get some breakfast in that pretty little belly of yours. We better hurry up before the line gets too long in the kitchen."

Gabriel hesitated. She felt an overwhelming sense of fear that she couldn't explain. It was as if a dark shadow was closing in on her, watching her every move. Suddenly, she was afraid to get off the mattress.

"Don't be afraid. Live a little. Take my hand. HA!" Melvin joked.

Gabriel stood up, wrapped her arm around his elbow, and followed his lead.

"So how 'bout it? You think an angel like you would ever consider going out with a bum like me?"

"Would you play your guitar for me?"

"Only if you sing along."

"I could sing."

"I can see that. You have a pretty voice."

As the couple walked towards the shelter dining hall, they passed right in front of the Black Angel. The angel of death was invisible to Gabriel, but the angel could see her. The Black Angel wore Gabriel's pearl laced sandals. They looked big on her, but she enjoyed airing out her feet. She looked forward to meeting with Gabriel again. But for now, she watched her and waited.

·············

Adam opened his eyes and drew breath again. His bones were fixed and he certainly did not have Scarlet's sword wedged between his eyes. He noticed he was naked as he stood up slowly. He contemplated his surroundings and quickly recognized the silver coated chamber as the throne room he once briefly ruled from. He knew he was not alone in that room, but he didn't have to face the throne to know who sat on it now.

"Why did you bring me back to life, Lucifer?" Adam asked.

"How fortunate to be gathered once again. This is a family reunion." Lucifer uttered. "Of course we are missing dear Lillith, but she is … out of my reach for the time being."

Lucifer had taken the form of the naked dark angel that once tempted Eve in the Garden of Eden. He sat on his throne, eyes fixed on Adam while he caressed Eve's blond hair. She was naked and sat on her knees at the side of the dark angel resting her head on his leg. The Weeping Queen held a wooden box in her hands. Her eyes were spaced out. She seemed to be under a spell.

"I've been so lonely for so long. I decided to take a queen." Lucifer declared, "There's always room for three if you're interested."

"You two deserve each other. Have a good life." Adam replied.

"I have always been so fond of you. You gave my life a purpose back when we used to play our little war games. I could use a man like you in my ranks. There is so much to do. The armies of Hell have been depleted and only four of the Deadly Seven remain alive: Greed, Sloth, Gluttony, and Envy. Greed already plans for insurrection. Bow to me, and help me restore order."

"I bow to no one. Not to you. Not to God."

"Don't be a sore loser. How about an incentive, then?"

Eve opened the wooden box in her hands, and a luminous red soul floated out from it.

Adam froze. After all his lover had suffered because of him, his soul could be condemned for all eternity at the hands of Lucifer. For a moment, he thought of giving himself up to save him.

"Steve…"

"If you refuse to do my bidding, your lover's soul will know suffering to the point of madness." the Devil threatened.

The first man clenched his fist, but remained unyielding.

"…Do with him what you want. I will never be yours to own"

Adam turned his back to Lucifer and took a few steps to leave the throne room.

"I will give you God's head on a silver platter" Lucifer continued, "You almost had Him with that stunt you pulled. But the final war will come one day. With you at my side, we can bring the gates of Heaven down and raise Hell."

Adam stopped, and looked back at the dark angel. He hesitated for a moment.

"I will never work for you" Adam said, "But what could I gain by joining you that I haven't achieved for myself?"

Lucifer laughed.

"Fair enough, my Pride."

Lucifer stood up from his throne and walked by Adam. Eve quietly followed.

"Come." the dark angel said to Adam.

A silver door opened and the three exited the throne room. The Devil led Adam and Eve down the tower towards an underground level where he had built a secret dungeon. As Lucifer opened the rusty steel door of the cell, Adam could hear loud inhuman growls coming from inside.

"Let me show you what I've done with the child you had with Lillith…" Lucifer smiled.

....

So the world didn't end, but there was a whole mess left behind we needed to fix. Millions of lives were lost all over the Earth; not to mention all that destruction left behind after the demonic invasion. There were even reports of random leviathan attacks here and there. People were pretty traumatized by something they could not understand. Prayers were at an all-time high, but they were not being answered in Heaven, 'cause there were no Cherubim to deal with them. And how could we possibly explain these events without revealing our existence to them? *"Hey, all that wild stuff that happened last night was kind of the final war between good and evil in the end of times, but we fixed it. False alarm! Our bad!"* This was not really something the Archangels could hide under a rug, right?

The six of Seven Lights assembled at the park in Sao Paulo that was destroyed during the earthquake almost a month ago. Evergreen and Blue finally got around to finish their reconstruction plans for Ibirapuera and thought we might get inspired by the place. We gathered at the hovering bridge lifted by powerful geothermal vapors, from Evergreen's geysers. The view of the city on the horizon was phenomenal.

The Black Angel offered ascending some of the best behaving souls into Cherubim so we could repopulate the Pax Dei. One of the first to be saved was the soul of a man named Jacinto. He was a saint that was trapped for many years in Hell by Eve, but his soul exploded to bits. Ricadel met him when she was Lillith and asked the Black Angel to help him. Azrael had to bring him back by assembling his skull like pieces of a puzzle. He was ascended to form of Cherubim and chosen to lead the angels as Amion II.

We all agreed that the angel of life and the angel of death would convene to separate those who should not have died in the war from those that were meant to, but that would take a while 'cause they had to check one soul at a time. They both seemed up for it, though, and very eager to work with each other. It was rare to see the angels of life and death getting along so well. The Black Angel even offered to help our white sister to find the child she lost to Lucifer.

I, on the other hand, got the task of finding the next worthy wielder of Scarlet's sword. I got the hang of it and got a bit attached to it, but I always knew it was a loaner. I suggested Isophie, who was still alive after all. Thank God that Fariphel or Envy or whatever didn't do a good job in killing her. She was badly wounded, and was taken to Heaven to rest and eat lots of fruit. The fire that burned her wings never went out, though, and the flames actually took the form of really cool fire wings. She looks so badass! I decided to wait until she got better to offer her the sword, along with Scarlet's ministry.

After all minor issues were resolved we got into the big matter at hand.

"Well, I think this is the perfect opportunity to introduce advanced space travel technology" Blue proposed, "I think it's high time the monkeys colonized other planets. We could let them believe they were attacked by aliens or whatnot. What better way to finally unite them all under one planet?"

Evergreen stared at Blue annoyed.

"First of all, stop calling them monkeys. It stopped being funny in the middle ages. Secondly, they cannot even take care of this one world, and you want them to go ruin others as well?! I vote that Blue makes a vow of silence for the next hundred years, who's with me?"

"Maybe it is not a bad idea to reveal ourselves to humanity." the White Angel suggested, "We should let them see for themselves that they are protected by God and the Seven Lights. If we vindicate their faith, surely they will choose to live their lives in the path of God. We could finally achieve peace for all mankind!"

"Too much... kindness... Must resist... urge to... punch her..." Blue whispered to Evergreen mockingly.

"Say, why won't ya let me take a crack at this world fixin' thing, ya mooks?" Goldie asked, "Why I could clean up this mess lickety split! Send those leviathan monsters back where they belong. I'll even make people think that all this hoopla was El Niño! Hocus Miraculous Presto!"

Evergreen and Blue looked at each other worried.

"I think it is a great idea! What worries you now, my siblings?" The White Angel asked dumbfounded.

Blue cleared his throat and paused before answering the query.

"See, honeybunches, there's a reason we don't let Goldie go crazy with Creation. Besides the whole danger of undoing the laws of physics and all that jazz, White (the one that came before you, I mean) -she told us that she restricted Goldie's role in this world because the last person to be the angel of miracles before Goldie went mad with power and rebelled against God."

"You mean Lucifer? He was the first angel of miracles?" The White Angel replied, "That is truly worrisome, I agree. But it seems to me that we should no longer trust the other White's judgment on account that she herself rebelled against God and almost ended the world."

"Aaaand how!" Goldie exclaimed.

Evergreen and Blue took note.

"That makes sense…" the green angel mumbled.

"And I think…" White Angel continued, "I think Lucifer is Lucifer and Goldie is Goldie, and there must be a reason why God trusted her with her ministry."

"What she said!" Goldie interjected again.

"I agree…" I finally spoke, "I trust Goldie completely. She bailed me out a couple of times with the other White. And she was the only one of us that didn't break her seal. I say we let Goldie do it. It's what she's meant to do."

My siblings all looked at me weird. It was the first time I actually let my opinion known in one of the many meetings we've had. But I had to take things seriously now. I owed it to them, to Ruth, and to God,

"Guys…" I continued, "I'm not feeling so good. I'm going to take a walk for a bit. I will be back. I swear."

"Oh, sweetie, of course!" Blue said, "You've done enough. We'll sort all this other crazy business out. But before you go, there's a little point in our agenda we need to coveeeer! We have to choose a new leader for the Seven Lights. I propose meeee, but you know, everyone that's interested can nominate themselves."

"I nominate my sister Evergreen!" White declared enthused.

"Evergreen" I said.

"Evergreen's got the knowhow, see?" Goldie seconded.

The Black Angel pointed at Evergreen.

"Well…" Blue reacted with a look over the shoulder to Evergreen, "That was fast! Congratulations are in order, I guess"

Evergreen stood silent for a moment.

"I thank you all, but I cannot accept." Evergreen declared, "I need to confess something."

"Oh, oh." Blue said, knowing the tone of Evergreen meant some bad news was coming.

"Some of you already know," she continued, "I fell in love with a human. His name was Paolo. When I was under Lust's control, I-I killed Paolo. I was made an offer by Lucifer to bring him back. I accepted."

"WHAT?!" Blue asked alarmed.

"This morning, Paolo rose from the natural grave I made for him. He is alive, and my soul now belongs to Lucifer."

Everybody fell silent. I should have noticed the pain in Evergreen's emotions, but I was so involved with mine, I didn't pay attention. Blue lowered his head. His complexion changed completely.

"When will he come to collect?" he asked.

"Paolo will live a long healthy life. I will perform my duties during that time. The minute he dies, Lucifer will come for me."

"We have to think of something! There's still time to plan! I could- I could-"

"Blue, no one outthinks Lucifer. I will be okay."

Blue couldn't contain the tears in his eyes, Evergreen hugged him.

"I'm sorry, little brother."

All of us were devastated by the news. After Ricadel was selected to lead us, we decided to stop for the day and parted ways.

I stayed at the park, thinking of all that had happened to me the last few weeks. I thought of Ruth and I cried. As I stood by the river that crossed the park, I felt a tug on my pants. I looked down. It was my sister Black. She took my hand and had me follow her. The Black Angel lead me to a nearby sitting area where there were many benches lined up against the river. Ruth sat on the third bench closest to the water. She looked calm, like she was waiting for someone. I held my hands over my mouth and cried some more, I slowly walked over and sat next to her. We hugged, we cried. Lots of OMG's were said.

"I thought you were-" I said

"Going to Hell?" she completed my sentence, "I thought that too. But it turns out what I did was more a sacrifice for mankind than an actual suicide, so... I guess I'm going to Heaven..."

"That is so awesome! We can totally see each other there!"

"I know." she smiled.

"And you'll totally love crossing the truth spirals."

"The what?"

"They're like flowing river waters in heaven, but they swirl upwards. Every soul that crosses the spirals relives its happiest and most loving memories until reaching its highest state of bliss, what some people call nirvana. It's the way each soul creates its own unique version of Heaven."

"Sounds nice"

"It is. That's actually how Lucifer got his idea for his creepy tower; only the opposite, you know?"

"Listen, I don't have much time, and I won't be seeing you for a while. I need to say something. I've been thinking about Jonah's tale. You were not the only one running away from your responsibilities. Ever since I had the dreams, I tried to ignore them for a while, but there you were on that train that day, just like in my dream. I got a second chance to make things right. But those people in Hell, the ones punished for committing suicide, they never got a second chance to do what God intended for them. When I go to Heaven, I'm going to plead for them. I'd like to ask God to give them that second chance. I mean, it wouldn't be everyone; not criminal assholes that killed themselves to avoid jail or whatnot. I'm talking those that really had it hard or felt truly lost and never got the help they needed. You think that's crazy?"

"Wow… No. I think that's really cool."

"You think He'll hear me?"

"He should! You just saved Creation, right? Just pray with feeling. I'll make sure He gets the message."

"Violet, thank you for everything you did for me, for saving my life."

"What?! Come on, no big deal really. It's what we angels do, you know?"

"You did warn me not to warm up to Adam!"

"Gramps was never in your league! Also, ew!"

We both laughed. It was so good to see her laugh.

"You were the one that saved me." I said to her.

We fell silent and held each other's hands. I took out my ipod and headphones.

"Hey, you want to listen to the Duncan? One last for the road?"

"I don't know. He's too dark. I don't want to feel dark anymore."

"Well, there's this Spanish pop band I like, Purpura Luz…"

"I love Purpura Luz! They're awesome!"

"You know Purpura Luz, too?! That's a sign right there! We're on a BFF level, you and I!"

"Yeah…" Ruth smiled and put on one of the headphones.

We listened to a song called *"Tu Corazon Baila Por Mí"*, and we sang and moved to it like two Japanese fan girls would for an anime theme song.

"Meh duell-eh no ten-her-teh cohn-me-go

Yoh-kee-eh-rou sah-behr see too meh kee-eh-rehs

See too meh kee-eh-rehs

See too meh ah-mahs, eeeeeee

Too coh-rah-zone bahla pour meee!"

"For the life of me, I don't know what I'm singing!" Ruth said with a cackle.

"I know! Me neither! I love it!" I laughed.

After the song ended, the Black Angel stood in front of us looking at us like we were crazy. We didn't care. The angel of death smiled at Ruth and extended her hand to her. Ruth and I stared at each other and then hugged again.

"Take care of yourself, Violet."

"You be good. " I said teary-eyed. "I love you."

"I know. I love you too,"

Ruth took the Black Angel's hand and walked in her steps. Just about the moment my sister opened a dark creepy tunnel, I saw Rob's spirit waiting for her with flowers. He wore a black suit with a red bow tie and pristine black shoes. Ruth and Rob held hands and together, they followed the Black Angel into the tunnel.

I got really excited for Ruth.

"Have fun at the Prom, my angel." I whispered.

I stayed a while on that bench after the tunnel closed and wiped my tears. I had to pull myself together before someone saw me crying. I am an Archangel, after all; emissary of the Presence and all that. I shouldn't let people see me all emotional and stuff.

ABOUT THE AUTHOR

Angel Fuentes is a writer from Puerto Rico who has authored several short stories and screenplays. His most notable work, *Santa Cristal* (2005), was made into an independent film. He also founded and served as publisher of RBA Comics, where he wrote several comic titles. Mr. Fuentes is currently living and writing in the Big Apple alongside his adopted cat Violet.

Violet Descends: A Seven Lights Novel is his first novel.